Sullivan's Scoop

Also by Geoff Daplyn

The Sniper, The Shopkeeper And Sami

The Man Who Nearly Had Everything

Just The Three Of Us

Publishing partner: Paragon Publishing, Rothersthorpe

ISBN 978-1-78792-059-0

Book design, layout and production management by Into Print
www.intoprint.net
01604 832149

Author's Note

THIS BOOK IS a work of fiction but based on facts already in the public domain. Characters, therefore, are fictional, except where the text quotes a public source for a real person/situation. As with many books of 'faction', time has been somewhat warped for dramatic effect.

It's primarily a story of a newsroom and the relationships between its investigators, who stumble across an astounding story. As it begins to be investigated, even they refused to believe it before digging further into the allegations. And the deeper they dug, the more they found.

A sorry story of our times which some readers might find distasteful at first but, unfortunately, the story is still alive so I encourage readers to push through.

All statistics quoted here are sourced from public domain literature and all acknowledgements are listed in that section.

Chapter 1

JOHN SULLIVAN ARRIVED sweating and breathing heavily as he approached his office at the Boston Gazette. He was returning from the local Courthouse, not three hundred yards away, where a reliable informant had earlier slipped him some interesting information. The investigative reporter had immediately left his desk and headed out to check. Confirmation of the court's records caused him to sprint back to his office, excitement pushing his inadequate lungs almost to breaking point.

A forty-a-day habit combined with a serious drinking issue were not uncommon characteristics of newspaper reporters back in the day, together with a divorce or two. Well, someone had to keep traditions alive and Sullivan excelled at doing his bit. Any ambition that he may have had for a level of physical fitness had long ceased. There was no-one at home to please or badger him any more, so it all seemed rather a waste of time to do it for himself. Even the promise of a healthier body and longer life were no longer relevant. He had more important considerations.

The ill-fitting jacket and jeans he usually wore indicated a rather carefree attitude to his appearance, except when he wanted to make a good impression, which was not that often. He had one daughter, Chloe, from his first marriage, the second not lasting long enough to produce offspring. He still somehow managed to stumble through a number of subsequent fleeting relationships, none of which had come to any fruition because there was only one thing that came first in his life - his job. Investigating corruption was his mission and he intended to die on the job, but not just yet.

The Boston Courthouse had just provided the next adrenalin rush he lived for. The jacket, which had trailed over his arm on his rush back to the office, was now reinstated to his shoulders as he began to repair his dishevelled state. He didn't even pause on the sidewalk outside the outer door of the Gazette offices before entering and, ignoring the astonished look of Jimmy the security man, began to tackle the stairs leading to the newsroom, two at a time. A mistake. He stumbled up the first flight causing Jimmy to stifle a snigger. He got halfway and, having turned a corner out of Jimmy's sight, took the wise decision to pause and catch his breath before attempting the second flight.

It took a few more minutes to wipe his sweaty brow with a well-used handkerchief as he struggled to get some semblance of order into his body. Whilst his lungs were still recovering, he tucked his shirt back into his pants and ran his hand through what hair he had left. In the end, he told himself, it didn't matter. He had a story and he was going to saunter into the heart of the Gazette in full control of his faculties. It was a great story, a scoop. Although his side was aching – he remembered from his high school days, it was called a stitch, wasn't it? - he gradually forced his breathing back to normal. Now on the stairs, he could hear the bustle of journalists in the newsroom working hard, no doubt heads down over computer screens, fingers skating over keyboards, cellphones jingling and occasional expletives as they fought with their words, all dedicated to getting their copy just right and submitted on time.

Sullivan was part of a two person team of investigative reporters – a cut above the rest, he maintained. It was they who could really increase circulation and bring the money in, as he had done some years earlier. That had been a particular gruesome story involving significant child abuse, and the circulation of the Boston Gazette had gone through the roof as he ran story after story, revelation after revelation which had rocked a certain element of the establishment.

Anything involving harm to children somehow touched him deeply. He didn't quite know why. His own childhood had been quite ordinary, as far as he could remember. No abuse there. Nevertheless, it was something that aroused his instant anger and a single-mindedness to expose the perpetrators. This particular case had involved a priest, which had turned the knife in his emotions even more. The fact that someone in a position of trust and respect, should betray not only the gospel he preached, but the confidence that parents put in him.... well, there was nothing worse in his estimation. If he had his way, they would all have been physically castrated or, at least, subject to the chemical equivalent.

He had been alerted to the activities of Father Richard Keating by an intelligent mother who refused to take the catholic hierarchy's reassurances that it was a 'one-off' and that the priest in question was having 'treatment'. The truth, however, was very different.

The investigator had received widespread praise from both his Gazette colleagues and across the US for his tenacious pursuit which had eventually led to a guilty verdict and a substantial prison term. The silence from the Vatican and its various outposts, however, was deafening.

But he was now ready for his next scoop. He took the rest of the stairs in more deliberate fashion intending to open the door on the first floor quickly but quietly. Instead, he lost his grip and the door slammed against the wall with everyone in the newsroom looking around to see what was happening. Just Sullivan happening again. Most turned back to their tapping and got on with making sure their deadlines were met.

Janice didn't. She knew where her colleague had been and, by his confident demeanour, was sure he had something. She wanted to be in on it, so quickly followed him into the Holy of Holies, the editor-in-chief's office. Janice Munroe was one of the few women to break the glass ceiling of investigative reporting in the early 'naughties'. She had been alongside Sullivan for a while, originally to keep an eye on him and rein in any exuberance in his pursuit of stories. Still a single lady at thirty years of age, she was not unattractive, with a number of males in the newsroom having expressed interest in pursuing a romantic relationship. She, however, had declined them all, not exactly knowing why. There had been a short romance with the editor-in-chief while he was going through his divorce, which didn't come to anything, more to do with him than her. Nevertheless, they remained on good terms. She knew very well the life that journalists lived, and she was not sure that environment would ever make the ideal partner. So maybe there wasn't a choice. She didn't know many eligible males outside the job and had refused point blank to use dating sites.

Janice had been in the employ of the Gazette for some years, working her way up from runner to court reporting and other mundane journalism. But she was better than that and everyone knew it. When the editor-in-chief wanted someone to 'look after' Sullivan, he chose Janice. She was very happy to become part of the investigation team and, in the beginning, did keep the boss in the loop until her loyalty to Sullivan began to outweigh her loyalty to the editor. Not a great move.

While she hadn't been around when the Keating story had originally broken, she knew all about it and both reporters had kept ears open for any possible follow-up opportunities. Nothing so far. Until today, possibly. Sullivan gave her a big smile and a thumbs-up as they both entered the editor's den. The forty-two year old editor, James H Porter, was a high flier and had been doing this particular job for eight years but had been in the print business man and boy. He knew that it was investigations that lifted circulation above its normal average, so both Sullivan and Janice reported straight to him. Nothing surprised him any more, or so he claimed. Still a church-going catholic himself, he was stunned at what he thought he heard Sullivan was now blurting out.

"Woah!" he intervened. He picked up a lit cigarette smouldering in his ashtray, took a long intake of smoke and put it back in the tray. "Start slowly and from the beginning."

Sullivan glanced at his sidekick and took a deep breath. He looked straight at his editor. "You remember that paedophile priest, Richard Keating, which we exposed a few years ago?"

"Yes. How could I ever forget it. I nearly lost my faith, such as it was." He sat back in his chair and lit another cigarette from the original lapsing in his ash tray. He was thinking this was not going to be short meeting.

"Well, I've just come from the courthouse where I've learned that not only did Keating molest five boys in his original parish but, after some 'gardening leave', was subsequently inducted into two more parishes and did exactly the same thing again: eight boys in the first and two in the second so far."

"Bloody hell," exclaimed Janice.

Porter was already thinking about lawyers. "Do we need to bring in the legal guys?"

Sullivan smiled. He had calmed down somewhat now he had his editor's attention. "I haven't finished yet."

"There's more?" exclaimed Janice.

"The Cardinal knew all along." Sullivan was triumphant. "He had been protecting this priest all the way and moved him around in the full knowledge that he was putting more innocent lives at risk of abuse."

Porter looked at Janice as if to say, "I told you to watch over this maniac."

Janice pursed her lips and shrugged.

"Do you have any evidence?" asked Porter. "And don't say, 'not yet', because I don't want to hear allegations with no evidence."

"O ye of little faith," said Sullivan lighting his own cigarette. "Yesterday, I got a tip-off that there would be a routine court filing today where it was acknowledged in black and white that the Cardinal knew about it all along and covered it up."

Janice whistled, while Porter reached for the phone to make a call to the paper's lawyers. Sullivan put his hand on the phone to stop the call.

"What are you doing?" asked Porter pushing Sullivan's hand away. "We need advice on this before we publish."

"Sure we do," agreed Sullivan. "But we need to decide what the story is and how we want to play it."

"But you've told us what the story is. It can't get much bigger than this." The editor paused looking at Sullivan's face. "Can it?"

"Think about it," encouraged Sullivan. "who's to say that Keating was the only one? Who's to say that there aren't lots more paedophile priests out there, doing what Keating was doing under the protection of this Cardinal or every other Bishop, Archbishop or Cardinal?"

"Surely not," exclaimed Porter, his faith beginning to shake all over again. Janice said nothing but her eyes were narrowing. "I think you may have got something there," she said quietly. "How do we go about proving that?"

Sullivan sat back. He knew he had demonstrated his point and was waiting for his editor to get to the same place.

"I suppose you want more people and a bigger budget?" he said looking at his reporter straight in the eyes.

"No and yes," said Sullivan. "Just Janice and me. We need to keep this tight for the moment. No one else except the three of us. Not even the lawyers yet until we've done some more digging."

"Can you keep your source at the courthouse quiet?"

"Yes."

"Were there any other media outlets there?"

"No."

"Hmm," said Porter. He was thinking and the others were waiting for his decision. "You said yes and no. What was the yes for?"

"It'll take some more expenses and time for the two of us," he nodded at Janice, "to work on this solidly until we have a result."

"How long?" asked the editor. As soon as Porter asked that question, Sullivan knew he had it.

"Don't know yet. Could all happen very quickly or it could be like pulling teeth," responded the reporter.

"OK. You have it for the moment but I want a meeting at the end of each week to assess progress. If it looks good, I can keep my publisher in the dark for a little while. If it's going to leak out you must let me know immediately, otherwise all our asses are on the line. Comprendez?"

"You got it."

With that Sullivan and Janice left the Holy of Holies smiling, leaving Porter to wonder what the hell was going on in his church.

Chapter 2

His Holiness moved slowly back down the corridor from the Vatican balcony where he had just given his Urbi et Orbi Easter message and blessing. His right knee was causing him some pain and it had been a busy time. Easter always was, and this year it had been even more difficult but not because of the message or the blessing. Those were the easy bits. He enjoyed interacting with his people, his loyal and devoted followers, even if it was at a considerable distance. He would have liked to get closer to touch them and they, him, but he knew that would never happen even on his various tours. Royalty, it seemed, could do it but not him. More than ever at the beginning of the twenty-first century, security demanded a 'Popemobile'. But if he had to have something, then the successor to the antiquated '*sedia gestatoria*' was gratefully received. Some degree of comfort was surely essential for an older man, and most Pope's tended to be of a certain age.

Each Pontiff in turn succumbed to the wishes of the Vatican's Swiss security guards, or whoever they had contracted with on overseas tours and rode in the vehicle designed to allow them to be more visible when greeting zealous believers. Jesus, he would explain to anyone who would listen, just had a donkey and that had been earth shattering, at least theologically. But, his listeners would say, Jesus never had to face snipers with a SAKO TRG 42 which, he was told, was a long-range sniper rifle made in Finland and apparently, one of the best in the world.

"Hmm," was his response. Popes on the whole, didn't tend to discuss the merits or demerits of sniper rifles. They were mostly interested in galvanising ordinary believers in their faith, especially pilgrims who had probably travelled far to hear an Easter message. For this Pope, it didn't matter where they came from, pilgrims invigorated him, at least temporarily. He could sense their adoration and even though he knew that should be redirected to the Divine, nevertheless, he accepted it personally on behalf of the Church.

Least interesting for him, and most of his predecessors, was managing the bureaucracy. It was what wore most Pontiffs down because most were pastors at heart, always willing to believe the best in people which was not always the most appropriate approach when dealing with the intricacies of the Vatican. Of course, being a white Cardinal in Africa meant dealing with politics and political men both inside and outside the Church but that, he was discovering, was child's play compared with Rome. His election had come as a complete surprise, at least until the last ballot. He suspected that they wanted him out of the African continent so that they could promote a black man to the position of Cardinal, and why not?

He was warned about the Curia, and the power-plays that dominated the Vatican bureaucracy, so he had brought his right-hand man from South Africa to Rome to be his private secretary. An understandable move, though not necessarily a wise one. Andrew Douglas-Scott had been a British diplomat based in Durban who had caught the eye of the Cardinal Archbishop Emeritus at several catholic fundraising events and they had become friendly. Douglas-Scott was a deacon in his catholic parish church and the Archbishop had met him many times, both as representatives of their organisations and latterly as firm friends, even though he was younger by some years. The diplomat had a reputation of using soft power to great effect, which was exactly what the Cardinal was looking for. However, it was not an easy hire. The British Foreign and Commonwealth Office also knew the man's capabilities and there was some pressure and a few inducements which made Douglas-Scott's decision protracted. It was two years later the diplomat eventually resigned from the British foreign service and, after a further period of study, was ordained as a priest in the catholic church. Shortly after, as if by careful management, he was appointed to be the Cardinal's private secretary.

Conclaves don't happen very often and it was some time later when Douglas-Scott became aware that a new gathering was imminent. He had some idea of the political machinations of such a decision but there had been no mention of his boss as the possible winner of the ballots. So Father Andrew Douglas-Scott remained in Durban whilst the Cardinal reluctantly flew to Rome to hobnob with his other namesakes and to cast his votes.

The ex-diplomat was sitting down at his golf club watching the television after a mediocre round as the white smoke had appeared.

"At last," he murmured to his foursome partners who were already tucking into lunch. He dismissed the usual banter, that is, until his Cardinal had appeared on the balcony dressed in white. He stopped eating and, with a full mouth, muttered a profanity. Very unusual for him causing his buddies to stop eating and look at him with open mouths.

From then on, things began to move fast. He had been effectively a chief of staff in Durban, not that there were many staff except for a few elderly priests and some nuns. Moving to Rome was an altogether different experience. He had no friends and his friend, now His Holiness, was in another orbit altogether. Their relationship had to change. Whilst Douglas-Scott did perform the role of 'gatekeeper' for His Holiness in Rome, a chief of staff he most certainly was not. A notion he was quickly disabused of by a few of the most powerful Curia prelates.

Three years later, dressed in his fuchsia-trimmed cassock and simar, he was accompanying his master back to his private quarters after the Easter 'rigmarole', as he privately called it, ready to see to his every need.

"Three score years and ten," intoned His Holiness as he made his way towards the lift which would take him to the papal apartments.

"Pardon, Holiness?" queried Douglas-Scott.

His Holiness turned around to confide in his friend. "I have already had my biblical time. I wonder how much longer." It was a question that had been on his mind for a while but unspoken to anyone, even his private secretary. His health was robust according to his physician but he sensed a lack of energy, and wondered if there was some underlying cause. He decided it was just age and continued the shuffle.

He went up in his private lift to the third floor of the Apostolic Palace, along the corridor, and round the corner to his office. He nodded to the Swiss guard outside and went inside to find a nun finishing the cleaning who, when she saw who had opened the door, went red-faced, bowed, and quickly disappeared. The Pontiff went over to his spartan wooden desk and sat down while his private secretary hovered nearby waiting for an opportunity to remind his boss of the one further meeting that was booked for the remainder of the day.

To his amazement, the Pope wrote a message on a bit of paper, folded it, and passed it to his Secretary whilst putting his finger to his lips. Douglas-Scott took it in his hands whilst looking quizzically at his master. He unfolded it, looked again at his friend, now enthroned as Pope who was raising his eyebrows in a questioning mode. The Private Secretary (PS) understood that His Holiness required a non-verbal response, so he nodded and took the paper away with him.

"Now," said the Pope slowly, "I want you to find out who leaked those papers to La Republica."

Douglas-Scott nodded, conceding that the silent conversation was over. He thought perhaps he ought also to play the game. "That rag," he exclaimed in response. "Holiness, surely you don't think the story is true?"

The Pope looked up and said in a tired voice, "It doesn't matter for the moment whether it's actually true or not. What matters is whether people think it's true."

"But people won't take it seriously, will they?"

"Come, come, Andrew. This is an institution comprised almost wholly of sexually repressed single men prohibited from the intimate company of women. It would be a miracle if there weren't some gay men among them."

His PS looked shocked. "But the report suggested that there was a network of gay prelates in the Vatican, some of whom were being blackmailed by outsiders." His voice had risen to a crescendo of disbelief.

His Holiness leaned forward, head down. "Let us pray not. But we need to protect the Church."

Douglas-Scott bowed in acknowledgement. He knew this story was not just being reported in Italy, but had been picked up by several international news outlets, including the UK Guardian. The paper had quoted a dossier compiled by three Cardinals who had been delegated to look into the affair which the papers insisted on calling, Vatileaks. They had delivered their verdict to the Pope's office and somehow it had got to the newspaper that prided itself on knowing all the Vatican gossip. It revealed, so ran the paper's story, that the Cardinals had described several factions within the Curia, including one whose members were 'united by sexual orientation'. It added that some Vatican officials had been subjected to 'external influence' from laymen with whom they had links of a 'worldly nature'. La Republica had reported that this was a clear reference to gay blackmail.

The PS left the Pontiff to rest for an hour before he was due to meet with the head of The Institute for the Works of Religion, more commonly known as the Vatican Bank. While his Private Secretary retreated to his own office to destroy the secret paper and work out how to accede to his master's request, His Holiness wondered how he could possibly get the Vatican Bank to reform itself. Certainly, he had the moral authority to instruct but not a great deal of power to make any changes.

At the appointed time, the PS showed Herr Erik Hoffmann into the room and took his seat at the side, while the President of the Bank made straight for His Holiness to kiss the ring as a mark of respect for the office. Respect, but not obedience since the Institution was run by an independent advisory board. Yes, it reported to the Pope and a committee of cardinals, but the assets of the bank were not the direct property of the Holy See, nor was it overseen by the Prefecture for the Economic Affairs of the Holy See. It was not, therefore, a department of the Roman Curia, nor was it one of the departments of the central administrative structure of the Roman Catholic Church. However, it did contribute millions of euros to the Vatican budget, making it one of its most crucial economic pillars. And, most importantly, if serious corruption issues did arise at the Institute, as had happened in the past, it was the Vatican itself that suffered the inevitable consequential damage, both to its financial probity and, just as importantly, its reputation. Hence the appointment of Herr Hoffmann, an experienced financial man rather than another priest. "And how is the pace of reform moving?" asked the Pope, looking at Herr Hoffmann intently.

"As well as can be expected, Holiness." said the non-committal Bank President.

"You are struggling with the senior management?" asked the Pope knowledgeably.

"Some are quite set in their ways," commented Hoffmann warily.

His Holiness looked Hoffmann in the eye. "This was to be expected. They have been in post for some time."

The financial man looked a little uncomfortable, shifting slightly in his seat. "I might need to move some on."

The Pontiff looked up sharply. "They are priests, are they not?"

"But perhaps those concerned should take their share of responsibility for previous scandals?" quizzed the Bank's President.

"The priesthood is a sacred calling," reminded His Holiness.

"But," replied Herr Hoffmann, "embezzlement, abuse of office, and bribery are still sins, are they not?"

"There is always forgiveness," cautioned the Pope.

Herr Hoffmann decided to push His Holiness a little further. "As you know, Holiness, as a Vatican entity, the Bank is beyond the reach of any independent regulatory scrutiny other than the Vatican's own supervision. Perhaps ….."

The implication didn't need to be spelt out. The prize jewel in the crown of the Vatican was effective immunity from any investigation by a national law enforcement organisation including legal suits. The Vatican had no extradition treaties with other nations, which meant that shelter for priests within the Vatican walls was secure as long as His Holiness maintained the Vatican's sovereignty.

If this was to be surrendered, the history of Vatican finances through the ages could be revealed. That history was murky to say the least, with numerous public corruption scandals and probably innumerable ones that had never seen the light of day. His Holiness was well aware of the past indiscretions of his church and the Vatican Bank, although perhaps not all the gory details. But he was not going to allow any accountability to move away to a secular authority.

The Pope looked sternly at his visitor. "Herr Hoffmann. You will be aware that because the Vatican is a sovereign nation, it is not accountable to any other system of national law, financial or otherwise."

He paused, as if searching for the appropriate words. "There may have been," he coughed, "irregularities in the activity of our predecessors, but you are here to fix those that emanate from your organisation. I will seek to do the same for the Vatican, but the sovereignty of the Holy See is not up for discussion and will not change on my watch."

These were the sternest words that Herr Hoffmann had heard His Holiness utter. He nodded his acquiescence. But looking at His Holiness closely, he detected a conflicted man who needed reform, but could not dispense with the secrecy and sovereignty which made reform virtually impossible. Secrecy always bred sin and corruption, whether minor or major.

The President of the Bank decided that the debate was for another day, maybe when the next financial scandal broke which, he thought, probably wouldn't be long in coming. He would have to think of a strategy to safeguard himself when the inevitable happened. In the meantime, he concurred, there would be no cull of guilty priests.

At this juncture, His Holiness struggled to his feet. The meeting was over and Herr Hoffmann retreated, shutting the door behind him. The Pontiff looked at his Private Secretary and sighed heavily.

"Make a point of bumping into Herr Hoffmann in say, a month or so, and see what his plans are. I don't want radical measures or rumours of a wholesale sacking of priests to get to the media. The Church must be protected."

"Yes, Holiness." The Vicar of Christ was then left to his own thoughts and to continue his private routine of reading and writing in his study, then prayers in his private chapel. Meanwhile Douglas-Scott departed and made his way down to his office. He happened to meet the Pope's butler, Paolo Gabriele, on the way.

"Paolo, do you have a minute?" asked the PS. The butler nodded and they went into Douglas-Scott's office.

"You've been here longer than I have," the PS started. "I'm hearing rumours of issues relating to the Institute for the Works of Religion."

"Ah. You mean scandals and corruption?" Paolo spoke English with a strong Italian accent.

Douglas-Scott cleared his throat, rather embarrassed at the willingness of a long time employee so ready to talk about the failings of the Vatican institutions. "I suppose so," he said hesitantly, wondering what was coming next.

"How much time have you got?" Paolo laughed. "Let's start with Mussolini."

"Mussolini?" echoed Douglas-Scott.

"He was the founder of fascism in Italy."

"Yes, I know that," said Douglas-Scott impatiently.

"Well, he wanted to eliminate catholic political opposition back in the 1920s. So in 1929 Mussolini and Pious XI signed a concordat and other treaties which included a lump sum payment of nearly 100 million dollars (equivalent to a billion in current dollars) to the Vatican, plus government salaries for the clergy, and the creation of the Vatican as a sovereign state."

"Ah. So that's when it happened," exclaimed the PS.

Paolo ignored the interruption. "A few years later, Hitler, Papen and Kaas also negotiated a mutually beneficial concordat with the Holy See.

"What?" exclaimed Douglas-Scott, incredulously and wishing he knew more about the Vatican's history than he did. "And what did Herr Hitler want?"

"Legitimacy of course. All German Catholic bishops were required by the concordat to swear loyalty to the Third Reich, rendering impossible any direct clerical opposition to the existence of his regime."

"What did the Vatican get in return?"

"The income taxes of all German catholics, amounting to about $1 billion from the beginning to the end of the war (equivalent to about 10 billion in current dollars).

Douglas-Scott was quiet. Paolo continued. "The tax income and contribution made at the time included money stolen from Jews by German catholics, but the Holy See made no attempt to use that money to compensate the victims after the war."

The butler was watching Douglas-Scott's embarrassment with amusement. The Pope's PS was about to get up but the butler hadn't finished. "You are English, no?"

"Yes," admitted Douglas-Scott.

"Then you will know about Roberto Calvi?"

"The so-called, 'God's banker', who committed suicide under a bridge in London? What of it?"

"Calvi teamed up with Archbishop Marcinkus, who headed the Vatican Bank then. They were both caught up in the collapse of Blanco Ambrisiano."

"Yes, I remember it now."

"The Vatican has always refused to disclose its full role in the affair, but it involved a billion-dollar bankruptcy of yet another major Italian bank. Apparently, it stemmed from the alleged direct or indirect ownership of Panamanian shell companies used to funnel $1.3 billion."

Douglas-Scott was shaking his head in some confusion. "Panamanian shell companies? What does this have to do with the Vatican?"

Paolo was clearly enjoying himself as he 'dished the dirt' on his employer and Douglas-Scott was becoming more uncomfortable.

"You see, Archbishop Marcinkus was found to have written dubious 'letters of patronage' that appeared to back certain loans..."

Douglas-Scott interrupted. "Surely, this is all speculation?"

"Well, there was enough evidence to prompt a Milan prosecutor to accuse the Vatican Bank of giving, and I quote, 'systematic support to Calvi in many of his illicit operations'. Apparently, Vatican bank officials played a much more prominent role than previously believed in the tangled, fraudulent schemes of Signor Roberto Calvi."

Douglas-Scott was about to intervene again and close down the conversation when Paolo overrode him. "Investigating magistrates concluded that the Vatican Bank had been an umbrella for Calvi's operations. Of course, it was all officially denied by the Papacy but interestingly, John Paul II paid $250 million to Ambrisiano creditors, shortly afterwards. A tacit admission, or what?"

Paolo sat back and looked at the Pope's PS. There was a look of triumph on his face, whereas Douglas-Scott was looking decidedly queasy.

"Oh. There's a lot more," continued Paolo. "It's all well documented by Gregory Paul on the 'Church and State' website. Take Poland, for example and the millions sent to Solidarity to 'overturn dictatorial atheism in eastern Europe, thereby inspiring a return to Catholic devotion in the west'. Guess who masterminded the scheme?"

Douglas-Scott had sat back in his chair resigned to hearing more. Paolo smiled. "Why our good friends, Calvi and Marcinkus. You can guess how legal or illegal that was."

"How much?" asked the PS faintly.

"A mere $100 million." With that Paolo got up to go. "*Buona Giornata*," he said, as he closed the door.

The following morning His Holiness woke early, as was his habit and, apart from his usual devotions, the following day was set aside for more internal affairs of which there were many; some serious, others potentially catastrophic, most entirely self-inflicted. None, at the moment, were financial, he was relieved to see.

The next issue to cross his desk was to do with American nuns. It was alleged by the Congregation for the Doctrine of the Faith, which was responsible for doctrine purity, that there were serious doctrinal problems with certain nuns' belief and behaviour in the US. His Holiness could do none other than agree to the proposed investigation, although there was more than a hint of suspicion in his mind over the underlying motives for the move.

The Leadership Conference of Women Religious, the largest organisation of US nuns, was now reeling from the news of a Vatican-sponsored visitation of all apostolic women's religious orders in the United States. It was, according to the National Catholic Reporter, designed to assess their 'quality of life,' when they learned that their leadership was under investigation. There were accusations that apparently challenged established teachings on male-only priesthood, homosexuality, and specific feminist themes such as abortion and the use of contraceptives.

The Pontiff had hoped that the investigation would be seen as a gentle shot across the bows of anyone deviating from acknowledged church teaching. However, the nuns themselves and the media painted it as a crackdown on radical feminism, arousing such strong feelings that a 50,000-strong petition had been raised with seven groups of US Franciscan friars condemning the crackdown as too excessive.

A heavy-handed approach was landing the Vatican in yet another fine mess...... but nothing like what was about to hit them.

Chapter 3

THE CITY OF Boston on the north-east coast of the US is a Roman Catholic stronghold with many claiming Irish Catholic ancestry. Indeed, the Kennedy family have their roots in the region, many still living across the water on Cape Cod. For priests, it was a sought-after place to serve, with many affluent families contributing generously directly to the church and towards many good catholic causes.

Cardinal Patrick Doughty was proud to claim such Irish ancestry and had risen through the hierarchy to become the resident Archbishop of Boston. He had entered seminary an era ago when the world was very different but the church very much the same. It had no need to change; in fact, it considered its unchangingness to be its strength. If asked, he might have admitted that the secular world outside of his ecclesiastical domain seemed to be increasingly at odds with his religion, but he saw his pastoral role to be towards his own kind. He wasn't particularly evangelistic, rather his primary focus was to protect Mother Church against the secularism around him.

He had called a special meeting with his Private Secretary, Gino Arata, a young priest on the rise, who was equally proud to claim his Italian ancestry from his great-grandfather.

"Gino, we have a problem," began the Cardinal as his Private Secretary came into the room.

"Eminence?" queried Father Arata.

"What do you know about Father Richard Keating?"

The young priest screwed up his face in an effort to recall the name. "Yes, he's in one of our best parishes, isn't he? I think he was installed a little before my time, though."

The Cardinal looked at his PS, "Probably," he said. "I appointed him to one of our more mixed parishes some ten years ago," subtly contradicting his PS.

"Is there a problem, Eminence?" Arata was furrowing his brow.

The Cardinal scratched his head. "Yes. We may have a problem on our hands which could cause the church much damage."

"I don't understand."

The Cardinal got up from his desk and walked around the room with Arata's eyes following him.

"We need to work out a plan to contain this issue," said the Cardinal, almost to himself. His PS was turning in his chair to watch his master as he circumnavigated the room and finally came to rest at a large window overlooking his opulent residence.

"What's the issue, Eminence?"

"*Mysterium Iniquitatis.*"

"What?" Father Arata was now thoroughly confused.

"That's what His Holiness called it," replied the Cardinal, still studying his gardens.

"Called what?" asked the PS.

"Paedophilia."

There was quiet in the room as Arata took in the enormity of the issue and His Eminence twisted and turned in his mind wondering how he might protect his church from a great calamity. The Cardinal turned around and looked at his PS wondering why the young man was so impacted.

"Are you so shocked Gino?" he asked.

Father Arata found his lips moving without much sound coming out. Eventually, he thought he'd better say something.

"What's Father Keating done?" he asked, already suspecting the worst. The question he should have asked was how long had he been doing it and how many young boys were involved?

His Eminence sighed. "If you're going to help me in this delicate situation, I suppose you need to know the whole truth. But this can go no further."

No answer from the young priest. "Can I trust you, Gino?" came the insistent question.

"Of course, of course," replied the Private Secretary pulling himself up in his chair so he was sitting ramrod, ready for business in front of the large, ornate desk where His Eminence was now seated.

"Our task is to protect the church from disgrace," began the Cardinal.

Arata instinctively asked, "But what about the young boys?" Then, as his master's eyes bored into him, realised he had asked the wrong question.

"The priesthood is not just for life," stated His Eminence. "A priest is a priest is a priest. Do you understand?"

"I think so," stuttered the young priest.

The Cardinal sat back in his swivel chair and looked at the ceiling before beginning to talk.

"It must be ten years ago that Father Keating was passed to me for oversight. He had..." At this juncture, the Cardinal coughed slightly, "he had... an illness." Now the Cardinal waved his hands in the air, as if to say, "What was I supposed to do?"

"What sort of illness, Eminence," asked the young priest, still not adding two and two together very well.

The Cardinal carried on almost oblivious to Arata's question. "You see, from my standpoint paedophilia is an illness, not a criminal condition, an illness." It was as if His Eminence was trying to convince himself, or a jury, of his argument. The PS sat and listened, thinking it was not his place to interrupt, yet.

"Of course," the Cardinal went on, "that's not to say that there would be no criminal liability...."

Now the young priest could sit still no longer. "But if it's not a criminal offence, how can there be criminal liability?"

"Ah. You haven't yet grasped it, have you?" replied the Cardinal. He went on. "Where such men were abused as children and then go on to become paedophiles, don't tell me that those people are just as criminally responsible as somebody who directly chooses to do something like that."

Arata was beginning to see the argument. "So you're saying that such a person doesn't deserve to be punished if he himself was damaged."

"Precisely, my young friend." He paused. "Do you understand what I am saying, Gino?"

"So Father Keating is essentially a good man who was abused and therefore open to temptation, eventually succumbing to that temptation, probably after months, maybe years of trying to resist?" It was a question, and the Cardinal nodded.

"... and which one of us can cast the first stone?" finished the young priest.

There was silence for a few minutes as both men reviewed their conversation, perhaps awaiting divine approval for their argument.

Then Arata frowned as he tried to remember something way back in his past. "Didn't all this come out some years ago. I was in Seminary. I don't remember Keating's name but wasn't there a media storm about this sort of thing then?"

"You have a good memory, Gino," began the Cardinal. "Yes there was, and the priest in question was moved to another parish after some gardening leave."

"Ah. So you had to move him on after the media got wind of his, er, illness?"

"Exactly so."

"So is the problem that he has started again?"

"Not exactly, although of course he has. This sort of thing never goes away. It will stay with him for the rest of his life."

"But he is a priest," murmured Father Arata. "So we move him on again?"

"Not that simple," said the Cardinal. The young Private Secretary was thinking that they were, at last, coming to the point of the meeting.

"I don't understand," Arata said, hoping his master would get to the point.

"The media have discovered that I, knowing Keating's behaviour, covered it up and, in their words, 'let him loose' on more unsuspecting boys in a new parish."

"Oh," exclaimed the Private Secretary.

"Indeed," replied the Cardinal. "I am now going to become the centre of the storm and it will all be muckraked up again."

Chapter 4

Josephine Sorento, known to her friends as Jo, lived in one of the poorer areas of Boston. Jack, her erstwhile husband, had long gone leaving her to bring up her two sons with little help. Ben was now thirteen and followed the Boston Red Sox basketball team avidly, though no chance of enough cash to see them play live. He had a shirt, albeit last season's variety, and wore it continually out of school. John was two years younger and idolised his big brother, except when they fell out, which was not that often.

It was a relatively happy home with Mom working two jobs to make ends meet, the second one not finishing until six o'clock in the evening. The boys weren't the only 'latchkey' children in their block so, in the summer months, both boys and girls would play outside, usually using the basketball nets which had been put up by one of the fathers some years before. In the colder months, the boys would huddle under blankets inside and watch cartoons on the television.

On Sundays, Mom would take them to church for Mass doing her best to ensure they would grow up to become good catholics. Father Keating was a kindly man with a welcoming smile that engendered the trust of his parishioners, having been inducted into the parish a few years earlier without anyone knowing of his past. As he bid his congregation goodbye at the church door on a Sunday, he would have a beaming smile for the single moms, with always a tousle for the boys' hair. He had a friendly air about him and an offer of help to Jo, if she ever needed it. Mom made sure the priest knew he was welcome to come round at any time, thinking that having a male father figure around now and again would help the boys.

She was delighted when Ben was invited to become an altar boy to join three other boys his age. To see her son helping the priest in the most important ceremony for catholics was tremendously reassuring to her faith.

"Ben," began Father Keating, when Ben turned up a week before it was his first time. "You will need to wear black trousers, shoes and socks with a white dress shirt."

"But," explained Ben, "I haven't got those things and I'm not sure my Mom can afford to buy them." Ben was concerned about any extra expense his mother might have to bear.

"Not to worry. I'll have a word with your mother and we'll sort something out." Father Keating was sure it wouldn't be a problem.

"Now, when standing and not holding anything, you'll need to hold hands together with your fingers straight." Ben was looking puzzled.

"Like this." The priest came behind the teenager and, pushing himself close to the boy, leaned over his shoulder and arranged his fingers just so. He stayed in that position for a little longer than was necessary but Ben didn't think anything of it.

"Also," said Keating, detaching himself from the lad, "you must arrive at least fifteen minutes before Holy Mass to prepare the altar and yourself. You'll watch David here do it for the first two Sundays, then it will be your turn."

After this meeting, Ben rushed home full of pride and importance at the role he had been selected to play in front of everyone at church. He couldn't wait for Sundays to come and go until it would be his turn to dress the altar. He talked non-stop to his mother, his brother, and his friends at his catholic school. The priest was as good as his word and the clothes Ben needed were provided with his mother having nothing to pay.

Father Keating seemed to be pleased with how Ben was doing and began to call in at their home just to make sure everything was fine. He would often go upstairs to pray with him and sometimes read him a Bible story. Every year in the summer, the church would have a garden festival to raise money for various charities and the priest would make sure that he bought both Ben and John ice creams. Their mother was so proud that her sons had been singled out for special attention.

In recognition of the help the priest was giving her family, Jo invited him to join them for the following Saturday evening meal. She only worked the morning on Saturdays, giving her time to prepare something memorable. She decided to buy some lamb and make an Irish stew and spent much of the afternoon making it while the boys made sure that the house was tidy. By the time Father Keating arrived, the delicious smells from the kitchen were pervading the whole house.

"Hello," he called out through the open door.

Jo heard him and rushed to the door to welcome their guest. "Please, please come in," she gushed.

"What a delicious smell. You must be a very good cook."

She blushed. "Not really. It's a recipe my mother used to make. It's our favourite for special occasions."

As he walked into the hall, he exclaimed, "Oh. I nearly forgot. This is for you," and he brought out a bottle of wine from his bag. "And I got some cans of coke for the boys. I hope that's alright? Are they allowed coke?"

"Of course."

Just then the two boys came in from the back garden to greet their guest.

"Now," said Father Keating, "I have something special for each of you. A little magic." He stretched out his hand to each boy's ear in turn and pulled out a coin.

"Wow," said Ben and John. "Can we keep them?"

"Well although they're magic, they're not worth much. I tell you what, why don't I buy each of them back for a ten-dollar note?" The exchange was made and Jo made sure that her boys thanked the priest. The evening went by quickly and before long it was time for the boys to go to bed.

"The boys really like your stories. Will you read each of them just a short one?" asked Jo.

"Of course." And upstairs the boys went, each to their own bedroom. John had his story first which was short, then Ben, which seemed to take much longer.

The weeks went past and, as far as Jo was concerned, all was well in the family, albeit Ben was becoming a little withdrawn. His mother just assumed it was the onset of puberty and teenage years, reinforcing her confidence that such a link with the church and Father Keating would help her son through these difficult years.

"Ben, will you help John clear up?" It was six thirty and she had come home from work to finish the evening meal which she had started early that morning before they had gone to school and she had left for work.

"Let John do it," came the blunt answer and he slouched off upstairs to his bedroom.

"Ben, I have to go out for half an hour," she shouted up the stairs. No response.

"Ben, you're the eldest!" her voice rising. No answer and no time to pursue the issue.

"John, be a darling and do what you can to help Mommy." John nodded as his mother swept out of the house.

On Sunday morning at the end of the service, while Ben was still changing out of his vestments, Jo had a word with the priest.

"Father Keating. I'm a little concerned about Ben. He's becoming quite distant and uncommunicative. Could you have a word with him and see what the problem is?"

"Certainly," said the priest with that winning smile.

Chapter 5

THE FIRST STOP for the Gazette's investigative reporters after leaving their editor's office was the local Irish pub. After ordering for them both, Janice joined Sullivan in a dark corner to plan their campaign.

"Cheers," said Sullivan. He lifted his pint of Guinness, with Janice lifting her white wine spritzer in response.

"Perhaps," started Janice, "we should begin by visiting the parish where Keating is currently."

"Yep. I was thinking the same thing," said Sullivan after taking a generous pull on his pint. "I suppose there's an outside chance that he might recognise me, so why don't you go to Sunday Mass?"

"I'm not a catholic."

"Just try to merge in with the rest of them. It won't be that difficult."

Janice grunted. Spending a precious Sunday morning in a catholic church was not her idea of a fun time.

"OK. There are a few things you need to know," said a smiling Sullivan, adopting his 'teacher' voice. "First, wear your Sunday best but not too flamboyant."

Janice lifted her eyes to the ceiling and said sarcastically, "But I've only got flamboyant clothes. Look at me."

Sullivan ignored her. "When you go in, genuflect in front of the sanctuary, both as you enter and as you leave."

"What?" queried Janice.

"It just means bowing to the altar, preferably with one knee touching the ground." Sullivan grinned broadly. He was enjoying the look on his colleague's face. "It's a whole new world. You'll love it."

"I'm not sure I can do that and get up again without falling over," exclaimed Janice.

"Well, just make the effort. No one's going to be watching you. If you wait outside in the car, follow someone in and just copy them."

Janice looked as if she was having second thoughts. "Oh," said Sullivan, "switch your phone off and don't wear a hat."

"But I love wearing hats. Now I'm really disappointed."

Sullivan ignored her again. "Now there will be two chances of getting a good view of the boys we need to identify. They will have to arrive, maybe fifteen or twenty minutes before Mass so that they can get into their vestments and dress the altar. I recommend that on Saturday evening you visit the church and find out where the entrance to the vestry is. It'll be somewhere round the side. Then if you arrive early on the Sunday, you can get a good photo of them as they arrive with no one else looking on."

"And if that doesn't work?"

"Plan B is to make sure you sit where you get a good view of the altar boys at the front. So don't get behind a pillar and try to remember their faces. After the service, they will go back into the vestry to change while the rest of the congregation is getting up to leave. Normally, the priest will already be at the door shaking hands with his flock as they leave."

"I suppose I will have to shake his hand as well?"

"Yes. Try not to get into a conversation with him but have something prepared just in case."

"Like what?"

"I don't know. You'll just have to think of something. Your main task is to get outside quickly and watch for the boys coming out of the side vestry door. Get a photo of them if you can."

"That won't be difficult," said Janice.

"Then decide which one to follow. I don't know how many will be on duty, so you'll have to make a decision about which one Keating will go for."

"What's his penchant?" asked Janice.

"It has been boys just moving into puberty." explained Sullivan. "So, say thirteen ish."

"So I follow one of them discreetly, either on foot or by car, and see where they live?" asked Janice.

"Right. If one is on foot and the other in a car, take the one on foot, and just note the car reg of the other one."

"And I suppose, if both are in a car, follow one and take the reg of the other."

"Exactly," said Sullivan. "Once we have an address, we can find out who lives there, and if it's a single mom, bingo."

They had both finished their liquid lunch and headed back to the office.

Sunday came and Janice arrived in the church car park twenty minutes before the start finding a great spot near the vestry door which she had located the previous evening. And there they were: two young lads, one certainly older than the other. The younger had blond hair and, she judged, looked about thirteen. Nevertheless, she snapped both of them and then decided that now she didn't need to go inside through all the catholic rigmarole.

But a few minutes later a man in a roman collar came around the corner to go into the vestry and nodded to her. She couldn't avoid being seen, so she nodded and smiled in return. Father Keating, she presumed. With his wispy, almost ginger hair, freckles and broad smile, he looked authentic enough. If she hadn't known his past, she would have taken him to be the genuine article. Now she would have to go in.

A further five minutes sitting in the car, saw most of the congregation making their way into the church. Moms, Dads, children, and older women members of the congregation, though not many older men. She followed them in, copied what they did, and took a seat next to the aisle for an easy getaway. She began to feel a little more relaxed and was now focussing on the altar boys. Yes, she could spot the younger one.

The service began and, to be truthful, she found it quite boring. She didn't have any faith of her own and couldn't possibly see how such liturgy and ceremony would generate anyone's faith. After an hour or so, it was finished and time to make her way out. Keating was at the door and she could see no way of avoiding him; she was going to have to shake his hand. Having laboured a little over what to say, it was all to no avail for while he was patting some lad on his head and speaking to his mother, she slipped past, breathing a sigh of relief.

She went over to her car and waited for the blond boy she had focussed on to appear from the vestry door. She got an even closer look as he wandered past the car and made his way over to where a mother and younger lad were waiting.

"Ah. You're part of the same family," she said to herself. "I bet she's a single mom who can't afford a car, which means they're walking home." Sure enough, they set off down the road together. Janice thought she should drive her car out of the church car park rather than leave it there, so she found a side road, parked, and followed the family, trailing them by about two hundred meters.

It might have been her imagination, but the older boy seem to go ahead of his mother and younger brother as if he was not speaking with them and wanted to be on his own. It was about half an hour's walk before they turned into a small run-down house with paint peeling off most of the woodwork. The reporter carried on walking, noting the road and number of the house on her phone. Excellent. Sullivan would be pleased.

Chapter 6

SULLIVAN HAD NOT been idle that Sunday. He arrived early at the office, surprising Jimmy on the reception desk in the foyer.

"Mr Sullivan, sir. Wasn't expecting to see you in today."

"Wasn't planning to come in till this morning," replied the reporter. "But a scoop's a scoop," he said winking at the man, whose name he had forgotten.

Upstairs, he settled himself down with a cup of black coffee and placed a newly opened packet of twenty on the desk to one side. His notepad at the ready, he opened his computer to search through the original historical records of the Keating case, looking for any other suspicious reports which had not been picked up at the time. He remembered that, once discovered, the Keating case had been the sole target of everyone. Something important could easily have been missed.

He also wanted to resurrect the emotions he had felt at the time – emotions of revulsions and anger. He wanted to feel that dark place again and, as someone once said, go into the abyss. This, he knew, would rekindle the flame which he would need if this investigation was to do justice to the victims. He had kept the pictures of the abused boys. They were still alive, as far as he knew, but the chances were that they were not enjoying life as they should have been. He dug out a picture of one of the boys, Michael. It was a school photo showing the lad in his school uniform smiling with braces over his front teeth evident. That did it for him. He was now stoked up.

He had arrived at about ten with a good idea of what he was looking for but, numerous cigarettes later, he had to admit to himself that he was nowhere. He looked at the clock on the wall and saw that Janice would just be leaving the church. He was hoping she would be having better luck. He needed a break and an early drink at the pub was in prospect, hoping that might provide him with some inspiration. It often did.

Two hours later, he was back at his desk and decided to look further back, before the Keating scandal broke. And there it was. Another paper had recorded a mother making a similar accusation about a different priest within the same Cardinal's jurisdiction, but outside the immediate Boston area. Odd, there was no follow-up story filed by the reporter. Perhaps it was a mistake, but Sullivan's gut told him otherwise. He decided to track down the mother in question and call her but, looking at the byline, he saw to his amazement that the reporter was known to him, but now retired. It didn't take long to find his phone number.

"Hello," asked a suspicious voice.

"Hi Fraser, it's Sullivan." There was silence. "From the Boston Gazette."

Recognition dawned, "My God, Sullivan. You're a blast from the past!"

"Yea. I need your help. Have you got a few minutes for me?"

"Straight down to business, as usual. You haven't changed."

"Er. Sorry," stuttered Sullivan. "How are you?"

Fraser laughed. "You're lucky to find me alive."

"What?"

"Had a quad bypass a month ago, but making good progress."

"Glad to hear it but sounds as if you've been through the mill." Sullivan was thanking his lucky stars that the only man linking him to this historical report was still alive. Anxious to make up for his earlier brevity, he asked, "How's the family?"

"Sullivan. What do you want?"

"OK, OK. Do you remember a report you did about a mother who accused her priest of molesting her son when he was an altar boy?" Sullivan had everything crossed, awaiting Fraser's answer.

"Sure I do," the answer came immediately. Sullivan raised his hands to the ceiling in a silent whoop.

"There was no follow-up that I could find" Sullivan asked the question as neutrally as possible. He didn't want to malign the man now he had found him.

"That's because my editor sat on it. Told me to move on." Fraser's voice had changed as he remembered the angry conversation he had had with his boss at the time.

"Why on earth would he want to do that?" asked Sullivan.

"Well, he was a staunch catholic but I think there was more to it than that."

"What do you mean?" Sullivan's heart was beginning to beat a little faster.

His antenna was up and he sensed something important coming.

"I thought I'd try just one more time to get back to the mom in question."

"So what happened?"

"She suddenly changed from wanting to out the priest to the world regardless, to slamming the door in my face."

"Someone had got to her?"

"That was my interpretation. So I left it a month or two and tried again to see if she had changed her mind."

"Had she?" Sullivan was looking for an answer in the positive.

"Never got to ask," said Fraser. Sullivan let out an audible sigh which Fraser was meant to hear.

"Because," he started. Sullivan's hope rose again. "Because outside the house of a single mom was a brand new Ford."

"Perhaps it was a visitor," suggested Sullivan, instantly knowing that it wasn't but needing Fraser's corroboration.

"Didn't think it was, so I waited down the road in my car. In about twenty minutes, out she came, got in, and drove off."

Sullivan was silent. He knew what that meant. "What did your editor say? You got yourself a big story there, maybe a Pulitzer."

Fraser snorted. "I tried to resurrect it, but.... That man was in the pocket of a very important person. I could smell it."

"What did you do?"

"Nothing. I had been told if I wanted to keep my job..... you know the score."

"Secret hush money," said Sullivan quietly, "probably with a gagging clause preventing the mother from saying anything."

"Yea, that's what I thought. Anyway, why do you want to rake that up again?" asked Fraser.

"Because I don't think that was an isolated case. I'm pretty sure abuse and private compensation deals from the church are still going on, and I intend to get to the bottom of it."

"Good luck," responded Fraser. "You're going to need it. The catholic church is very powerful in these parts. They play dirty when their church is in trouble."

"I know," said Sullivan. "Man, I wish you the best. Thanks a lot. You've been a great help."

He put the phone down and laid back in his chair. The whoops were over. Now was the time for some serious thinking. Another single mom! Was that their *modus operandi*, no husband to come banging on the door and making a fuss? He looked at the clock. Wow! Four o'clock already. The afternoon had flown past and he decided to go home but not before calling his co-investigator.

"Janice, how did you get on?"

"Made some progress," said the reporter with uncharacteristic understatement.

"What does that mean?" asked an impatient Sullivan.

"Just got the lady, the boy, and their address," replied a satisfied Janice. "What have you been up to?"

The chief investigator reporter filled his colleague in with his morning's work. When he told of the cover up and a brand-new car, Janice whistled. "This is amazing. How many more do you think we'll find?"

"Don't know, but I think there's a way of finding out. See you in the morning?" With that Sullivan signed off but had no intention of having a relaxing Sunday evening himself. When he got home, he booted up his computer and searched for the annual directories of the archdiocese.

"Now," he whispered to his computer, "talk to me."

After only an hour of searching he had a list of priests who had inexplicably left one parish only to turn up in another a few months later. Sometimes, he noted, the same priest was moved around several times. Gotcha! He stopped and looked at the names. Although the individual names meant nothing to him, the total number of them did and the fact that the pattern had been going on back in the 1980s appalled him. For the first time, he began to appreciate the scale of what had been happening.

He sat back. This was just in one archdiocese. What about all the other ones in the US? There could be hundreds of priests who had been abusing kids, then been protected by their bishops and archbishops and released in another unsuspecting parish to do the same all over again.

"There could be hundreds, maybe thousands of children abused by men who preached the gospel of Christ up and down this country," he breathed.

Then he stopped.

"What about Mexico and other catholic countries in South America? What about Spain, Portugal, and Italy?" He was beginning to feel dizzy. He shook his head and looked at the results of his research again, asking himself if he was making all this up? Could all this possibly be true? He stared at his computer and his notes for a while before deciding he needed a drink, then an early night. He would look again at it in the morning before going into the office. There were five days before he had to meet with his editor to substantiate these suspicions.

He left a text with Janice to meet early at seven o'clock in the office to share progress and prepare a plan. He wanted an empty office to work in, at least while they did all the desk work. Then, he anticipated, they would be out of the office much that week chasing down each story, hoping that at least some would come up trumps.

Chapter 7

EVERY WEDNESDAY, HIS Holiness would give a Papal General Audience from the Vatican Balcony. It didn't require a great deal of preparation on his part, but it meant a great deal to the populous who had come to witness the event. Even as he was walking to the balcony, he was mindful of the internal issues which would consume the rest of the week; issues that continued to need careful thought if the church was to avoid more scandal. He was hopeful that the Vatican Bank would recover from its low ebb of a year ago but he was yet to hear from his Private Secretary how Herr Hoffmann intended to deal with middle-management priests who had been in office during the last scandal. This was crucial, for he shuddered at the thought of papers like La Republica shooting another salvo across the Vatican bows reporting lots of priests being sacked.

Neither had he heard who had leaked the confidential papers about a cabal of gay priests in the Holy See. He knew that the bureaucracy was slow, not that he criticised this. It was better to be publicly slow for it often took the sting out of negative media stories, but he needed to know himself. The issue of the nuns in the US was annoying but he believed that if the Congregation for the Doctrine of the Faith could be persuaded to soft-pedal the issue, at least publicly, they might get away without a major media storm.

"Have you my blessings?" He asked his Private Secretary, as he moved towards the balcony, referring to the blessings he would offer in a multitude of different languages to the assembled throng in St Peters Square.

"Yes Holiness, here they are." And he passed a document in large type to his master for him to read out. Just before he appeared on the Balcony, at exactly 0900 hours, he turned to Douglas-Scott.

"I wonder how many pilgrims think this is all I do?"

The Private Secretary replied, "I think most will be well-versed in what Your Holiness has to do."

"Hmm." The Pope sighed. "Perhaps I should just be content to be the PR front man for the church and leave internal reforms to someone else."

"There is no one else who can do what you do." Douglas-Scott wanted to be encouraging although he knew the weight his master carried.

"Maybe so." And with that, he went through the curtain and blessed the crowd. Invigorated, he moved back to his office with his Private Secretary in attendance. As they were moving back through the corridors of the Vatican, Douglas-Scott whispered that he had the item that the Pope had asked for.

In turn the Pontiff whispered, "Charge it up and to start with, put your own number on it."

When they had reached his office and settled down, His Holiness asked about the Vatileaks issue.

"I've been talking with Steiner, commandant of the Pontifical Swiss Guard, and he believes they are very close to identifying the culprit."

The Pope looked up. "It must be done quietly. We cannot keep sustaining scandal after scandal."

"Yes, Holiness."

"And what about the nuns?"

"Do you want me to have a word with the Congregation for the Doctrine of the Faith? They say that the whole move was authorised by you."

"Yes, yes it was. We must protect the traditional doctrine of the Church which we have inherited, but this thing has gotten totally out of control."

"I agree, Holiness," said Douglas-Scott. "It's been handled very badly almost as if they were making a point."

"Of course they were," murmured the Pontiff. 'Probably at me', he thought. "Yes, have a quiet word that thanks them for their diligence but, at all costs, avoids feeding the media scrum."

"Yes, Holiness."

And the Private Secretary departed, leaving the Pontiff to his private thoughts. He made his way back to the office allocated to him, wondering why scandals always seem to revolve around money, sex, or power – sometimes all three. Money and power were somehow understandable, not acceptable but conceivable. But there was something about sex that somehow trumped both the other vices. The PS couldn't exactly put his finger on it except he knew that it sold papers.

Before he knew the Archbishop of Durban, as he was then, he had been married. No children since his wife wanted to pursue her career and, with the rigours of the diplomatic service and being assigned to a series of third world countries, the relationship had fractured and divorce had followed. His non-virginal state was seemingly no bar to his becoming a priest and so his catholicism led him out of the diplomatic field into the priesthood, though he had never served in any pastoral capacity. He embraced his new singleness as part of his commitment to God, so could never understand why some of his fellow priests turned either to each other or to pubescent boys. To him, such behaviour was completely unacceptable, particularly the abuse of children.

When he eventually got to his office, he sat down heavily in his chair still puzzling over the delicate line His Holiness was trying to follow in these sex cases. He wanted to serve his master effectively but was at a loss to understand him sometimes. He turned on his desktop and glanced at the emails that had come in whilst he had been with His Holiness. Among the dozens of emails listed as having arrived over the last two hours, there was the normal media digest waiting for him where the Holy See press office collated world-wide news which directly or indirectly impacted the Vatican.

He opened the email intending to glance at the headlines so he could delete it; one more email dispatched from the mounting list he had to work through. However, there was one headline reporting a story from the Boston Gazette which made him shudder. He immediately extracted the story and printed it ready to take upstairs to his master, who didn't use computers. The Pontiff's daily diary was always in front of him and a glance revealed there was an empty slot just before luncheon.

He denied several other requests for others to use that slot such was his anxiety to brief His Holiness. For the next two hours, he busied himself by chasing up Steiner about Vatileaks and trying unsuccessfully to contact anyone of seniority in the Congregation for the Doctrine of the Faith. He had no doubt they were at their desks but had probably been told not to reply to the Private Secretary to His Holiness. They didn't want to hear any instruction contrary to how they perceived their current mission.

Finally, the time came for him to go upstairs and share his news. The Pope was sitting at his desk writing when he knocked and went in. The Pontiff looked up, surprised to see his PS come in with a rather serious look on his face.

"What is it, Andrew?" asked the Pope.

"I've just seen this news report from Boston," said the PS, and handed over the piece of paper as well as a small black box. His Holiness nodded his appreciation.

"Hmm," murmured the Pontiff as he read the details of the report. "Nothing to worry about, Andrew. Just one priest and I'm sure His Eminence, the Cardinal will sort it out."

"But, Holiness, the report says that there may be many more priests involved in …. such behaviour."

"On the same basis, there may not be," countered His Holiness. "Don't worry yourself unnecessarily. Just concentrate on finding the person who leaked those documents from my office."

Chapter 8

GINO ARATA MAY have been a priest but he was no stranger to the world of intrigue. His father was a leading catholic businessman in Boston and, while he had been disappointed that his son had decided to become a priest instead of giving him grandchildren, he had come to terms with the situation. Perhaps his daughter, Angelica and her husband Mattia, would do what was necessary. Italians loved their *bambinos* and, whilst they themselves only had two offspring, Gino's parents wanted grandchildren to make a fuss of and pass down their wealth.

Arata Sr., known to everyone simply as Arata, openly admitted that it was difficult to get to the top in business without occasionally sailing close to the wind or, as he eloquently put it, 'being a little sporty'. In the world of corporate entrepreneurial business, all sorts of games were played, for the benefit of shareholders of course, he being the major shareholder in this instance. The portfolio was mainly in real estate but a successful diversification strategy meant when real estate values were not growing as much, other sectors made up for it or otherwise absorbed much of the tax due. Mattia had been recruited some years ago as a finance whizz-kid and was now part of the family and privy to most of the issues in the business.

It was a Sunday lunch for five, which was unusual but very welcome for the parents. The conversation around the table had turned to what Gino was doing.

"We might be facing a few challenges in the coming months," he said as he munched his way through the *antipasti* his mother had prepared.

"By 'we'," began his father, "I'm assuming you mean the church?"

"Yes, but probably closer to home."

"You?" queried his father a little sharply, putting his knife and fork down.

"Well, possibly. But more the Cardinal."

"That doesn't sound good," interrupted his mother. "I've always thought he was such a nice man."

"He is. But the more I do the job, the more political it seems to get."

"Every job has its politics," contributed Mattia, drawing a sharp look from his father-in-law.

"Let's change the subject, shall we?" said Arata Sr. with a knowing look at his son.

Both men then listened to the ladies talk about the new house Angelina and Mattia were moving into until the meal was over and they were able to retire to the drawing room. Gino's father was never one to beat about the bush, so came straight out with it.

"Anything we can do to help?" It was a question aimed at Arata Jr. with his eyes firmly on his son while setting light to his cigar.

"Not sure," said the young priest, following the same procedure with his cigar. He was thinking furiously about how much he should divulge.

"You raised the subject at the table," encouraged Mattia who already had his lit and was pushing smoke into the room at a furious pace.

"The thing is," he started, "some years ago, a priest was found to have transgressed with some altar boys." He stopped and looked at the other men. Mattia stared but his father nodded.

"Yes, I know."

"You know?" questioned his son incredulously.

"Of course. Keating, wasn't it?"

"Yes," confirmed Junior, totally taken by surprise. "How did you know?"

"I think it was in the papers," said his father airily, not admitting that he had helped the archdiocese with some funding at the time of the compensation award.

The priest stared at him for a moment, then looked at Mattia who, knowingly, raised his eyebrows.

"What would help at the moment?" asked his father, thinking real estate.

"Well, we're anticipating that the Boston Gazette will begin raking up the old stories in preparation for releasing new ones."

"What new ones?" asked Arata Sr.

The priest coughed. "It seems that the Cardinal moved him several times after each transgression only for him to do it all over again."

"So he's now in the firing line," concluded the businessman calmly. "Stupid fool."

The room went quiet for a few moments. Mattia was shifting in his chair signalling that he wanted to say something, but not sure what his boss was thinking.

"What about the boys who've been abused?" he asked the priest, thinking it seemed like the right question to ask and looking at the two other men in the room.

"What about them?" asked Arata Sr. No response. He waved his hand in the air. "Of course, someone should see to them," he said, not very convincingly. Mattia looked at the young priest who met his eyes but conveyed nothing. He knew his father.

"And if," he addressed his son-in-law, "you have any male children, I'll thank you not to allow them anywhere near the altar."

At that moment the ladies entered the room, complained about the smoke, and began talking about something else. After a reasonable amount of time, Arata Jr. looked at his watch, hugged his mother, shook hands with his father, nodded to Mattia and left. He made his way back to his rooms at the Cardinal's mansion, said to be worth over two million dollars. He wondered what his father was going to do.

Doing was his father's motto and, once he had set his mind on something, it would get done, somehow. It came as a bit of a shock to hear his father call a senior catholic cleric a 'stupid fool'. Perhaps he had been. It caused questions to arise in his own mind. Why would he move Keating around? Why not put him on permanent gardening leave or give him a job in his office to keep an eye on him? Did Keating have something on the Cardinal?

Father Arata had a diaried Monday morning meeting with the Cardinal each week, mainly to discuss the week ahead and, after he had spent a few hours thinking about what his father had said and the subsequent questions it had raised in his mind, he had decided to raise the issue with His Eminence. However, he didn't quite know how to do that, nor did he want to lose his job if he was seen as poking his nose in where it was not wanted. Not to worry. The Cardinal raised the issue himself. It was not on the published agenda for his daily meeting, but it was evident that the Cardinal had been giving the subject a great deal of thought over the weekend.

"I've been thinking," he started, "I should give you the whole picture if you're going to work alongside me to limit the damage to the church." He neglected to admit that his and the church's interests were very much aligned but his PS immediately understood. After all, this was a man that the Holy Father consulted. His fall would instantly question the judgement of the Pope, who might himself have to step down. That would have huge consequences for the whole church as well as being a tragedy for the men themselves.

"The thing is," the Cardinal moved uncomfortably in his chair, "the press will find out that Keating wasn't the only one."

The young priest sat back in astonishment. In his naivety, he had just assumed that priests were honourable men who had counted the cost of celibacy and taken an oath of service to God, the church, and their flock with Keating being just one 'bad apple'. Clearly, that was not the case.

"Why?" asked the Private Secretary, rather open-mouthed.

The Cardinal shot a glance at the young man ready to put him in his place, but relented and sighed.

"Why did I move Keating on?"

"No, why cover it up and all the other cases.... how many cases?"

The Cardinal waved his hand as if waving the question away. "Maybe it was weakness on my part. I didn't want a scandal and my previous Private Secretary recommended that we give Keating some time to come to his senses, then move him to another parish to see if he could conquer his …. tendencies."

"And the other cases?"

"The same process was followed. Of course, having done it once, it became the thing to do. If I'd have changed it, everything would have come out."

"As it has done," murmured the young priest.

"I did find out later that the recommendation was given by a person, a priest indeed, who had the same affliction."

"What?" Arata's voice rose almost to a scream. "Your previous PS was a paedophile?"

The Cardinal's face instantly changed and an angry expression spread across it. "He was a good man. Don't forget, these are priests we're talking about."

Chapter 9

THE GAZETTE WAS a weekly with its edition coming out on a Friday. So at seven o'clock on a Monday morning, the office was usually completely empty. Just what Sullivan wanted. He had left his apartment and driven his ancient Chevy through the early morning rush hour traffic for twenty minutes, to arrive before anyone else. Although the Suburban had been in production since the 1935, Sullivan's was a mere fifteen years old, only round the clock one time. Of course, he would have given a lot of money to own an original but not on his pay. It was his type of car: longest nameplate in the world, one of the first metal-bodied station wagons, a progeniture of modern SUVs (and better, in his opinion) with the chassis and power-train of a pickup truck.

A quick nod to Jimmy on Security, who never seemed to go home, and he bounded up the stairs to the newsroom. He looked around.

"Good," he said to himself. "No one's here yet."

Sullivan wanted absolute confidentiality. In fact, he wished he could have done all this without even showing his editor, not that he distrusted him personally but you never knew from where pressure might come. He trusted no one. Maybe Janice, though not in the beginning but she had earned his trust. He correctly suspected she had been put with him to report back to management and had been pleasantly surprised when she showed herself to be a savvy reporter with good instincts.

He gathered his notes on the desk and waited for Janice. He didn't have to wait long. On the dot of seven, the newsroom door opened and in she walked with coffee takeaways and bagels. He put his cigarette down and smiled. She settled down in front of Sullivan's desk, pushing her dark, shoulder-length hair back behind her ears and taking a large swig of coffee.

"What's the plan then?" she asked.

He looked up. The triumphant look he had on his face when they were in the editor's office had been replaced by an assured seriousness.

"This is going to be big," he whispered confidentially. Janice looked around and raised her eyebrows. They both knew no one was there.

"We might be bugged," he whispered again, looking up at the ceiling. Janice rolled her eyes and he smiled at the joke.

"So," he began, a little more seriously. "Look at this list and tell me what you see?"

It didn't take very long for Janice to see the pattern that he had spotted. She whistled quietly and read through it again just to make sure.

"It's the same pattern. Priests in a parish for a few years, then have some months off, then inducted into a new parish, where the same pattern reoccurs." She sat back thinking deeply. "Is there another explanation?" she asked.

"Not that I can think of," replied Sullivan. "But we need to check it out."

"But these are all over the US," Janice exclaimed. "This one," and she pointed to the top one, "is in Illinois, this one in Maryland. There are two here in Louisiana."

"My God," she exclaimed, "there are eight here in Texas. More in Kentucky, California, Oregon, Colorado, Arizona, and Washington State." She paused, looked up at him, and continued, "Also Minneapolis, New Jersey, Philadelphia, Florida, even two here in Hawaii." She stopped, shook her head, and rubbed her eyes.

"What the hell is going on, Sullivan?"

"Hell is going on, that's what," replied the veteran reporter.

"This can't be true – there must be another explanation."

"That's what we're going to find out."

"But we're saying," she started. "Let's be clear what we're saying, that dozens, maybe hundreds of catholic priests, probably in every state in the US, are paedophiles."

She looked up. "I don't believe it." She finished with an emphatic wave of her arm which landed with a bang on her desk.

He took a deep breath. "We can't go to every state listed here, so let's list those most likely to prove the pattern. So, we need to identify any local paper who may have run the story, then call the reporter named on the byline."

"What question are we asking and why are we asking it?" Janice was already anticipating reporters doing what reporters do i.e. answer a question with a question that would get them nowhere.

Sullivan thought for a bit. It had been a coincidence that the story he had come across had been written by an old friend. That was not going to happen again.

"Why don't we say that we're writing a book about the catholic church and came across this report? If we get lucky that will open up the conversation."

Janice nodded. "OK. So what do we want to know, besides any further detail the reporter had that he or she didn't publish?"

"Most importantly, we want to know if they had a story for a follow-up piece which they never published and if not, why not."

"Got it. That will tell us if there was any underhand stuff going on."

The newsroom was still empty although they could hear blurred conversations as people were coming up the stairs. No one interfered with them as they got to work listing the various newspapers in each of the places where priests had been removed. There were still numerous papers to examine in each place as well as online editions from some of the larger publications. Once done, the next stage was to access an online digest of stories for that paper within certain date parameters, and search for words such as 'catholic', 'priest', 'altar boys', or maybe even 'paedophile'.

Gradually the newsroom filled up until there was a buzz of activity that they were completely unaware of. So engrossed were they in their work that they hardly noticed what was going on around them. James H Porter, editor-in-chief, came in at about ten and made to come across the office floor but changed his mind and went into his office when he saw the concentrated looks on their faces. Janice didn't have the stamina that Sullivan had built up over years and by ten thirty was desperate for another coffee and to stretch her legs. Both were achieved by walking around the office the long way and getting two cups from the machine, one for herself and the other for her boss. She hung around the coffee area for a few moments stretching her arms and legs before returning to place one cup on Sullivan's desk. He grunted his thanks, leaving the coffee untouched on his desk where, over the next hour, it gradually assumed room temperature. He was getting somewhere and didn't want to break the momentum of discovery.

By lunchtime, they had both unearthed several probable leads within a reachable radius. Sullivan didn't want to push the budget flexibility he had too far too early. This investigation was going to be the proverbial marathon.

He knew how it would go having gone through the same or similar process many times in his career; hard slog desk research to begin with gathering data, then seeking out the victims, before confronting the perpetrators, whoever or whatever that might have been at the time.

Victims were important. They would both corroborate his hypothesis and provide juicy copy for the eventual stories. So he wasn't yet interested in the religious men at the heart of this scandal. They would come later and be the centre of his anger and vitriol. Right now, he was seeking the single moms who had willingly offered their sons to the various priests having no idea how their lives would be ruined. To do that, he had to carefully stroke a few fellow reporters who, he knew, would be as suspicious and cynical as he. Giving away their suspicions would mean losing the story and a possible Pulitzer. Some were free with the information they had, many others wanting good reasons and, even then, reluctant to share anything. It was like pulling teeth but it was only just a first tranche. When they had a pattern to share with their editor, then there would be more time to dig into the others.

It was time for lunch and to share what they had got. Sullivan nodded to his compatriot and they quietly gathered their stuff together and decanted to the pub.

"How many have you got?" he asked, once they had their drinks.

"Five good ones and four possibles," replied Janice. "What about you?"

Sullivan puckered his lips and estimated, "Probably ten, but a couple of real gems." He took another pull on his pint and added, "Don't forget, all we need to do by Friday is proof of concept, so go for the tastiest first." Janice nodded.

Chapter 10

FATHER ANDREW DOUGLAS-SCOTT was disturbed. Since his friend had a white robe placed around him, he had changed. Was that, he wondered, how it was with every Cardinal who had the Fisherman's Ring put on his finger? Was it something spiritual that had happened to him, just the weight of the responsibility he held, or was he just over-anxious to keep the senior prelates who held key positions in the Curia on side? He remembered that back in Durban, the Cardinal had stood up for human rights. And there were certainly lots of human rights to stand up for in South Africa. But now.....

Sitting at his desk, he decided he needed a break from the claustrophobic atmosphere of the Vatican. He needed to talk with someone to get his head straight for maybe the future for him in the Vatican was drawing to a close. He wasn't speaking to his ex. or rather she wasn't speaking to him. He recalled how she had laughed when he let slip that he had resigned from his diplomatic career and gone to catholic seminary. It wasn't a laugh of happiness rather one of derision. He should have known. She was career-led and would never have understood that there was something more to life than career and status, such as a calling. Thank goodness they had never had children. What a disaster that would have been!

He glanced at his diary and saw that he was free for a few hours, so he made his way out of the walls. He decided to change into his lay clothes and exit through the Vatican Museum entrance and lose himself in the crowds whom were pressing to come in. Once on the Viale Vaticano, he made his way down the Via di Porte Angelica and just walked, not really caring where. He was out. In the real world. He looked back at Vatican City and the Piazza San Pietro from outside in, rather than the inside out view that he normally saw. He examined the pilgrims and tourists with their maps, sunglasses and backpacks. Normal people. Suddenly, he wanted to be normal. Who could he talk to? He carried on walking, breathing the disgusting fumes of Rome's streets, but he felt free. He was enjoying it. No one approached him or took any notice. No one knew who he was and he enjoyed the anonymity.

He glanced at his watch and knew he had to return. The fleeting temptation just to disappear had to be controlled and, brandishing his ID, the Swiss guard let him through. After a three hour excursion in normality, he was back in his office, preparing to ring his sister back in the UK. There seemed to be no one else he could talk openly to. Yes, he had friends in Durban who were good company in the bar. They could talk golf, politics and women but none of them confided in him or anyone else that he knew about. He recalled that he had tried to confide in one friend whom he thought might have some wisdom and discernment only to be disappointed at his response. He seemed to be embarrassed to be asked about something a little deeper than general 'pub talk'. That were certainly not what he needed now.

There were colleagues back in the diplomatic service with whom he had got on really well, but were they the right people to disclose his uncertainties? Mostly, he remembered, they were good people but all dedicated to climbing the greasy pole for status and pension. He couldn't remember anyone who had congratulated him on his change of career. On the contrary, not one of them seem to understand what he had done or the reasons he had done it. He recalled how lonely he had felt and how it had pushed him into questioning again if he was taking the right move. But he had committed himself and quite looked forward to studying at the seminary, being a student again with no responsibilities, and no one except the lecturers to tell him what to do. He could express his own thoughts and opinions in his essays and no one could gainsay them, unless they were badly argued or heretical.

And here he was, still lonely. Perhaps, he thought, this was part of his make-up. His father, God rest his soul, had been a private man. His fatherhood was composed of providing the income for the family, insisting they go to Mass, and leaving everything else to his wife. His mother, admittedly, was more outgoing and fun with plenty of friends. Maybe that was the way she coped with his father. It was a Mars and Venus marriage but it seemed to work as far as he could remember. At least, they never divorced so, he supposed, that was a good thing. On reflection, he concluded, he had more of his father's DNA than his mother's.

His sister, on the other hand, was the reverse. She was outgoing but also thoughtful and that's what he wanted, needed. In his mind, this was a pivotal moment for him and his future. Now, he was not so sure that the move away from the diplomatic service had been a wise one. Yet he had grown dissatisfied with that role because increasingly he was being told what to say and do, with very little opportunity to be heard and express how he felt about situations and issues. And here, in the Vatican, it was turning out to be the same. Whilst he had some influence on the Cardinal in Durban, as Pope in Rome, he didn't seem to have any.

His thoughts turned to Kent, where his sister and family lived. What was he going to say to her? What would Trevor, her husband, say? He got on reasonably well with him but never knew whether that was real or he was just making an effort to be pleasant for the sake of his sister.

He rang her number. "Hi Jo," he said as cheerfully. He could fake it with the best of them. After all, he was a diplomat.

There was a pause at the other end. "Andy?"

"Sorry to call you out of the blue,"

"Wow. Great to hear your voice. How are you? How's the Vatican?"

"Busy of course. Look," he said, wanting to move away from church stuff, "I have the opportunity for a short break and I wondered whether I could call in and see you all while I'm in the UK?" Expressed like a true diplomat!

"Yes, yes. Be delighted to see you, as will the children. When were you thinking?"

"I've yet to make final arrangements but I can be flexible so I thought I'd ring you to see if there was any time I should avoid?"

"No. I don't think so."

"Great. I'll email you with the dates I'm in the UK and perhaps you and Trevor can check your diary and see when might be free?"

"OK," said Jo, hesitantly. "Is everything alright?" There, she had already picked up that something wasn't quite right. If only he had married someone like that.

"Perfectly. The Vatican is only a small place and it gets quite claustrophobic, so it's good to take a break now and then." He was upbeat in his answer but also conveyed a concern which he knew she would pick up. "I'll email you shortly. Thanks."

Jo put her cellphone down and thought about what he had said. He was also running what he had said through his mind searching for any misstep he might have made. Part of his diplomatic training. No, he couldn't think of anything. He was now cheerful. All he had to do was to have a word with His Holiness.

Chapter 11

JANICE'S CHOICE WAS straight to a single mom in New Jersey. She had called the original reporter who had been quite free with his information, even as far as a phone number, on the basis that she gave him any feedback so that he might file a follow-up story for his paper. There was no timeframe mentioned and, whilst Janice would certainly keep her end of the bargain, it would be at a date and time of her choosing.

She made the call to the lady. It rang for quite a long time and, just as it was about to go to voicemail, it was answered. Janice surmised the number was not in her contact list, provoking a little hesitancy in answering an unknown caller. Janice spun the story she had worked up and, after some hesitation, she agreed to the interview as long as it was when her children were at school. She didn't want to upset them again. Good. She was in.

It was very early Tuesday morning. She had made a breakfast sandwich the evening before including a can of diet coke, for an early start. It was still dark when the alarm went off, but she heaved herself out of bed, took a fresh towel off the shelf in the closet, showered, got dressed, and exited her first floor apartment. Her ride was just around the corner in its bay with a full tank of gas ready for the journey. She put the zip-code into her satnav and headed down Route 95 in her VW still yawning. She was surprised to see trucks already racing each other north to south and south to north but, fortunately, not many other vehicles. It was a good run and, even though traffic going in and out of New York City was heavier, there were no hold ups. She passed the turn-off for her parent's place, just glancing down that highway before returning her eyes to the road in front. She had already consumed her pre-prepared 'breakfast' but her stomach still complained of hunger. However, she decided to push further to get on Route 80 before finally stopping at Wendys. Not her favourite by a long way, but she didn't want much.

She sat away from other customers to consume her coffee and bagel, enabling her to review the notes she had made. It was important to be fully briefed and ready for any comeback for there was usually only one chance. This lady seemingly had a son and a daughter, both in their early teens, the daughter eighteen months older which caused her to wonder whether girls were also targeted by priests as well as boys. Perhaps, if the conversation went well, she would ask.

She began looking at a website called www.nj.com. It appeared that two Roman Catholic dioceses in New Jersey had been pressured into naming priests who had been "credibly accused of sexual abuse of minors." It was unclear to her whether the Cardinal, one Joseph Tobin who led a flock of more than 1.3 million in four counties, had protected these priests. It appeared things were moving fast. If the Gazette were to get exclusives on this story, they would have to move quickly to get ahead of the game. Fortunately, none of these stories had reached major media as yet, but she knew it wouldn't be long. As she read down further she saw that a list of some sixty-three priests had been released who were guilty of abusing minors dating back to the 1940s, including several clerics accused of abusing multiple children. She was stunned. Odd, though, that the actual number of victims was never included. Perhaps they did not know, or maybe they knew but declined to add fuel to a fire that was already burning quite well.

The reporter was heading to interview the mother of just one of these victims who had gone public with her complaint. Maybe she knew of other moms whose children had been abused.

"Yes," murmured Janice, "she must surely know of others. If she was still antagonistic to the catholic church, she might be persuaded to tell."

She tucked her notes away, left the restaurant, and jumped back in her VW. She headed out towards Dover and, looking at her satnav, saw that she was only about thirty minutes away. She found the dwelling first time, pulling up slightly beyond a small house with a patch of green in the front and two bikes lying on the drive, but no car. Janice checked her watch. It was well past school start time so, just taking a small notebook and audio recorder, she stepped out of her car and knocked on the door.

"Excuse me, are you Brenda?"

A middle-aged woman appeared a little confused until the reporter said, "I'm Janice. We spoke on the phone yesterday?"

She looked at Janice for a moment as if deciding whether or not to let her in. Then she stepped aside, "Come in."

There was no offer of coffee perhaps indicating the lady didn't want this to last very long. When they had settled on the sofa, Brenda asked, "What is it you want to know? I don't want it all dragged up again."

Janice had been anticipating such a response. "My colleague and I are writing a book about how the catholic church has tried to cover up what their priests have been doing. Do you mind?" she asked as she put her recorder on the coffee table. Brenda shrugged.

"I don't want our names in any book," said Brenda quickly.

"No. We've explained to everyone that it's all confidential." Janice hoped that by implying Brenda was not the only parent cooperating with them, she would be more amenable to talk freely. It seemed to have the desired effect.

The next hour was a harrowing story of initial trust, abuse, lies and deception, more abuse, then public accusation, lawyers involved, then a settlement offer. The more the mother talked, the more she seemed willing to spend the time. Janice listened with increasing horror at what Brenda, a single mom, was made to endure to get any sort of justice for her son and family. She was ostracised by the local parish, threatened by church lawyers, her son stigmatised at school and herself having former friends publicly turn away from her.

Brenda was close to tears as she said, "JJ, that's my son, will never get over it. He might never have a fulfilled marriage and, I'm told, the chances are that he will somehow inherit the evil that was done to him."

"Has anyone offered counselling or help like that?" asked Janice.

"I was finally offered a settlement if I agreed to drop any legal claim and keep my mouth shut," said Brenda.

"How much, if I may ask?"

"I refused."

Janice was taken aback, raising her eyebrows. Brenda continued, "I wanted to tell the world through the courts what had happened. Yes, I got something from the courts but it won't make up for the damage it has done to my family."

"That's terrible," sympathised Janice. Brenda was now sniffing and left the room to find a tissue.

"If it's any consolation," started Janice once Brenda had returned, "in New

Jersey alone, some sixty-three priests have been convicted of abusing young boys, going back decades. The church has never admitted how many children have been damaged for life."

Brenda stared. "I had no idea," she said.

"Everyone seems to have been told that they're the only one and the priest would be moved. Unfortunately, only on to another parish."

Brenda continued to stare. Janice continued. "We have reason to believe that this is replicated across the whole of the US," admitted Janice.

"They're evil," said Brenda, shaking her head. "How that church manages to keep going is a mystery to me." Both were silent for a moment until Brenda spoke up again. "I guess lots of people don't think it's going to happen to their kids. I didn't, and look where it got me."

"Do you know of any other moms who have been in the same situation as you?" Janice was drawing on the bank of goodwill she had built up.

"Yes, now you come to mention it. There were two others who came to court at the same time as me. I wasn't in for their hearing, but we shared a bit outside the courtroom."

Brenda seemed open to talk so Janice thought she would keep pushing. "I'd like to talk to them if I could. Do you have a contact number?" Brenda hesitated and Janice held her breath.

"Why not?" She got up to retrieve what looked like an address book and read out the numbers.

"And the surnames?" asked Janice, and Brenda obliged.

"I haven't been in touch since," Brenda admitted. "To be honest, I'm trying to put it all behind me."

"I understand completely," said Janice getting up. "I really want to thank you for your time and I'm sorry to rake it up again for you." As Brenda also got up, she added, "unfortunately, there are still moms out there who don't know their children are being abused, which is why we're doing this."

As they both moved towards the door, she tried to affirm the lady again, "You've been a great help to other families." Janice then turned back for one last question.

"By the way, why did you not use a lawyer?"

"Because I don't trust any of them either." Janice must have done a good job at looking puzzled because Brenda added, "They stitched me up on my divorce. Snakes, they are."

Janice left and Brenda shut the door without saying anything further. Janice walked down the road and got into her VW. Throughout the interview, her adrenalin had been pumping and now she was temporarily exhausted. She shut her eyes and took some deep breaths. It had been a harrowing story and it had left this single mom bitter and negative, but she couldn't blame the woman. If it was to happen to her someday if she ever got married, she might well react similarly. For someone in such a position of trust to do this to a child, what could be worse?

Having worked with Sullivan on numerous investigations, she couldn't remember anything that had impacted her like this. She had worked on environmental issues where a big corporation had dumped toxic material in a local river which had a calamitous impact on yet unborn children. Their response, she recalled, had been to deny, obfuscate, blame someone else, and eventually try to settle with local people offering a pittance with a gagging contract. The holy catholic church was doing exactly the same thing. It was just another multi-national organisation seeking to avoid doing the right thing and, when faced with the inevitable, tried to get away with paying the smallest amount of compensation as possible.

It was so unjust. She took a few moments to record some of her reactions in her notebook. Being objective about facts was one thing but, in her humble opinion, there could be nothing objective about the impact on hundreds of trusting lives, now lying in ruins. She wrote and wrote, paragraph after paragraph, using it as a kind of therapy. She knew such a story would never get through the Gazette's editorial process and be published as news, at least in that form, but maybe as an opinion piece in the future. It is said that everyone loves a good story, even at the expense of the truth. Well, if a good story, how much more a bad one? And this was really bad. So exactly how much truth was being covered up by the catholic church?

As she turned the pages of her notebook, she began to think of where to go next. A decision formed in her head to do one of the possibles where the local journalist had warned her of an unsympathetic welcome, so she hadn't called ahead hoping to use surprise as a tool to gauge reaction. The lady was going to be 'doorstepped', where she would try to get as much information as possible by challenging her rather than being sympathetic.

"Yes," she thought, "I might enjoy that."

It didn't take long to get to Bridgewater, just thirty-four minutes or so, and a few more minutes to locate the place. Janice parked her car outside a small block of red brick apartments, called Squires. She examined the plate near the main doors and saw there were just twenty-four dwellings on two floors with plenty of well kept gardens surrounding the building. It certainly wouldn't have been in the top echelon of apartment blocks, but nicely kept.

No.8 was on the second floor and, taking a deep breath, she climbed the stairs and knocked on the door. An African-American woman in her late fifties answered it, which took Janice a little by surprise.

"What can I do for you? We don't buy anything at the door." she said in a reasonable tone of voice.

"Sorry, I've not come to sell anything. My name is Janice Munroe and I'm a writer for the Boston Gazette." She avoided the word 'journalist' or 'investigator' for obvious reasons.

"Well, you've come a long way," was the woman's answer. "And I hope it's not for nothing." there was a hint of challenge but still said in a respectful tone.

"I'd like to talk with you about Kevin."

"That's a closed chapter."

Janice took a deep breath and asked a personal question. She needed to know. "Are you his mother?"

The lady laughed a deep laugh. "You think I had a child when I was forty three? No. I'm his grandmother. And just so you know, his mother has gone and so has his father for that matter, my son." At this point, her lips began to tremble and her voice waver. Janice took the opportunity.

"May I come in?"

"No. But if I change my mind, I'll call you." She now seemed very tired.

Janice looked at her more closely. Yes, she was looking quite worn-out. She guessed looking after a boy who'd been through such an experience was not easy. Janice felt sorry for her but she had a job to do.

"My partner and I are writing a book about...." She was interrupted.

"I know what you'll be writing about if you want to talk about Kevin," said the lady.

"It might help other parents and grandparents to be aware of priests."

"Maybe. You have a card?"

"Yes," said Janice, and fished one out of a pocket and handed it over.

"Thank you," responded the lady and shut the door.

Chapter 12

ARATA SR. WAS more than annoyed with what his son had revealed at Sunday lunch. The Roman church had been his family's church for generations, back in the homeland as well as now in the US. It seemed to him that senior clerics were complete novices when it came to running a multi-million dollar organisation which, in his humble opinion, is what the church was. They couldn't control their bank, couldn't control their personnel, and certainly couldn't control the media. It was all so amateurish. Such colossally bad decision-making. The only thing they had going for them was the undying loyalty of most ordinary catholics, and the public face of the Vatican, the Holy Father himself, who always polled higher than most Presidents or Prime Ministers.

As soon as everyone had left lunch, and his wife had retired to lay down for an hour or two, he made a call to a trusted friend who was a member of the same club as himself. After a few minutes of speaking in his mother tongue, he put his cellphone down and poured himself another brandy. He sensed an opportunity. Each archdiocese was a legal entity in itself and owned much real estate in their area besides the churches where congregations met. Perhaps he could repeat the deal he had done with Boston some years ago and offer some financial protection from the media – no guarantees, of course – and, at the same time, develop his real estate portfolio. The media would be the easy part; the difficult part would be the negotiation to take a charge on certain catholic real estate should an archdiocese need funding to ensure 'out of court' settlements for the activities of errant priests.

The venue was a gentlemen's club with lounges and dining spaces – no music or women allowed unless special permission had been given. The dark mahogany dining room with its hushed lunch ritual was quite a formal place but dedicated to conspiratorial conversations which could, and did, change the course of lives, including politicians, business people, senior churchmen, and media publishers. A meeting had been arranged for the following Tuesday.

"*Buongiorno*, Arata. *Chiedo scusa.* " His guest was a few minutes late and full of apologies. Rossi was also an entrepreneur of sorts. Import-export mainly, although very interested in the right kind of real estate.

Arata Sr. waved away his apology, smiled, and immediately put his guest at ease. He signalled with his hand that they should bypass the bar and go straight to their table.

"Thank you for coming. How are you and the family?"

"You know. Grown-up children that still aren't grown up!" They both laughed.

Their waiter was invited over and they made their choices. Sami bowed his head in mock appreciation, expressed his thanks, and headed off to the kitchen to deliver his orders. A few more minutes of small talk and Sami was back with their *antipasti*.

Arata began. "You remember that business involving a catholic priest some time ago who got caught acting....er shall we say, inappropriately?" Arata was pushing some mozzarella around his plate as if the question was of no real consequence.

"Hmm. Keating, if I remember correctly," said Rossi not looking up.

"Yes. Well, we managed to enable the church to settle the thing out of court to avoid unnecessary embarrassment. And, if you recall, it also enabled us to expand our influence in that direction."

"It worked out rather well, didn't it?" said Rossi, approvingly.

"It's quite possible we may have further opportunities in that field shortly," said Arata. "I thought you might be interested?"

"Yes, of course. Delighted to help."

"Good."

Just then Sami came to clear away, leaving a clean table cloth ready for *il secondo*. Conversation was paused for a moment.

"*Grazie*, Sami," said Arata to the waiter.

"What has the man done this time?" asked Rossi when Sami had retreated.

Arata paused. "This is where it gets interesting." Both men relaxed a little before Arata outlined what his son had to say at lunch the previous Sunday.

"What is wrong with these clerics?" began Rossi. "It's bad enough that their sexual foibles are becoming plain for all to see, but when their masters behave so ineptly..." He shook his head in disbelief.

Arata continued. "I have a suspicion that this is far more widespread than we first believed."

Rossi looked up and raised his eyebrows. "Indeed?"

"I don't know for certain but it wouldn't surprise me if the Gazette will be doing some digging into this.... you remember they exposed the original goings-on with Keating."

"Yes, I remember. So how can I be of help this time?"

"We don't want to stop the reporters..." Arata was interrupted by Rossi.

"Are you sure?" he asked, reacting as a staunch catholic.

"Yes, sure. At the moment, we don't know which archdioceses are affected and until we do, no approaches can be made to assist them," explained Arata.

"I see," said Rossi, beginning to understand where Arata was going. He wasn't going to allow his faith to get in the way of some business. "So, let the Gazette do the research, we get hold of their findings and then we stop them, or at least slow them down until we can complete our negotiations."

"*Esattamente.*"

Sami had returned with their Capri lobster with tomatoes, rocket salad, and marinated spring onion and the men sat in silence enjoying their lunch, but thinking hard.

"How much funding are we talking about?" asked Rossi in between mouthfuls of lobster.

"Difficult to say at the moment. We know the Vatican encourages each archdiocese to be self-sufficient in their finances and, in my opinion, it is quite possible that Rome will refuse to step in to bail out Cardinals who have protected certain priests who are now out of control."

No riposte from the guest, so Arata continued. "The last time it was only one priest. If there were more....." He left the thought hanging.

"So," continued Rossi, "there would be more compensation required, more funding to be put in place, but more business to be done."

"Indeed," confirmed Arata. He continued. "it's highly likely that some archdioceses might face bankruptcy, so the timing of our approach will be crucial if we are to maximise the opportunity. I have an envelope with me which outlines some possible approaches."

"On the way out," murmured Rossi.

The club was not a place to be passing envelopes across the dining table. The friends had passed on the *frutta e dolce* and *caffe*, opting to retire to the easy chairs of the lounge with a cigarette. It was only lunch, after all.

Chapter 13

FATHER ANDREW DOUGLAS-SCOTT was on his way to Fiumicino – Leonardo da Vinci International Airport feeling relieved. He had been dreading asking His Holiness for a break, but the Pontiff had been generous and just asked him to find someone suitable to stand in for him, which he had. His Holiness was also someone who could detect emotional disturbance, if that's what the PS was suffering from, but hadn't said anything except wishing him a relaxed and enjoyable time.

"Are you going back to Durban?" he had asked.

"No. To the UK, to visit my sister and her family."

"That's good," he had said.

When the door had closed, the Pontiff had put aside what he was doing and thought about his friend, wondering whether he was finding Rome more difficult than he had thought. However, he parked those thoughts with the promise that he would have a more in-depth conversation when, or was it if, he returned.

Douglas-Scott's sister lived in Tunbridge Wells, not far from Gatwick so he initially booked himself to arrive there, then a room at the Royal Wells Hotel. He didn't want to stay at their home, despite a probable invitation to do so. All he needed was peace and an opportunity to talk and getting that at the house was unlikely.

He rang Jo from the hotel once he had settled in to ascertain when would be convenient to call.

"Depends on how long you want to talk," she said.

He smiled. "Could never keep much away from you, could I?"

She laughed, "Well, you did signpost it quite skilfully. Come around for our evening meal tonight and say 'Hi' to the kids. They've been looking forward to their famous uncle coming. I think they might be looking for a present each," she warned.

"Yes, I had that in mind," he said, ruing the fact that he hadn't thought of it whilst in Rome. He had been much too immersed in his own situation. He'd better go out and get something quickly.

"Nothing expensive, please. Otherwise that will set a precedent for every visitor we get."

The evening was very pleasant and once the children had gone to bed, he had a friendly chat with Trevor about life at the Vatican, a subject on which he was happy to share, both good and not so good. But it was the next morning's walk with Jo that he most wanted. They agreed to meet at Dunorlan Park at 10.

A quick hug, then down to business. Looking at his sister he said, "I suppose you're familiar with the current scandal we're dealing with?

"Paedophile priests?"

"Yes." He paused. "By the way, how are you with your priest?"

"What on earth makes you say that? Do you know something?" Jo was alarmed.

"No, no. Nothing like that." Andrew hastened to assure his sister. "I'm sure he's a good man." He sighed. "You see, this is part of the problem. Because I'm dealing with reports of abusive priests, I'm beginning to suspect every priest. It's not good."

"I see," said Jo. "As a matter of interest, how many are there?"

"I don't exactly know but one is more than we need," admitted her brother.

"So there's a lot?"

He stopped walking and looked his sister squarely in the face. "I'd put money on it. A few years ago the Boston Gazette published stories about a Father Keating who had been accused of molesting at least one lad. Cardinal Doughty sent him on some gardening leave before putting him in another parish."

"So it's only a matter of time before he does it again." She was already ahead of him.

"Yes. Him and maybe a lot of others."

They were both silent as they began to walk around the lake passing runners, pre-school children with their parent or child minder, and retired people getting their daily exercise.

The priest started again. "The thing is that, even at the Pope's level, there seems to be a deliberate strategy to do nothing. They believe that it will all blow over and any damage to the church will therefore be minimised. The more they say, especially to the media, the more the likelihood of greater scandal for the church."

"But what about all the boys that have had their lives ruined?"

"Exactly. But I'm afraid that their only concern is to 'protect the church'.

"At any cost?"

"The greater the exposure, the greater the cost, both in terms of reputation and finance."

"So I guess victims, or their parents, are suing for large amounts of compensation."

"If they can't be persuaded to settle quietly."

The priest, still dressed in 'civvies', walked along silently, looking at the view but not seeing it. His mind was going over the arguments he had concocted to see it they held up. His sister was also quiet, giving him time to think.

"You see," continued Douglas-Scott, "I also want to protect the church, but I don't think that this is the way to do it. As long as these men are in positions of trust with minors, there will be no end. It's like someone has placed a cookie in their brains and they can't delete it. In fact, the more they do it, the more they want to." He shuddered.

Jo was still quiet, wanting her brother to get everything off his chest.

The priest continued. "We need to authorise bishops and archbishops to take immediate action when a complaint is made and suspend the person. That's what would happen in any other organisation. It would be a straightforward safeguarding issue."

"Why don't they?"

"If they want to try to keep a clean sheet with Rome, they move the offender on to another parish, where....." He stopped as the implication was clear. "Eventually, it all gets referred to Rome. They don't seem to want to listen and I'm not sure I want to be a part of that."

Jo gave a big sigh. "Now I begin to understand."

"They think that because someone has taken Holy Orders, they can be absolved without any criminal sanction because they're a different class of humanity."

She gave her brother a friendly punch on the arm. "I always knew you were a man who wanted to do the right thing."

"The question is: what is the right thing to do here? Stay in to influence, or resign and be on the outside?"

"But you're a priest now. Can you make individual decisions or are you bound by your superior?"

"To be honest, I've never really thought about it. If there was pressure to go against my conscience, I'd had no alternative but to resign the priesthood."

"Would that be a huge decision?"

"Yes, I suppose so. But it would strongly indicate that I was wrong to become a priest in the first place, wouldn't it?" He looked at his sister.

"Of course not. You went into it with the best of intentions to serve people to the best of your ability, and you still could."

He looked wistful as he remembered those early days believing he was making a difference. "Yes, and I still want to make a difference," he concluded.

"There will be many others who think the same way that you do," reassured his sister.

"Yes, there must be. Of course, you probably already know about the report of a 'gay cabal' inside the Curia?

"Is that really true?"

"The Holy Father said to me, and I quote, 'this is an institution composed of almost wholly of sexually repressed single men prohibited from the intimate company of women. It would be a miracle if there weren't some gay men among them.'"

"Oh!" said Jo. "Perhaps I shouldn't be so trusting,"

"Well, I'm in a special position of trust. But I don't want to go back to 'diplomat days' where I was told what to say, even though I thought it was wrong and didn't accurately reflect what was happening on the ground."

"No. I understand that."

"But if I can't believe in the Vatican's position, I don't think I can serve anywhere in the catholic church with a clear conscience."

They had completed their walk around the lake and Jo was leading them to the small coffee shop near the car park. For once, he was happy to be served, as his sister went to order and pay. Whilst she was waiting for the barista to prepare a latte for her and an espresso for him, she thought about Helen, his ex. As two women, they had kept in touch, though just birthdays and Christmas cards. Should she mention it to her brother? Perhaps not. It was not her responsibility, but....

"Have you talked to Helen?" She had returned with the coffee and couldn't help say what she had been thinking.

He looked at her sharply. "No. We didn't part on the best of terms."

"How long is it now?"

"What? Since the divorce or the affair?" he asked cynically.

Jo apologised. "I'm sorry. That was very clumsy of me." She took the opportunity to drink her latte and wait for what her brother might say next.

"It must easily be eight years or so now," he reflected. Then grunted as he recalled when he told her he was changing job. "She was very catty about my moving out of the diplomatic service into the church. I think she'd already said hello in her heart to someone else, and just wanted to give me a good kicking. For what? I have no idea."

"I don't think that relationship lasted." Jo looked down at her coffee rather than look at her brother.

Her brother immediately looked up, accusingly. "How do you know?"

"We still exchange Christmas cards with a short message and I'm pretty good at reading between the lines, as you know!"

"The Helen I knew was never up for changing her mind. She was always right, never acknowledged another point of view. Either she ignored you or trashed your point of view."

"There must have been something you liked about her. After all, you married her."

Chapter 14

SULLIVAN HAD, IN the meantime, headed to the nearest airport and flown to Chicago. A cheap flight, no more costly than Janice driving to New Jersey, he claimed. Of course, a cab at the other end might push the budget a little, but he could always submit that outside of this project if necessary. United's on-line ticketing was easy and the flight departed on time. Settled in his seat, he began to review his notes ready for any question or confrontation.

He had discovered that there was a group called Survivors Network of those Abused by Priests (SNAP) based in Chicago which, he was hoping, would provide a goldmine of information for him. On the other hand, the lady in charge might be so protective of her members that she might immediately clam up. For that reason, he had not called her in advance trusting his journalistic skills to persuade her to open up at the door.

After half an hour he was ready for a nap, catching up on lost sleep the previous night. The flight was just under three hours and he slept well, waking up just as they descended into Terminal 1 at O'Hare International. He grabbed a cab and made for the Chicago SNAP office. He had researched the organisation on-line the evening before and knew that the idea for SNAP had come from a lady called Barbara Blaine, after she had been abused as an 8th grade child by a catholic priest in Toledo, Ohio who taught in the catholic school she attended. Years of pain, depression, and shame followed the abuse with no response from the local catholic bishop who, presumably, hoped she would just 'go away'.

As an adult, she began researching the subject and realised that she was not the only one to be preyed upon by catholic priests. Survivors of clergy abuse like her, she declared, needed to help each other. By mid 1988, she had built a network of about two dozen victims, all of whom were told they were the only one. But it was not until 1991 that the very first SNAP Meeting was held at the Holiday Inn, Chicago. Since then they had grown as more and more victims contacted them.

The cab stopped outside Suite 810, at 205 N. Michigan Ave and Sullivan entered. Contrary to his negative expectations, once Sullivan had made his intentions clear, he was welcomed into the small office.

"Let's go into the back room," said Sarah, who seemed to be in charge. "Normally, we use this room for listening to, and recording the stories of those who come to us." She led the way with Sullivan following obediently.

"Can I offer you a coffee? I think there might be a donut or two as well?"

"Coffee would be great, but perhaps not the donut," he said patting his stomach and smiling. She smiled in return and went out to get the drink. He looked around a room conspicuous by the absence of people's faces. Confidentiality. However, there were statistics, graphs, and maps relating to their mission.

So, how can we help?" she asked once they had both sipped their respective drinks.

Sullivan decided to discard his pre-prepared cover story and be honest about who he was and what he wanted to achieve. In a few minutes, he outlined who he was, where he was from, what he and Janice suspected, and what they wanted to prove.

"Well, I think we're ahead of you in some regards," she explained.

She settled down in her chair and began. "Our primary purpose is to support survivors and protect children, but in doing that we also want to expose the truth of what has been, and still is, going on inside the catholic church."

"Have you noticed any patterns of response by church officials?" asked Sullivan.

"Oh yes," replied Sarah. "Essentially there is one response. Never admit anything. If there is any allegation, firstly deny it, then if witness statements are made, claim it was a 'one-off' with a 'rogue priest' who would be taken out of the parish."

"Yea. Heard that one before."

"Of course, the 'rogue priest' being taken out of the parish proved to be not just an empty promise, but a very deceitful one. There was never any intention of taking these men out of the ministry."

"Yep," confirmed Sullivan. "They just send them to another parish to do it all over again."

"Right," confirmed Sarah. "So we then tried to get various individual bishops and cardinals to acknowledge the truth about many of their own priests, but to no avail. Eventually, we decided that we had to travel to the National Conference of Catholic Bishops in Washington D.C. to confront them."

"I bet that went down well!" said Sullivan sarcastically.

She snorted at this point. "Of course, we knew they would refuse to see us, but we stuck around with the media and finally somebody decided that perhaps we were an embarrassment and the media would weigh in, so three of them finally agreed to meet with us and to listen to our stories."

Sullivan was listening carefully but also making his own audio recording. "What was their reaction?"

Sarah retorted, "What do you think? They said they would take what they had learned 'under consideration.' And they made that statement to the media in an attempt to sideline us and defuse the whole thing."

"And," prophesied Sullivan, "that was the end of that!"

"Precisely. We then decided to hold what we called a 'Listening Session' in New Orleans the following spring and all bishops were invited. Guess how many bishops came?"

"None?" prophesied Sullivan again.

"Correct," confirmed Sarah. Sullivan was shaking his head, while Sarah continued. "Abuse gets power from silence and we were determined not to go away quietly."

They were both subdued for a few moments; Sarah re-experiencing some of the conversations she had encountered with various catholic bishops, whereas Sullivan was thinking of the width of this story and how best to frame it. Then Sarah spoke up again.

"NPR Illinois reports that our state's Attorney General, Kwame Raoul, has got his teeth into this and found that nearly 2,000 minors were sexually abused by catholic priests in Illinois over 69 years. Cardinal Blase Cupich said the church had nothing to hide."

"69 years!" Sullivan was incredulous, not quite echoing the probable reaction of his sidekick who would have exclaimed, "2,000 kids damaged for life!"

"How does this church survive?" he asked, shaking his head in disbelief.

But Sarah had more. "Did you know that, according to the Washington Post, Cardinal Theodore McCarrick, Archbishop of Washington, was accused of allegedly abusing a minor while he was a priest in New York City nearly 50 years ago."

"What happened?" asked Sullivan.

"He stepped down." She paused. "Are you going to tell me that it was only the one time?" she asked rhetorically.

"Highly unlikely," agreed Sullivan. "This thing is in their DNA."

"And before he became Archbishop, he was bishop of Metuchen." Sullivan must have frowned, for Sarah went on, "it's a suburban borough in Middlesex County. And was he whiter than white whilst there?" There was a cynical tone to her voice as she clearly thought not.

"Then, there's the Maryland story. Their Attorney General's Office has released a report detailing accusations of sexual abuse against 160 catholic priests involving more than 600 victims across 80 years."

Sullivan was leaning back in his chair as if he had been hit around the head. His brain was having trouble taking all this in. He couldn't believe the extent of such behaviour and why no one had done anything about it for decades.

"I've not finished," said Sarah, observing her visitor's reaction. "www. nbcnews.com reports that Pennsylvania's supreme court issued a report stating that over 300 'predator priests' in six dioceses abused at least 1,000 children over 70 years. I could go on."

"This is more than shocking. It's......" Sullivan was incredulous, words failing him. The hard-bitten reporter was staggered at the dimensions of what he was finding. They were both quiet. Sarah had known all this, and more, for some time, yet it still hit her in the stomach every time she rehearsed it.

"Hang on a sec," said Sullivan thinking hard. "There's another aspect to this which no one has raised.

"What?" asked Sarah.

"I wonder how many paedophile priests that bishops and archbishops have protected and proceeded to move around?"

"We'll never know," admitted Sarah.

Sullivan smiled. "Do you want to know?"

Sarah stared at him. "You know?" she asked, her voice rising.

"No. But I'll show you how to find out," said Sullivan and explained how to interrogate the annual directories of a diocese.

"Amazing," said Sarah. "We can do this for the whole of the US. I'll get someone on it."

"Perhaps you can do me a favour in return?" asked Sullivan.

"Anything," replied Sarah.

"As a journalist, I need stories. Can you point me in the direction of a couple of your members who would be willing to tell me their stories?"

Sarah thought for a moment. "Yea, I think so."

"If possible, make them as different from each other as possible?"

"In what way?" Sarah didn't quite understand.

Sullivan explained. "Maybe how they reacted. You know, lawyer up and go to court or settle quietly, for instance. Or maybe good, well-off families versus struggling single mom ones."

"OK. I get it," replied Sarah. "Leave it with me."

"If you have an obvious one that maybe I could squeeze in this afternoon while I'm here, that'd be great. Otherwise, I'll have to fly back over."

"I'll try. But you could always zoom them."

Sullivan pursed his lips. "In person is always better. You know, body language, state of the house, car or no car on the drive. It all helps me to get a picture."

"OK." Sarah looked at her watch. "Why don't you step out for a bite while I have a word around and see what I can find. By two o'clock, I should know if I have something or not."

Sullivan agreed and after securing a recommendation for a quick lunch, he left the building. He tried to get through to Janice but there was no answer so he left an upbeat message hoping she was also doing well.

He was back in the building on the dot of two o'clock and in luck. Just a short distance away was an affluent neighbourhood where there was quite a vociferous mom who would talk to him provided Sarah came along too, so off they went.

"Dad," explained Sarah, "works at McKinsey's and Mom is an accountant who primarily works from home. She will give an hour. No more."

Sarah explained more on the way. They have two sons, both of whom went to a prestigious catholic boarding school where they were weekly boarders, that is, until 'the incident' with the younger son, Joe. He was too traumatised and scared to talk to anyone at school so it was not reported directly to the institution but the parents noticed something was wrong immediately he came home that weekend. The elder son said he knew nothing except that his brother was unusually quiet and a bit upset. He didn't take much notice and assumed that maybe he'd done badly in a test, or done something to annoy a teacher, many of whom were priests. All this background allowed Sullivan to make the most of the time allowed and, instead of the time-consuming process of establishing the facts, could probe the emotional impact on everyone and their reaction to what had happened.

Here they were. They advanced to the door where Kate, who had heard the car coming up the long drive, was waiting for them. Sarah introduced Sullivan who was brusquely invited in by the lady of the house, politely offered tea which was politely declined. Sullivan wanted the whole hour and more if he could get it.

"Sarah has graciously given me the bare facts without divulging any confidences," started Sullivan, hoping to strike the right note as well as shielding his source.

Kate looked at Sarah, who explained, "I thought it would save time. We will not stay a minute longer than the one hour you've given us ….. and I'm very grateful. Mr Sullivan, here, has already given us a lot of help and I believe can help many more families who have been and are going through what you went through."

"May I use my recorder?" asked Sullivan.

"Provided no names are recorded or released. I want total anonymity." That assurance was immediately forthcoming.

"Then fire away, Mr. Sullivan," said Kate.

"Can I ask how you first noticed a change in your son's demeanour?"

From that point and for the full hour Sullivan peppered Kate with questions to which she gave succinct and incisive answers. Sullivan was hoping that they had taken the school and the priest to court for she would make a superb witness. It turned out that, whilst they had been begged by the school to settle, they refused and were determined to go all the way. The school held their own investigation, mostly to protect themselves, as their insurers' legal team advised.

Although that investigation discovered at least two priests were involved, one being in charge of physical education, the school hierarchy denied any knowledge of paedophilia on their premises. It was the lesser of a number of evils, admitting to lack of oversight, duty of care etc., claiming that the priests were under the oversight of the bishop primarily. The lawyer for the catholic church, however, counter-claimed it was the school's total responsibility and had nothing to do with the bishop or archbishop.

Having done some significant digging in conjunction with SNAP, the lawyer for Kate and her husband, produced evidence that at least one of these priests, allegedly, had done something similar in a previous pastoral role and had been moved. It was then the catholic church that found itself firmly in the dock whilst the school was let off lightly.

But the emotional turmoil in the family whilst this was going on was horrendous. Joe regressed severely. Bed-wetting, crying for seemingly no reason, not able to go back to any sort of school, and distancing himself from his father, which was highly distressing for both parents. Initially, they hadn't told the full story to the elder brother, but it soon became obvious that strategy was not going to work. Once told, he too, became suspicious of men as a whole and Kate put her business on hold to home-school both her boys. The payout ordered by the court, which was considerable, did much more than cover Kate's lost business income but money was not what it was about. A family had been emotionally ripped apart and two promising young lives had been devastated for the fleeting sexual pleasure of an adult priest. For the family, religion as a whole was now an anathema.

Towards the end, Kate was beginning to look teary and Sarah called a halt even though there was ten minutes to go. Sullivan acceded but just as they were going back out of the front door turned with one more question.

"If I write this up could I send it to you for your scrutiny?"

Kate hesitated. "Send it and we will look at it."

Sullivan stayed overnight using the time to write up his story, catching a return flight the next morning. Janice also drove back to Boston after her overnight stay and both were back in the office after their usual lunch rendez-vous at the pub, where they brought each other up to date.

"I think we've got enough to demonstrate our case," said Sullivan.

Janice agreed. "Perhaps we each ought to précis our findings – no names, just facts, and figures so we can give him something to chew on."

Sullivan screwed up his face. "I'd prefer not to give him anything."

"But if you were in his chair, what would you want?" asked Janice.

"Good point. But I still don't like it."

Janice said nothing but waited for the inevitable capitulation.

"Alright," said Sullivan, getting up. "Let's give him both barrels."

Chapter 15

ARATA SR. TOOK a day to think about the best way to get the publisher of the Gazette to do what he wanted. The man was a business friend rather than a personal one, an important distinction meaning he needed to mull over his exact pitch. Yes, Carl Meyer was a member of the same club as he, but they had never done business before. In his favour was the fact that, as far as he knew, Meyer was of German extraction, but a catholic as were most, if not all, members of this particular club. But religion did things to friendships, both negatively and positively. Nothing could be taken for granted.

"Carl, how are you?" Arata Sr. opened the conversation expansively when the publisher picked up his cellphone. Meyer knew who was calling which immediately put his business antenna on alert. Trust is at the heart of business, especially the sort of business Arata was into, and Meyer was not entirely sure of his ground with the Italian entrepreneur. It was the same for both men, but there had to be a first time and perhaps this was it.

"Arata, how nice to hear from you," replied a neutral-sounding Meyer. "How are you, and the family." Carl was a big man of German extraction with blue eyes and hair that looked as if it wasn't naturally blond. He knew how Italians loved family and instinctively mirrored his friend's cultural norms.

"Good, good," replied Arata, "although my son was talking to me over Sunday lunch a day or so ago which got me thinking about a potential business opportunity, and your name came to mind."

"What sort of opportunity?" asked the publisher cautiously, knowing Arata's record for wheeling and dealing.

"Look, you're probably busy right now. Why don't we meet at the club for a spot of lunch and I can explain fully? My treat."

"Of course, my friend," said Meyer, who loved nothing more than a free lunch which, of course, Arata knew full well.

"I'll get my personal secretary to call yours and get a date set up."

"Looking forward to it," replied the publisher.

Arata gave precise instructions to his personal secretary as to what dates he wanted, namely as soon as possible, and left him to get on with it. As it happened, Meyer decided he would be available whenever Arata was free. The date was set for the following day, Thursday.

"Why wait," thought Meyer. "This could be just what I'm looking for."

All Arata wanted was a small favour, but it had to lead somewhere big for Meyer to cooperate. The publishing magnate was something of a bully when it came to getting what he wanted. His empire didn't just consist of a few regional newspaper titles. He was into radio and cable but known to be looking for investment in a struggling TV news channel which, he believed, could be turned around.

Thursday lunchtime arrived and Arata had already secluded himself in the club's bar ready to meet his guest. He had given Sami instructions to direct the publishing man there for pre-lunch drinks. Arata had chosen just tonic water although it looked to any onlooker like a large gin and tonic. He wanted to have a clear head but would invite Meyer to order whatever he wanted.

"I'll have the same," said Meyer. So Arata ordered a large gin and tonic for his guest.

"How's the publishing business these days?" asked Arata, opening up a business conversation. He had Mattia, his son-in-law, do some research into Meyer's business and knew where the publishing magnate wanted to take his empire next.

"Newsprint is dying, of course. Not completely though. In my humble opinion, it will always be around, just at a smaller volume." Meyer was rarely humble, so it brought a knowing smile to Arata's face.

"I suppose the trick is to find the business model that will sustain it at that level," replied Arata, trying hard to be supportive.

"Sure," said Meyer. He shifted in his seat ready to get down to business. "What business opportunity did you have in mind?" He was anxious, even curious, to find out why Arata had approached him rather than someone else.

Arata got up from his seat and said, "Let's go through and I can explain." So both men went through to the dining room, Meyer taking his drink with him. As soon as they were seated, Sami came across with the menu and the men took a moment to order.

"And another bottle of that delicious white I had the other day, please

Sami." The waiter nodded.

"I didn't know you came here that often," commented Meyer.

"I don't regularly, but I find it's a good place to explore business opportunities." Arata was indicating that he was ready to talk.

He waved his hands. "It's a small favour I need, for which I would like to invest in your TV and film production company."

Meyer's mouth dropped open. "It's not mine yet, but how did you know I was interested?"

"I make it my business to know what's going on," replied Arata evenly.

Meyer grunted, clearly not enjoying the fact that his business plans were that transparent. "You said a small favour?"

At that juncture, Sami interrupted with the starter but as soon as he had disappeared, Arata reminded Meyer of his conversation with his son over last Sunday lunch.

"Ah yes," confirmed the publisher.

"You might not know but he's a priest."

"No, I didn't know," replied Meyer, now puzzled as to where this conversation was going. Religion and business rarely mixed, at least in his life.

"Well, he said something highly confidential which I now need to share with you."

Meyer had finished his starter in double quick time, pushed his plate away, and leaned forward intrigued.

"Do you remember that priest who was in the papers a few years ago for an incident with one of his altar boys?"

"Of course, my paper exposed it. Did a damn good job too. Got a Pulitzer for the investigation and doubled circulation overnight. Fallen back a bit now but still better than before the splash."

"There could be another in the offing. Even bigger."

"Really? My editor has said nothing."

"This is where the favour comes in," Arata stopped rather dramatically. He could see Meyer's eyes bulging a little at the thought of another coup at the Gazette.

"What do you need?"

Arata paused again as plates were cleared and the main course was served.

"I would like you to lean on your editor a little and get copies of whatever that investigator fellow..."

Meyer interrupted between mouthfuls of salmon, "Sullivan."

"Yes, Sullivan. I would like copies of whatever he finds out before it is published." Arata went back to his plate.

"That's it?"

"That's it! But I don't want Sullivan to know his editor is leaking stuff to you."

"OK," said Meyer. "I don't fully understand, but I can certainly do that. What is so highly confidential?"

"You'll see when you read it. I need to protect my son," replied Arata. "But I must have your assurance that it will not pass through any other hands, not even your personal secretary."

"OK," said Meyer, still rather mystified.

"Can you do that right away?"

"Sure. Will call him when I get back to the office. He won't like it, though. Have never done it before."

The men finished their meal before Meyer began to enquire as to the nature of the quid pro quo Arata had in mind. The entrepreneur asked some general questions about the TV and Film venture, demonstrating to his friend that he knew quite a lot already about the business and its issues. Meyer, in turn, mentioned the sum he was looking for and Arata already knew it was much more than he needed, but he didn't argue at this stage. That would all come later.

"Will you send me any due diligence paperwork you have and I will prioritise it."

Meyer was in deep thought as he was driven back to his opulent offices. It seemed a small thing he was being asked to do and out of kilter with the investment offer on the table. Of course, it was just an offer at this stage – no promises. It might never materialise but he needed more capital to fulfil his dream. Yes, he would do it.

He called the Gazette editor from his car.

"Porter!" his voice boomed out from the editor's phone such that he quickly held it away from his ear.

"Afternoon sir. What can I do for you?" James H Porter knew his place and that he served at the pleasure of his publisher.

"I understand that Sullivan guy of yours might have another catholic scoop." It wasn't a question. Meyer was grinning as he visualised his editor's face. Sure enough, there was silence on the other end of the phone. Meyer's grin got larger and he began to chuckle.

"How did you know?" spluttered the editor.

"Doesn't matter," replied the boss.

"I want you to get copies of whatever that hound dog of yours finds, as he finds it, and quietly pass me a copy so I can see where this is going."

Porter was getting himself back together again. "Well, I don't know yet what he's got. Maybe nothing."

Meyer interrupted. "It won't be nothing, believe me. When are you due to meet him?"

"Tomorrow, as it happens," admitted Porter, adding, "This could be very lucrative and therefore needs to be kept completely confidential."

"Good. Tomorrow then. Get it over to me by close of business." The line was cut and Porter put his phone down wondering what the hell was going on. He had no choice.

Chapter 16

FRIDAY'S MEETING CAME. As a weekly, the paper was put to bed on Thursday night and the first edition on the streets early Friday morning. A skeleton staff was still around if a new story broke which meant a new front page was needed for a second edition but that wasn't often. The rest of the paper would remain the same unless the original front page needed to be slotted in somewhere, but it would be tailored to fit the space available. Rarely did the whole paper go in for a complete rewrite. It was intended for a weekend read and so had many non-news pages such as book, music, and film reviews, plus the inevitable real estate and auto ads.

Many of the staff would not even come in on a Friday, especially if they had been up most of the night before. It was, therefore, a quiet time in the office, and after lunch even the skeleton staff had disappeared to the pub. The editor strode in at two o'clock, surprised to find Sullivan and his sidekick hard at work in their corner.

"No pub lunch today," he thought. "Must have something. That bastard," exclaimed Porter as his attention switched to his publisher.

"When you're ready," he shouted across to them and he settled himself in his office ready for the fight he knew was coming. He certainly wasn't going to tell them about his publisher's interest, or that he intended to leak their findings, but he did want to have a copy of what they had and he knew Sullivan would not like that.

Five minutes later, all were gathered in the Holy of Holies. "So what have you got?" barked Porter. Janice went first and recounted her visit to the catholic church where Keating was currently installed, and the single mom with two young boys of which one was suspected of being abused.

"That's not evidence," stated her editor. She then tried to counter with her visit to New Jersey.

"New Jersey, eh?" Porter was building his scepticism in order to pull out everything his reporters had got. The last thing he wanted was to leak half the story only to find that his boss knew more.

Janice recounted her trip and interview with Brenda. She outlined the abuse and the toll it had taken on the family, especially as she was a single Mom. She detailed the approach taken by the catholic authorities to cover it up and how she was persuaded to settle for a very modest sum, compared with what other victims had got when they had lawyered-up.

"Why didn't she?" asked Porter.

"It seems she was shafted by her husband's lawyer during a messy divorce and became very cynical about lawyers as a whole."

"Huh," grunted Porter. "Court records would be better for us."

"There was talk, " Janice continued, "that there had been sixty-three priests who had been guilty of abuse in that archbishopric."

"Talk is not evidence," said Porter looking hard at Janice. "I hope you have something better?"

Sullivan took up the story with his research and the link with an old colleague Fraser.

"Fraser, Fraser," repeated Porter. "That name rings a bell."

While his editor was trying to recall where he had heard that name, Sullivan recounted how this Mom wouldn't talk but had a brand new Ford outside her house.

Porter came to himself again. "Still not evidence. She could have inherited the money."

"No," contradicted Sullivan. "She initially went to court but settled before any legal process could begin.

"Difficult to prove," growled Porter. "And I bet she signed a gagging contract." Sullivan looked at Janice and grimaced.

Sullivan was getting a little exasperated with the continual knock-backs and decided to talk about facts and figures instead of stories.

"Look, we've got lots of stories but we've also got facts and figures."

"Let's hear them," challenged the editor.

"One more story first." The editor sighed and leaned back in his chair, having lit yet another cigarette.

"I went to Chicago...." Sullivan started.

"You went where?" Porter's chair came back to its standard position and he was now leaning over his desk. "I said you had a small budget extension, and you go off to Chicago?"

"It didn't cost more than Janice's trip to New Jersey."

Porter's eyebrows were raised as he looked at both of them with an expression that said, "And I guess you both had to stay overnight?"

"Just hear us out," pleaded Sullivan, thinking this meeting was getting away from him. He then told the editor about SNAP, how many victims they had uncovered and his meeting with Kate, the abuse at the catholic school, how she and her husband had lawyered up and got a substantial payout from the court as the catholic church was found guilty of covering up previous paedophile behaviour by the very priest who had abused their child.

Porter said nothing and Sullivan began to feel he had control back.

"These are just a few stories that we could have told, but here are the facts and figures." He then outlined his analysis of the catholic church's annual directories and demonstrated the pattern that catholic cardinals had adopted in these cases. He listed the following: Boston, Chicago, Honolulu, Los Angeles, Orange County, Palm Beach, Philadelphia, Portland, New Jersey, Minnesota, Arizona, Washington, San Diego, Colorado.....

"Gimme that," Porter stretched out and snatched the crib sheet that Sullivan had been using. He looked at it.

"Are you telling me, that you have evidence that catholic priests have been abusing kids in all these places?" Porter was looking directly into Sullivan's eyes, challenging him to substantiate his claims.

"I'm saying," said Sullivan quietly, "that the pattern we have discovered in the directories matches up with the stories we have tried to outline to you."

Janice felt she had to come in and support Sullivan. "Every story we have found matches the pattern of abusive priests being found out, accused, dirty tricks by the catholic authorities, hush money payments being made, the priest having some gardening leave then, when the dust had settled, being placed in another parish to do the same thing all over again."

The editor gave in. He got up from his chair and moved to look out of his window at the car park below, most of which was still empty. But he wasn't taking any notice of that. He was trying to get his head around what his reporters had found. He couldn't gainsay it. It was a massive story. Meyer had been right. That son of a bitch. How did he know?

Sullivan and Janice said nothing but looked at the back of Porter's creased suit as he stood by the window.

The editor turned around. "Bloody hell," he said to himself. He sat down and looked at his reporters. "You realise what you've got, don't you?"

Sullivan looked at Janice and said, "Lots of big, juicy stories."

"No. What you've got is a declaration of war against the catholic church."

Chapter 17

PORTER DISMISSED HIS reporters with a "Well, get on with it then." As an after-thought shouted through his door, "And give me a publication strategy that doesn't tell every other media organisation in the land where to look for more stories. I want this as an exclusive for months and months. Do ya hear?"

Sullivan looked as if he was going to demand his notes back but, looking at his boss, decided that now they had the go-ahead, he should quit arguing while the going was good. Porter sat in his office wrestling with how he was going to effect the leak. It went against everything he stood for, and what he thought the principles of his publisher were. He moved over to the small printer in his office with clean vinyl gloves on and made two copies; one he put in his safe, one was going to find its way to Meyer and the original was going to be returned to Sullivan.

He put the copy for Meyer in a plain white envelope, took the gloves off, and walked out of his office towards his top investigative reporter with the original. "Sullivan, I believe this is yours. Take good care of it. I don't want to hear that this stuff has got out." He walked away as Sullivan answered.

"Sure," said Sullivan, looking surprised.

"I thought he was going to keep it," whispered Janice.

Sullivan looked at the disappearing editor. "Don't forget, he's got a printer copier in his office."

By six o'clock, Porter still didn't know how to do it. The issue for him was that, with a clear conscience (or nearly clear), he wanted to be able to deny to his reporters that he had anything to do with it if it leaked any further than his office. He wanted to show Sullivan and Janice the copy in his safe, dated and signed. Deniability. If the catholic church played hard in court, he wanted a cast iron case that all he had done was instruct his reporters to continue digging. Not a crime.

By seven that evening, James H Porter, editor-in-chief of the Boston Gazette, was in his favourite bar plucking up the courage to make a call to his publisher from the pay phone at the rear.

"You're late. I said by the close of business."

"My business hasn't closed. In fact, it never closes." replied the editor. Porter could hear his boss snort in the background.

"So what have you got?" asked the impatient magnate.

"Tomorrow morning you will receive in a clean white envelope, something that did not come from me." And he hung up.

He needed another drink. Was he going over the top or was it a sensible precaution? He didn't know. What he did know was that this was by no means the end. Once done, his boss could do this as many times as he wanted. If he objected, another editor would be thrown to the wolves as had many others in the industry before him, and possibly after him. After several more drinks, he decided to take a trip out of town to mail his envelope. On the way, he passed the residence of the Cardinal. Lo and behold, a mailbox! Now if that wasn't divine guidance, he didn't know what was. In went the letter and he hoped to hear no more about it.

The following morning at eight o'clock, USPS delivered a white, legal size envelope to a private address in Boston. A housekeeper, who had been told to look out for it, carried the mail safely to the addressee who was in his private office still in his purple-coloured dressing gown.

"*Danke*, Hilda," said Meyer, already opening the envelope as if it contained a winning lottery ticket. He brought out the enclosed single sheet of paper and began to read.

"My God," he breathed. "This is dynamite. I never did think much of those senior clerics who seemed more to delight in dressing up in their costumes rather than engaging with the real world. What a load of morons."

He moved over to his copier printer, made a copy, and deposited it in his safe. He glanced at the clock wondering whether Arata would call him or wait to be called. Let him stew for a bit.

"Hilda," he called.

"Yes, sir."

"I'll have breakfast in twenty minutes, *bitte*."

"Yes sir."

Having showered and dressed, Meyer was ready for the day. He had been thinking about the revelations he had in his safe and desk drawer. Although he stood to make a lot of money out of them through the increased circulation of the Gazette, he thought he could make more. He had already emailed his private prospectus for the TV and Film production company and wanted to make that the major subject of the next conversation with Arata.

He waited until Arata called him. He didn't have long.

"Carl," said an upbeat Arata. "What have you got for me?"

"I have to say," began Meyer, "I can scarcely believe what I've read. It's dynamite. By the way, what did you think of the prospectus?"

Arata smiled at the tactics. It would have been what he would have done himself. He assured Meyer that it all looked good.

"What timetable are you looking at?" asked Arata.

"The end of the month," replied Meyer, which was a mere ten days away.

"That's not a problem," reassured Arata.

"Great," confirmed Meyer. "How shall I get this paper to you? I presume you don't want it in the mail?"

"No," confirmed Arata. "I'll send one of my staff to your office, or perhaps home, to pick it up."

"My home if it's today," said Meyer.

The deal was done. Meyer had his timeline and Arata had not committed the amount of investment he would make.

The Italian entrepreneur received the package at midday and he too, was blown away by the dimensions of the paedophilia among catholic priests. "If I had my way......" he murmured. His next move was to contact Rossi.

"Morning Rossi," greeted Arata.

"I assume you're instincts have proved to be correct?" asked the import-export man.

"More than I had thought," replied the entrepreneur. "I think our first approach ought to be Chicago. They've already paid out a significant sum to one couple who lawyered up. I imagine a few more like that and the Cardinal will be facing bankruptcy."

"Will that be problematic to arrange?"

"I don't think so. I have some good lawyers in the city who would love to get involved to help."

"By the way," asked Arata, "Have you heard of SNAP?"

Chapter 18

FATHER ARATA HAD a lot to think about. His Cardinal was in the firing line but seemingly unrepentant. He had referred to paedophilia as an 'affliction' and seemed to think that because a priest was involved, somehow that made it different. He shook his head as he sat at his desk in his little office. As far as he knew the Cardinal was not in the building and he didn't know where he was which, was worrying for a personal secretary. He looked again at the diary. Nothing. Where was he?

A legal charge had been laid and he was expecting lawyers for the catholic church to interview the Cardinal himself in preparation for his, as yet, undated court appearance. Perhaps that's where he was. He'd just assumed that the Cardinal's very position, and the privacy this matter required, made it imperative that the interview be held on church property. In any event, an interview with him, as the Personal Secretary was very likely, if not by them, certainly by the police.

He needed to prepare himself and began walking around his little office. What line should he take? On the one hand, he could defend his boss up to the hilt. Perhaps not. He might not be a criminal in the church's eyes but he was almost certainly guilty of something in the secular law's eyes. On the other hand, he could make his personal disgust plain and distance himself from what his boss had done. Smacked a little of saving his own skin.

The truth was that he didn't know the full totality of what his boss had done because he wasn't in post at the time. But surely, he didn't need to know anything except what had happened to Keating, did he? His mind was going in circles. What didn't help was that the previous priest in post, who was seemingly also 'afflicted' (he couldn't even mention the word), had made the recommendation. His body involuntarily shook itself as he remembered what the Cardinal had said about him. Were there things his boss had still not told him?

Perhaps he should try to tread a middle course. Find some form of theological words which would not implicate the Cardinal but also not compromise his own situation. Hmm. That might work in clerical circles but shuddered to think how he might be torn apart by some high-powered state prosecutor seeking to make a name for himself.

But didn't his career depended on it? Certainly, his career as PS to the Cardinal was in undeniable jeopardy. If the boss was found to be guilty, any new appointee by the Vatican would want a clean sweep of the staff. He could be transferred miles away, perhaps to a lonely outpost to meditate on the sins of his master. And what about the Holy See itself? There was very little coming from Rome about any of this. The current Pontiff had not offered a great deal of encouragement that any change in policy was on the way. What had he said to some reporters?

"The problem of abuse will continue," he remembered it being reported. "It is a human problem." It sounded to Arata Jr. as though even the Vatican accepted the practice as somehow inevitable.

"They're still in denial," thought the young priest. "Just wanting to try and protect the catholic church. But it's not going to work." He remembered reading a review of a book by sociologist Frederic Martel. He recorded the comments of Pope John Paul II when the first shocking disclosures of clerical abuse emerged back in the 90s.

"Just a few bad apples," he had said. Father Arata shook his head. The next Pope had been no better. Benedict XVI had pointed an accusing finger at the high number of closeted gay men in the clergy. Martel had commented,

"Though it flies in the face of all secular, scientific and psycho-sexual orthodoxy, the leaders of catholicism (as many as 80% of them gay themselves) persist in equating same-sex adult sexual attraction with the violent rape of children by grown men.... It will involve rethinking an entire approach to sexuality that is peculiar, punitive, and often plain perverse."

Another explanation given by certain other Cardinals, no doubt approved by the Vatican, was that it was the fault of the devil - a malign force tempting otherwise good priests to sexually abuse children. As if, thought Arata, human beings didn't have a choice in the matter. What a mess!

No. He would tell the truth. He had to for the sake of his own conscience, not to mention his immortal soul. His boss was surely not worth that much. He looked across his desk as his internal phone rang, breaking his deliberations.

"Hello,"

"Father, will you come in, please," said a familiar voice. So he was in. Maybe he had been in his private chapel. That would explain everything – well, not everything.

"On my way, Eminence," replied the Private Secretary.

A few minutes later, Arata walked into the Cardinal's office. The man sitting behind his desk looked in charge and confident as if he had been sitting there all morning. Arata did his best not to gape.

"You have a clear day, Eminence. Nothing in the diary," began his PS, as if everything was normal.

"Thank you, Gino." He paused and looked at his young protégée, perhaps wishing he was still young and could have his time over again. Arata looked more closely at him. Now he really scrutinised the prelate, he did seem rather tired with the beginning of black rings around his eyes. He had always been a little overweight, but now the fleshy folds of his face were looking decidedly limp. So not as serene as he first thought.

"He's trying to put a brave face on it all, but this business is starting to tell on him," thought Arata.

"Gino," the older man started again, in a fatherly voice. "I have been in touch with Rome. To be more precise, with the Cardinal Secretary of State of His Holiness."

"Oh!" stuttered Arata.

The Cardinal Secretary of State is sometimes described as the prime minister of the Holy See. It is the oldest department in the Papal Curia, the central governing bureaucracy of the Vatican. He performs all the political and diplomatic functions of the Holy See. If there is a potential legal issue in another government's jurisdiction, he must be informed. Eventually, His Holiness himself would be informed as might other dicasteries.

"Don't look so down-hearted, Gino," the Cardinal smiled. "This business will soon be over."

Arata didn't respond simply because he didn't know quite what to say.

"I'm sure the media will soon be in full cry, so I want you to prepare a short statement."

"Of course, Eminence. What would you like to say?"

"Something along the lines of ......" The Cardinal paused for a fit of coughing had started.

"I'll fetch some water," said Arata and dashed out. Even in the corridor, he could hear the retching and hacking coming from the Cardinal's office. He re-entered with a tall glass of cold water and the older man quickly drank, finally pulling out a rather stained white handkerchief and passing it over his lips.

"You see," started the Cardinal, "I'm not that well at the moment."

Arata stared and said nothing, waiting for his boss to continue. "I've been to the hospital this morning for a check-up." Arata's mouth dropped open. "I'm sorry I didn't tell you but it was a personal matter I had to deal with."

"And..." Arata didn't quite know how to phrase his question. "Did you receive some medication for your cough?"

"Yes," replied the Cardinal looking up. "I'm sure you've noticed that I've been getting a little slower these days."

Arata had, but he didn't see it as part of his duty to comment on the health or age of his boss.

"I guess we all get a little slower as we age," said Arata a little lamely.

The Cardinal smiled thinly. "I have cancer," he said outright.

"Oh no!" said Arata out loud. He was now troubled. All thoughts of the paedophilia issue had gone with concern for His Eminence.

"Nevertheless," continued the Cardinal, "our work must go on a little longer. So this statement needs to say....." At this point the Cardinal leaned back in his chair, looked up at the ceiling, and almost began to dictate.

After a pause, he continued. "We recognise the distress that has been caused by a few priests and we will continue to investigate... No, continue to thoroughly investigate any allegations that may come forward. We take all such allegations seriously and the safety of our parishioners is paramount. We will continue to learn from these episodes and have strengthened our processes. The measures we are now taking are part of the continuing process to build a healthy and transparent culture of life in our parishes and institutions."

His chair came down and he looked at his PS. "How does that sound?"

"Er...fine. But what measures are we taking?"

"That's for you to decide. I want you to write up some policies which will demonstrate our determination in this area."

Arata stared at His Eminence. He stammered, "But I don't know where to start."

"I'm sure you'll find a way," said the Cardinal. "Now, you must excuse me, for I need to rest."

The young priest made his way back to his office in a daze and sat down trying to process what he had heard. It had been only ten minutes, but ten minutes that had changed everything. Was His Eminence going to resign? Was he going to die? What had he said to the Cardinal Secretary of State and, just as importantly, what had the Cardinal Secretary of State said to him? And how was he supposed to pull policies out of thin air?

Chapter 19

SULLIVAN AND JANICE were having some concerns about Porter but didn't know what precisely. Their reporters' antenna was up but they couldn't quite put their finger on it. They were in their corner of the office tapping away, doing the grunt work of the job. This was the bit of the iceberg invisible to everyone else but without it, what was visible wouldn't amount to anything substantial.

Sullivan chuckled. Janice looked up

"What's so funny?" she asked, implying she couldn't see much funny about this assignment.

"Something just came into my head which my father once said," replied Sullivan.

Janice looked up sharply. "I've never heard you mention your father before. Not once."

"Well, we disagreed a lot," stated Sullivan.

"Why does that not surprise me," commented Janice wryly.

"He's dead now, but at one time he did do a lay preachers course in some church. I can't remember which."

"So, what did he say that was so funny?"

"He was commenting on the catholic church. He called it the biggest Christian cult. And if you think of some of the things they get up to, you can see some parallels."

"Like what?" Janice had moved from being interested in what Sullivan had to say about his father to what his father had actually said.

"Well, the way they indoctrinate the kids through their own schools. You see my dad grew up in the UK and we moved over here when I was about three or four."

"So you're a Brit really," interrupted Janice.

"In fact, I have dual nationality. But that's beside the point. What he told me was that when he was young, the Brits used to have a 'Christian' assembly every morning before lessons in secondary schools. Apparently, there was an Act of Parliament which made it a legal requirement."

"Really?" said a disbelieving Janice.

"If you'd stop interrupting, I could get to the point. Because there wasn't a catholic school in his neighbourhood, all the catholic kids that attended that school were allowed to skip the morning assembly. Either the assembly wasn't 'Christian' enough for them, or maybe too 'Christian' to come to a Protestant one."

He thought for a bit, then added. "And, if you ask them their religion, they don't say Christian do they? They say catholic."

"Interesting," said Janice, now thinking about the cult idea. "They do have ways of holding in people, don't they? I mean, as long as you get baptised, go to church, attend confession, etc. etc. you can do what you like and you are absolved of your sins, and guaranteed to go to heaven, aren't you?"

"I think it's a bit more than that, but you got the general idea," confirmed Sullivan.

There was quiet for a few minutes as they both picked up from where they had left off. Then Janice spoke up, "So is that where they get this thing about priests being absolved, meaning they can carry on doing what they do as long as someone absolves them again?"

"Well, they certainly regard 'holy orders' as something which sets them apart from us ordinary mortals."

Janice hummed and all went quiet for a few more minutes. Then she piped up again, evidently not getting on with her research but rather gone back to thinking about Sullivan's dad.

"So, you're dad was a preacher?" she asked.

"Nah. He never went through with it, but he was quite learned and knew a bit of Hebrew and Greek."

"Such as?" Janice was getting quite interested now.

Sullivan thought for a few moments, and looked as if he was delving into a long distanced past. "OK. This is interesting considering what we're dealing with. You know that the Pope is supposed to be the spiritual successor to the Apostle Peter, right?"

"Sort of," said Janice screwing up her face. Her face then lightened, "Yes, the Fisherman's ring. That's it, isn't it?"

Sullivan looked to the heavens in fake frustration, disregarding her ignorance. "Anyway, they trace it back to a verse in the New Testament where Jesus is supposed to have said to Peter, something like, 'You are Peter and on this rock I will build my church.'"

"I don't understand. What rock?"

"Peter's name in Hebrew or Aramaic, I can't remember which, means 'rock' or 'stone' or something like that."

"Aramaic! What on earth is that? asked Janice flaunting her ignorance as far as she could.

"It's the language Jesus was supposed to have spoken," explained Sullivan, not understanding that Janice was now leading him on.

"Really?" said Janice.

"So that is their claim to be the original and only church," finished up Sullivan, pleased that he could remember all that. "But my father disputed that."

"What did he say?"

"Well, he maintained that the Greek word which is translated 'church' in our Bibles, doesn't mean 'church' as we know it."

"So how did it get translated as 'church'?" Janice was now beyond her knowledge base.

"Guess who did the first translations of the New Testament from the Greek into Latin?"

"Ah. The catholic church." Janice was cottoning on.

"Right. It was called the Vulgate and Latin is still used in many catholic churches today. I guess it gives some sort of authority to their ceremonies."

"So what was the Greek word, and what did it mean?" Janice was now interested, thinking it might have a bearing on their investigation.

Sullivan was suddenly conscious of other people around and looked up to see if anyone else was listening to their weird conversation. No-one was. So he continued. My father said it was 'ecclesia'."

"OK. I get it. Ecclesiastic. Ecclesiastical. Refers to church-type stuff. Right?"

"Wrong. He says that the word was hijacked to reinforce Rome's claim to be the central authority for Christianity. If I remember correctly, and it's been a long time, it literally means 'those who are called out to serve.'"

"So it could mean anything – any public official could qualify under that definition, especially if they've been elected."

"I suppose so," said Sullivan. "Anyway, enough theology for one day. What's the time?" He looked at his phone. "Another half an hour, then lunch?"

"Sure," replied Janice, and the two of them got their heads back down.

Just then Sullivan's phone rang. Glancing at it he saw it was from Sarah at SNAP in Chicago. He mouthed S N A P to Janice, who looked rather bemused.

"Hi Sarah, what can I do for you?"

"Have you told anyone about us?"

"No. Oh, except for my editor. Why?"

"I'm not upset at all. Rather the reverse. A well-known firm of lawyers has made contact, said they appreciated the work we're doing and would like to help any of our clients (we don't call them that) if any of them wanted to be represented against the catholic church."

"That's very kind of them," said Sullivan, racking his brains as to how that might have come about.

"But that's not all," said Sarah. "They said they would do it on a 'no win, no fee' basis."

"Wow. That is interesting. How much of the compensation do they want to swallow?"

"That's the most interesting bit. They said they'd like to do it *pro bono* but would have to cover some of their costs."

"How much do they want?"

"Just 10%."

"Wow. That sounds like a great deal. I expect they're thinking every case is going to be a slam dunk."

"Well, it probably will be," agreed Sarah. "Anyway, if it was anything you've done, I wanted to thank you."

"Wish it was," replied Sullivan. "Anyway, great news. Hope you guys get a lot of money."

Sullivan put the phone down. He looked at Janice, "Did you get that?"

"Most of it," she answered.

Sullivan was silent. "Something smells," he said.

Chapter 20

ARATA SR. HAD pinpointed Chicago, Illinois for a very simple reason. He had taken Sullivan's report from Chicago and began to dive into what was happening with the catholic church in that state. He saw the reference to SNAP and immediately saw a ready market for some good lawyers. What he found was elsewhere alternately shocked and delighted him; shock because of the scale of abuse that was coming to light, and delight at the prospect of the business that could be done.

He began to discover what Sullivan already knew but in more detail. The recently issued report by the Attorney General in the state alleged as many as 451 of the church's clergy members and lay religious brothers in six dioceses had abused 1,997 children between 1950 and 2019.

"Unbelievable," he muttered to himself as he worked through the 696-page document. The report accused Illinois catholic church leaders of being 'severely slow to acknowledge the extent of the abuse', and of 'frequently dragging their feet' to confront accused catholic clergy. Moreover, the report went on, the catholic church failed to warn parishioners about possible abusers in their midst, sometimes taking even decades to respond after allegations had emerged about a clergy member. Unfortunately, the report noted, the statute of limitations had expired in many cases and those abusers would never see justice.

The Archbishop of Chicago said, in response, that he had not studied the new report in detail but took issue with how the statistics were presented, saying "it isn't fair or wise to focus only on the catholic church." In his own statement, Cardinal Blase J Cupich "apologised to the survivors and pledged that the church would root out abusers and continue to investigate allegations."

"Presentation of statistics! Is that the gist of his defence," Arata Sr. had no sympathy with such men. "If there was just one such allegation against me, my board would at least try to fire me and investors would probably withdraw their money and we would be toast. End of. These people seem to carry on regardless."

He put a call through to Chicago. Anthony De Luca was a partner in a prestigious law firm in that city that Arata Sr. had used before, but not for a while. When asked for his name by reception, it didn't take long for De Luca to answer. He could already sense dollars.

"Arata, my friend, how are you, and that son of yours, Gino?"

"Very well, Tony. That is what I wanted to speak with you about. Do you have a minute?"

" I certainly do, but let me say that I'm due over in Boston next week. Why don't we catch up, maybe go out for the evening?"

Arata smiled. The wheels of business were the same no matter what the product or service. "Yes, that would be good. It would take too long over the phone anyway."

"That's great," replied De Luca, "I'll let your secretary have my schedule, but keep your evening free. Should be fun."

"Will do. Ciao." The phone went dead. Arata could envisage De Luca getting back to his profitable meeting having quickly told his secretary to clear his diary for Friday morning, book a flight to Boston on Thursday late afternoon arriving not later than six, and reserve a room at the Boston Harbor that evening. He also made a note to mention to his wife to say he would be away on Thursday night but back Friday afternoon. De Luca knew it would be worth his while.

A few minutes later an email arrived and Arata nodded, updating his laptop diary which would automatically transfer to his Private Secretary ready for Monday morning. The next job was to survey the catholic property in Illinois. Enter son-in-law Mattia.

It wasn't difficult for Mattia to obtain a list of the properties which housed the Cardinals themselves. CNN had done a very thorough investigation of these properties back in 2008 and Mattia was staggered at what he found. At least 10 of the 34 active archbishops in the United States live in buildings worth more than $1 million and that didn't count hundreds of retired and active Catholic bishops in smaller cities, some of whom live equally large properties. Cardinal Timothy Dolan of New York, for example, lived in a 15,000 square-foot mansion on Madison Avenue, one of the priciest areas of Manhattan, worth at least $30 million. This neo-Gothic mansion was reportedly filled with thick red carpets and priceless antiques.

"Incredible," murmured Mattia to himself. "The boss is going to love this. Now, where is the data on Chicago? Ah! Cardinal Francis George, what have you got? Here it is."

A mansion in Chicago's ritzy Gold Coast neighbourhood with 19 chimneys sitting on 1.7 acres of prime real estate and worth $14.3 million. Three nuns who care for the Cardinal and his mansion live in a 5,800 square-foot coach house near the main residence.

"Phew!" breathed Mattia. "That value must have doubled by now." At this point, the son-in-law had no idea what his boss was thinking about, but he knew the corporation was into real estate, and here was a lot of it. He was getting carried away with what he was finding.

"While I'm here, let's look at some of the other Cardinals."

According to the same CNN investigation, Archbishop James Sartain of Seattle lived by himself in a three-story house worth $3.84 million; Archbishop Leonard Blair of Hartford, Connecticut, had a nearly 9,000 square-foot mansion, appraised at $1.85 million; Archbishop Thomas Wenski of Miami lived with his secretary, a priest, in a six-bedroom, six-bath house, a tiki hut and pool in the backyard overlooking Biscayne Bay, coming in at 5,350 square-foot and worth more than $1.38 million and St. Louis Archbishop Robert Carlson had an 11,000 square-foot home, worth $1.4 million.

"Poor man," said Mattia, sarcastically. "Has to live in only 11,000 square-feet!"

At this point, Arata's Private Secretary, Anita, came in. "Look at this," called out Mattia. "The Archdiocese of Los Angeles spent $7 million building a 26,000 square-foot rectory for its former archbishop in 2002. Not bad for a retirement home, eh?" They both laughed.

Anita said, "I heard once that a century ago, catholics decided to celebrate the success of their church in the United States by building mansions for their archbishops, as a way of saying, "We've made it, and we're here to stay.""

"Hmm. They certainly stayed, that's for sure," grunted Mattia. "And they certainly moved into some large and valuable real estate, but where did they get all the money from?"

"They probably have lots of millionaire donors," said Anita.

"Yea. Maybe they came from Italy and wanted to receive absolution for how they got their money," said Mattia cryptically.

"Woah. You don't know that," objected Anita.

"Well, my folks came from the home country as did our boss's. We know how things tend to work."

Anita decided this was not a discussion for her and moved away to get on with her job when Mattia shouted out again.

"Hey. This is even better. Listen to this. Archbishop Gustavo Garcia-Siller of San Antonio lives in a 5,000-square-foot residence, which includes a court-yard, a private chapel, and a wet bar."

"And get this," said an excited Mattia, "At the time of building, the archdiocese was facing a budget shortfall that resulted in the firing of eleven full-time employees. You couldn't make it up!"

Having had his fun, Mattia now had to dig into Illinois a bit more fully. There were plenty of church buildings for sale but unlikely to fit into their portfolio easily. Not a lot else was publicly available without trawling through government records which he was loath to do without knowing more about what his father-in-law wanted. The obvious approach would be to talk to their Chief Capital Assets Officer. He had found a name and contact details, but such a direct approach might not be appropriate.

Chapter 21

IT WAS EVENING in the middle of the following week and Sullivan was poring over documents relating to his crusade. They had done a whole lot more desk research into other US States ready for another meeting with Porter the following day. Sullivan was in his bachelor apartment with his vinyl turntable providing the soundtrack to his efforts. Tonight, it was Miles Davis and he was playing one of Sullivan's favourite tracks: Blue in Green. It was a haunting sound which somehow excited the reporter and, whilst others of a different disposition might think it rather dreary, it encouraged him to think. He was feeling upbeat and had decided he deserved a cigar which he was gently puffing with no partner any more to turn up her nose. He turned in at about midnight.

Overnight, a thought had been growing at the back of Sullivan's mind which continued to incubate when he was back in the office the next morning. He put another document he had just printed off to one side and brought the incubated thought to the front of his mind. He would readily admit to being something of a conspiracy freak, suspicious of everything he heard and read. And his conclusion was that it had to be Porter! Why would a law firm in Chicago suddenly approach SNAP directly after he had been there and, more to the point, just after he had talked to Porter about it? No one else knew about SNAP, did they? He looked over at Janice. No. It couldn't be her. He trusted her, didn't he?

Janice was beginning to tire. Week after week, the pressure they had put themselves under had provided little rest as they conducted their mission. A phone rang. It was her cellphone with its familiar ringtone of waves crashing against rocks. Well, it was better than the traditional chimes and it reminded her of summer holidays surfing in California. She hadn't done that in a while and made a mental note to plan a trip when the warmer weather finally emerged. May wasn't the ideal month.

Such thoughts only took a millisecond to pass through her mind before she glanced at the number even though she had every intention of answering it. A journalist answers every phone call just in case there was a story – well, maybe not every call, especially if your editor was on your back and you weren't as ready with your copy as you should have been. She answered pleasantly with some curiosity. That demeanour quickly changed. Sullivan was watching her and sat up when he saw his colleague suddenly arch her back and put her hand to her mouth.

"Oh no!" she exclaimed. "I'm so sorry."

There was quiet as she listened to the person on the other end of the line. "Yes, of course. I'll be there first thing tomorrow."

She clicked the phone off and put her hands over her face. When she took her hands down, Sullivan was expecting to see tears and was ready with a word of support - consolation was not in his DNA. It was obviously bad news. However, what he saw was a different Janice than he had seen before. She was angry. Her teeth were gritted and her whole bearing looked ready for a fight.

"What the hell was that about," he asked wondering what had caused such a change in her appearance.

"Kevin's committed suicide," she answered, standing up.

He began searching through his mind for a Kevin and was coming up with a blank. Janice looked at him and understood the blank look on his face.

"Kevin was the African-American lad in Bridgewater, New Jersey who lived with his grandmother."

"Oh shit." Sullivan suddenly understood. He also got to his feet and began moving around muttering to anyone who wanted to listen. "We'll take them to the cleaners on this. Now their problems have gone into the stratosphere."

But Janice wasn't reacting just as a journalist, rather as a human being. She said nothing further but picked up her bag and stepped out of the office to get to the restroom.

"Janice," called out Sullivan after her. No answer and she was gone.

"Shit," he said again.

He quickly sat back down and began to dig into the New Jersey situation while Janice locked herself in a cubicle, and put her hands over her face again. She didn't understand herself. Having never seen the lad, nor having children of her own, why was she so upset? She rose to her feet but, hearing someone else come in, decided to wait for them to finish so she could exit without facing awkward questions. However, her anger had not dissipated, rather morphed into a cold, calculating tenacity. She was an investigator, now on the same page as Sullivan. She returned to the office and sat down.

"Sorry if I was out of order." Sullivan was conscious that he was not the most pastoral of people and wanted to empathise with his colleague. She waved her hand.

"She didn't want to talk about him when I saw her last," she said firmly. "But she does now! You're right. We need to get these bastards." It was said with a steely determination that again surprised the cynical investigator. "I'm going to drive down, stay overnight and be there first thing to get this story." It was not a question requiring Sullivan's authorisation, nor did he seek to challenge her decision.

"Go girl," he said. "This could be our opening salvo." He didn't think it would, but wanted to encourage Janice in her pursuit of the story. Thinking about his publication strategy, this was just the story to launch when initial interest was fading.

Janice drove back to her apartment, gathered just what she needed for one night, jumped back in the VW, and pointed it in the direction of New Jersey. She had booked the same motel as before online and resigned herself to negotiating rush hour traffic most of the way. The car was on autopilot most of the way as Janice allowed her mind to wander. She had felt a tenseness in her body ever since the phone call and knew a period of relaxation was key to on-going physical and mental health. She didn't want to go down the Sullivan route of fags and booze, although he didn't seem to be doing too badly on it. The key for her was to turn off from the immediate source of stress and think about something entirely different, like surfing in California.

This strategy, however, was not altogether successful on this occasion. Her mind insisted on returning to Kevin, and what had made him take his own life. She knew nothing of his background. Why he was living with his grand-mother? Did he have any siblings? Where were his parents? Who had abused him, how many times and where had it happened? She breathed a deep sigh and looked out of the window wondering where on earth she was. In a four-lane queue – she knew that much. A quick check on the dash showed she was fine for gas, so settled down again.

It was late evening when she arrived within reach of the motel and decided to begin looking for a restaurant for an evening meal. She fancied Italian. Porter would have to swallow the expense tab. This was going to be a big story, possibly the biggest of the campaign so she stopped at Maggiano's Little Italy for a plate of spaghetti carbonara. She had a glass of Chianti but no desire to find another drinking hole which is what Sullivan would have done. She went straight to bed ready to be up early to spend some time working out the pattern of questioning that she wanted. The perennial assumption was that you only get one chance.

She arrived at the requisite door at precisely nine o'clock and knocked. Although it took a few minutes for the door to open, she didn't repeatedly press the bell. She was expected and knew that the occupant would be in mourning. The door opened slowly and she was beckoned in. Janice followed the grandmother down the hall as she steadily made her way to the living room. Janice thought the lady seemed to have aged terribly since the last visit.

"I guess that's what bereavement does to you," thought the reporter, having never experienced it yet. "Shall I make a coffee for us?" she asked, wanting to do something.

The lady nodded. "It's all in the kitchen," she said not moving, just inclining her head. "Sorry, haven't slept since..." she stopped herself and started weeping.

Janice came back with coffee and set the cups down. "Is there anyone I can call?" The lady wiped her face and shook her head.

"My husband has passed and Kevin's parents split up. I have no idea where they are."

Janice needed to keep the conversation going so began asking more questions. "So how did Kevin come to live with you?"

The lady was quiet. "Sorry. I asked you to come, didn't I?" Janice said nothing.

"Well," continued the lady, "I'd better start at the beginning." She sniffed. "Excuse me a minute, would you dear?" She got up and made her way to the restroom where Janice could hear her shuffling about. After what seemed like a long time, she emerged looking more together and ready to talk. In the meantime, Janice had looked around the room and had spied a picture of a young lad whom she supposed was Kevin.

"Is this Kevin?" she asked. The lady nodded.

"May I borrow this? It's a lovely photo." She nodded again.

Janice continued. "What's Kevin's surname?"

"Webster," said the lady. "I'm Dora Webster."

"So Kevin's father was your son?" She nodded.

"What happened?"

"My son got in with a bad crowd, eventually got caught, and is serving three years somewhere out West."

"Oh!" said Janice, not knowing quite how to respond. After a moment, she asked, "So that was what caused the breakup of the marriage?"

"Yes. My daughter-in-law couldn't cope and had what might be called a breakdown. I was asked to look after Kevin on a temporary basis, which," she smiled weakly, "turned out to be permanent."

"How did you get on?"

"Very well, at least to begin with."

Janice leaned forward. She sensed a critical point in the story was about to be divulged.

"What happened?"

"I took him to church. That's what happened." Her tone began to change as she began to relive what had happened. Her outrage began to grow.

"I go to a black gospel church, but my daughter-in-law was catholic, so that's where I took him."

"What about your son?"

"He was never interested in church, any sort of church. Maybe that's why he went off the rails." She began to get a little wistful as she recalled her son as a little boy, wondering what exactly she had done wrong for him to go the way he did.

"What happened at the catholic church?" asked Janice, trying to keep her impatience in check.

"They run a boys club with one of the priests leading it. Kevin wanted to join and I was happy that he would meet new friends after he moved in with me. Also, it meant he could continue with the club without me having to go to that church every Sunday."

"When was the club?"

"Monday and Thursday evenings, which suited me. It meant I didn't need to leave work early on those days." She stole a glance at the journalist and added, "I always left early if he was home from school, even if it meant a drop in pay."

Janice smiled and nodded, understanding that Mrs. Webster didn't want her to think she was unfit to have Kevin.

"Did Kevin like the club?"

"Yes, for a year or so. Then things began to change."

"In what way?"

Dora Webster took the cup of coffee to her lips, not seeming to notice that it was already cold. Janice waited.

"He seemed to be the only black boy and would often come back with cookies or candy. I thought it was a sign that he was getting on well. You know, maybe they were prizes for something he had done well. So I congratulated him."

"Was it?" asked Janice, knowing full well how this story was going to develop and end.

"Of course not. I didn't think for a minute that a priest....." She paused, "that a priest would abuse my Kevin."

"Were other boys involved?"

"I don't know. All I do know is that boy changed from having a sunny disposition to sulks, back chat, refusing to do anything to help around the house like he used to do. I mean, he was not Kevin any more."

"What did you do?"

"I went to see the priest who was running the club."

"And what did he say?"

"He waved his hand and said Kevin was just going through puberty and this sort of behaviour often happens. I should wait it out."

"I guess I took his advice, but it got worse. Then the school reports started coming in. He was truanting and sometimes wouldn't come back home until seven o'clock at night."

"What did you do?"

"I tried everything. Nothing worked. Then I began to hear other stories about this priest in previous parishes, so I went to their church on Sunday morning determined to have it out with the senior priest which I did at the door after the service."

"He got quite angry as did some other parishioners, but I was not going to let up. I wanted to know what this youth priest was doing with the boys and if had he done this before."

"What happened?"

"Kevin was banned from the club and shortly after that the youth priest was moved on."

None of this was enough for Janice. A good story but no evidence yet and she had Porter's scepticism ringing in her ears.

"So what is the name of this youth priest?"

"Er. Father Graham, I think."

"And which church is this?"

"The Holy Family Church or something like that."

"Thanks Dora, that's great."

Janice shifted in her seat wondering how to ask the next question tactfully. She looked up and smiled encouragingly as she asked, "so how do you know that Kevin was being abused by this priest?"

At this point, Mrs. Webster pulled out an old-fashioned handkerchief to wipe the tears now falling down her cheeks.

"I cornered him and insisted he tell me what was going on. Eventually, he did. All the details." She stopped again. "And the next morning he didn't come down for breakfast, so I went upstairs." This time, she burst into tears and there was no consoling her for at least five minutes. Janice tried providing her with some tissues from her handbag but they seemed incapable of doing the job. Eventually, Mrs. Webster calmed down, wiped her face, and apologised.

"There's nothing to apologise for, Dora. You've had a traumatic experience."

"It looked like he had planned it for there were empty pill bottles every-where." The grandmother was beginning to recover herself. "I can't tell his mother because I don't know where she is."

"Did you call the police? Was there a note of any sort?" asked Janice, still needing evidence that it was the abuse that caused the suicide.

"Yes, but they didn't stay long. An open and shut case, one said to the other. And no, there was no note, but he did have a laptop. I'm not an expert, but it looked like it had been wiped. There was nothing there."

"May I take it? We have experts who can deal with this sort of thing."

Mrs. Webster shrugged. "I don't know anyone who could do it. But I do need it back," she added.

"Of course. I will personally bring it back." At last, Janice felt she had something. She was invisibly crossing everything, hoping this was the silver bullet. She wanted to get back to base and get someone to look at the laptop.

She got up. "Are you sure there's no one I can call for you?"

"I have the pastor from my church calling in this afternoon, and I have friends."

"Well, thank you for your time. I appreciate how hard this must have been, but you need to know that there are a lot of parents and grandparents whose young boys have experienced what Kevin did."

Janice moved towards the door with the laptop safely under her arm and added. "We want to expose it and try to put a stop to it. You have my number. Call me if you need anything." Mrs. Webster nodded but stayed sitting on her chair whilst Janice quickly let herself out.

Chapter 22

HIS HOLINESS WAS not having a good morning. Come to think of it, he had not been having a good year so far but perhaps not an *annus horribilis* just yet. He knew everyone else had bad days so why should he be an exception to the rest of the human race? The Vicar of Christ certainly didn't feel like an exception. He was sitting at his simple desk – not writing, not reading, not even thinking. Just sitting. He looked up as there was a knock at the door and Douglas-Scott, his Private Secretary, entered with a file of papers and with the intention of talking to His Holiness about his conscience.

"Ah. Andrew," he started. "Have you ever considered your mortality?"

His PS looked startled and began mumbling something that His Holiness could not hear, which was just as well. Louder, he replied, "Of course, Holiness. Surely every priest has, otherwise they couldn't fulfil their calling."

"Quite right, Andrew. But I wonder what reception we will get when we arrive at the pearly gates?"

Douglas-Scott looked at the Pontiff closely, wondering if he was ill or perhaps depressed. His Holiness chuckled. "I mean, do you think we, being priests, will get an easy pass because of the Holy Orders we have taken upon ourselves."

"So he wants to talk theology," thought Douglas-Scott to himself. "I'd better watch myself."

His master continued. "Perhaps you think, perhaps everyone thinks, the Pope will get a special pass."

"I believe Genesis 18:25 says, 'Will not the Judge of all the earth do right',", replied Douglas-Scott, cautiously.

"Excellent. I see you've been reading your Bible. Unfortunately for us, it doesn't say anywhere that we, as priests, will receive favourable treatment."

"Oh!" said Douglas-Scott.

His Holiness quoted 2 Corinthians 5:10. 'For we must all appear before the judgement seat of Christ, so that each one may receive good or evil, according to what he has done in the body.' "You see, nothing about priests or Popes for that matter."

"Holiness, may I ask what stimulated this train of thought?"

"Andrew, you and I will receive good or evil according to what we have done on earth. How does that make you feel?"

"I'm not sure," said Douglas-Scott beginning to cotton on. "But for priests who have abused young boys for their pleasure......" he didn't finish the sentence.

The Pontiff looked up, pleased with his protégée. "But," he continued, "we are all priests and, in the Holy Church, we have traditions." He added, "although I'm not sure that God approves of all of them. But the catholic church is the Bride of Christ. We must not forget that." He finished quietly as if trying to ponder the mind of the Divine.

"My, excuse me, our primary task is to protect the catholic church, regardless of its foibles, whether that be in terms of process or people. Everyone and everything must have redemptive possibility. Our duty is to find that, not merely accuse and judge."

"Yes, I wanted to talk to you about that," responded Douglas-Scott, seeing an opening to talk about his visit to the UK.

"What are those papers you have brought in?"

"Er." He quickly turned to the papers. "Cardinal Patrick Doughty of Boston has been in touch with the Cardinal Secretary of State about his situation and His Eminence would like a word with you today if possible."

The Pontiff looked up, "Of course."

"Looking at your diary, would two o'clock be suitable. Holiness?" There was no further opportunity for the PS to talk to his friend.

At precisely two, the PS entered the Pope's office and announced the Cardinal Secretary of State. Douglas-Scott watched as the two men metaphorically danced around each other for a few minutes before the Vatican's Prime Minister saw fit to bring up the subject he wanted to talk about. There was respect for each other's office, but they were not friends. Although the Pontiff had the opportunity of moving the Secretary of State on his election, he had decided against. The man was good at his job and maintaining good relationships with other governments was important.

"Holiness, Cardinal Doughty had expressed his wish to step down."

The Pope pursed his lips. "Is this to do with his errant priest?"

"Not entirely," responded the Secretary of State, carefully.

"What then?"

The Secretary of State settled himself in his chair for a moment. "There are two other factors, one of which is almost certainly going to cause us some pressure."

The Pope was ahead of his Secretary of State, knowing the routine that many Cardinals had with such priests. "And the other one?" he asked.

"He has cancer." The Pope immediately crossed himself and Douglas-Scott observed him offering a silent prayer for the man. Opening his eyes again, he asked, "how many times did he move Keating on?"

The Secretary of State let slip a millisecond of astonishment, then quickly assumed his diplomatic face. "Many times, Holiness." Then added, hoping to surprise the Pontiff, "there have been and are many other Keatings."

His Holiness kept his face down without showing any reaction. He looked up. "Perhaps you would see what influence we might bring to bear which might limit the damage and make arrangements to appoint a successor. I shall write a personal letter to Patrick."

"Very good, Holiness." And with that, the meeting was over and the Secretary of State left the room.

The Pontiff turned to his PS. "You did warn me, I suppose."

"I'm not sure how successful His Eminence will be in trying to limit the damage. The information I have here," he proffered the bunch of papers he had brought in with him, "suggests that the local paper," he looked down, "the Boston Gazette," he looked back at His Holiness, "is preparing a further campaign against His Eminence."

"Against him, or the church as a whole?" It was a sharp question.

"He will be the touchstone of an exposé of what the church has allowed to happen," replied the PS.

The head of the catholic church left his desk and went over to the window where a couch was positioned and sat down. His PS had never ever seen him sit on the couch before, so he watched carefully and said nothing, conscious that his master was thinking at a deeper level than just errant priests. He said nothing for a while, then spoke into the air.

"It seems everything we hold dear is being challenged."

"There certainly seems to be a moral shaking taking place," contributed Douglas-Scott, trying to move the conversation in the direction of what his conscience was telling him.

The Pontiff smiled. "I'm glad I have you for a Private Secretary. You're right, of course."

The PS took that affirmation as a green light to extend the discussion toward a subject that he was particularly concerned about. "Perhaps, that is just one manifestation of an existing order which needs to be replaced and not necessarily the most important one."

The Pontiff looked up, interested to see where his PS would go.

"Is this what you've been wanting to talk to me about?" asked His Holiness.

"Partly," admitted the PS. "In many aspects of life, we can no longer rely on the past to predict the future. Take climate change, for instance. I was reading yesterday that the past data on the climate is worthless in predicting extreme weather, flooding, wildfires, or any number of things and events."

It seemed to be at a tangent to what His Holiness was saying, so the Pope wanted clarity.

"Are you implying that our traditions, based on centuries-old 'data' as you call it, should be re-thought? And that the Church is part of an infrastructure propping up an old order?"

"That's not my place to say," responded the PS rather lamely. "But perhaps we might start with some vision of what a new order might look like."

"Ah. That requires imagination and I'm afraid the Vatican is fearful of imagination. One never knows where it could lead." The Pontiff was smiling and getting up.

"Now, we have some urgent issues to solve. Where are you with *Vatileaks*?"

The PS shuffled his bunch of papers. "It seems, Holiness, that your butler is the prime suspect."

"What, Paolo?" He expressed complete surprise.

"He is being interrogated as we speak and, from what I understand, it is very likely."

"Why?"

"We don't know yet. I don't really know him personally, but the one conversation I've had with him suggested to me that he was not altogether happy with how the Vatican was dealing with certain issues." His Holiness glanced sharply at his PS, but no further amplification was forthcoming from the ex-diplomat, neither did his boss ask for one.

Chapter 23

As WELL AS preparing the front page spread for the coming weekend paper which was easily done, Sullivan was also delving into victims in the Boston area. This would be the follow-up for next weekend. He did most of it by phone using one victim to identify a further one. Some were dead-ends, others provided a rich source of leads. They all had one thing in common: after complaining, all had been offered compensation on the basis of an out-of-court settlement with a gagging clause. The church had even suggested lawyers who would work freely on their behalf. It was more dynamite against His Eminence and fodder for upcoming Fridays' editions.

"Are you ready yet?" yelled Porter across the newsroom.

"Shortly," yelled back Sullivan. Janice had just arrived back and he wanted to brief her before entering the editor's den.

"You need to see this," she announced to Sullivan when she came into the office.

"What is it?"

"It's Kevin's laptop. We need someone who knows what they're doing to interrogate it. It looks as if it's been wiped."

"Shouldn't be a problem. Computer files are a bit like sin."

"Pardon?" queried Janice.

"They can be absolved but they never really go away." Sullivan was smiling broadly at his joke.

"What does that mean?"

"It means that nothing is ever lost unless a real pro has wiped it."

"And you know a real pro, who can do this confidentially?"

"I certainly do. Let me have it and I'll get Iqbal on it.

"Iqbal?" questioned Janice.

Sullivan ignored the question. "I'll bring it back tomorrow."

Janice stared at him before handing over the device.

"Now," said Sullivan, "we have to persuade Porter to let us have the front page this week to launch our campaign."

"What's the main thrust?" asked Janice, recognising she was out of the loop and Sullivan had done the copy himself this time without her input.

"The Cardinal knew everything," he said simply. Janice nodded and they both trooped into the Holy of Holies. The editor-in-chief looked up.

"You're back, I see," he said to Janice rather grumpily.

"One of the lads has now committed suicide." It was said with a little hostility as if Janice was daring Porter to challenge her.

He quickly looked up first at Janice, then at his chief investigator. It looked to both of them as if their editor was truly shocked.

"Bloody hell," he said. "This changes things." Then quickly reverting to his normal cynicism he asked, "You have proof?"

"He confessed everything the night before to his grandmother, with whom he was living. He didn't come down for breakfast. She went upstairs. There were empty pill bottles everywhere."

"He'd been planning it," said the editor-in-chief.

"And we have his laptop."

"Which says?" asked Porter.

Sullivan butted in. "It's been wiped but I'll get our friend to open it up."

Porter grunted. "Right. This is a runner. You've got your front page with you?"

Sullivan handed it over and waited. Porter read it quickly.

"It's good. Enough detail to grab attention, but not too much to give away what we've got." Porter was grunting again.

"Yes, a bit of history, that's good. Gives us the right to open up the subject again." More grunts.

"Don't like this accusation here." He jabbed his finger at the bottom of page two which alleged the Cardinal's involvement. "Leave this to next week. You don't need that now. You've got enough to whet the appetite. Just start asking questions. Everybody will be waiting for the answers next week."

He finally looked up and added, "which better be good." Sullivan nodded.

"What pics have you got?"

Sullivan showed him his own pictures of the Cardinal's mansion where, his front page suggested, the Cardinal was hiding from public view.

"No. Not good enough. Get Harry to dig up some good library pics as well, and I'll make the final call tonight."

He paused. "You realise that although I'll let this go tonight, I'll have to talk with legal before next week."

Sullivan nodded. "We'd both like to be in the meeting," he said.

"Don't worry. You will be."

The intrepid investigators went back to their desks where Sullivan booked his 'friend' to persuade the laptop to give up its information. He had no doubt that it would – whether there would be anything useful on it – well, they would have to wait and see.

"Are you OK?" Sullivan was quizzing his sidekick. Janice looked at him and decided that he really was concerned for her, so instead of a sardonic reply, she nodded, "Yea. Thanks."

"What do you think he's going to do with my copy?" asked the chief investigator, his head slanted towards Porter's office.

Janice looked across at him. "Put it on the front page, I hope," she said, not understanding.

"Remember what happened last time?" reminded Sullivan.

"Hmm. Probably coincidence."

"You don't believe that and neither do I," rejoined Sullivan, then added. "Let's watch him."

Janice stared at him. "Are you talking about surveillance?"

"Why not?"

"You've been watching Homeland again, haven't you?"

"OK. Just me then."

Janice's mouth dropped open and gaped at her boss. "My God, you're serious. I don't believe it."

"Somebody is leaking. I know it's not you, and it's certainly not me."

"Thank you for that expression of confidence. It means the world," responded Janice sarcastically.

Sullivan continued to look at her in a questioning manner. She was now in a quandary. Could she be party to secret surveillance on someone she had known intimately and still liked, a lot? And would he do such a thing? Her answer: probably if he was put under pressure.

She sighed. "I suppose I can get another job at Walmart."

"That's my girl."

"I'm not your girl and this is a one-time shot," said Janice fiercely.

In his office, Porter was struggling with his conscience and not for the first time. He stepped over to his printer/copier and took two copies again; the original for his main sub-editor to do the final editing of the copy prior to releasing it to the pre-press team, one copy for his safe and the other into a plain white envelope which he folded and put into his inside pocket. Once done, he did his best to forget what he was going to do after he left the office and concentrated on getting his paper out.

He didn't leave until eight o'clock when all decisions had been made and it was just down to the technical people to do their stuff. Sullivan and a reluctant Janice had left earlier to take up positions outside the office. All they had to do was wait. Sullivan was conscious that Janice might get fed up and leave, but she didn't.... and here was their editor.

Porter had left the building and was on his way, somewhere. Sullivan nodded to Janice on the opposite side of the square. They moved slowly only to follow Porter to a bar where he sat on his own drinking a bottle of Sam Adams. Sullivan expressed some frustration and indicated to Janice that she should go, and she gladly obeyed. He, however, was determined to see it through. Thirty minutes later, the editor-in-chief left the bar and walked to the same postbox, dropped the envelope in, and made his way home. Sullivan, watching all this, felt he had been foiled. He didn't know what was in the envelope, although he could guess. He didn't know to whom it was addressed and could not predict where the information in the envelope would eventually reside or for what purpose.

He allowed his boss to leave the area before getting his phone out and relaying what had happened to Janice who, much to his annoyance, didn't seem to share his anxieties.

The following morning (Friday), Meyer received the envelope delivered to him by Hilda before he departed for the office. He recognised the envelope and tore it open.

"My God. They've started running it." He asked Hilda to pop out to get a copy of the Gazette and began reading the front page. He rang Arata who was still getting over a good night with De Luca from Chicago. They had renewed their friendship with Arata only hinting about business. The formal meeting would be this morning at his office.

No small talk with Meyer. "Suggest you get hold of a copy of the Gazette pronto," said the publisher. "It's started." Arata Sr. needed no further words. He got a copy and began reading its front page.

"Interesting.," he mused. "Doesn't give me any more information about Chicago, but does raise some other prospects close to home."

He looked at his watch. De Luca would be arriving at the office in thirty minutes, so he called his chauffeur, quickly finished breakfast, and left for his office – only ten minutes drive away. The meeting with the Chicago lawyer wasn't long. After he had brought Arata up to date with SNAP progress, the discussion began to centre on the front page of the Gazette. When Arata started to talk about other possible catholic archbishoprics, the lawyer began to lean forward as he began to see the dimensions of the business that his firm might have on their plate.

Another firm of lawyers were ensconced with Porter, Sullivan and Janice. It was an all-day meeting with sandwiches brought in at lunchtime. No break allowed. The lawyers wanted to keep the Gazette as clients but, just as importantly, wanted to cover their backsides. They were certain that the catholic church would try to challenge the Gazette. The first front page was fine since it had rehearsed the previous story and asked follow-up questions, implying they had a lot more to publish.

The second was trickier. It alleged the Cardinal's role which was backed up by evidence already in the public domain, but also that after complaints, he had authorised secret payments to settle claims of abuse against multiple priests over a period of years. No public record of the ugly truth but suggestions that the victims' lawyers were receiving a third or more of the financial settlements without ever having to go to court. The Gazette lawyers were hesitant to allow the Gazette to go after professional colleagues.

But Sullivan had names, dates and amounts from victims who were willing to trash their gagging clauses and blaming their church-appointed lawyers for not having explained it all to them. It looked like the various lawyers could also be in the dock at some point or at least sanctioned by their professional body. So the paper's lawyers advised Porter to concentrate on the catholic church and they would take it upon themselves to see if there was any evidence to take any further action against the church lawyers. Privately, Sullivan wasn't holding his breath on that one.

The rest of the day was taken up with stories and statistics about other US states, including Illinois. At about four o'clock, the meeting looked as if it was winding up when Sullivan began outlining what he believed could be happening in Europe and other mainly catholic countries.

"Woah!" one of the lawyers almost shouted. "This involves other legal jurisdictions. We're now in a whole new ball game."

The senior partner of the law firm stepped in, "We can't represent you if you print anything relating to any jurisdiction outside the US. But we can probably recommend a firm in whatever third country you decide." He looked at Porter, who responded, "Clear!" as he looked purposely at Sullivan and Janice.

It was one evening a week later when Porter stayed late to watch over the paper as it began to take shape. As Sullivan left, Janice said she had a little more to do. The reporters had finished their stories and the news floor began to empty as Janice knocked on Porter's door.

"I'm busy," came the perennial grunt.

Janice ignored it. "I hope you've not leaked any of our stories," she said, in a matter of fact voice.

That got Porter's attention. "What?" he almost shouted.

"I said, I hope...."

"Yes, I heard what you said. What on earth makes you think that?"

Janice mentioned that a high-powered lawyer had contacted SNAP the very next day after Sullivan had been there.

"You think I contacted a lawyer to call SNAP?"

"Of course not. But there's more than one way to skin a cat."

"Get out. I'm busy."

She left the door open, gathered up her things and made her way home. Left behind, was one very troubled editor.

Chapter 24

CARDINAL DOUGHTY WAS indeed hiding. He had spokespeople to deal with lowlife like reporters, so no possible need for him to appear in person. Father Arata, his PS, had issued his statement before the latest revelations which, unfortunately for him, had now been overtaken by events and shown to everyone as being mere window dressing. He was frustrated that it was all getting away from them. They were behind the curve and the Gazette was having it all their own way. His statement looked crass and all the so-called policy documents not much better. Indeed, they might have now put him squarely in the 'cover-up' firing line.

For the moment, however, the media scrum had turned its attention to the Cardinal himself. Now they were asking about how many other Keatings were there, and had he, as Cardinal, followed a policy of letting paedophile priests loose on unsuspecting boys in parish after parish. The Cardinal also seemed to be hiding from his own staff. No one had seen him for days and, according to one informed source which wasn't his PS, he didn't want to see anyone except his doctors.

"He would have to make himself available for the police at some point," Father Arata thought. "If he lives that long and if it ever gets that far."

Out of sheer self preservation, the PS fervently hoped it didn't get that far, but if the paper was to be believed, it looked like a slam dunk. What was he going to do? What do you do when you're in a sinking ship? With the paparazzi firmly encamped outside the building and nothing on which to fix his attention, his mind was running riot thinking of all the ways he might be found culpable in a court of law.

The weekend had come and gone. Everyone in the mansion had read the Gazette over and over, Father Arata included. They were just as astonished as he had been when first disclosed to him, although the paper disclosed things that even Arata didn't know about. It was all just terrible and there was nothing they or he could do about it. Just as he was musing disconsolately about his future, his internal phone rang unexpectedly. It was Tuesday morning, the first time in days that anyone had wanted to speak to him. All the staff were keeping their heads down, hoping that tomorrow would bring some relief from the siege.

"Gino," said a voice. It was the Cardinal, sounding quite weak.

"Yes, Eminence."

"I have to go into hospital tomorrow for treatment." He paused. Arata could hear coughing in the background as His Eminence tried to muffle the sound by covering up the speaker on the old handset. Arata waited.

"Gino. The doctors are positive they can catch this before it spreads any further." There was a little laugh. "But medics are always positive, are they not?"

"That's good, surely," responded Arata, not really knowing what to say. If his boss died or retired, would that prolong the crisis or bring it to a swift conclusion? He knew which he would prefer. Suddenly, he felt ashamed that he was so concerned about himself, after all, the man had cancer. But the Cardinal was still speaking and he hadn't heard what he had just said.

"Sorry, Eminence, I missed that."

" I said that I will, almost certainly, not return to my post. If they give me more time, I will retire and if they don't, well my soul is in the hands of God."

"Oh!" responded Arata.

"You have been an excellent Private Secretary and I will write a letter to that effect for you."

"Thank you Eminence."

"One final thing. Father Keating has been arrested. I thought you ought to know."

"Oh!" responded Arata again.

The following morning, many of the staff lined up in the hallway as Cardinal Patrick Doughty passed slowly out of his residence to his waiting cab with the help of a walking stick.

"Why on earth do those photographers take all those pictures?" muttered Arata as flash after flash, and click after click continued until the cab had departed.

"Perhaps they'll go away now and we can resume our lives," said one of the other staff, rather unkindly.

They all looked at each other and, without further conversation, were swallowed up by the mansion as each disappeared into his/her own area. Arata also retreated into his small office. There was still nothing to do. About an hour later, he went to the Cardinal's office to look outside. It seemed everyone had their wish. All journalists and photographers had gone, just like leaves blown away in the wind.

"Probably encamped outside the hospital," murmured Arata. He needed to get out. The air inside the building seemed stale and the atmosphere claustrophobic. He called his mother and said he was coming over.

"That's nice," said his mother. "We don't see much of you any more." This, despite a series of Sunday lunches in the past few months. Arata planned to spend a few days at home, out of the morbid mansion that had become a second home. He had his laptop and his phone so if anything happened or anyone wanted to contact him, he could still be available.

The following Friday's Gazette was eagerly anticipated by the Boston populace. Porter had ensured a bumper edition with more revelations about priests in the Boston archdiocese. Maybe not so eagerly by the Cardinal's staff but, nevertheless, each bought a copy as soon as the first edition came on to the streets and gossiped among themselves about their boss. Some were supportive, but many were of the opinion that he had brought it all on himself and them. Those who either had children or grandchildren were horrified and immediately took steps to protect their families. They would never see the catholic church in the same light again. For many, it would never be forgiven.

As Father Arata read the front page, he knew that it couldn't be long before the Cardinal was questioned and probably charged with something. The people would insist on it. His turn would come next. Maybe the lawyers would also be prosecuted for covering up crimes with blood money and gagging clauses. They had done well out of it all financially, if the Gazette was to be believed, and most did.

Father Arata may have been disconsolate, but Sullivan and Janice were upbeat despite their differing opinions about their editor-in-chief. The first edition sold out almost immediately and a second edition was hastily printed.

Meyer was apoplectic with joy. His paper was making more money than it had done the first time around and he wasn't short of praise for his editor who was tasked with keeping this momentum going.

It didn't take long for the city's prosecuting authorities to contact the Gazette's editor-in-chief as they looked for hard evidence of what had been printed. Porter was happy to oblige, knowing that Sullivan could work that into the next front page. He insisted that the paper's lawyers were present, as was Sullivan. Janice was excused. Meyer also had to be informed but, as he had seen the written note from the lawyers to Porter giving the go-ahead, he declined to attend.

Before the session with the city, Porter, Sullivan and their lawyer had a pre meeting where both made it clear to Sullivan that he could only talk about what had been published to date.

The lawyer was firm. "They will want written evidence, not just verbals. So as well as the stories that have been published so far, you will need to reveal any other background evidence you have. It will be to your benefit in substantiating what you have now, and giving credence to any future revelations."

Porter added, "This will be a win-win for us." Sullivan nodded.

Prosecutors seemed satisfied with the material that Sullivan provided and went away to decide whether the evidence reached the required threshold. There was little doubt in the room that it had.

Chapter 25

ARATA JR. MAY have been in a slough of despond but his father was upbeat, turning his acquisitive attention from Illinois to Massachusetts, and Boston in particular. He wanted to approach the Boston catholic authorities again about potential financial support in the certain event they needed lawyers to defend them, and had to find large amounts of compensation for the families of victims. However, he had a problem. If he did so through his own organisation, he was acutely aware that his involvement might make his son vulnerable to charges of insider knowledge and risk his priestly career. He decided to ask Rossi to take the lead on this one, which he was quite willing to do, since it would land him with a greater share of the subsequent profit.

Rossi wasted no time in getting on the phone. He asked to be put through to the Chief Capital Assets Officer, or the person who headed up that department. He was listened to with respect but Rossi had the distinct impression they were in denial about the serious nature of their potential financial situation. He left his details, together with the implication that they were already looking at working with Illinois. It was the nearest he could get without outright lying. True, Arata had made a similar call to the Chief Capital Assets Officer in Chicago and had experienced the same polite rebuff.

As he and Rossi mulled over their options, they decided to up the pressure on each of these catholic archbishoprics. It was important to begin working with one so that they could use that as leverage for the rest of the states who they knew were in line for victim compensation.

First, they decided to research the Chief Financial Officers of each archbishopric and tailor a personal approach to them based upon the financial probity of having a backup plan should they need finance of some sort. Second, they would write formally to each CFO outlining a better deal than they could get on the open market. Thirdly, they would get De Luca's legal firm to approach each of the victims, either through SNAP or directly. Once representation had been agreed, to fast track court proceedings claiming millions of dollars in compensation for each victim. They examined each case, as they knew it, to hand-pick the most egregious one. Once they had one success, that case would be used as precedent and a model for the rest. It would surely be sufficient to bring these catholic organisations to their door.

When Arata Sr. arrived home that evening, he was pleasantly surprised to find his son there. He listened closely as his son outlined what had been going on at the Cardinal's mansion. It was cathartic for him but invaluable for his father, who was gaining a better understanding of the emotional and psycho-logical state of the catholic organisation in Boston. His mother, however, was operating at a more human level, expressing her deep distress at the news of the Cardinal's cancer diagnosis, suitably ignoring his 'faults', as she perceived them.

"And that paper, the Gazette, is just part of the gutter press, wanting to tear the reputations of decent people." Father and son looked at each other.

"Mother, I'm afraid everything the Gazette had published is true," said her son as gently as he could.

"I don't care. As far as I know, he's a good man. Why do they have to do this when a man of God is probably dying of cancer in hospital as we speak?"

Father and son didn't look at each other this time. Arata Sr. changed the subject and enquired when dinner would be ready.

Douglas-Scott had received the full, unexpurgated version of the Gazette's revelations, as had most of the Cardinals around the world. Shock waves were being felt from individual parish priests right to the top of the organisation. As far as the general population was concerned, the revelations were limited to the populace of the greater Boston area, but those in the know were certain it wouldn't stay that way for very long. Meyer was making the most of the opportunity his other media outlets afforded to spread the gospel, hoping to capitalise of the investigations from Boston and promising new revelations each Friday.

The Pontiff's PS hurriedly arranged a meeting with the Vatican Press Office prior to him advising His Holiness what, if anything, they should do.

"Usually in these circumstances, we make no comment," said a senior spokesperson who had been there for years and seen it all.

"But I think this is on a different scale to anything we've encountered before, isn't it?" persisted the PS.

"The more we comment, the more the media will want. It's a vicious game and we will lose."

The PS was somewhat taken aback. "Don't we have some obligation to our congregations who will be looking, as a minimum, for some reassurance?"

"Reassurance from what. Precisely?"

"Reassurance that their local priest isn't a paedophile, for a start," snapped back Douglas-Scott. "And that their children are safe in the catholic church."

"I think you're exaggerating, don't you?"

"We already know..." The PS was interrupted.

"That's the point. We don't know anything at this juncture. All we have is the front page of some rag in the United States about a few priests in Boston."

They stared at each other for a few moments, neither backing down. So, with not much more to say, Douglas-Scott left for his meeting with His Holiness. On the way, he ruminated about the strategy expounded by the Vatican Press Office. There was no doubt that this had always been the way the Vatican had treated adverse press reports and perhaps they were right. But wasn't this in a different league to previous scandals? He believed it was. But did His Holiness?

The more he thought about it, the more he felt that the plan of silence and 'no comment' would inevitably prevail. What could they say? He had seen the statement put out by Cardinal Doughty's office and he had to admit that it fell way short of what was needed. Perhaps they had to wait until further revelations appeared which might indicate the scale of what they were dealing with.

He knocked on the door and went in. His Holiness was writing at his desk.

"Andrew, come in."

"I've just come from a meeting with the Vatican Press Office about the goings on in Boston."

"What goings on? asked the Pontiff.

"We now have two consecutive front pages from the Boston Gazette about errant priests that His Eminence saw fit to move from parish to parish."

There was a long sigh from the occupant of the desk. His Holiness looked up.

"And what did our esteemed Press Office recommend?"

"Say nothing," stated Douglas-Scott, starkly.

"And you disagree?"

"I understand that such a strategy has been followed in the past," replied the PS cautiously. "And even if that is what we decide to do now, I believe we need to map out a response if this issue grows, which I suspect it will."

"I have no problem with that," responded the Pope.

"The thing is," started the PS again, "our congregations, families, parents will surely want some reassurance that this thing is under control, not to mention wealthy donors who may well stop supporting our good work."

"Of course. Why don't you suggest to the Press Office that they contact His Eminence's staff to offer any advice they might need."

"Thank you, Holiness."

Douglas-Scott left the room and once the door had been closed, began shaking his head. The subsequent conversation with the Vatican Press Office was brief. The PS conveyed His Holiness' wishes for some thought to be given if this issue grew in magnitude and also to offer any advice as might be appropriate to His Eminence's staff. The spokesman smiled, perhaps a little too triumphantly.

Douglas-Scott was dismayed. A quote came to mind often used in his diplomatic days. "A fish rots from the head", meaning that if an organisation, a political party, a government, even a church is found to have serious issues, it inevitably stems from a lack of leadership from the top. However, he acknowledged to himself that he didn't have the temerity to say it to the Vicar of Christ. He had offered his advice – what more could he do?

Chapter 26

TWO FRONT PAGES done. Now they were looking for victim's stories to paint the emotional picture of what had been happening – something that people could identify with. Janice decided to head to another parish in Boston to seek out further victims. Illinois and New Jersey were fine, but Boston was where they were and Boston was their immediate audience,

It wasn't far from the Keating parish but this time a different priest was involved. She set out in her VW and thirty minutes later, she was outside the house. With her audio recorder at the ready, she approached the door and knocked. A smart lady opened the door and with a pleasant smile said,

"Hello,"

Janice was taken aback for a moment, expecting a rather ruder greeting.

"Mrs Middleton?"

"Oh no. They moved away a few months ago. Can I help at all?"

"Sorry to have bothered you. Can you recall exactly when they moved?" Janice thought she saw an opening.

The lady knew instantly. "Yes. The day before we moved in. September 9."

The lady looked pleasant enough so she pushed a little more. "Er, was there anything odd or rushed about the move?"

"There was, as a matter of fact. Can I ask why you need to know?"

Janice thought quickly. She hadn't been prepared for this eventuality and, more often than not, she knew from bitter experience that if nothing was prepared, it was best to be as truthful as possible, else she would be found out quickly.

"Well, yes. I'm researching for a book on the catholic church and I understand Mrs Middleton was involved in an issue with them. Are you a catholic, by the way?

"Goodness no," she replied. " I read about her story in the paper, of course, but didn't know we were moving to her house until the conveyancing was all finished."

"Any idea why she moved?" Janice pushed a little further.

"Well, the rumour was that she got a rather large payout from them."

"Really," Janice was hoping her surprise was coming across as genuine. "How much?"

"Don't really know, but enough to move from this three bed house to a large five bed house with a double garage in a much better neighbourhood.

"Which neighbourhood?"

"I'm not sure I know, but my next door neighbour would. I believe they are still friendly." At this point the friendly lady nodded to the left side and signalled the end to the conversation by saying goodbye and shutting the door. Janice just managed a "thanks very much," before she was standing alone on the doorstep. Stepping back, she reviewed the neighbour's house before going over to knock on the door. Despite pushing a little harder, not much more information was forthcoming from the lady next door except the name of the neighbourhood.

"Good enough," murmured Janice, "I can work with that." She looked at her phone and decided that she had at least two hours before children came home from school, so began researching from her phone. It was surprisingly easy since all house purchases were logged by the state and were a matter of public record.

It was a mere ten minute drive to the house in this upmarket neighbourhood. On the drive, Janice could see the brand new SUV as she passed and parked a suitable distance away. Identifying vehicles was not Janice's greatest suit, but she thought it looked like an Audi or maybe it was a Mercedes. Whatever, it looked at least a six figure motor. She made her way to the house knowing exactly what she was going to say, but not how it would be received. She knocked.

"Hello," she said, in an officious tone and quickly flashing a lanyard of indeterminate origin. "Mrs Middleton?"

"Yes," said the woman, rather taken aback.

"My name is Janice Munroe. My job is to follow up from the court to check that everything is working out well. May I come in?"

"Er. Yes, I suppose so."

"Thank you," said Janice as she moved beyond the door into a spacious hall before entering into a well furnished lounge. "This shouldn't take long.

I understand, correct me if I'm wrong, you didn't go through with the court action?"

"No. We settled."

"Yes, that's sometimes the best thing to do." Janice smiled. "Can you tell me why?"

"Well, my lawyers advised me to settle."

"Ah. Yes," said Janice pretending to rummage through her papers. "Remind me, who they were?"

"Ericksons."

"Yes, I have it here."

"And were you happy with their service?"

"I think so."

"Usually the deal is that you, as the plaintiff, also sign a confidentiality agreement with the defendant." It was a statement which Janice hoped Mrs Middleton would interpret as a question.

"Yes."

"That's good. And you have kept to that agreement?"

"Of course."

"I see from the record that it was a considerable sum. Remind me how much?" Janice was rummaging through her papers again.

Mrs Middleton was becoming a little tense now and didn't answer. Janice pushed forward.

"The thing is this, Mrs Middleton. How can I put this?" Janice paused. "Were you aware when you signed that agreement, that the priest who cruelly abused your son had also done it to multiple other boys in previous parishes? And that the bishop had simply moved him on every time there was the beginnings of a complaint?"

"No, I didn't."

"In fact, I have here details of Father John Geoghan. He was the priest in question, wasn't he?"

"Er. Yes I believe so," said Mrs Middleton, quite confused as to where this was all going.

"Well, after your case, he was subsequently found guilty of sexually abusing 150 young boys during his 30-year career within the catholic church that spanned across six different parishes. It was all published in crimemagazine.com."

Janice went on and Mrs Middleton stayed quiet. "And did you know that those 150 other families endured the misery that you have, most without any redress whatsoever?"

"Er. No I didn't."

Janice pressed home her advantage. "If you had knowledge of that, would that have made any difference to you signing that confidentiality agreement?"

"I don't know. Possibly."

"Do you think the catholic church should be able to cover up the activities of priests who are child molesters and allow them to move priests on to commit more abuse to more young boys?"

"Of course not."

"Would you be willing to stand up to them and talk about what happened?" At last Janice had got to the point. What would the woman say?

"But I've spent the money."

"I don't think they will have a leg to stand on if they try to take it back. If you like I can give you the name of a lawyer we're working with who can independently advise you."

Suddenly, the woman woke up from the spell that Janice had successfully weaved. "Who are you? You're not from the court?"

"No I didn't say I was. I said I was following up from the court."

Janice showed her the lanyard with the Boston Gazette details on it. "You've seen our front pages over the last two weeks?"

The lady nodded.

"Well, in the coming weeks, there will be lots of stories from abused victims of catholic priests and how the church hierarchy has consistently denied, then tried to settle outside of court, anything to keep these paedophile priests from being exposed, even to the extent of allowing them to abuse other boys in another parish." Janice paused to see if Mrs. Middleton was following her. It looked as if she was, so she pressed in one final time.

"I would like you to think about letting us tell your story."

"Oh. I don't know. I don't want to drag it up again after all this time. He's just getting settled into a new non-catholic school."

"That's fine. We can make it anonymous. No real names will be used." Janice got up. She didn't want the woman to say no. As they went to the door, Janice passed over her business card and added, "Please think about it. You can help other families avoid going through what you've been through."

The door was shut and Janice made her way to her VW and sitting down in the driver's seat found that she was trembling all over; so much so that she was incapable of driving. She sat there for fifteen minutes taking deep breaths, trying to get her body under control before driving back home rather than the office.

Chapter 27

JANICE REPORTED BACK to Sullivan the following day. With what he had also managed to do, they had enough stories to fill the front page for some weeks. They spent the morning reviewing them and allocating each to a front page for the coming weeks and months. The key was to classify them in ascending order of horror. Too many stories which sounded the same would tire readers, reduce circulation, and lose momentum. And, as every campaigner knows, momentum is crucial to longevity and a successful campaign.

Sullivan described some of the stories he had unearthed.

"Here's one," he said as he dug into a pile of seemingly random papers all over his desk. "this victim, John, who is now," Sullivan broke off as he struggled to find the right page of notes. "Ah. Here it is. Twenty-six years old and says he has contemplated suicide many times after being abused, turning to drugs and alcohol in a bid to cope with, quote 'anxiety and feelings of unworthiness.' He contacted SAMHSA. (Substance Abuse and Mental Health Services Administration) many times. Never got free."

"I did a story on suicide once," said Janice. Sullivan didn't look up but grunted that he'd heard his colleague. "Did you know that last year, according to the Samaritans, 48,183 Americans committed suicide?"

Sullivan looked up. "Hell, that's a lot of people."

"Yep," confirmed Janice. "that means that there is one suicide death in the US every eleven minutes."

"Really?"

Janice was waxing lyrical now, quoting figures off the top of her head. She knew her stuff.

"That's 132 Americans every day. But get this, suicide is the third leading cause of death for 15-24 year-olds."

"Because of abuse?" Sullivan was seeking more ammunition.

"Stats not available," responded Janice. Sullivan grunted again. If it didn't fit his current need, he wasn't really interested.

"Anyway, to get back to this victim," continued Sullivan. "He says his life is ruined and he's very happy to give a full interview. Interestingly, and you'll like this, it concerns a priest we've not heard of before, so that's good."

Sullivan looked up quickly, conscious that his remark could be taken in the wrong way. Janice nodded. She had worked with him enough to know how his mind worked and didn't take offence.

"Another one here," continued Sullivan, picking up another set of notes. "Didn't want his name to be released, so let's call him David. He said that the priest's sexual abuse of him as a child directly affected his career, financial well-being, and ability to hold jobs. He told me he has 'left, quit, or was fired from every job he's ever had.'"

"That's a good one," contributed Janice. "We need to get his employment history both to verify his statement and to get the story from their side." Sullivan nodded.

"Here's another one, Michael. He says he was singled by Father Thomas Francis Kelly." Sullivan looked over to Janice who was still listening carefully. "We know him from other survivors, don't we?"

"Yea. I remember him. He was listed in the 'clergyreport.illinoisattorney-general.gov' report," said Janice. "He was the one who assaulted more than fifteen boys aged 11 to 17 in various parishes during the 1960s and 1970s."

"That's him." Sullivan snorted. "What an animal! Do you know what his modus operandi was?"

"No. I can't remember," said Janice. "You know, we've got so many stories, that I'm finding it difficult to distinguish between them."

"Well, if we can't," responded Sullivan, "our readers won't. So we have to make each story unique."

"The problem is, though," commented Janice, "many of them have very similar experiences. We might struggle here."

"I've thought about this," said Sullivan confidently. "It's a matter of what we lead on and what we put further down in the report. So with David, for example, we lead on the jobs front, but put the other stuff in the small print."

"OK. So what was Kelly's particular way of working?"

"He would pick 11 year-olds and invite them to drive-in movies and a sleepover at the rectory. He would offer beer, which put the boy out for the count so that when the boy woke up he'd find the priest performing oral sex on him."

"That's disgusting," reacted Janice.

"Pretty gross, isn't it," agreed Sullivan.

"I mean," continued Janice, "what were these priests thinking? Were they so predatory that they specifically joined the priesthood specifically so they had easy and safe access to boys?"

"I don't know," rejoined Sullivan. "My question would be, 'how in earth did they get through whatever selection process the catholic church has?' Incidentally, that's a good angle."

"What is?" asked Janice.

"Let's dig into how the catholic church recruits, selects and trains these priests. There's got to be something wrong there." Sullivan was busy writing this new line of inquiry down in his notebook.

"Yea," agreed Janice. "Unless....."

"What?" asked Sullivan.

"Unless," continued Janice, "those who do the selecting and training are themselves paedophiles?"

"Good point. We need to look into all that," said Sullivan, making further notes. "This is good."

"Just to finish on Kelly," Sullivan wanted Janice to know everything he had. "Despite his abuse being well known in the community, he was never prosecuted."

"Why the hell not?" protested Janice.

"Well, he was moved from parish to parish until he died in 1990. Some of his survivors who I've spoken to report suffering from, and I quote: 'insomnia, anxiety, trust issues, nightmares, suicidal impulses, guilt, addiction, alcoholism, depression, post-traumatic stress disorder, issues creating and maintaining relationships, and sexual side effects.'"

"Unbelievable. All that suffering and no closure for them." Janice was shaking her head in disbelief.

"Here's another one that gives us a slightly different angle," said Sullivan.

"What's that?" asked Janice.

"It's to do with the confessional," said Sullivan. "this is a former altar boy who was allegedly sexually abused by a serial paedophile priest who says he could have been spared if the catholic church enforced mandatory reporting of crimes admitted in the confessional."

"Is he suggesting that this paedophile priest went to another priest to confess and gain absolution so he could do it again and that priest should have told the police, but didn't?"

"That's what he's saying," confirmed Sullivan.

"That was never going to happen. A priest shopping another priest. Never."

"But it's a good headline," responded Sullivan. "Anyway, this guy, Father Michael McArdle who had allegedly targeted this 12 year-old for oral sex, had been molesting children for a decade and no one did anything when they must have known."

"Did he also get the lad drunk?"

"Don't think so. Apparently, the abuse was done at the sacristy and presbytery of the Holy Rosary Church, as well as during an overnight school camp. It was reported by 'abc.net.au/news'."

"That's Australia. We're not meant to go there," protested Janice.

"But we can just refer to it generally," countered Sullivan.

"You know," said Janice, thinking aloud, "there's no justice anywhere in this, is there?"

"Unless you believe in a righteous God who judges what we do," said Sullivan. Janice looked at him rather nonplussed.

"Are you getting all religious on me again?" she asked caustically.

"No. Just saying. None of us knows what happens when we die."

"You are!" accused Janice. "I would have thought that this investigation would be enough to put you off religion completely."

"Believe me. I'm not into religion, catholic or any other version," said Sullivan, defending himself.

"What are you saying, then?"

"Forget it," said Sullivan as he got up to get another coffee.

Janice looked at him as he disappeared out of the office with disbelief on her face. This was a hard-bitten investigator who took no prisoners, now expressing religious thoughts that had never come out of his mouth in all the years she had known him.

She started looking at his notes, trying to put them in some sort of order.

"You know, there's another way of doing it," Janice said quietly to herself.

"Why don't we change our approach and begin to major on the priests rather than the victims?"

Chapter 28

FATHER ARATA'S WORST scenario had come to pass. It had been the police rather than the prosecuting authorities that had contacted him, giving him a date and time to be available as a person of interest in what might end up as the State v Catholic Archbishopric of Boston. That was interesting in itself. He didn't know that the archbishopric was a legal entity, but now he thought about it, the setup made sense. They had their own treasury, after all. The downside was that with all the legal fees and potential compensation payments, they might well go bust.

Immediately, he began to understand his father's interest. The archbishopric had a lot of real estate beside church buildings which might prove interesting if there were to be a 'fire sale'. He already knew many wealthy donors had given their apologies for non-appearance at some of the recent fund-raising functions. Numbers at Sunday congregations had also fallen slightly. It was very likely, therefore, that the inflow into their treasury would be consequentially lower.

His mind shifted to the Cardinal; firstly to wonder how he was, but secondly, about his meeting with the police. Had he already been questioned or would he escape interrogation due to ill-health? Was he a person of interest or a suspect? Had he been charged and given his Miranda warning? He felt helpless and completely in the dark. Perhaps a call to his boss might be wise, to see how he was and, if the subject came up, to discover what he had said to the police – to get their stories straight. He quickly chastised himself for his paranoia. It would be the first question the police would be likely to ask him. And, in any case, he had no case to answer. It was all down to his boss. He knew nothing!

At the hospital, Cardinal Doughty had also been given his date and at a time which had reluctantly approved by his doctors. The prosecutors had been direct with the police chief; they wanted nothing to mar the handling of the case, nothing that might allow this man to get off the hook they had painstakingly prepared for him. Careers were on the line.

In anticipation both of his interview, or was it an interrogation, and his possible early demise, the Cardinal had asked a fellow priest, of the parish variety, whom he had known for a long time as an upright and righteous man, to hear his confession. Duly made, the Cardinal had received absolution and felt he could face the police and be completely honest with them. He didn't waste his time wondering what his fellow priest thought of him. That was of no concern. God was his judge.

"Your Eminence," started the senior detective. "By the way, is that how you'd like to be addressed?"

"That, or Cardinal will be fine," said the churchman, weakly.

"You are entitled to have legal representation."

"Yes. She should be here by now," replied the Cardinal.

"Would you prefer we wait?" The question remained unanswered as the door of the private hospital room opened and Ms Shirley Clarke strode into the room, her red high heels clacking on the linoleum floor, hair perfectly lacquered in place, and her tailored business suit making the consummate finish to her professional figure.

She stared at the two detectives aggressively. "You haven't started yet, have you?"

"Ms Clarke, how lovely to see you," said the senior detective dryly, looking at his watch.

There was no response from Ms Clarke, preferring to turn her attention to her client.

"Patrick, I'm so sorry I'm a little late. Do you want a few minutes with me before facing these gentlemen?"

The Cardinal waved his hand, "That's alright, Shirley. We can stop at any time if you feel we need to. Let's get on with it."

The detectives looked at each during this exchange, the junior one mouthing 'Shirley' to the other and suppressing a snigger.

"Detective Royston, you can go ahead, but I will call time if I need to." Ms Clarke didn't even look at the detective, sure that she was in control.

Royston cleared his throat. "Much obliged Ma'am," he said, tongue in cheek. "We will be recording the session, as a matter of policy." It wasn't policy, of course, but the detective wasn't going to ask permission and Ms Clarke didn't object. Cardinal Doughty had already told her that he would truthfully answer all their questions to the best of his ability. There was to be no cover-up this time.

The recorder was switched on. "Actually, Detective Royston," It was the Cardinal. "Could you pass me that bottle of water? My mouth's a little dry." The detective, a little exasperated, nodded to his colleague to retrieve the bottle while he switched off the recorder.

"Are we ready now?" He asked, looking around when the older man had sipped some water. He switched the recorder back on.

"Interview with Cardinal Patrick Doughty. Also present: Ms Shirley Clarke, Detective McGowan and myself, Lieutenant Detective Royston."

Royston's rank raised the Cardinal's eyebrows, although his lawyer seemed to be well aware of who he was. It was an indication of how serious the department was taking this case.

"Your Eminence," he started again, delighted to be able to have a little fun at the expense of this criminal without any recourse. "May we start with Father Keating." It wasn't a question.

"When did you first meet him?"

"How did he seem to you?"

"What exactly did you know about him?"

"Were there any reports from the seminary about him?"

The detective peppered him with such questions for about thirty minutes without seeming to get anywhere. Then,

"When were you aware of his criminal tendencies?"

Ah! Now we were getting to the heart of the matter, thought the Cardinal. They weren't. Father Keating was the hors d'oeuvres, the main course was yet to come.

The Cardinal didn't rise to the challenge of the question. "I presume you know Father Keating was abused when he was young?"

The detective gave nothing away. "Tell us about it," he said.

"I don't know. You'll have to ask him."

The detective reminded him that he was on record and they would be asking the same questions to Keating. "I'm sure you would prefer if all your answers lined up?"

The Cardinal didn't answer. It was a rhetorical question, wasn't it?

"So you know quite a lot about Keating, don't you?"

No answer. The two detectives looked at each other.

The churchman stirred himself as his legal counsel looked on anxiously. "As far as I can remember, Father Keating came to Boston straight from seminary and, as far as I know, there were no," he paused, "no 'irregularities' mentioned on his reports."

"Was there any verbal communication between anyone in your employ, including yourself, which indicated that there might be, irregularities as you call them, in his behaviour?"

"Not with me, certainly. Perhaps with my Private Secretary at the time."

The detective looked down at his notes. He had done his homework. "That would be Father Michael Kearns, would it not?"

"Yes."

"Would that be the same Michael Kearns that you subsequently appointed to a parish within your archbishopric?"

"I believe so."

"You believe so?" questioned the detective, raising his eyebrows.

"Apologies, detective. Yes, it was," confirmed the Cardinal, in a slightly stronger voice.

"When did you have suspicions that Kearns was also a paedophile?"

At this point, Ms Clarke jumped in. "Detective. Do you have evidence that Kearns molested children?"

"We have serious allegations from one of his flock to that effect," said the detective.

"So no evidence?"

"We have a written statement and are currently having the young lad in question interviewed by a psychiatrist."

No response from Ms Clarke.

"So let me summarise so far," said the detective. "Your Private Secretary is alleged to have been a paedophile, which you knew and your records will show that he recommended to you that Keating, another paedophile, be allocated a parish?"

Ms Clarke sat up straight. "You have not established that my client knew Kearns was a paedophile."

Royston ignored her and went on. "Your records will also show," he said directly facing His Eminence, "that once Keating was unmasked by some of his parishioners, the same Father Michael Kearns, recommended that he be transferred to another parish after a few months of gardening leave. Correct?"

Ms Clarke was about to jump in again when her client lifted his hand.

"Father Kearns did indeed recommend that Father Keating be given time to overcome his urges and make a new start," confessed the Cardinal.

"Let me get this clear," said Detective Royston. "We have one paedophile, Kearns, recommending to you that another paedophile, Keating, be allowed to move to another parish to sexually assault more pubescent altar boys. Is that correct?"

His Eminence was silent for a moment. "Yes," he said quietly.

"Cardinal, would you please speak a little louder for the tape? "Is that correct?"

His Eminence looked up sharply just for a moment, not used to being spoken to in such a manner. He then lapsed, looking like a defeated man.

"Yes. You see, Detective. In my world, there is such a thing as confession and forgiveness. I believed Father Keating was a good man but injured by his own abuser when he was young. Yes, he struggled to control himself but we don't throw people out because they are injured. We try to heal them."

It was the longest reply that the Cardinal had given so far and one which set the junior detective on edge. He was desperate to attack the churchman, but Royston held up his hand.

"And what about the victims?"

"Of course, they also need healing and we have policies and programmes to help with that."

The younger detective could no longer sit quietly. "Policies and programmes," he shouted. "In the real world, these men," he spat the words out. "these men, are guilty of the most horrendous crimes against innocent children and, not only did you cover it up, you organised for them to do it again and again."

Royston made no attempt to intervene and was watching the Cardinal for any sign of remorse, and his lawyer for any objection.

"Effectively, you pimped him around your archdiocese," accused Detective McGowan.

At that, Ms Clarke asked for a recess of twenty minutes for her client. It was agreed.

Chapter 29

FATHER ARATA ARRIVED back at the Cardinal's mansion to be met by a substantial police presence and an officer at the gate who challenged him as he tried to enter the grounds. Arata produced his ID, causing a hurried phone call to the senior officer within the building, whereupon he was allowed in. Dressed in his black cassock, he was easily identified as he moved up towards the building to be met at the front of the building by a burly plain clothes detective.

"Father Arata, please come with me." The PS obeyed without comment. "Unfortunately, you will not be allowed in any offices while my team continue to examine various files. I'm sure you understand."

Arata was looking quite confused, partly counterfeit and partly real, wondering what they were looking for and might subsequently find.

"I understand," continued the detective as they walked through the magnificent atrium, "that you have been given a date and time to come to the precinct as a person of interest?" Arata nodded. The detective stopped and turned to the PS. "Would you mind if we had a preliminary conversation now, as you're here?"

"Do I need a lawyer?"

"That's entirely up to you. We do not suspect you of any crime so will not be cautioning you, but we need to cover all bases as I'm sure you will appreciate." The detective was cordial and respectful, offering a smile to put Arata at ease.

"Sure. Let's do it."

"Is there a comfortable room where we could talk away from the melee?" There was indeed a lot going on, with boxes upon boxes of paper files being piled up outside various offices, ready to be taken away for examination.

"They'll all be returned in due course," assured the detective. "And we'll need to take the computers as well."

"I assume you have a warrant?" There was a flourish of paper waved in front of him, which Arata didn't bother to examine.

"Where shall we go to talk in private?"

"Er. Yes, follow me."

As they were settling, another officer appeared and the three of them sat down on some very comfortable chairs in a spacious room with paintings on every wall and *objet d'art* on most work surfaces. The third man sat a little apart, clearly not going to be part of the conversation.

"This is some room," commented the detective, who had introduced himself as Detective Sergeant Holdon. He was surprised at the opulence of the place. "This is like a palace," he commented.

"Yes, archbishops' dwellings have always been called palaces," said Arata, "though not all are this grand," he added.

"Where does all the money come from to buy this stuff?"

Arata suspected that this question might open up a whole new area of investigation, so he side-stepped. "To be honest, I don't know. You would have to ask the Finance people."

"But you attend all those fund-raisers where millionaire donors come to support your catholic charities?"

"Yes, of course," admitted Arata.

"Where does the money go?" persisted the detective.

"Into the Treasury, I guess," said Arata.

"And exactly how much of the 100% that goes in, eventually comes out for the good causes?"

"Sorry, no idea."

"By the look of the stuff in this one room alone, not 100%, that's for sure." The junior detective was nodding furiously. Arata said nothing.

Holdon looked at his colleague, "Maybe we ought to get the fraud people in to go through the books," he suggested.

"Excellent idea," agreed the other officer.

Arata spoke up. "I'm sorry. I'm just the Private Secretary to His Eminence."

"Of course. Why don't we start there? How long have you been Private Secretary here?"

"Three years."

"And did you know that your predecessor was a paedophile?"

Arata was startled by the bluntness of the question. He sat bolt upright, his demeanour suddenly changing. Now wary of this softly-spoken detective, he recognised that he had been taken in by the officer's courteous approach. How should he answer? Did he now need a lawyer? No, surely that would signify some sort of guilt. He quickly thought about it. There seemed to be no risk to him, so he answered guardedly.

"His Eminence told me last week when he began to anticipate your involvement."

"So, to be clear. You did not know that your boss was hiding paedophiles in his churches?"

Arata winced. At this point he should have refused to answer, citing lack of legal representation. But he was relatively new to the post and still rather naïve, so he carried on.

"No, but I'm not sure 'hiding' is exactly the right word."

"What would you say was the right word?"

"I think you'd better ask the Cardinal himself."

"Did you know that Cardinal Doughty was protecting paedophile priests and moving them from one parish to another, with terrible consequences?"

"I knew he was involved in appointing priests to parishes, but that process also involves the appropriate Bishop."

"So who has the authority over the priest?"

"The Bishop."

"And who has authority over the Bishop?

"The Archbishop, or Cardinal."

"So when would the Cardinal interfere with the appointment of a priest?"

"Again 'interfere' is not the correct word. There might be a dialogue between Cardinal and Bishop and they would come to an agreed decision as to who to appoint."

"But if a Cardinal specifically wanted a priest appointed, it would not be wise for a Bishop to dig his heels in?"

"Not if he wanted to move up the organisation."

"So, if we were to examine the instances where the Cardinal put pressure on the Bishop to appoint a particular priest, would we find that many, if not all, would be paedophiles, which he was protecting?"

"I couldn't say," replied Arata.

Detective Holdon paused for a few moments to ponder Arata's answers.

"As Private Secretary, you don't seem to know much, do you?"

Arata decided that this was the time to get out of this interrogation. "If that's all officer, I'd like to go now. I assume I can't use my office?"

"I'm afraid not."

Arata got up and walked out of the room slowly and with as much dignity as he could muster, while the detective watched him. Once he was out of the room, the detective stood up and walked around the room, deep in thought.

"You aren't telling me anything like the whole truth, are you?" he said, as he watched Father Arata making his way out of the grounds. His colleague nodded in agreement.

Chapter 30

SULLIVAN WAS NOT a fitness fanatic by any stretch of the imagination, but he randomly thought one day that a jog to his office in the morning, rather than using his car might be good for him. It wasn't something to be rushed, but he had decided to take a spare set of clothes and leave them under his desk to be retrieved when he needed them. This morning, he looked out of the window of his apartment and it seemed the ideal opportunity to give it a try. A clear sky not too warm, a little breeze and he could see others doing the same thing. Yes, he would do it, but he had to move quickly. He wanted to get to the office before anyone else.

He made himself a light breakfast, dressed in his new jogging outfit and set off. He couldn't understand it. Others were flying along, clearly enjoying their constitutional, whereas he was finding it tough going. He jogged for a bit more before coming to his senses and stopping to light a cigarette.

Arriving at the office, he caught the surprised looks of Jimmy, the security guard, who he ignored as he made his way upstairs. Janice was, unexpectedly, already at her desk, with her head down. She stifled a guffaw when she saw her boss arrive in shorts, a T-shirt, and trainers all looking brand new. Sullivan hadn't been expecting her to be in and looked rather embarrassed. Nevertheless, he retrieved his workday suit, now suitably crumpled and departed to the restroom without a word.

Looking fresh and with his thinning hair still wet, he re-emerged into the office and sat down ready for work. Janice took pity on him and went straight into a work conversation.

"Do you think we should begin featuring more stories about the priests rather than just the victims?" she asked.

"Yea. Good thinking," responded Sullivan glad to talk about something other than his new hobby. "Maybe we should mix it up a bit. Readers could get a little punch drunk with all the sob stories, even though they are all slightly different."

"Right. I've been going through all the stories we have and allocating each of them to a front page. At just one a week, we have enough for a year," said Janice. "Maybe we should suggest to Porter that he should consider a mid-week special occasionally."

Sullivan looked across at Janice. "That's a great idea." He sounded as if he meant it. "Why don't you pitch it to him yourself?"

Janice saw Porter was already in his office and went straight to his door which was already open, signalling to the floor that he was available. She knocked and went straight in.

"No Sullivan? I thought you two hunted in pairs," said the editor-in-chief, who had glanced up then back down to his desk again.

"I'm not hunting at the moment," she said. "I have a suggestion."

"Oh?" questioned Porter, still not looking up.

"Why don't we do a mid-week special?"

Now he sat up and leant back in his chair. "Go on," he said.

"We have enough stories both about victims and priests to last the rest of the year, plus we haven't yet started on the rest of the States."

"Hmm," said Porter. "Are you thinking it would be exclusively for you?"

"Not necessarily, but it would be the main feature. I think it could make a bit of money," she added.

"Maybe," admitted Porter, "but there's also more costs involved." He turned in his chair to look out of the window and think.

Janice stayed and waited for what might come next from the editor's mouth. She had thrown her line out and he had taken the bait. At least, she thought so.

"If we did it, the feature would need to be different from the regular front page," mused Porter.

"What if we used the mid-week editions to cover other States?" asked Janice. "We've got stuff on most of them?"

"Yes, but you still have to make it interesting for readers in Boston. If they get bored, they may stop buying the main edition."

Porter didn't want to dismiss the idea. He certainly saw benefit but the proposal needed more thought. He said so to Janice.

"I like the idea, but I need a thought-out proposal which is different and doesn't risk the weekend edition. Chat with Sullivan and come back to me."

Janice turned to leave the office and just as she went back through the door, he said, "Good thinking. Well done."

Although he may have appeared lukewarm, inside he was excited. This was the sort of business proposal that Meyer would love. He knew his investigators would come up with something he could work with. In the meantime, he called Mackie, his Finance Manager, and asked him to scope out the costs of a mid-week special edition, potential readership, additional advertising, and work out possible pricing options. He then contacted Production for them to scope out their incremental costs. He wanted it all before Saturday.

Janice made her way back to their corner where Sullivan was on the phone. He lifted his eyes to acknowledge her presence and mouthed SNAP. Her puzzled face changed as she remembered the organisation in Chicago trying to get justice for the victims of clerical abuse.

Sullivan had been listening for a few minutes before he started to speak.

"That's amazing. How much did you say?" Eyes widened and eyebrows went up. He began to fidget in his seat, a sure sign that he was excited at what he was hearing. When eventually the phone went down, he turned to his junior who already had an inquiring look on her face.

"That was SNAP in Chicago."

"I got that," replied Janice dryly. "What about SNAP in Chicago?"

"You remember that lawyer I told you about who wanted to sign up their members?"

"I remember that you were immediately suspicious about how that came about," replied Janice.

"I'm still suspicious, but a guy called De Luca from a hotshot legal firm has signed up three families and has lodged court proceedings for one of them, claiming $1m in compensation."

"That's unlikely," said Janice.

"Why?" questioned Sullivan.

"According to my research, the average compensation being awarded so far is about $268k, depending on the severity or duration of the abuse and the treatment costs for mental and physical injuries resulting from the abuse."

"That's ridiculous," objected Sullivan. "We can show that victims are marred for life."

Janice agreed. "I suspect there is a great deal of lobbying going on behind the scenes to keep these awards down."

"That would figure," said Sullivan.

"There was a recent case in Newark, where I went recently, which awarded $400k between five claimants."

"That's preposterous." Sullivan was getting emotional.

"That, is not our business," reminded Janice. "Our job is to sell newspapers by revealing what paedophile catholic priests have been getting up to with children in the US."

Sullivan was back to grunting as Janice brought him down to earth.

"But," she went on, "there's no reason why we shouldn't do more research and devote a front page to it."

Sullivan was warming to the idea. "It would make a change from the stories we have been publishing. Then the following week we could hit them again with that suicide story you got."

"Or," speculated Janice. "We could use a mid-week special to highlight it? Porter was keen to do one, maybe more, but wants a 'thought-out plan', his words."

Sullivan thought for a moment. He wasn't into drafting plans and strategies, Janice would have to do that. But he did have good journalistic ideas. "Why don't we make the first one about the catholic church itself? We can work up a dozen different stories on subjects from how they recruit priests, train them, appoint them to parishes, their safeguarding policies, their legal and moral duty of care towards their parishioners, especially minors, their strategies for obfuscation and covering up, etc. etc."

"I'm guessing you want me to do all that?" Janice was beginning to feel overwhelmed.

"You put the proposal together and we'll do the research and writing together. How does that sound?"

"Deal," agreed Janice.

"Don't forget, we're not here to be kind to them. We're here to expose them."

Chapter 31

IT WAS ARATA Sr.'s role to find a way of getting inside the machine that was the Archbishopric of Chicago. He decided to lean on De Luca.

"Anthony, how are you?" asked Arata, not really wanting to know how the lawyer was.

"Arata, how good of you to call. We are making good progress." He went on to explain that they had signed up three excellent clients through SNAP and picked the best one to launch their legal action.

"Excellent news," responded Arata. "I don't suppose any of your partners have any friendships with any senior figures in the catholic hierarchy there?"

"I'm not sure. I can certainly find out easily enough. What do you want to know?"

"We're trying to get a meeting with the Chief Finance guy or possibly the Capital Assets Officer, or anyone who might be senior enough to persuade those gentlemen to grant us a meeting."

De Luca understood and immediately saw an increase in his fees. "What approaches have you made so far?"

"I have called the men personally, but they still seem in denial as to the exposed financial position they're in."

"Understood. Let me make some enquiries and I'll get back to you." Both put the phone down without any further pleasantries. Time was money, after all.

It was towards the end of the day when De Luca called back.

"I don't have very good news," said the lawyer.

"You don't have anyone who can get into this catholic organisation?"

"It's not that," explained De Luca. "Bankruptcy is not my area...."

"Bankruptcy?" responded a surprised Arata.

"It seems as though, deliberate strategy or not, dioceses and archdioceses are going for Chapter 11." (Chapter 11 bankruptcy is used to protect businesses that are struggling financially. The process evaluates and reorganizes an organisation's assets. In doing so, an entity can pay off debts while maintaining enough capital to continue operating.)

There was silence from Arata, almost disbelieving what he was hearing.

"As I'm sure you know," continued De Luca, "when a catholic diocese files for bankruptcy, all civil lawsuits against the diocese are suspended, including clergy abuse lawsuits. The diocese's assets are also partially frozen and reviewed by the bankruptcy court."

Arata was still not speaking, coming to terms with the fact that lots of potentially lucrative real estate opportunities seemed dead in the water.

"Of course," continued the lawyer, "victims may still be able to get compensation but they need to file proof of their claim with the bankruptcy court. If that victim's proof of claim is accepted, he or she becomes a claimant in the bankruptcy case. It's then up to federal judges handling the case to review the diocese's assets. Once the deadline to file claims expires, the court will allocate money to claimants while ensuring the diocese retains enough money to continue operating."

Arata finally found his voice. "That means that payouts will be considerably smaller?"

"Considerably," confirmed De Luca. "But hear this. Bankruptcy can also protect their reputation since, in a civil suit, a court may order a diocese to release sensitive documents that could negatively affect the diocese's reputation, whereas in bankruptcy proceedings, a diocese could be protected from any negative exposure."

"This must be a deliberate strategy. So they can continue to operate and maintain their reputation." Arata was thinking as he spoke. "But what about their assets, principally their real estate? I don't want their churches, but do they have to sell their assets?"

"Now you've put your finger on it," said De Luca. "Organisations can transfer assets prior to filing for bankruptcy. By doing so, unless the transfer is contested, a business can protect certain assets from the scrutiny of the bankruptcy court. Historically, some dioceses have transferred assets to parishes, education trusts or any other legal entity for protection."

"Have they indeed?" echoed Arata.

But De Luca hadn't finished. "A recent Bloomberg article, which one of my partners came across, has found that catholic dioceses in America have shielded about $2 billion from abuse victims by transferring assets prior to bankruptcy proceedings."

"Bloody hell," exclaimed Arata.

"I'm sorry," said De Luca, "I'm not sure there is a business opportunity here for either of us."

"Seems so," said Arata, sounding disappointed. "Send me your account to date and I'll settle it immediately."

"Sorry to the bearer of bad news," said De Luca, and rang off.

Arata settled down to think about what he had just heard and what, if anything, he could do about it. Nothing came to mind except some disquiet about the dimensions of the financial re-engineering being done by the catholic church just to avoid paying out to their victims. Arata wasn't a soft liberal rather a hard-nosed businessman, but even he wondered about the morality of what his church was doing. Yes, he would admit a little hypocrisy in his business but wasn't the church supposed to act in a different way? After all, most businesses didn't abuse little boys.

He had to call Rossi. Perhaps there was some chance that some diocese or archdiocese would want to talk seriously to them. But it would involve more of a mailshot approach rather than individual phone calls. Rossi immediately picked up on the gloom exuded down the line by Arata.

"That's very disappointing," he said after Arata had summarised the position. "I'll put everything on hold for the moment until you come back to me."

The entrepreneur was in deep thought as he drove home that afternoon. Part of him was still trying to figure out a way to make his idea work, but another part of him was becoming more than a little concerned about the ethics of his church. He determined to tackle his son about it.

"I'm home," he called as he came through his front door into the large foyer. He looked up the stairs which swept gracefully up and around a large balcony to the bedrooms. No immediate answer. He walked further in to see if his wife was out in the garden, which he could see through the array of triple-glazed windows and saw her walking near the lake with his son, still dressed in his cassock.

"Excellent," he murmured. He went upstairs to change ready for their evening meal which he assumed they were sharing with his son. By the time he had showered and changed, his wife and son had come in and they gathered in the drawing room for drinks. After a few minutes, his wife left the men and went to check on the meal. She still did most of the cooking, but had help in to do all the other chores.

It was a good time for Senior to tackle Junior about what he had learnt from De Luca in Chicago, but perhaps not the financial impact it would have on his business. That might not impress the young priest.

"What are you going to do if you have to pay out large amounts of money in compensation for your Cardinal's errors of judgement?" As usual, his father came directly to the point.

Junior looked at his father, better understanding his father's interest than he had previously.

"It's not my area of expertise," he replied evenly. "We have a Finance and Assets department who look after all that."

His father picked up on Junior's reluctance to open up on the subject and assumed that he had figured out what his own interest had been.

"Just so you know, I'm not interested in church real estate, at least not now," said his father opening his hands in a manner designed to tell his son that he was telling the truth. Junior looked at him carefully.

"Not now?" queried Junior.

"Initially, I thought there may be a way to help dioceses and archdioceses to fund any large payouts which they might incur." He paused.

"Now?" persisted Junior.

"I didn't appreciate the financial jiggery-pokery that our church would indulge in, just to avoid paying out compensation for molesting young boys."

Arata Jr. looked sharply at his father "What do you mean?"

"Simply," started his father, "that many dioceses and archdioceses plan to go bankrupt, thus significantly reducing their capability to pay out."

"Oh!" said Jr. "I'm not sure what that means?"

The businessman began to recognise that his son knew very little about finance or business. So he decided to spell it out rather than just dropping hints.

"It's a simple way of covering up the detail of the claims, reducing the level of payouts and keeping all their assets intact."

"Sorry, I don't understand. How can they go bankrupt and keep all their assets?"

"That's the trick. It's done in business all the time, but I didn't think our church would stoop so low."

"I'm sorry, but you've lost me," said the priest, realising that his knowledge of the world his father lived in was a complete mystery.

"You simply transfer all your assets to another legal structure prior to declaring Chapter 11, thus they are no longer your assets and no longer to be considered accessible for claims."

"What's Chapter 11?"

His father looked on as if to say, 'Are you kidding me?' But looking more closely at his son's open face, he saw complete transparency. The priest truly did not know what his father was talking about.

At that moment, dinner was called and they made their way into the dining room.

"Look it up," Senior said brusquely on the way in.

The conversation changed as they reached the table – it was not the kind of discussion that his wife approved of, which was why most of the time not a lot was said unless they had guests. Now that her son was here, she was anxious to know how the Cardinal was getting on.

"Such a nice man," she said echoing her previous opinions.

Junior brought both parents up to date with his health and his police interview.

"For me, the main one at the station is yet to come, but a preliminary session with a Detective Sergeant Holden put me on my guard."

"You're not a suspect, surely," exclaimed his mother.

"No," he reassured her, "I'm just what they call a 'person of interest.'"

"You'd do well to be on your guard," said his father. "It's better you say nothing to them without a lawyer present. There's no doubt that the police and prosecutors want a cast iron case here. They've all been put on the spot with the revelations from the Gazette."

His wife turned up her nose at the mention of the paper. "Rag," she mumbled.

"At any point," continued his father, "a 'person of interest' can easily become a suspect. Any little omission might be turned into an infraction or even a felony misdemeanor."

"Surely not a felony?" his wife protested.

"Often depends on the judge," responded the husband.

"Can we change the subject, please?" asked Junior.

"Of course," said his mother. "This is not appropriate at the dining table."

The family lapsed into the usual silence.

Chapter 32

PORTER, THE EDITOR-IN-CHIEF of the Boston Gazette, had been stunned at Janice's questions about the leaking of their work. He knew that she knew, and he was not happy. On the plus side, it seemed as if she hadn't told Sullivan for which he was very grateful.

"Janice is a loyal person," he thought to himself, "I could have done worse than make her a fixture in my life, but that boat has probably sailed." The last thing he wanted was his top investigator knowing that he, contrary to his express promise, had leaked the scoop even if it was just to his publisher.

The issue was: what had Meyer done with the information? Who had he passed it to? And what had they done with it? Well, he knew what they had done, but why? Why did a top-charging lawyer from Chicago, suddenly offer to fund the claims of some victims of clerical abuse? There was a link somewhere but no matter how long he thought about it, he couldn't figure it out. He decided to ring Meyer and say there would be no more envelopes.

"Hi Porter," said Meyer, then responding to his editor's declaration of intent, said, "That's OK." He was very happy at the increased revenue the paper was already making. "As long as you keep the lawyers informed so that we're clean. I'd like to be kept in the loop as it all develops, but I don't want you to be uncomfortable."

"Great. Thanks," said Porter and put his phone down.

Meyer then called Arata Sr. hoping that the investment in his TV production company was still on, to which the entrepreneur replied that unfortunately, it would have to be smaller than he had originally envisaged because a real estate opportunity that he had been banking on, was now off the table.

"If it comes back on," said Arata, reassuringly, "I'll be able to up my investment."

Arata had asked Mattia, his son-in-law, to look at the prospectus and he reported that while it was a business that could be quite volatile, the projects currently planned and scheduled looked good, at least on paper.

"How much may I expect?" asked Meyer.

"Half a mil." Arata thought this would be a good investment since he still wanted to keep tabs on the catholic investigation.

"Much appreciated. I'll get the paperwork over to you soonest."

Porter was left to get on with his job free from any further encumbrance. He had Janice's mid-week proposal in front of him and it looked good, with a few provisos. He called her in towards the end of the day.

"Please sit down. Can I get you a drink?" He got up and opened a cupboard at the back of his office. There was not much there except a bottle of Jack Daniels. He apologised.

"It's one of those drinks where you don't need mixers," he said and Janice nodded, wondering where this was all going. This was the first time she had been invited to have a drink in his office.

"Sure, just a small one."

Porter took his time, wondering how to say what he wanted, no, needed to say.

"Janice, I don't think I've said it but, er, you're doing an excellent job with Sullivan. Er, I know he's a bit of a maniac and I'm grateful to you." He was stuttering now in his embarrassment as Janice waited until he said what he evidently wanted to say.

"I'll just come out with it," he said, eventually.

"Please," said Janice.

"Well, I appreciated that you came and talked to me about the leak and I'm sorry I didn't respond well. You took me a little by surprise."

"I guess we owe something to each other," she said. He looked up after taking a large swig of his whiskey.

"Yes, perhaps we do," he said. Then as if a thought just struck him, "Why don't we have dinner tonight and I can explain a bit further?" Out of the corner of his eye, he saw Sullivan looking up and probably wondering what was going on.

"He'll be adding up two and two and making six," thought Porter. Then said out loud, "I think Sullivan's speculating on what's taking us so long. So let's look at this proposal." Now Porter was on firmer ground. Personal relationships weren't his forte, which was what Janice found endearing about him, not that he knew that. He went on.

"It's good in that it doesn't compromise the main edition, but it can't just be a documentary. It's got to have bite. Each story has to be going in the same direction. I want readers to be talking about it over breakfast, lunch and dinner, saying how they never knew this and no wonder the catholic church is full of paedophiles."

Janice raised her eyebrows. Porter paddled back a little. "OK. I exaggerated, but you know what I mean. This is a crusade for us. I want us to be building a case story by story, a case which puts the truth out there." He had been leaning over the desk in his enthusiasm and now coolly leaning back in his chair, trying not to concede how much the alcohol was doing the talking.

"Got it," said Janice.

"And about dinner?" asked Porter.

"Is this a date?" asked Janice, provocatively.

"Just friends having a meal together and enjoying each other's company, if that's OK?"

"OK. Text me details," said Janice and walked back to her desk.

Sullivan was quick to get in. "What was all that about?" Janice threw back her hair.

"He wanted to say how grateful he was that I was keeping you under control."

"He what?" exclaimed Sullivan.

Janice laughed at Sullivan's face. "He loved the proposal. He just wants it to be a crusade. I think he's after a Pulitzer."

Sullivan grumpily looked at his watch, logged off his computer, and picked up his jogging stuff making a mental note to put them on eBay or some other site. He was not going to use them again.

"See you in the morning."

Janice also took off, back to her apartment to shower, change, and await Porter's text. If it didn't come through within the hour, she would make her own arrangements and switch her phone off. There was no need to worry. Within ten minutes Porter had sent a text and within a couple of hours, both were sitting at a table in the Thai House near the railway station. He had remembered that she liked Thai food, which was impressive.

"I wonder what's this all about," she asked herself as he settled down smiling at her across the table. They ordered and clinked their glasses.

"I expect you're wondering why suddenly I suggested we have dinner together?" he began.

"Just a bit," responded Janice cautiously.

"Well," he hesitated. "I need to explain about the leak and....."

"You're the editor-in-chief. You don't need to explain anything."

"But I do. I gave my word, then had to break it."

"Had to," queried Janice.

Porter pursed his lips and shook his head, not in denial, but to say, "I wish I'd never done it." He stayed silent.

"Are you OK, Jimmy?" asked Janice, suddenly wondering whether the pressure of the job was getting to him at last. Only a few people were allowed to call him Jimmy and Janice was one of that small circle. She used to use it all the time when they were an item.

" Meyer insisted and I broke a cardinal rule – no pun intended." They both smiled at that. It seemed to break the tension that had been building. "He wanted to know exactly what we had."

"You don't have to answer to me," Janice reiterated.

"The thing gnawing at me is, what did he do with the information?"

Just then their food arrived and they tucked in. That spicy jungle curry was to die for.

"I did appreciate that you didn't tell Sullivan," said Porter after a pause.

"I suspect he knows, but can't prove it," responded Janice. She wasn't about to tell Porter about their surveillance activities.

"Well, no more," declared Porter. "Meyer will have to sack me if he wants more."

"That's unlikely given the increase in revenues you're generating. Just as you wouldn't sack Sullivan just now."

"Hmm," Porter's trademarked grunt seemingly said, "Nothing's impossible."

That was the end of the work conversation and it moved on to other things; relationships, attachments, each sounding the other out. The meal came to an end and Porter settled the check, with a half-hearted protest from

Janice. They parted at the door with Porter giving her a peck on the cheek, but no promises expected and none given.

Chapter 33

Sullivan appeared in the office the next morning carrying Kevin's laptop. No sign of any jogging outfit just his ageing jacket and usual jeans. Getting his body into some kind of normal shape had been put on the back burner, where it had been for some years.

"Anything significant on it?" asked Janice, anxious to be able to take it back to Kevin's grandmother and to keep her promise.

"Some social media rubbish from some bullies, and it seems he'd been having an online conversation with someone called Father Graham."

"I think that's the priest," said Janice.

"Very likely, but can't be proved yet."

"What do you mean, 'yet'?

"The hard drive has now been copied and it might take a while to track the details down," answered Sullivan. "There are also some inappropriate pics on there, but that might be just kids messing around and not related."

"So can I take the device back to his grandmother? I did promise to."

"Sure."

"I've written up his story for a front page at some point," said Janice. "Have a look and see if there are any other questions that I need to ask. I don't want to keep pestering her."

Janice added her file to an email and sent the story over to her boss headed, 'The Suicide'. Sullivan promised to get to it by the end of the day.

"I also did some work last night on our mid-week edition," said Sullivan. "By the way, where were you? I tried calling you, but no answer."

"Went to bed. Needed an early night, then got up early to finish off Kevin's story."

Sullivan seemed happy with the fictional explanation she had given. It was the first thing that popped into her head, not that she needed to justify where she was out of hours to Sullivan.

The man's desktop pinged, which meant an arriving email.

"Looks like our Cardinal is being charged, but his PS is not," he said quickly reading the message from his court source.

"Good," said Janice. "Who is his PS?"

"A Father Arata, only been a priest for a few years." Sullivan kept on reading.

"Wait a minute. The Cardinal is being charged with, listen to this: 'violating non-profit and estate, powers and trusts laws' and is being 'barred from any future service in a secular leadership role in the state, and the state is also seeking damages against them for the waste of charitable assets caused by their misconduct'." Sullivan sat back and shook his head.

"That's all?" exploded Janice. "did you say 'banned from any secular leadership in the state'? That's laughable. He won't last a couple of months."

"I agree," said Sullivan still studying the email. "It says, by failing to refer priests, the diocese prevented 'determination of the merits of the allegations', and 'deprived the accused and victims of an opportunity to be heard'.

"That's certainly true," said Janice.

"And," added Sullivan, "in addition, the suit seeks to hold the two bishops who oversaw the alleged cover-up individually responsible."

"What does that mean?" asked Janice.

"I think we need some legal clarification on this," exclaimed the determined investigator. "Either this is truly the extent of the law or there's been some secret deal done with catholic lawyers." Sullivan was apoplectic. "This is unacceptable."

He stomped into Porter's office demanding to see their lawyers. As he began his rant, Porter looked up towards Janice who raised her eyebrows and shrugged, mouthing, "Nothing to do with me, guv." He turned his attention to Sullivan who had calmed down a little and gave him the number of one of the lawyers, with the advice, "Calm down a little or he will put his phone down."

Sullivan rang through to be stopped by the gatekeeper, or secretary as they are usually known. The lawyer wasn't available but would certainly read his email before close of business, if he would like to send one. Janice just prevented him from throwing his phone across the newsroom saying, "We're the client. He will come back because he's being paid to. Every fifteen minutes!"

Sullivan was somewhat pacified and sent the email, then decided to take a break and a smoke, to calm down and think. He turned his attention to the mid-week edition. There were lots of articles and websites which purported to address the questions that he was asking, but he needed a 'true' catholic to review what he was going to say, preferably a priest who had recent knowledge of the system and how it had changed over the years, if at all.

Suddenly, he wondered about Father Arata, the Cardinal's PS. He was in the clear. Maybe he would talk off the record. Worth a try. With these thoughts, his excitement was back and he bounded back to his desk and shared his idea with Janice who agreed. But what was to be the approach? He couldn't doorstep him. A phone call might do it, especially if a female made the call – less intimidating perhaps?

"I'm thinking you might be the best person to approach him," said Sullivan. "Might be less alarming?" Janice thought about it and said she would do it if they could compile the questions between them. So it was agreed.

After a little thought, Janice made the call. "Hello, is that Father Arata?"

"Yes. Who's calling?"

"I'm Janice from the Gazette." She stopped to see if he would put the phone down. If he didn't she had permission to push him a little.

"I'm not sure talking to you is a good idea," he replied tentatively.

"May I tell you what I need?"

"OK."

"We want to do a mid-week special which will outline how the catholic church recruits, filters and trains its candidates."

There was silence on the other end of the line.

Janice jumped in again. "We are trying to understand how the catholic church got itself into this mess and be as fair as possible."

Still silence. Sullivan who had been listening was encouraging Janice to keep going with his gesticulating hands. She almost laughed at his efforts before there was an answer to her request.

"OK. I think I can do that on one condition."

"Which is?" asked Janice.

"My name is not mentioned anywhere, nor even hinted at."

"I can live with that," said a relieved Janice, hoping her relief hadn't been transmitted to the priest. "When would be convenient?"

"Well, as you probably know, there isn't a lot to do here at the moment until an interim is appointed to take the place of Cardinal Doughty. So let's say tomorrow at my parent's home. Both will be out all morning at least."

"Perhaps you could text me the address." Janice gave her number, and finished with, "Shall we say 10?"

"That will be fine."

While Arata was wondering if he had made the right decision, high fives were going on in the newsroom of the Gazette. Porter looked up to see what was going on. It seemed the whole newsroom had been listening and willing Janice on. He smiled with beneficence at the camaraderie. In the midst of it all, Sullivan's phone rang. It was the lawyer.

"I've read your email and what the charges are against the Cardinal. I know you'll be disappointed but they are the most the prosecution could do. If he had been charged with personally molesting a minor then it would have been a lot more. Sorry, not what you wanted to hear, but I'm sure you'll use that information to ask why harsher charges couldn't be levied." The phone went dead and Sullivan shrugged. Yes, he would be asking big questions about precisely that because he knew his readers would be asking themselves the same questions.

Back to the present. It was already Wednesday and stories need to be submitted ready for final editing, especially the front page. So a new front page had to be scrambled now there was a breaking story about Cardinal Doughty. Both investigators worked on separate stories for the front, page 3 and the centrefold, detailing his past, present and future and asking why more serious charges couldn't be levelled at him. Apart from the back page, traditionally reserved for the sports headline, these pages were the most looked at.

After a furious three hours of writing and re-writing, they were ready to go to Porter. There was a minimum of amendments to be made before he emailed them over to the lawyers for approval. By now this was becoming a regular occurrence, costly but necessary. Both breathed sighs of relief. They could now get on with putting together a question track for Janice's interview with Father Arata in the morning. Fortunately, it would happen before the Gazette hit the street on Friday for Janice had no idea how the priest would react once he had seen the headlines about his Cardinal. It was another one-shot interview and she was anxious to get it done.

The question track they were working on covered all the elements they wanted to cover which would be the backbone of the whole edition. They had plenty of third-party information already in the public domain, but they needed confirmation, and hopefully amplification, by a living, breathing priest.

It was nearly midnight by the time they had finished. They both knew an interview could easily go off track and, sometimes, it furnished valuable information. But the interviewer had to know how to get back on track indiscernibly, to ensure every area was covered in the time allowed.

Janice left with a print of the notes intending to go over them again at home before meeting Father Arata at his parent's home.

Chapter 34

JANICE ARRIVED ON time at an enormous stone house where the Aratas lived. She had to be buzzed in from the private road so that the electronic gates would be opened allowing her to drive in. Having parked her VW on the gravel outside the triple garage, she made her way to the imposing front door but before she could press the buzzer, Father Arata opened it dressed in his black cassock. He was a lot younger-looking than Janice expected, almost boyish.

"What a shame he's a priest," she thought as he welcomed her inside.

"Good morning," greeted the priest, with a guarded smile. "You found you're way in, then?"

"What an amazing house!" responded Janice.

"Yes, my father is a businessman who has had some success." Arata was leading the way into a side room which had its own fireplace, some easy chairs and a coffee table set on what looked like a very expensive rug. "May I offer you some coffee?"

Normally, Janice would have declined so that she could make the most of the time in conversation, but now she wanted to get a better sense of this house, the background of this priest, and look at the photos on the mantelpiece which showed the family on various holidays around the world.

"Thank you. That would be welcome." Arata left and she made the most of the time, and not just in that room. The more she wandered, the more she felt a little overawed. Arata returned to find her in the hallway.

"I can't say I've ever been in such a house before," she exclaimed.

"I trust that won't be held against me?" responded Arata, looking at her sternly.

"I apologise," said Janice, hurriedly.

"Let's get to it, shall we?"

"Certainly, but I'd love to know why you went into the church."

Arata paused for a moment. "Is that part of your piece?"

"Gracious no. Just interested. I imagine you went to the best schools and could have done anything you wanted, and yet.....” She left him to complete the sentence if he wished.

Arata smiled a little.

“He's warming up,” she thought. “Even priests like talking about themselves.”

“I don't think I was suited to business.”

“Why?”

“The cut and thrust of it mainly,” replied Arata. “It didn't sit well with my outlook on life.”

“And yet....?” Janice waved her arms around.

“Indeed,” responded Arata.

That seemed to bring an end to that line of enquiry, so Janice asked if he minded if she used a recorder. He did.

“I could be identified from my voice,” he said firmly.

“That's fine,” said Janice. “Just means I'll have to do a bit more writing.”

From there, she guided him through his own experience of applying, being interviewed, selected, trained in seminary and eventually receiving the sacrament of Holy Orders. It all seemed straightforward and confirmed much of the processes that she already knew. It seemed almost therapeutic for him to revisit his choices and comment on his journey since deciding to approach his priest at Harvard.

Two hours had passed by this point and Janice's hand was getting tired. She hadn't done this much writing for a long time, but he was certainly becoming more settled and relaxed with her, and she didn't want to break the mood. However, she needed more, so decided to ask the killer question which would either see her out of the door or unlock lots of precious information.

“So how did the church manage to get itself into this mess?” She waited, unconsciously holding her breath.

“Ah!” he laughed. “I wondered when you would get to that. You might have left it a bit late.” He looked at his watch. “We've probably only got another thirty minutes.”

“Why, if I might ask?” queried Janice.

He laughed again. “Because my mother will be home at lunchtime and she hates the Gazette.”

"Oh!" replied Janice.

"She calls it a 'rag'. Not very complimentary, eh?"

"Not very," said Janice, now squirming a little and anxious to move on quickly.

"Having said that," his turn to pause, "whilst I think your headlines have been a little racy, everything you have said up to now is true."

Janice was stunned for a moment.

"I don't write the headlines, just the copy," she said. "So tell me what you think about it all?"

Arata sat back and took a deep breath before launching into his explanation.

"Look. I can go through the history if you like."

"That would be nice, but briefly and in simple English if you would."

Arata looked troubled. "History is one thing, but to have it happening on your doorstep is another." He grimaced and shook his head.

Janice said nothing. Arata took a deep breath. "OK. This is what they teach you in seminary. We need to go back a bit."

"No problem," said Janice.

"Right. Since 1917, the church dealt with accusations against sexual abuse of children through rules that barred priests from soliciting sex when they were in the confessional."

"Excuse me! This has been going on since 1917? And in the confessional?" Janice had lost her objectivity for a moment.

"I'm afraid, well before 1917. That was just when the church started to take any notice." He carried on. "If priests, when taking a confession, solicited sex, they were viewed as having committed a particularly egregious sin. The confessional is a sacred space and confession a sacred act."

"I get that," said Janice writing furiously.

"The thing is," said Arata, hesitantly, "that the concern was all about the priest sinning, not about abuse being perpetrated on another. You see, the 1917 code did not have any canons that dealt with sexual abuse outside the confessional or sexual abuse of minors."

Janice was gaping. Arata couldn't help but notice. "Yes, it's horrifying, isn't it."

"Almost like a green light," commented Janice, once she had got herself under control.

Arata went on. "In 1922, the then Pope issued a set of guidelines, formally called an 'instruction', which tried to deal with cases in which the priest did not directly solicit sex during confession. So clerical sex abuse of minors was only a crime if the act was somehow associated with the sacrament of confession."

"I understand," said Janice.

"So from 1922 onward, investigations of clergy suspected of sexually abusing children were cloaked in secrecy, limiting bishops from reporting cases to the police, or even to parishioners."

"Even if they were criminal acts?" asked Janice. Arata ignored the obvious inference and carried on.

"Now this instruction was reissued by Pope John XXIII in 1962, although not officially incorporated into the Code of Canon Law nor, I'm afraid to say, was it widely circulated. So it was only in the 1983 code that child sex abuse was listed as a crime within the canon about clergy violating their obligation to not have sex.

"Sorry, let me stop you there," Janice held up her hand. "Let me get this right. This obligation not to have sex — are we conflating sex between consenting adults, male or female, with sex between an adult, even a priest, and a child?"

Arata was now looking a little uncomfortable. "You have to remember, that it was a different time back then."

"I'm sorry. You don't believe that and neither do I." Janice was looking straight at him.

"But the new code did give the Vatican much more control over the fate of accused clergy."

"Not that it did much good," commented the reporter.

"You're right," admitted Arata. "There was then a canon about avoiding scandal which compounded the secrecy of it all. It became a sin and a violation of canon law, to do anything that would cause 'scandal' to the faithful by leading them to sin or question their faith."

"What does that mean?" asked Janice.

"Well, if a bishop, for example, were to make known that a priest had sexually abused children in his diocese, the bishop, and not just the priest, would be guilty under canon law of causing scandal – because information about the abuse might cause catholics to question their faith."

Janice continued to write furiously. "As it would do," she commented dryly.

"Also included, was a requirement that bishops provide such priests with funds when they were removed from ministry."

"But they were not dismissed from the priesthood?"

"The term is 'defrocked'," said Arata patiently.

"Sorry again. Let me get this straight. This morally dubious practice of paying child sex abusers is, to the hierarchy, a fulfilment of their obligations?" Janice was transfixed at the twisted nature of it all.

"Let me go back to 1917 for a moment." Arata continued with his lecture on church history. At this juncture, he didn't seem touched by the iniquity of it all. "You see, under the 1917 code, bishops, under certain conditions, could dismiss priests from the clerical state, and without a canonical trial. But it could be done only after it was determined that there was no possibility of reform. If a priest claimed his abuse was due to paedophilia or other psychological disorders, canon law provided for a more lenient punishment. The priest could be regarded as not being fully responsible for his actions."

"Excuse me," Janice almost yelled. "Not responsible for his actions! A psychological disorder! Do you agree with that?"

Now Arata was looking very uncomfortable and Janice was worried that her interventions were upsetting the priest. "No, of course not. I'm giving you the history."

"Sorry. I apologise. Please carry on."

"The revision in 1983 put forward by Pope John Paul II made it impossible for bishops to dismiss priests. Authority for doing so became centralised in the Vatican."

"Why? Most people saw him as a good man." Janice was hoping to reinstate her objectivity.

"Well, my reading of it, and I wasn't around at the time you understand, was that the Pope was responding to a wave of good priests abandoning the priesthood. But the change ended up constraining the bishops. Now they had to retain abusive priests unless they were found guilty at a canonical trial and the Vatican agreed to dismiss them."

"Which they didn't want to do," guessed the reporter.

"At most, bishops could suspend priests' clerical faculties: that is, priests' authorisation to say mass and administer other sacraments, or present themselves publicly as priests, for a short time. But they could not do so permanently."

"I see," said Janice beginning to see how it was the Polish Pope who had made it all worse.

Arata continued his lecture. "The 1983 code also_reduced the maximum time within which proceedings could be initiated against priests having sex with a child to five years."

"So," Janice concluded, "if victims didn't come forward, it would mean that these would escape accountability and any punishment."

"Especially as canonical trials require the cooperation of the victim as a witness," Arata added.

"That's crazy. So that's another obstacle to holding priests accountable." Janice began to look very serious. "This is terrible. The code has encouraged the very inaction by bishops that the Pope said he condemned. Why? It's baffling."

Arata said, "I must agree. You see, there are no provisions in canon law that specify what is to be done if a bishop has failed to act on a case of suspected or actual child sex abuse."

"But common sense says something must be done, surely?"

"You would think so," said Arata. "But you must understand that most, if not all, catholic churchmen live in a catholic bubble. They are more concerned with canon law than with secular law."

"Are you saying that they consider themselves not under the law of the land?" asked Janice.

Arata thought for a moment. "I think many older priests, bishops, even archbishops and Cardinals might do, to a limited extent." He looked at his watch.

"OK. Let's quickly bring developments up to date. In 2001, a couple of years ago, there was a further centralising move from the Vatican which required that bishops send all cases of substantiated allegations of child sex abuse to its Congregation for the Doctrine of the Faith."

"That's the people who police possible heresy in the church?"

"Among other things, and the most powerful department in the Curia."

"How does it fit into sex abuse?" asked Janice.

"Its job is primarily to promote and safeguard the faith. So it may tell a bishop to conduct a canonical trial of a priest accused, or it may conduct one itself. It may accept or reject a request for dismissal of the priest and apply conditions to him. There is also the possibility of the verdicts and sentences being appealed."

"But that would take years," objected Janice.

"Time, in the Vatican, is not viewed in the same way it is for other institutions. Remember, it thinks in terms of centuries, not even decades."

"So this is the way the Vatican controls the process," mused Janice. "So, that means it is able to overrule what a bishop or archbishop wants."

"Exactly," confirmed Arata. "Although it is entirely within their power to do so, no Pope since has altered the Code of Canon Law about clergy child sex abuse and how it is handled by bishops."

"Why?" asked Janice.

"That I don't know. It would seem an obvious thing to do. Maybe it will happen soon and maybe you might play a role in that?" He raised his eyebrows and smiled at her.

Suddenly, Janice realised that she'd been played. She stared at his smiling face. Arata wanted change in his church and saw the Gazette as one way to push for it. She began to look at him in a different light. He smiled again as if he knew that she knew.

"I hope that's all been useful," he said as he got up. The interview was over and he offered his hand to Janice as she exited through the front door. "I shall read your 'mid-week special' with interest."

She stumbled back to her ride, quite shocked at how he had somehow turned the tables. She sat inside trying to make sense of this highly intelligent man. Then she laughed out loud as she thought of Sullivan's face when he was told. Nevertheless, she had what she wanted.

It would be dynamite.

Chapter 35

CARDINAL PATRICK DOUGHTY was externally comfortable in bed, but internally racked with all sorts of emotions: guilt, regret, even anger. Most of all though, he felt shame. Shame, not about boys who had been abused, but that he had let the catholic church and the Pope down, bringing scandal upon it. His only consolation was that he knew he was not the only senior churchman to have moved paedophile priests around. What else was he to do? The Vatican had given him no leeway to do much else. They were priests after all.

"Eminence, you have a visitor," said a nun who was there to look after his non-medical needs.

"Who is it?" said the Cardinal, struggling to pull himself up in his bed and putting his prayer beads aside.

"It's only me, Eminence," said Father Arata, at the door.

"Ah! Gino. How good of you to come." The PS came fully into the room and alongside the bed but didn't sit down. He would wait until invited.

"How are you? Are they treating you well?" Arata was hopeless at visiting people in hospital. He never knew what to say, so he started with the kind of banal question that everyone asks of patients. Fortunately, after this small talk had been accomplished, he would be able to talk work with his erstwhile boss.

"Yes, can't complain. Except for the food, of course." He gave a little laugh which promoted a coughing fit, bringing in the nun and a nurse. He waved them away with a little movement of his hand.

When they had gone, he said conspiratorially, "They say I've got some time left," Arata didn't quite know what to make of this. Was that good or bad? He decided to be positive.

"Good," he said watching the Cardinal closely. Then, "I hope the police treated you appropriately?"

"They have a job to do," said the Cardinal. "I made my confession before they came and said that I would answer all their questions truthfully before God."

"It seems the prosecution authorities are determined to proceed despite your ill health," said Arata, not quite knowing whether the Cardinal was up to date with developments.

"Yes, it seems so. But Shirley, Ms Clarke, was there and kept them in order, although the younger detective was quite disrespectful at one point." He did not enquire as to whether his PS had been charged or even questioned, but lay back on the three or four pillows that were propping him up, awake but with his eyes closed.

"I'd like to think," started the young priest, "that all these struggles you've had are not in vain and that some sort of new order will emerge."

The Cardinal opened his eyes and looked sharply at Arata. His physical weakness belied a mental toughness despite everything on his mind. "What do you mean by that?"

Arata hesitated. He'd been thinking deeply about this for some time, even before the invitation from the Gazette. He wondered whether the Cardinal, now approaching the end of his life, would be able to view the issues within his church from a different perspective.

"I'm not sure the church can continue to tolerate the scandal of priests doing unspeakable things to children." He used the word 'scandal' deliberately, referring to the canon issued by the Vatican about avoiding 'scandal', which Arata knew the Cardinal would understand well.

"Hmm," grunted His Eminence with his eyes shut. The PS had tried to make it an objective statement with no personal inference for His Eminence. It looked as if he had succeeded, but he didn't quite know what to make of this response, so said nothing and waited. Then, the Cardinal followed up his grunt with, "it's not good to criticise the Holy See."

Arata felt emboldened. "I agree, but we are at the coal face whereas Rome, and those living within the walls, are far from the world in which we have to live and act."

"Are you saying that the canons that are issued from Rome are wrong?" His Eminence was beginning to get worked up.

"I'm suggesting," explained Arata patiently but boldly, "that the existing ones that relate to this matter, are out of date and unless they are changed, bishops and archbishops, even Cardinals, will continue to be prosecuted, and we will continue having to pay out huge sums in compensation to an ever-increasing number of victims of priests, who should no longer be allowed to be in the ministry."

There. He had said it and it felt good.

"Father Arata," said the Cardinal, no longer calling the young priest by his Christian name, "you are young and do not know what you are saying."

"How so?" asked Arata, knowing he was getting very close to contradicting what His Eminence was saying, but since he was going to resign and a new archbishop would be appointed, he felt safe.

"This church relies for its law and practice on His Holiness and those who serve him in Rome. It has done so for centuries through scandals, corruption, wars, etc. These things have come and gone, but the church is still here, is it not?"

Arata was silent. He wanted to ask, "and how many innocent lives have been wasted, lost, irreparably harmed just because senior churchmen said 'nothing can be done'?" But he thought better of it. He realised that the Cardinal was of an old order and was not going to change. No matter what the pastoral pressures the Congregation for the Doctrine of the Faith placed on bishops and archbishops, this Cardinal was not going to be the one to put his head above the parapet, even though he didn't have long to live.

Although the young priest knew his master, he was still disappointed in him. The Cardinal also had nothing to lose by speaking up for change. Arata had misjudged him. He was totally conformed to the existing order of things, whereas Arata wanted things to change. He wanted a new order to replace the old, a church more attuned to the needs of its flock, especially the children, rather than to its own.

What had Jesus said? "*Whoever receives one such child in my name receives me. But if anyone causes one of these little ones who believes in me to sin, it would be better for him to have a millstone fastened around his neck and to be drowned in the depths of the sea.*" (Matthew 18:5-6)

The Cardinal had closed his eyes and was lying back on his pillows. He seemed exhausted by the conversation, so Arata sat in the visitor's chair and prayed silently for his soul. As he was doing so, another Scripture came to mind, almost as if the Holy Spirit was speaking directly to him. It was so real that he had to open his eyes to make sure there was no one else in the room.

It was James 3:1 *"not many of you should become teachers, for you know that we will face a more severe judgement."* He knew every priest was a teacher, whether directly in the pulpit or by everyday example. Indeed, he himself was a teacher. This realisation drove him to more urgent prayer, not only for the Cardinal but for himself.

Then another verse from Scripture popped into his head. What was going on? Again, he looked around - only a nurse passing the window of the Cardinal's room. What was it again? He had nearly forgotten it. Oh yes! It was the Apostle Paul in 1 Cor 6:9. He shuddered as he recalled it. *"Do you not know that the unrighteous will not inherit the kingdom of God? Do not be deceived; neither the immoral, nor idolaters, nor adulterers, nor sexual perverts."*

What was he supposed to do with all this? He quickly felt under his cassock for his phone and, opening the Notes app, he began to tap out the references before he forgot them. Were they from God? Was he supposed to relate them to the Cardinal? With whom could he share his dilemma? He didn't know anyone who shared his reservations and who would be open to discussing them with him, but he had to find someone.

Chapter 36

PORTER WAS YELLING for the mid-week special copy. Other departments were all ready and waiting for to go. It had been trailed in last weekend's edition and advertising interest had been high. Porter had promised Meyer a bumper edition. He was on edge and it showed. The rest of the newsroom looked on with a mixture of jealousy and sympathy as the investigation department had their heads down furiously working to a deadline which had come and gone.

"Send it to me now," yelled Porter again. Sullivan had sent in one of his stories and had three more to send. Janice's story was going to be the centre-fold and she was still typing and re-typing frantically. She had not the time to explain much to Sullivan except that she wanted the centrefold. Sullivan had looked at her with some curiosity. Normally, he would have had the pick of the pages, but she hadn't asked and he didn't have time to argue or check her story. He had to trust her which was a big ask considering this was a high profile edition. If it wasn't right, there would be hell to pay.

Sullivan pressed his Send button. His remaining stories had gone for approval, giving Janice some cover for her big one. Neither knew exactly how the front page would eventually look or what the headline would be. Porter wanted to read it all and this time he also had one of his sub-editors along-side. It was important to get this right. Everybody's reputation, including the Gazette's, was on the line and stress levels were high.

Finally, Janice also pressed her Send button. Her story had gone. She sat back, breathing heavily, which was just as well, since she had hardly breathed at all for the last hour, or at least it seemed like that.

"Send me a copy, will you?" said Sullivan, exercising some measure of authority over his junior. He knew it wouldn't be long before the editor-in-chief yelled again for them to enter the Holy of Holies. So he began to scan Janice's story. There were two stories: the side story covered the path of a young man who wanted to become a priest, highlighting the lack, as she saw it, of much in the way of safeguarding policies and training. But the main story was the historic inability, or was it reluctance, to deal with paedophilia among the priesthood. It seemed to have been just accepted as inevitable.

Sullivan was completely captured as he read the copy. He hardly heard Porter's next yell to come in. Janice gave him a friendly punch on the arm and nodded in the editor's direction.

"My God," he started, "You've certainly got something here." He was excited for her as they entered Porter's office.

The editor-in-chief turned to Janice. "How much of this is research and how much from a reliable source?"

"Except for the odd comment here and there, entirely from the horse's mouth."

Porter looked at her in disbelief. "You got a catholic priest to give you all this?"

"Completely."

His eyes narrowed. "Why? What possible motive could a priest have for dishing the dirt on his own church?"

"It was interesting. I thought I was using him to get the story until right at the end when I realised that he was using me!"

Sullivan was listening. He had the same questions in his mind since he had not had any briefing from Janice. So he jumped in, knowing who the informer was.

"Let me guess," he said. "He wanted to get his own back for being let down by his boss."

Porter leaned towards his chief investigator. "Are you telling me," he started, "that you hadn't read this or checked it out before it came to me?"

"Didn't need to," said Sullivan. "She's just as good as I am." Then added, "In fact, I think she did a better job with this source than I could have done?"

"So you know the source?" Porter said accusingly.

"Yes."

Porter paused his interrogation and looked at Janice, "I don't know what the lawyers will say, but I think it's brilliant."

"And so do I," said Sullivan to Janice's blushes.

" In fact, regardless of what they say," continued Porter, "within reason, I'm going to get this out there. Everybody should know this."

Janice raised a cautionary point. "There will be many people who won't like it. The mother of the priest I interviewed still thinks Doughty is a good man and that we're wrong."

"You won't convince everyone," interrupted Sullivan. "If they're in their religious bubble, truth won't come into it. All they will want to hear is stuff that reinforces their point of view. They will close their ears to anything contrary, arguing black is white if they have to."

Porter nodded. "They're not our readers. If they've supported this church regardless of what we already published, there's nothing we can do to persuade them. We have to accept that."

He stood up and unexpectedly stretched out to shake the hands of both his investigators.

"Do we get a raise?" asked Sullivan, cheekily.

"Get out," said Porter. "Go home and have an early bath. You deserve it. We've got lots to do here."

Both investigators moved back to their corner. The adrenalin was beginning to dissipate and each was beginning to feel very tired.

"OK. It's Tuesday," said Sullivan, thinking ahead. "We've already got the bones of what we need for the weekend, haven't we?"

Janice agreed. "We can finish that off tomorrow and still have time to spare before Thursday's deadline." They both left the building going their separate ways.

It was only when Janice got home that she began to wonder if anyone would be able to identify Father Arata. The more she thought about it, the more uneasy she became. She decided to ring him.

"Hello," She recognised his educated voice immediately.

"Father Arata, it's Janice from the Gazette."

"Hello, Janice. What can I do for you?"

"Well, the copy has gone to press and the edition will be on the street tomorrow morning."

"I shall buy a copy,"

There was a pause before Janice said, "Er. I was wondering," she started, "whether you would like to see what I've written?"

"Why?"

"Obviously, it can't be changed, but it might alert you if you felt you could be identified."

Arata's voice changed. "Is there something I should know?"

"No. But I want to protect you as best I can."

"Perhaps you had then. Send it as a WhatsApp." Then the phone went dead and Janice sent it. Once done, she felt she had done as much as she could and went to have a shower before changing and going for a walk to the Waterfront.

On the way back, her phone rang. It was Arata.

"Hello Janice, I think you did a good job. Should put the cat among the pigeons."

"At first, I didn't realise that you were using me."

"'Using' is rather strong, don't you think?"

"Well, I hope you succeed in your quest to change the church," said Janice.

"Ah. That's an ambition much too far," admitted Arata.

"We can only splash a story for a short while until the agenda moves on," explained Janice.

"You do yourself a disservice. I have some hopes this edition will reach Rome. I'm sure your headlines have already been noticed."

"You're going to send them a copy?" Janice was incredulous. "I had no idea. So it will have an impact."

"Certainly. For good or ill."

"How do you mean?" Janice had now found a seat and sat down. She needed to concentrate on this conversation. She sensed there might be another story here.

"Well, the Holy See doesn't change overnight. In fact, it tries not to change at all. It hates change. The best that can be done is to sow some seeds."

"I understand," said Janice.

"So, thank you for what you've done so far. Incidently, I will write to your editor-in-chief. Porter's his name, isn't it?"

"Yes," said Janice, wondering what was going to come next.

"I will complain that you are dragging the catholic church into the dirt and exaggerating this whole business for the sake of increased circulation and more money."

Janice was dumbstruck for a moment until she realised what he was up to.

He continued. "I trust that, in the interest of objectivity, your editor will publish it." She detected a smile on his face as he said it.

Janice burst out laughing. "I shall suggest he does, though it's not my call."

Sullivan had no such qualms about his stories. He didn't like the catholic church, but then there were lots of things he disliked; big industrial corporations, political elites of both sides, young Silicon Valley millionaires, white supremacists, pharmaceutical companies and the list went on. Some originated in pure jealousy, but others were more about his personal morality and supporting the underdog.

Instead of going straight home, he stopped off at the Irish pub for his usual liquid lunch, then drove back to his apartment, keeping a wary eye out for any police patrols. He was in no hurry and started thinking about Janice. She had come a long way and certainly had what it took to be a top investigative reporter. Porter obviously saw something in her that he hadn't seen, but then he didn't see much other than the next task ahead. He was a loner or had been until Janice. Now he was pleased to have someone who was reliable and whom he could trust to give him good feedback. It was all about the job.

Porter didn't have to stay around the office. Once he had approved the copy and some of the page layouts he could have gone home, but he was caught up in the excitement of his first mid-week special. He treated himself to a 'wee dram' in his office, although when he poured it, rarely was it a 'wee dram'.

He started thinking about Janice as well. Had that boat really sailed? Could he recover the situation? Was it wise for him as editor-in-chief? He didn't know any of the answers, but he did know that since their dinner engagement, something was stirring in him that wasn't the Gazette.

Chapter 37

As far as the Vatican was concerned, reports of child abuse within its ranks came and went. Whatever the issue, the strategy was to say as little as possible and not feed international media machines. The UK was not the centre of the catholic universe by any means but, nevertheless, an important opinion former in the English-speaking world and Andrew Douglas-Scott, the Pope's Private Secretary, was anxiously awaiting a report. As an English national, he had a specific interest in the outcome of the Independent Inquiry into Child Sex Abuse (IICSA). It had been set up to examine child abuse in England and Wales in all institutions, but it was the catholic element that he was concerned about. Cardinal Vincent Nichols was the leader of the catholic church in England and Wales and he had earlier flagged up to His Holiness that he might come under some criticism.

Sure enough, it was a damning report claiming that the church 'repeatedly prioritised its own reputation over the welfare of child sex abuse victims'. In its final review, it said 'the Vatican's failure to cooperate with the investigation passes understanding'. The Pope's PS decided to take a précis of the report to His Holiness.

"What are you going to do with Cardinal Nichols?" Douglas-Scott asked His Holiness as he read the précis. "He has offered his resignation," he added, expecting his master to accept and appoint another.

The Pope looked up pointedly, surprised by the question. "Do?" he asked. "I'm going to 'do' nothing."

"But," said his PS, a bit taken aback, "the report says that under the Cardinal, the church 'neglected the physical, emotional and spiritual well-being of children and young people in favour of protecting its reputation' and 'was in conflict with its mission of love and care for the innocent and vulnerable.'"

"That does seem to be the view of Professor Jay," agreed the Pontiff.

"But I'm afraid the Cardinal comes in for specific criticism," said the PS. "The report says, 'there was no acknowledgement of any personal responsibility to lead or influence change. Nor did he demonstrate compassion towards victims in the recent cases which we examined.'"

"A Cardinal can't possibly know what every priest in his archbishopric is doing, nor to whom he is doing it." The Pope was adamant.

"But there are calls for him to resign, even by parts of his own church," continued the PS.

The Pope sighed. "There are always calls for people to resign but we can't just give in. He may not be the most pastoral of men, but I know he will defend the church."

"But they are saying that the catholic church is not a safe place for children," insisted Douglas-Scott.

"Andrew," said the Pope sternly, "Enough. I've read your report and yes, there are things to do there, but I want Cardinal Nichols to do them. We will not give in to those who want to attack the church."

Douglas-Scott was about to leave the papal office when His Holiness added, in a softer tone, "Andrew, I've heard what you've said and I know you have great concern for this situation. I shall pray for more guidance. In the meantime, would you encourage our Cardinal to liaise with the *papal nuncio* (Vatican Ambassador) to put out a comforting statement?"

"Yes, Holiness."

As Douglas-Scott returned to his office, he wondered exactly what kind of guidance God would give His Holiness. Maybe if he had given his master all the facts and figures he might have come to a different conclusion. They didn't make pleasant reading.

The church in England and Wales had received more than 900 complaints involving more than 3,000 instances of child sexual abuse, which included priests, monks and volunteers. On occasions, the inquiry said, the abuse was accompanied by "sadistic beatings driven by sexual gratification" as well as "deeply manipulative behaviour by those in positions of trust".

One child estimated that between the ages of 11 and 15, he had been abused hundreds of times by a priest. His testimony was:

"After each incident, I was required to say three Our Fathers and a Hail Mary, or it was one Our Father and three Hail Marys, I can't quite remember. Apparently, it was so God could redeem me of my sins, if you can believe that."

He also testified that the priest concerned made it plain that his sister's place at a local convent school depended on his compliance.

Douglas-Scott sat down at his desk his hands over his face. He had no children of his own, but he thought of his sister and the three children he had met not long ago. The odds were that their priest was a good man, but what would he do if his nephew was molested and he had done nothing about it? He put the thought aside – for the moment.

He had a job to do and prepared himself to write to the Cardinal and Ambassador. He knew that the Pontiff had instructed the Vatican Secretary of State to ensure that neither the Cardinal nor Ambassador should take part in the Inquiry which had not gone down well with Professor Alexis Jay, the chair of the Inquiry.

The statement was sent and duly issued, saying the comforting things that His Holiness wanted said. The report was 'welcomed', it would 'inform' improvements and 'apologies' were offered to those who had not been properly listened to.

The PS thought it was what His Holiness wanted, but he retained deep concerns.

In the US, Sullivan had been tipped off a few days earlier by a journalist friend, Jerry Harris, on the staff of the UK Chronicle, that a long-awaited report was about to be released, which he might find interesting. That morning, there was an email from the UK containing a URL, giving him access to the report. The subject immediately grabbed his attention. The Independent Inquiry into Child Sex Abuse (IICSA). In the past, he would have kept this to himself as a valuable source for a front-page story, but now he had changed. He saw Janice almost as an equal, although she didn't have the years of experience that he did. He forwarded it on and indicated that she should read it as well.

"But this is about the UK. Will our readers be interested?" Janice saw the size of the report and baulked at spending the morning ploughing through it.

"If Jerry says it will be interesting for us, it will." stated Sullivan confidently.

"Who's Jerry?" asked Janice.

"A good friend across the pond who knows a story when he sees it," was all Sullivan would say.

"If you say so," said Janice reluctantly.

"I do."

They both downloaded it and began reading, ensconced in their corner of the newsroom. Sullivan was speed reading to find the relevant bits for him, whereas Janice was slower, ready to make notes for another story if there was one, but was yet to be convinced. That is, until she read the Executive Summary. Then, she was hooked. The following pages reminded her of all the stories that she had researched and written from the US. They were exactly the same, the methods were the same, the reaction of the catholic church was the same, and the impact on the children was the same. As she was coming to the Recommendations, she was interrupted.

Sullivan suddenly jumped up and shouted out, "I don't believe it!"

Almost everyone in the newsroom at the time looked up to see Sullivan waving his arms and walking around his desk in an agitated state,

"What on earth is it?" Janice asked, a little concerned. "Calm down. What have you found?"

Sullivan looked around and mouthed 'Sorry' to the newsroom, most of whom had already gone back to what they were doing. Just Sullivan again.

"The catholic Brits actually sent paedophile priests over here to cover up what they'd done over there. I can hardly believe it."

"Excuse me?" asked Janice, who was way behind Sullivan in reading the report. "That can't be right. Show me."

"It says it right here," said Sullivan jabbing his chubby finger over the offending paragraph of the report.

Janice read it slowly on his screen, then found the page on her screen. She read it again to make sure she fully understood what the report was saying. She sat dumbfounded for a few moments thinking.

"Does this mean," said Janice slowly, as she was coming to terms with the implication of what she had seen, "there could be some sort of international market for paedophile priests?"

She looked at Sullivan. "I know that sounds ridiculous, but what else can it indicate? I mean, how many are we talking about? Who organises this? Where in the US do they go? Have they come in from other European countries as well? And have any US priests been sent over there?"

Sullivan hadn't got that far, but he quickly saw where Janice was going. He began shaking his head.

"No sooner do we think we've got to the bottom of this, than a new dimension arises. I'm going to call Jerry."

"Jerry, it's Sullivan from Boston."

"Sullivan, nice to hear from you. Did you like the report?"

"Sure. The thing that jumped out to me, and which our readers will be interested in, is that paragraph where it says paedophile priests in the UK were sent over here as part of a cover-up."

"Yea. Only one, as far as I know, and I've not got much information on it. The catholic church is not known for being transparent about its activities."

"Tell me about it," said Sullivan.

"It concerns a guy called Father Quigley. A complaint which led to his removal to the US, was made by a third party about Quigley's relationship with a sixth-form student. But there were multiple offences in a previous role in Warwickshire. Anyway, he was 'removed from high priesting' and sent to an institute in the US for six months."

"Where did you get this?" asked Sullivan.

"It's from a catholic newspaper called The Tablet."

"OK. What institute and what for," asked Sullivan.

"Don't know about where. All I can get at the moment is that it was for some kind of 'therapy', although it could just as well have been the sort of 'gardening leave' that many paedophile priests did when they were found out."

"How long did he stay here? asked Sullivan.

"Again, don't know, but he did return to the UK and was allowed to resume school work with children."

"For God's sake, why?" asked Sullivan.

"The church seemed to believe that it had met its duties."

"What happened to him?"

"Oh. He was jailed for eleven and a half years."

"At least that's something."

"Anything else you've come across which might be useful?"

"Oh, there was a priest who was sent to Toronto. Are you interested in that?"

"Sure."

"OK. Look up Father Paul Moore from Scotland. It all came to light following a BBC investigation. They found that Moore had admitted in 1996 that he had abused more than one boy years earlier, and it was initially covered up by the bishop. The then Bishop of Galloway, Maurice Taylor, did not contact the authorities about the priest's confession until eight months later. Instead, he sent him to a treatment centre in Toronto."

"Do you know what treatment centre and what they did there?"

Jerry laughed. "Of course not."

"Do you have anything else for me?"

"Just one thing which you might find amusing, concerning one of your own catholic priests."

"What has he done?" asked Sullivan.

"He hasn't done anything that I know about. He's an academic and psychologist."

"Has he come up with a theory as to why so many of his compatriots are sexual deviants?" Sullivan's cynicism was showing.

"Ha. Ha. His name is Rossetti and he has reported that the frequency of paedophilia amongst the catholic clergy is no higher than among the general population, and a catholic priest is no more likely to be a paedophile than the average male."

"Now I've heard it all," said Sullivan.

"Well, both you and I could be paedophiles, Sullivan." He laughed.

Chapter 38

FATHER ANDREW DOUGLAS-SCOTT had come to a conclusion. It was the biggest decision of his life and it had taken him some time. He had decided to wait until Paolo, butler to His Holiness, had been charged and found guilty of stealing the report into a gay cabal within the Curia from his master's office and the trouble with the American nuns was partially under control. Two difficult issues had been dealt with and felt he could leave somewhat of a clean slate, at least for the present.

He agonised over his letter of resignation for days, and nights. He wanted it to be professional without that 'preachy' element that featured in many politicians letters published subsequent to their sacking. He wanted to try one last time to influence the way his church was proceeding and not just with the paedophile priest issue. Maybe a 'new order' was an impossibility; maybe the wrong phrase, but some change was urgently required, in his opinion. It couldn't start anywhere else but the top.

His Holiness had been expecting it and upon reading the letter, in the presence of his PS, was visibly downcast.

"I'm sorry to read this letter, Andrew. You have been a good Private Secretary and I know how hard this must have been for you."

"I was also sorry to have to write it," said the soon to be ex-PS. "Maybe, I had unrealistic expectations of what we could do together."

The Pope shifted in his seat at the implication. "There are so many things which have to be balanced," he explained. "That's why the Cardinals have an incentive to choose an older man, like me." He stood up and went over to the couch again, signalling he was happy to have an informal 'off the record' conversation. It was as if he wanted to unburden himself.

"Holiness, you don't need to explain yourself to me."

"You see," The Pontiff continued, "an older man makes a better candidate to navigate the differing factions within the Curia. If it turns out they do not like the one the Cardinals have chosen, they can easily wait out a few years to revisit their options sooner rather than later, hoping their lobbying might provide one suitable to maintain their status quo."

"But you have the authority to do what you think is right?" It was a question which had long provoked the PS as he saw his friend merely sustain what he had inherited.

"Ah!" replied the Pope. "I may have the authority but not necessarily the power. They're two different things. In order to exercise power you must have instruments that you can wield. And to do that successfully you need to divide and conquer, and to do that you need allies. Without that, one is limited to gentle cajoling rather than outright confrontation."

The Pontiff sighed. "It all takes time; time that most Popes don't have." At this point, he looked a lonely and defeated man. The PS almost wished he hadn't written his letter. Almost.

"It doesn't sound as if the Holy Spirit has much to do with it," said Douglas-Scott. "The same comments could, and have been made by government ministers about their civil servants. I've seen it in the Foreign Office back in the UK. The church is supposed to be different."

"Well, we have to believe that regardless of the will of man, the will of God must prevail."

"But as long as there is a battle of wills," argued the PS, "the will of God is delayed by men and people get hurt."

The Pope immediately connected the comment to the paedophile priest scandal. "That is true. Our Lord once said, 'The poor, you will always have with you.' And it seems it is the same with those who are injured and hurt."

"But surely, not by our hands?" Douglas-Scott was a little too strident, but His Holiness didn't object.

"The Bride of Christ is not perfect, at least not yet."

Douglas-Scott decided that the cut and thrust of debate was not going to change what he saw as a grave passivity embedded in the catholic church. He thanked His Holiness once more, bowed and left the room with a thoughtful elderly man in white still sitting on his couch.

Once back in his office, he picked up a small suitcase already packed with all his civilian clothes, documents and personal cellphone, then exited the building, nodding to the Swiss guards who knew nothing of his resignation and probably didn't care. Still wearing his everyday vestments, for he was still an ordained priest in the catholic church, he stood outside the walls and took a deep breath of real air. He filled his lungs in a symbolic act of emancipation but Rome's characteristically fume-filled air soon put a stop to that. Nevertheless, he felt a sense of freedom he had not felt for years; no one to report to, no one to tell him what to do, and no one to please. For how much longer, he didn't know.

He was never a man who acted impulsively which certainly suited him for the UK Foreign and Commonwealth Office right at the start of his diplomatic career. A first-class degree in philosophy from Exeter University had equipped him intellectually, but he soon realised that most of his fellow interviewees in those early days were Oxbridge graduates, some even post-graduates and a few having relatives already in the service. From the off, he knew he was at a distinct disadvantage but with studious preparation of current world affairs, a honed ability at debate, and a steadiness even when attacked verbally at the interviews, he was finally, if grumpily, accepted.

His parents were enormously proud, he being the first of his wider family to go to university, let alone be accepted for the diplomatic service. His sister would follow the university trail a few years later, though at St Andrews. Education would be her career until marriage and offspring came along. Children had never been on the radar of either him or his ex., Helen. Both were wedded to their careers; his in the service of his country and hers for Accenture, formally Andersen Consulting. Fortunately for both, Accenture had offices in most major cities and so they managed to co-habit most of the time despite the seemingly random diplomatic postings around the world which he was subjected to. It was almost as if they were trying to be rid of him, and perhaps they were. Such a vicarious existence didn't help their relationship and soon, Andrew began to suspect an affair. He began to test out his wife with questions such as,

"Work must be very busy at the moment?"

To which, she would reply, "Yes, very busy."

Not a satisfactory answer for her husband, but he was not looking for any answer just, not so subtly, indicating his disquiet at the late evenings and over-nights which seem to be getting more regular. It wasn't long before her situation became an open secret, with Helen almost revelling in her extra-marital adventure. Divorce followed relatively quickly and assets were divvied up between them with some harsh words thrown out by each other.

These reflections and more went around his mind as he made his way to Roma Termini to catch his Leonardo non-stop train to Fiumicino Aeroporto. Yes, he was hurt. Who wouldn't be? Maybe his friendship with the then Cardinal had been on the rebound, and he should have given himself much more time to come to terms with his divorce and the impact it was having on him. And if that was wrong, maybe the whole priesthood decision had been wrong.

He shrugged his shoulders even as he was walking into the rail terminus as if giving up on the rationale for his past decision-making. He made straight for the rest-rooms to change out of his cassock into normal dress. Another symbolic act of freedom. There was some time before departure, so he sat down and switched his mind off the past and on to the issue that had led him to resign.

What he couldn't understand was how such harm to young children could be talked about within the catholic church in such academic, quasi-theological terms when young lives had been, and were still being, wrecked by men supposedly preaching the gospel of Christ. He had never had children, but he could almost feel the pain, confusion and anguish that victims of errant priests were still experiencing. He knew he wanted to do something about it, but what?

His airline ticket showed London Heathrow as his destination, but the more he began to think through how he might be received by Cardinal Nichols and the catholic structure in the UK, the more he began to doubt whether they would be receptive to his views, in fact, quite the reverse. He wondered whether his friend in the Vatican might notify Nichols of his arrival and the reasons for his resignation. But what was the alternative? He had no other relatives other than in the UK and friends in Durban hadn't kept in touch, perhaps out of embarrassment. There was no other place, was there?

Then into his mind came one word. Boston.

Chapter 39

IT WAS ONLY a few days later that Cardinal Doughty passed away. Father Arata, nominated as next of kin, was woken up at three in the morning to be told the news. It had been a combination of conditions, undoubtedly caused by his cancer which was quite widespread. Typical of the man, he had not signalled any ill health until absolutely necessary. By then, of course, any real hope of remission had disappeared and it had been an end-of-life regime that the medics had recommended.

"There is no need to come to the hospital immediately," the voice told him, "but if you could get here mid-morning, we would appreciate you formally identifying the body."

"Of course. What about his personal belongings?" asked Father Arata.

"Yes, we'll have them prepared for you to pick up when you come."

"Are there any other formalities that require my presence?" Arata wasn't familiar with the procedures around death, this being the first he had experienced. He wasn't even sure if he wanted to see the Cardinal's body.

"Yes, as nominated next of kin, you will need to obtain the death certificate but that doesn't have to happen tomorrow."

"Thanks. I'll be in tomorrow morning."

Father Arata wasn't grief-stricken but certainly sad. They hadn't had many disagreements since he had been appointed; the Cardinal was experienced and he was young with his career in front of him, and he hadn't wanted to overstep the mark. That is, until the issue of paedophile priests was reignited. On the whole, they had a professional relationship and any decisions the Cardinal had made that might have been considered marginal, he had kept away from his Private Secretary. Whether that was from a desire to protect his protégée or because he was embarrassed to admit them, would never be known. The young priest wanted to think the best, except he knew the older man was a product of his generation and things had to change. But on a personal level, the Cardinal had been a good boss.

He lay in bed with a hundred thoughts competing for attention. It was now nearly four o'clock with no chance of getting back to sleep. So he got up, showered and dressed wondering how long he would be living in the Cardinal's mansion. He was sure that the new Archbishop, whoever he was, would want to bring his own Private Secretary, someone probably more experienced than himself. Where would he go? Would he have any choice in the matter? Perhaps the contents of the Cardinal's letter of recommendation, which he had never seen, would say that he was a troublemaker, an idealist with newfangled ideas, someone who should be inducted into a parish far away from where he might ferment disorder and disobedience.

He dragged his mind back to more immediate concerns. The Gazette would, no doubt, hear of the Cardinal's passing and feature it in the next edition which was due out in two days' time. He wanted his boss to get a fair write up and he wasn't sure he could entirely trust the paper to do it on their own.

"Hello Janice," greeted the priest. "Sorry to call you so early in the morning."

He heard the reporter grunt at the other end of the line. "What time is it?" she asked sleepily.

"I believe it is time for lectio divina," said the priest chuckling.

"Time for what?" muttered Janice.

"My apologies," said Arata.

There was a silence at Janice's end, as she tried to figure out who it was. Just as she was about to terminate the call, she twigged.

"Is that you, Father Arata?"

"I'm sorry if I woke you prematurely," he said. "But I have some news and a request."

Janice was well awake now. "OK?" she said tentatively.

"The news is that Cardinal Doughty has died."

Janice responded in the only way she knew how. "Oh. I'm sorry for your loss."

Father Arata pressed on. "The request is that I write an obituary piece for your paper."

"I'm sure that would be welcome," Janice said encouragingly, "though I'm not the one to say yea or nay. That's the editor's prerogative."

"But you have a good relationship with your editor?" It was an innocent comment but it startled Janice.

"I'm sorry, what do you mean?"

Father Arata suddenly felt that he had trodden on a land mine. "Oh, nothing," he said hurriedly, "except he allowed you to write what I said almost verbatim, so I assume he has confidence in you?"

Janice tried to backtrack a little. "Yes, yes of course. I'll ask him. I'm sure he would agree. Of course, we will probably write our own editorial."

"I understand," said the priest. "And sorry for waking you so early." He rang off.

Unlike Arata, Janice went back to sleep, ostensibly just for an hour but she overslept and, although rushed her bathroom routines, had to miss her breakfast, still arriving at the office late. She was going to dive in through the newsroom door full of apologies to her boss but then remembered she had a story, a good one. That trumped almost everything in her business.

Sullivan lifted his eyebrows as he saw her saunter in, thinking she's got something. He decided to get in first.

"So, you've got a story?" he asked looking up.

She stopped, surprised. "How do you know?"

Sullivan put his finger beside his nose, indicating he could smell it. "Am I right, or am I right?" he asked, teasingly.

"Maybe," she said. "What if I told you that the Cardinal is dead and that Arata wants to do an obit?"

Now it was Sullivan's turn to be surprised. "What?" He had raised his voice in disbelief.

"What's he going to say?" he added, thinking the paper was not going to allow catholic propaganda to be spread through its pages.

"I suspect he's going to be traditional, tell the man's personal story, probably with a little twist of his own."

"Hmm," responded the veteran reporter.

"He's quite an intelligent man if you think about what he's already given us."

"But what about that letter he wrote? Even with Porter's cut-down version, it was a spirited defence of current catholicism."

"That's what I mean – a very intelligent man."

"Hmm," responded Sullivan again, not understanding at all. Suspecting there was an angle he wasn't getting, he said lamely, "Better take it into Porter and see what he thinks."

Porter asked his usual sceptical questions but his eyes were sparkling. He already had an idea of how to play it. After her pitch, Janice got the go-ahead with the usual proviso of a word count and deadline. Just as she was leaving the Holies, he added, "And I'd like you to write a draft ed. on this."

Janice looked back quickly, taken by surprise, but Porter had his head back down and wasn't looking for an answer. Clearly, it wasn't a question requiring agreement.

Sullivan raised his eyebrows in questioning mode as she got back. "Apparently, I'm drafting the editorial on this one." He took a moment to lean back in his chair weighing his boss's decision. "Hmm," he grunted again. "Not an experience I've ever had but I'm sure you're up to it."

"Glad to know you approve," said Janice in sarcastic mode.

She made a quick call to Arata to say he had a go-ahead outlining the editor's provisos.

"I've already written it," said the priest. "Just need to cut a few words and it will be over to you in an hour." It wasn't easy to impress Janice but she was impressed with this man.

Sullivan began putting the front page copy together featuring another paedophile story whilst Janice began to think about the line she would take in the editorial whilst waiting for Arata's copy to come over. She had no doubts that it would arrive when he said it would. Sure enough, it did. She read it and thought it was perfect. Those who wanted to support the catholic church would see something they could agree with, whilst those with a keener eye would see another strand altogether woven into the piece.

"This man can write," she said to herself. Sullivan overheard and looked across his desk.

"What was that?" he asked.

"Arata's already written the obituary. It's a masterclass of writing when you want to satisfy both those pro-traditional catholicism and those looking for a change. I'll send it across."

Sullivan read it and grudgingly admitted the fact. "Is he putting his name to it this time?" he asked.

"Of course. He was Personal Secretary to the Cardinal and the right person to do it."

Something was bugging Sullivan that he wasn't going to acknowledge to anyone, not even himself so he restricted himself to another grunt. When Janice passed on their usual lunch at the Irish pub citing working on the editorial, he became quite discontented. Was Porter favouring Janice over him? He was the senior, after all. Perhaps they had started their affair again? Yes, he knew about it the first time, not that anyone knew he knew. Over his pint of Guinness, he determined to keep an eye on those two. His career might be at stake.

Chapter 40

ARATA SR. WAS sitting in his opulent office in front of a couple of computer screens; one tracking his Wall St investments and other related stocks, the other the latest monthly results from his own various enterprises. There was some satisfaction to be had but he was not a man to be complacent. He didn't get to where he was today by being content. Businesses didn't run themselves and profit didn't come without careful management of both strategy and people. Anyone who walked in would have thought he was studiously analysing the data on the screens, but the truth was that his mind was far away.

He had no heir to pass on his businesses and, now approaching his sixtieth birthday, he was beginning to be consumed by the issue. His son had come into the business and just as promptly come out of it.

"It's just not me," he had explained to his father. "I see what you do but my brain doesn't work the same way as yours. I'd only make bad decisions and ruin what you've carefully built up over the lifetime. I'm sorry."

Arata Sr. remembered how displeased he had been, especially when his son decided he wanted to go into the church. Some harsh words were said, which he regretted now. However, his son hadn't taken them to heart, almost as if he expected them and saw them as a cathartic reaction to a major disappointment. Perhaps he was better off in the church. He had always been a sensitive lad, very intelligent without a doubt, and able to write and speak much better than his father. Maybe it was the very catholic school he had chosen for him that had turned his head. His thoughts had strayed well beyond his computer screen when his cellphone rang. It was Rossi. It pulled him back to the current reality.

"Rossi, what have you got?" asked Arata. His occasional partner had been mulling over their options for pulling in some real estate business from the catholic church. There didn't seem to be that many.

"I've identified a few archbishoprics that are seeking to avoid bankruptcy and I've opened negotiations with them. I'm hopeful that we can salvage something."

"I guess it's better than nothing," replied Arata, "but nothing like the scale of what might have been." He knew Rossi could finance these himself without any help so, in his mind, he had mothballed the partnership for the moment. But Rossi was evidently still actively pursuing and Arata was happy to let him whilst he turned his attention elsewhere.

"Excellent. Let me know if you need me to close any of the deals."

"Sure thing."

Arata was certain that his fellow-Italian businessman had picked up his lack of interest in pursuing these leads but if he was unable to finance it all himself, he would have to come back to him. Once the conversation had concluded, the office became quiet again and the elder Arata's mind switched to the catholic church. He found himself getting more annoyed and exasperated at the financial tactics used by the church to secure its wealth and limit compensation. It definitely wasn't because of a deep concern for the victims, more some degree of moral indignity that his church should use such tactics. Combined with the fact that it had ended one of the best business opportunities that had presented itself for some time, he was ready to exact some retribution if he could.

He had an idea of what he wanted to do. The question was how to do it? He needed to talk to his son and quickly decided that home was not the appropriate venue as his wife would not approve if she got wind of what he was proposing. So the club, it had to be.

"Morning, son," the father was upbeat.

"Morning," responded Jr. cautiously, already thinking about what might be the hidden agenda.

"Look, I know you've been through the wars with the death of the Cardinal and the police investigation, etc. So I'd like to take you to lunch at the club, if you'll allow me?"

"That sounds very thoughtful of you," said Jr. still suspicious of his father.

Senior knew what his son would be thinking, so he put his cards on the table. "I want to discuss something with you about the church, not real estate," he hastened to say, "but what's been in the news," he added.

"OK," said Jr. "When did you have in mind?"

"Whenever you're free – today, tomorrow?"

The priest paused for a second, "Yes, today is fine. In about an hour then?"

"Looking forward to it," said Arata Sr. ending the call.

Jr. didn't like the club. It was full of old men, as he saw it, engaged in conspiratorial discussions and pulling strings to try and enrich themselves mainly at someone else's expense. It proffered all the reasons why he declined to follow his father into the business. He also guessed that what his father had to say needed to be beyond his mother's hearing. But he had nothing else to do, not until a new archbishop was confirmed and he knew whether he was either in or out. Lunch with his father would be the highlight of the day, if one could call it a highlight.

By chance, they arrived at the entrance at the same time. Senior opened the door and led his son, now dressed in civvies, into the foyer where he nodded to the concierge and proceeded to sign both in.

"I've booked a table," said the businessman "So shall we dispense with the bar and go straight in?"

"Fine with me," replied Jr.

Sami came over to greet the pair and offer some menu cards. "Sami, this is my son," he said. Sami greeted Jr. and departed to await his guests' menu decisions.

"Let's choose first shall we, and then I'll share what I'm thinking." Jr. didn't think an answer was necessary and so carried on scanning today's offerings. When they had ordered, father sat back and looked at his son.

"You know, I'm very proud of you and the course you've chosen. Disappointed in the beginning, sure. But I can see you're going to make a real difference." Senior wanted to warm his son up to be receptive to his idea. Junior, constantly wary of his father, responded guardedly. "I appreciate that."

"The thing is this," Senior started. "As you know, I was looking to help the church over these compensation claims they've been getting by a mutually beneficial scheme." Even to his son, Arata Sr. couldn't help selling the scheme.

"I would inject financial stability by taking a charge on some of their real estate." He looked at his son for any sign of distaste. He saw none, so pushed on.

"But the more I looked into it, the more uncomfortable I felt." He paused as he saw puzzlement on his son's face and Sami arrived with their *antipasti*.

"I'm listening," said Junior, once Sami had retreated.

"You may want to call me a hypocrite, but I believe the church, our church, should uphold standards which are higher than we might have in business."

The priest said nothing, so his father continued. "You remember what I told you about their financial moves to hide their assets?"

The son nodded, but then asked, "Is that legal?" to which his father replied, "Yes, but that's not the issue. Surely the church has a moral obligation higher than that which businesses have. What might be legal, might not be ethical. Do you agree?"

"Yes, I do," said Junior, digging into his fresh pasta alfredo with added bacon. "So what do you have in mind?"

Senior paused, partly for effect and partly to finish his mouthful of broccoli and salmon pasta. "I wondered whether the Boston Gazette might be interested in the story?" There, he had said it. Now to wait for the reaction.

His son was nodding. "Yes, I think they might. How were you thinking of doing it?"

"That's where I thought you might have some ideas. I read the obituary you wrote for the Cardinal, and very well written it was. So somebody there contacted you?"

"I approached them," clarified Junior. "I knew they would want to cover the death as part of the whole paedophilia campaign they're running, but I wasn't sure what angle they would take and I wanted a fair and balanced account, rather than a biased one."

"Perhaps you would write this one up?" asked Senior.

"No, I couldn't do that," declared the priest. His father looked disappointed until his son added, "but I could talk to them, highlight the issue allowing them to do their homework, and write the copy."

"Great," said his father. Then added, "Are you sure this doesn't put you in an awkward position?"

"Not at all. It'll be done on a no-names basis," assured Junior.

"That's good." His father was smiling. Mission accomplished.

"I might include my own view as well which they may or may not publish."

"Of course."

Business having been transacted, there was no need to stay much longer, both declining the delicious selection of *frutta e dolce* and *caffe*. They embraced each other in the foyer, something they hadn't done for some years. At last, they seemed to be on the same page but how long that would last was anyone's guess.

Arata Jr. didn't take long to call Janice at the Boston Gazette. It was becoming a strange friendship.

"Ms Munroe," he began when she answered her cellphone.

"I wasn't expecting to hear from you so soon," she quipped. "Did you have an objection to the editorial alongside your obit.?"

"Ah. I thought I could detect your hand in it," he said playfully.

Janice was taken aback again by this man. "How do you know I had a hand in it?"

"Well, many of your editorials are blunt and rather forthright – something of a male speciality, I think. This one was different. More nuanced, more subtle, more readable," explained Arata, and added, "in my humble opinion."

"Hmm," said Janice not confirming but not denying either.

"So I was right!" laughed Arata.

"Father..." started Janice.

"Please call me Arata."

"Arata, what can I do for you?"

"Write another story, if you like the sound of it. Anonymously, of course."

"Which is?" questioned Janice dubiously.

Arata then began to explain what his father had outlined to him. Janice was quiet, then began scribbling furiously.

"Think of this as a tip-off, but please do your own research and write accordingly," cautioned the priest.

"I appreciate it," said Janice before Arata ended the call.

She sat at her desk for a moment looking at her notes, wondering if this was a wind-up or if there was any truth in it. Only one way to find out.

Chapter 41

FATHER ANDREW DOUGLAS-SCOTT landed at Boston's Logan International mid-afternoon after a long transatlantic flight. He had not been enthralled by the latest Mission Impossible movie or the best episodes of Friends which the in-flight entertainment purported to offer. In fact, his consul never got switched on, much to the puzzlement of the teenager sitting next to him who was intrigued by such behaviour. This man was actually reading an old fashioned book!

'Why We're Catholic' by Trent Horn was normally a book given to non-catholics or fallen-away catholics to help them understand what the church teaches and why. Father Douglas-Scott was re-reading it to confirm whether he really believed it all. It was not yet a crisis of faith but, having made one life-changing decision in Rome, another was looming in his mind. He had read the book before and knew it well, so finished it fairly rapidly. It had done its job and, yes, he still believed. The volume was put away in the seat pocket of the seat in front of him and he shut his eyes with the intention of beginning to meditate and pray. Unexpected turbulence quickly disrupted his exercise as cabin staff quickly moved around the aisles, waking passengers up if necessary, to check that seat belts were fastened and seats were in the upright position.

When normal service was resumed, he decided to read another of his favourite books: 'Mere Christianity' by C S Lewis. Quite an old book but, as far as he was concerned, still had a rare lucidity as the author, patiently and flawlessly, detailed his rational defence of the Christian faith. He admired Lewis greatly and, although not a catholic, he regarded him as a giant of the faith and his book as the epitome of Christian apologetics. Again, it was a book he knew well and it had always settled his mind that Christianity made perfect sense. The question for him was whether the catholic version of it made sense as well. He had no issues with the basic doctrines of the church, but there were so many 'add-ons' that had accumulated over the centuries which, it seemed to him, weighed the whole church down. In fact, faith seemed now to be the least important element for the church, the most being keeping to the policies and practices laid down from the Vatican over centuries.

He knew many excellent catholic priests, full of love and devotion, and he felt they needed much more support, principally by weeding out sexual deviants. As long as such men were part of the priesthood, all were suspect. The institution to which they had yoked themselves seemed more focussed on protecting itself than protecting its righteous priests or its flock. Simply put, Rome seemed to arc towards more law and less love. Yes, he was sure. It was an institution unwieldy in structure with a centralised hierarchy, continued blatant corruption and a refusal to change that was incomprehensible, at least to him.

He had no doubt that it was tradition that was holding it back, traditions which might have been useful when they had been adopted, but had now well passed their sell-by date. Celibacy would certainly be one of those, in his mind. He knew the Apostle Peter himself had been married whereas the writings of St Paul expressed support for celibacy. The oft quoted rationale of being 'married to God' seemed at odds with the current spate of sex crimes in the priesthood. Surely it was time for a new order.

After all these thoughts and quasi conclusions, he was still at a loss to know what to do next. If he was expecting an epiphany on the journey to Boston, where God would show him the way forward, he was disappointed. Currently, the only plan he had was to book into a hotel and contact the Boston Gazette. The first part went well and he booked in at the Comfort Hotel at 900 William T Morrissey Blvd, a mid range hotel at about $200 per night. He didn't know how long he would be staying and his natural instincts were on prudence but with some creature comforts, so motels were definitely out. The second part posed something of a problem. He wanted to see first hand the devastation that paedophilia was having on victims and their families. Yes, the Boston Gazette would have those details but now he doubted whether they would ever release any such details to him. They probably wouldn't even believe who he was, er, had been.

By good fortune it was a Friday, and he found the latest edition of the Gazette in the hotel lobby. His face lit up for now he could see for himself what they were saying. He paid for his copy and settled himself back in his room to read the latest exposé featuring the financial engineering many archbishoprics had been involved in to retain their wealth and minimise compensation payouts to victims of catholic clerical abuse. He suddenly felt ashamed. This was exactly what had brought him to this crisis in his life. He just couldn't be a part of it. Looking at the byline, he saw the name, Janice Munroe. Perhaps he should call her. No. His explanation would be too long. He would email her at the Gazette's generic news address and explain who he was, er, had been, why he was in Boston and perhaps they could meet up. It took over an hour to compose the email to his satisfaction, leaving his cellphone number at the foot for her to call back.

Janice, for her part, had finished for the week and was not due back in the office until Monday, although she was thinking about options for the following week's edition. Work rarely stops for investigative journalists. It was Porter's secretary, a mature lady called Layla, who received all emails that came to the news email address and she was still at her desk. As the email was addressed to Ms Munroe, it was immediately forwarded to her. Janice had half expected Porter to suggest dinner together that evening, but that invitation had not come. So she looked forward to a long, lingering, fragrant bath, then flopping on the couch to watch a couple of old episodes of Sex in the City, one of her favourites. The forwarded email arrived while she was in the bathroom and so it was about eight o'clock before she realised there was an email. She opened it and read it with amazement. Then read it again. Surely this had to be Sullivan yanking her chain.

She quickly put Father Andrew Douglas-Scott into her search engine and, sure enough, he was, or had been the Pope's Private Secretary. She still required proof that the sender of this email was authentic, so she looked at the cellphone number at the bottom of the text. It started with 39, so she looked up a table of international call prefixes to discover that Italian numbers started with 39. OK. Probable, but not yet definitive. The search engine showed her a picture of him, so she emailed back and asked for a photo of him with today's edition of the Gazette. Two minutes later she got her definitive answer. It was him. Bloody hell!

This was a story. She now texted back, showing him her cellphone number, suggesting coffee at a certain Starbucks at 10.30 the next morning. Once she

had put her cellphone down, she began to think through what she had potentially. This will get up Sullivan's nose, she thought playfully. Sex in the City
was suddenly rejected as the evening's entertainment. Instead, she curled up
on the couch and listed the areas of questioning she would take the priest
through. From her conversations with Arata, she recognised she would need
to have her wits about her. She didn't want to be used again. Sullivan would
jump on that straight away. Having spent a few hours with her notepad, she
retired to her bedroom at about ten-thirty.

She had decided to arrive early at the coffee house and sat where she
could see the entrance, sipping a small latte. She would order another when he
arrived. As she watched Saturday shoppers coming in, she began to wonder
what was going on inside the catholic church. First Arata, now Douglas-Scott.
Were they representative of a new order, or just outliers who would be briefly
listened to, then forgotten as the catholic machine rolled on from one century
to another ignoring everything in its path except its own rules?

There he was, easily recognisable but not looking like the confident Arata.
This man was decidedly alone and hesitant. It looked as if he'd never been
in a Starbucks before. Thinking about it, he probably hadn't. She got up and
greeted him with a handshake, introducing herself and guiding him back to
her table in the corner. Asking him what drink he would like produced more
confusion as he looked at the variety on offer on the wall above the baristas.

"I'll just have tea, please," he said eventually.

"You're from Italy, perhaps you would like a cappuccino or a latte?" she
asked inquisitively.

"I'm really a Brit," he confessed. "Tea is good. Thank you."

Once Janice had returned with the drinks, she got down to business. "So
Father, what can I do for you? I presume you are still a catholic priest?"

"Just," he said, to which Janice raised her eyebrows.

"I suppose I should explain," said Douglas-Scott. Janice took a sip of her
second latte of the morning and settled down to listen. She decided to leave
her notebook in her bag not giving him any impression that she was interested
yet. That would come later. He needed her at the moment. She was in the
driving seat.

"I'm sure you've read up about me, so I'll skip the history. Suffice to say that His Holiness was the Cardinal of Durban in South Africa where we met. We became friends and I was offered a job as his private secretary. Long story short, I then left the UK diplomatic service, was ordained, he was then elected Pope and invited me to go to Rome with him."

"You were obviously happy to go, but you resigned. That doesn't happen very often."

"No, probably not," admitted the priest. He was looking decidedly uncomfortable and shifting in his seat. "The thing is that he is, perhaps was, my friend. I don't want to betray him or my church, but there are things which must be said and I don't know anyone else who is saying them."

Janice knew, but now was not the time to show her hand. She had more questions to ask.

"So, why?"

"I had no idea that there were priests in my church who were ….. er practising paedophiles." He seemed to flinch as he said the words. "It was a total shock to me, but not to him, the Pope. He seemed to think it was inevitable with men who couldn't marry women." The English priest shook his head in disbelief.

"So, why?"

Douglas-Scott seemed to break out of his hesitancy. He looked straight at the journalist and said, "Because there was no sign of anyone acknowledging the need for change. The strategy, if you can call it that, seemed to be: 'keep heads down and it will go away,' eventually". Having blurted out his damning indictment, he seemed to retreat inside himself again.

Janice watched him, saying nothing but witnessing the immense struggle that was going on inside the man. Nothing like Arata. Here was someone at the heart of the papacy, now questioning its whole approach to the biggest scandal it had ever faced.

He carried on, almost oblivious to the presence of a journalist. "What about the victims, I asked him? He said, 'the poor we will always have with us and maybe the injured as well.'"

Janice kept her silence allowing this man to unburden himself as much as he could struggle to do in the melee that was happening on a Saturday morning in Starbucks.

"'We must protect the church', he said."

"Who said," asked Janice.

Douglas-Scott looked up at her. "His Holiness." He paused before continuing, "But how do we protect the church by harbouring priests," he almost spat out the word, "priests, who preach the gospel of Jesus on Sunday and bugger little boys on Monday? God help us!"

He looked as if he was about to cry. Janice put out her hand and said, "Let's go." She helped him up and led him out of the building with most onlookers not taking any notice.

"Where are you staying?" she asked.

"The Comfort Inn," he replied.

"I'll take you back. My ride is on a meter just around the corner."

A few minutes later they were heading for his hotel. The priest seemed to be emotionally exhausted, his eyes were shut and his hands tightly held together. Janice was becoming a little concerned but as they approached the hotel, he pulled himself together. She stopped the VW outside and looked across at him.

"Are you OK?" she asked.

"Yes, thank you," he replied.

"So what do you want from me?" asked the reporter.

He was quiet for a moment, looking down in his lap. "I'm going to resign from the priesthood. I shall write directly to my friend in Rome and then I would be happy to be interviewed by you for your paper." He looked up and smiled at her.

"I believe I can trust you," he said.

She looked straight ahead at the hotel entrance. "You have to understand how reporters work." She turned to face him. She wanted to make sure he knew how it would be.

"Yes, I would be happy to interview you on the record, and ask all the difficult questions but the eventual copy will need to be approved by the editor-in-chief."

"I understand." he said.

"Right. In that case, I will need a day to prepare. Shall we say, tomorrow at 10 in your room? Sorry, it's Sunday. Perhaps Monday would be better for you?"

"No. In fact," he smiled, "I think Sunday would be perfect."

She watched and wondered as he went into the hotel. What was going on in the catholic church? And why did they come to her? Anyway, these might be questions for tomorrow. Today, she had to call Sullivan. No answer. She left a message and then tried Porter who picked up immediately.

"Hi Janice. Just the person. I was going to call you and suggest dinner tonight." Janice's first reaction was to smile – her instincts about last night were spot on, just a day late.

"Sure," said Janice, and they arranged the date there and then. She would drop her bombshell over dinner.

Chapter 42

SULLIVAN, OBLIVIOUS TO the story Janice was working up, had been toiling over another story that he thought could become the next mid-week special. He had received a call from Jerry Harris in the UK mid-afternoon Friday which would have been breakfast time in the UK.

"Sullivan! How's it going? Glad I caught you before you went home for the weekend. I know how you guys like to take off early on Fridays."

"Hi, Jerry. Couldn't be better. We're breaking all records over here." Sullivan was wont to exaggerate a little when speaking to fellow journalists.

"Look. I'm about to publish some data in the paper this Sunday about naughty priests in other European countries and my boss wondered whether the Gazette would like to be a part of it?" Jerry was being circumspect but, essentially he was asking for rights money.

Sullivan knew how the business worked. "What does the data say?" he asked knowing that would be the first question Porter would ask.

"All I can say is that it will blow your socks off." Jerry could outplay Sullivan on exaggeration anytime.

"Are you publishing all of it or keeping some back?" This was important because if they published it all, it would be less valuable. Exclusives meant money.

"If we can make a deal, we can give you some exclusive stuff, then you can pack the rest of the page with what we've released.

"OK. I'll speak to the boss. He's gone now but if you send me the contact details of your guy, I'll call him right away and they can make the deal."

Porter was looking forward to his date tonight – at least, that's what he was hoping it might turn out to be. Janice was giving the right signs so his confidence was high. The weekend edition had been put to bed and, after a hard week (weren't they all?), he wanted to escape business and enjoy himself. He thought he deserved it.

His cellphone rang just as he was at his closet deciding what he should wear and agreeing with himself that now he was dating, he ought to replenish its contents. Bachelor stuff had to be put to one side. He glanced at his cell-phone. Sullivan. Bother, didn't he know it was the weekend? He debated whether he should let it ring out. Eventually, he decided to answer just as it moved to messages. He never listened to those so he waited a few minutes for Sullivan to leave his message and then he rang back.

"Sullivan, what do you want," he growled. "It's the weekend. Get a life!"

"Just had my contact from the UK call me with a proposition." He then outlined the conversation together with the benefits, as he saw them, of taking the offer. Porter's interest was peaked and he sat down to pepper Sullivan with all the questions the investigator knew he would ask.

"I don't have all the answers," Sullivan started.

"You don't have any of the answers," growled back Porter.

"I'm thinking this could be another mid-week special with all the additional revenue that would generate." Sullivan was trying his persuasive best.

"Don't forget all the additional costs as well," shot back Porter.

"Whatever," Sullivan replied. "I'll send over the contact details of his boss and you can sort it out. It's not like we haven't done this before."

Porter looked at his watch. It was lunchtime over in the UK so he decided to phone now otherwise his evening was going to be ruined. In fact, it may have already been wrecked because if it looked like a good deal, he would have to contact Mackie, his financial director. He, in turn, might want the comfort of the publisher's go-ahead depending on the size of the monies involved.

The call was made and Porter was liking what he was hearing, especially the exclusive element and the fee they were looking for.

"OK. I like what I've heard. I just need to run it past my financial guy and if it's a goer, I'll get him to send across our standard contract." Porter wanted to pass it off to someone else and still save his evening if he could.

"Fine. I'll send over our paperwork as well and we'll let the financial guys agree the details between them." The Brit wanted it done before the end of his day because his paper's deadline for what they might include or exclude would not be far off.

Porter knew time was of the essence and rang Mackie, who was a family man looking forward to an evening with his wife as his teenage children were out at the movies.

"It won't take long," promised Porter. "Just call this guy. Have a look at his paperwork and if similar to ours sign it and tell them to get the story over to Sullivan pronto."

With that instruction, Porter left for his evening date whilst Mackie also promised his wife he wouldn't be long and decamped into his study to finalise the deal. Porter decided not to contact Meyer or the lawyers and Mackie thought that with any luck, he might get back to his wife before the whole evening had been squandered and his wife again tried to persuade him to change his job.

Janice didn't mind that Porter had booked the same place. She liked the cuisine and knew that Porter was a man of habit and probably never went anywhere else. Janice had been at the table only ten minutes before Porter arrived puffing and panting from running from the parking garage.

"Sorry, sorry, sorry," he started.

"I thought you were going to stand me up," said Janice in jest.

Porter took it at face value and began to explain. Janice stopped him, "I was joking. I know you would never do that." She put her hand on his across the table. A pulse of electricity passed through his body.

"Let's order, shall we?" proposed Janice. "I've got some news I want to share."

Porter was on the defensive, willing to go along with whatever Janice suggested. They ordered virtually the same as before, almost as if the meal had never been the main event of the evening. They smiled at each other as the meal progressed, each enjoying the other's company. It was as they came to desserts that Janice broke her news.

"I've just had a long conversation with the Pope's ex-private secretary," said Janice. nonchalantly. Porter stopped with his spoon half-way to his open mouth.

"You what?"

"I had an email last night from someone claiming to be Father Andrew Douglas-Scott. I checked him out and he's in Boston wanting to talk."

Porter was still coming to terms with what Janice had revealed. "Why?

How? I mean, what on earth is going on?" He was shaking his head, also thinking about what Sullivan was about to bring to the party.

"I sense he's a broken man," Janice went on. "I was prepared for an intelligent priest who wanted to use me, us, to contradict everything we have been exposing."

"And?" questioned Porter.

"Quite the opposite. It sounds like he's completely disillusioned and needs to unburden himself before he can move on with his life. Once he's given me the interview – on the record – he says he's going to resign the priesthood. That's how strongly he feels about the catholic church's failure to deal with paedophilia in its ranks."

By this time, Porter had put down his spoon, his dessert virtually untouched. He was manfully struggling to get his head around someone from the Pope's office travelling to Boston and asking to be interviewed by the Gazette, and on the record as well. It was mind-blowing.

"Janice. I don't know what to say. This might be the biggest story you'll, we'll, ever write in our lives. This has got Pulitzer written all over it."

"I explained how it works, that you as editor-in-chief have the last say on what gets published and he was fine with that."

"How have you left it with him?" asked Porter.

"We'll meet on Sunday morning at the Comfort Hotel, in his room. I need tomorrow to prepare."

A thought suddenly occurred to Porter. "Does Sullivan know?"

"No. I called him and left a message but he hasn't got back to me. That's when I called you."

"He never bothers to listen to his messages. Probably because he's working on something else at the moment, so leave him be. When you and he have got your stories, we'll meet together in my office to share what we've got." Porter didn't want either reporter to be caught up in something else. Each needed to be totally concentrated on their own story. They quickly finished their desserts, passed on the coffee, paid the check and moved out into a lamplight street holding hands after Janice agreed to have a nightcap at his home.

Unbeknown to them, Sullivan had his own date that evening. His teenage daughter, Chloe, had just turned eighteen and he had offered to buy her dinner by way of a celebration. Her mother had been rather sarcastic, but said she could accept and the two were walking back to his old Chevy on the other side of the street.

He couldn't help but see Porter and Janice hand in hand walking in the opposite direction.

Chapter 43

IT WAS GONE ten o'clock at night that Porter received a curt text from Mackie, his financial director, which read,

"Deal done. Have texted Sullivan. You owe me!"

Porter was otherwise engaged and didn't get the message until early Saturday morning. Janice awoke first and tiptoed to the shower as Porter continued to sleep with his mouth open, his breathing hoarse. Not snoring, because, according to him, he never snored. He came to just as Janice was about to leave, explaining that she needed to get home to prepare for her 'Pulitzer' interview with Father Andrew Douglas-Scott. As she slipped out, Porter went back to dozing and thinking about the night before. Maybe?

The city was still quiet, even at eight o'clock on a Saturday morning as she navigated her way to the car, paid the ticket and drove home. The sun was bright and she was happy. The evening had been fun and the night very satisfying. But that was yesterday. Today, she was now looking forward to getting down on paper all the thoughts that had been randomly generating in her head overnight. Even with all the technology she had, notebook and pen still came out on top when drawing up an interview strategy.

She stopped on the way for a black coffee and salty toasted bagel with cream cheese, smoked salmon and avocado to go. It was a treat but she thought it was deserved. By the time she had arrived at her apartment block and parked her car, she had scoffed the lot, leaving the empty containers on the passenger seat for the next time she passed a bin. She quickly made her way to her first floor front door, entered and sat down at her desk. She began to visualise her interviewee.

Starting with the personal was her natural approach. It settled people down because everyone liked talking about themselves. Then she would move on to Rome and what the job of a Private Secretary entailed and finally what made him come to Boston and what did he want to achieve. That was the bare bones settled for the moment. It might change but it was the obvious strategy bearing in mind the fragility of the man. If he had been more bullish, she might have reversed it and asked him outright what he wanted to achieve, taken him by surprise. But not this man. He needed to be groomed rather than confronted.

Having done that, she could now have a shower and change into jeans and a T shirt ready to take each section and list topics she knew her readers would love to ask if they were the ones asking the questions.

Sullivan had got back to his apartment at about nine thirty, having dropped Chloe off after their meal. He had enjoyed it and he had high hopes that their relationship might develop further as she went to college and into the workplace. Her Mom was still bringing up kids from her second marriage but Chloe was his, so he felt he could play the role of a Dad even if he wasn't living with them. He knew that teenage girls didn't always like to be seen with their Dads so he tried hard to think of things to ask her rather than talk about himself. What university was she thinking of? Did she need internships? Maybe a bit of about journalism on the way. However, it didn't exactly go to plan.

"You know, Dad, my friends think you're really cool."

Sullivan was taken by surprise. "Me? Why?"

"Because you exposed those perverts in the catholic church. Mind you, some parents didn't like the fact that you caned the church."

"Well, the catholic church should have been safeguarding the kids in their congregations a whole lot better." Sullivan retorted, adding, "and sacked those priests instead of protecting them."

Chloe was silent for a while. She had questions to ask but didn't quite know how to ask them. She decided to broach the subject of journalism.

"What about journalism as a career?" she asked, eventually.

Sullivan looked at her wondering if that was the question she really wanted to ask him and why she had agreed to go out with him.

"Ah! You'd probably better ask my colleague, Janice."

"Why?"

"Well, it has probably changed now, but when I started, women didn't really get a fair deal. It was quite a male-dominated atmosphere with all the kinds of banter that goes on in those situations."

"Perhaps, it needs more female reporters," she suggested.

"I'm sure that's right. But it's a profession that requires everything of you. There's not much time for other relationships or family, as I'm sure you've noticed." Maybe they were getting close to what she really wanted to ask.

She eyed her father as he concentrated on his meal trying to avoid her gaze.

"So is that why you and Mom split up?" she was asking the question every child wants to ask their parents if they've separated or divorced. So this was the real question she had wanted to ask. Sullivan didn't blame her. He had anticipated these kind of questions and knew he had to answer them properly if he was to stand any chance of retaining and improving their relationship. Yes, he had thought about how to answer these questions for a long time, but still didn't have the ready answers he knew she wanted.

"Have you spoken to Linda, your Mom?" Sullivan needed to establish the ground on which he was about to tread. The last thing he wanted was for Chloe to see him at odds with her mother. After all, she had brought up Chloe herself, albeit with alimony from him.

"She says she doesn't want to look backwards," Sounds like she hadn't spoken about it, so maybe the ground was solid enough for him to tentatively move forward.

"Well, that's a good principle," He said, knowing that such an answer was not going to cut it.

Chloe said nothing but continued to look at him. Sullivan was beginning to feel a little uncomfortable. When he didn't say anything further she prompted him again.

"So?"

He put his knife and fork down and gave her his full attention. "From my side, there was never any other woman." He felt this was the first thing to say. Yes, there were flings after they had separated, but they didn't count, at least in his mind.

"What was it then?" she asked, open-faced.

"There's rarely one thing that closes down a marriage. Usually it's a whole host of factors." Chloe was not going to accept a non-personal answer.

"So what were they?"

"I suppose I gave more attention to the job than I did to your Mom. I guess I took her for granted and we gradually stopped talking."

"So, it was the job?"

Sullivan nodded.

"What about the job?"

Sullivan sighed. Chloe was not giving up.

"Well, I was trying to get my career going and spent far too much time concentrating on that than you guys." Sullivan was hoping this would be sufficient, but teenage girls never gave up, did they?

"Mom said you drank a lot." So she had made some comments on him. If the ground was to remain firm, he had to acknowledge it. He thought she would make a good interviewer, tenacious and never accepting the first answer.

"I probably did," admitted Sullivan. "I would have a drink at lunchtime, then a few after work each day and when the paper was put to bed on Thursday evening, we would all go out to the pub for a few hours."

"That's quite a lot," observed Chloe.

"That's part of what I meant when I said it was male-dominated. If you wanted to get on, you had to be seen."

"Well, it worked. You got on," stated his daughter baldly.

Sullivan's level of discomfort was rising. He was wishing the conversation would move on, but thinking it probably wouldn't.

"Yes," said Sullivan. "But there was a price to pay, most of it not by me."

"Do you still drink?"

"I have a pint of Guinness at lunchtime, but nothing after work. I go straight home to my apartment."

He added, "And I've never done drugs. That's stupid." As an afterthought, he said, "You haven't, have you?"

Chloe smiled. "Nicely done," she said. Then, "No, I haven't." He smiled back. It seemed he had passed the test. After that, the evening went well and they bantered back and forth as father and daughter do from time to time, but all in good fun.

Having reached his apartment at nine thirty, he put on some Brubeck and paced up and down waiting to receive a text from Mackie. It came just before ten and he whooped his way around his apartment which he had never done before.

"My daughter must be making me happy," he thought.

But it was also about evening things up with Janice. If she had the kudos of the first mid-week special, he would have the second. He would have denied any accusation of a race between them, but there was no doubt that he felt he needed to keep his end up as Janice was very capably demonstrating her investigative skills to the boss.

He had his laptop open ready to receive Jerry's story. After ten minutes, it had not arrived and he felt it necessary to call the Brit, not to pressure him, but just to say he was waiting.

"Hi Sullivan. I'm told the deal is done, but I'm under pressure to re-jig my story to leave more exclusivity for you."

"Oh?" exclaimed Sullivan.

"Yea. I don't know who you have negotiating these deals but he's good. I'm having to leave out more than I would like to, But I get to release that stuff next week, so I suppose it equals out."

"So when can I get the exclusive part?" Sullivan was impatient.

"What's the hurry? It must be nearly midnight over there and you don't publish until next Friday." Jerry was standing firm. His deadline was going to come first.

"I'm thinking we do a mid-week special," said Sullivan.

"Good idea. Well, I'll be finished in an hour or so. Normally speaking, it would all have been put to bed a while ago, but the pressure's on now that your guy screwed us a bit."

"In an hour, then?" persisted Sullivan.

"For heaven's sake," said Jerry, losing it a bit, "Go to bed and when you wake up in the morning, it'll all be there. I've got work to do." He cut the call.

Sullivan understood Jerry's situation but was still annoyed. He wanted the story as early as possible so he could read it and allow it to ferment in his head whilst he was sleeping. But there was nothing he could do except switch his attention to Janice and Porter. What was going on there?

Chapter 44

PORTER WAS SMILING to himself as he shuffled around his apartment in his PJs. Not only had it been a lovely evening and a great night, but his two investigators were each working on stories which would be major exclusives for the Gazette. It didn't get much better than that. He was a happy man.

Janice was spending most of Saturday morning drilling down into each of the three areas she wanted to explore with Douglas-Scott. She knew that many of the questions might never be asked since it was important to flow with the answers that her interviewee gave. Nevertheless, she never left anything to chance. Again, she knew she had one shot at it and needed to get the maximum out of it – enough to publish several different stories over the coming weeks.

At two o'clock she leant back in her chair and looked at her notes. Was it enough? Should she take a break or press through? Her yawn told her that a break was needed. She had done enough for the moment and now was the moment to get some fresh air, do some shopping, then come back to go through it all again with a renewed perspective. Walking around the park, close to her apartment block, she tried to 'live' inside the Vatican and 'feel' what it would be like to be the head of this church. What would her priorities be? Who would be pressurising her to follow a certain line? And why? From their point of view, was closing ranks and trying to cut out the media the correct strategy? She admitted to herself that if they really didn't care about the victims, maybe it was the best strategy. After all, it hadn't seemed to make much of a dent in the overall number of the faithful.

On Saturday evening she decided to call the priest to check he was ready for the interview.

"Father, er Andrew," she remembered how he wanted to be addressed. "Have you had a good day?"

"Yes, thank you. I took a bus tour of the city. It's beautiful. I especially liked what the city is doing at the Waterfront."

"There's certainly lots to see; for example the place where Cheers was filmed. But you probably don't know Cheers."

He laughed. "Of course I do. I was a regular citizen once upon a time." At that point, he became quiet as if remembering what he had lost by going to Rome. Janice saw a change in his demeanour and decided to keep quiet, allowing him time but also interested to see what he might say next.

"Anyway," he said, recovering himself, "looking forward to meeting you tomorrow at 10."

"Me too," said Janice.

"Would you do me a favour?" he asked.

"Sure, if I can," replied the reporter.

"I think I might like a real coffee this time. Could you bring me a takeaway cappuccino – or as you say, a cappuccino to go?"

She laughed. "Sounds like you're preparing for a change," she suggested.

"You may well be correct," he said before ending the call.

She decided not to look at her notes at all that evening but to do something that would completely take her mind off work. She would go to the Emerson Colonial Theatre to see Madama Butterfly. It was not her normal entertainment genre but would certainly fulfil her objective of focussing her mind on something completely different. She hoped it would also be enjoyable, although some quickly scanned reviews suggested it should have been put on the shelf due to its alleged peddling of sexual exploitation, racial stereotyping and suicide. But after what she had been exposed to in her work, she thought coping with that would be child's play. Besides, wasn't that what all operas were about?

She surprised herself by thoroughly enjoying the production and thinking it might be a point of banter with Sullivan on Monday. As soon as she exited the theatre and met the cool air, tiredness took over and, by the time she was back at her apartment, it was all she could do to undress and flop into bed. At some point in the night, she awoke. Something in her conscious told her that she had not set her alarm. Fumbling with her phone, she set it for seven thirty and immediately fell asleep again.

She woke well before the alarm, content to continue dozing and waiting for the cellphone to buzz her into life, which it did. By eight, she was at her desk reviewing her work. A few amendments later, she was out and heading for breakfast at The Thinking Cup where she enjoyed a breakfast burrito. At $5.95, it was excellent value and, with an americano for $2.75, Porter would surely appreciate her mercenary approach.

By nine thirty, she was ready to go and make her way to the nearby Comfort Hotel. She texted Father Douglas-Scott to say she might be a few minutes early and asked if that was convenient. He immediately texted back in the affirmative giving his room number, so she went through reception to the lift and made her way to his double room on the top floor, cappuccino in hand. He had made the bed and tidied the room ready for his interview. He invited her to sit on a small two-seater couch whilst he sat in the armchair with a small coffee table between them.

"This is a lovely room, Father," remarked Janice looking around. She was making some small talk just to establish a connection with him again.

"Please call me Andrew. I've only booked this for two nights and so tomorrow morning I will be moving on," he said.

"Where will you go?" asked Janice.

"Not sure yet," he replied.

Janice was on the point of mentioning Father Arata but decided not to, at least not yet.

"Andrew, do you mind if I use my recorder as well as take notes," she asked and added her usual excuse, "My writing isn't as fast as my typing!" It was a light-hearted joke at her expense, again meant to put an interviewee at ease.

"Of course," replied Andrew, taking a sip of his coffee.

She took her place on the couch leaning slightly forward, with her interviewee settling himself with his feet crossed and arms resting lightly on the sides of the chair. She then took Father Andrew Douglas-Scott through his journey from student days to a Cardinal's PS.

From University to Durban. What did you study at university? Why the diplomatic service? What countries were you sent to? Did you enjoy the Foreign Office? What was Durban like to work in? How much was moving around from country to country responsible for your marriage breakup? Any children? Are you still in touch with your ex.? How did you meet the Cardinal? Why change career? What were your responsibilities as PS? How much was that training for PS to the Pope? How much of a surprise was his election?

Did you ever think of not going to Rome?

This had been the easy bit, albeit with a few intense moments around his marriage breakup. She looked carefully at him as they took a break for 10-15 minutes to have coffee/tea and relax. He looked as if he had enjoyed the session overall, so that was good. Objective achieved. Now it was to become more poignant.

From Durban to Rome. What were his first impressions? Who gave you a friendly welcome and who didn't? Did you enjoy it? What were the pressures? How much power does the Pope actually have? Is he just the front man for PR purposes? Do Popes speak 'ex-cathedra' any more? What is the Pope's primary responsibility – to the flock, the priesthood or the money men? What were his specific concerns in his post? What reaction was there in the Vatican to allegations of clerical abuse? How far do ancient traditions in the church rule its approach to modern issues? How does the known gay presence in the priesthood sit alongside the church's doctrine which outlaws gay sex? Do you put it all down to celibacy?

The knock on the door signalled it was lunchtime and an opportunity for a break. The priest had asked for a finger buffet to be brought to the room at one o'clock and here it was. Janice moved into the bathroom as a trolley was wheeled in, partly because she wanted to use the facilities but also because she didn't want unsavoury gossip to spread around the hotel staff should someone have known Douglas-Scott was a priest. As she was sitting, she mused about the man and his answers. He seemed much more together today than yesterday, perhaps because of the preparation he had done, or maybe it was her laid-back style! She'd like to think so. In any event, the crucial section was yet to come. She emerged and walked around the room, looking out at the view of Boston as she ate a few sandwiches and drank some juice. It didn't take long to finish lunch since both of them wanted to get the interview over and done.

From Rome to Boston. What was the tipping point which made him write his resignation letter? How was it received? Did he think anything would change? Did he have faith in his friend, the Pope, to tackle this scourge? So why choose to come to Boston? What did he think needed to be done? What did he personally want to achieve? How did he think he could do it? Was he in touch with any others in the church who felt the same way? What about staying inside to work for change? If he resigned as a priest what impact did he think he could have?

Janice could see that he was beginning to tire, whether from lack of sleep or stress, or both. So at half past three o'clock, she called a halt. He looked relieved but wanted to say one last thing.

"The church needs a seismic culture shift, especially at the top. If there is any hope at all of real change it will require some relinquishing of power, and a will to treat survivors as human beings."

She was rather taken aback at this bald prognosis and, to be fair, he looked pained to say this of his church. Janice said, "I'd like to quote that verbatim, if I may." He nodded and Janice began to get up.

"May I call you if I need any clarification?" she asked.

"Of course," said Andrew. She collected up her things and headed for the door. Just as she was shaking hands at the door, she took out a note that she had written in the lunch break. She pressed it into his hands.

"Ring this number and say that Janice from the Gazette recommended you call."

He looked a little wary. "Who is it?"

"Someone who has the same views as you. It might help you decide where to go tonight." Then she left and the door closed.

Father Andrew Douglas-Scott put the note to one side and lay down on the bed. Within minutes, he was fast asleep. The early evening sun began streaming into his room at about six o'clock which woke him. He looked at his watch – he still used one to gauge the time – and roused himself. He quickly used the bathroom to wash his face before sitting down to review the interview. He liked Janice. There was a humanity about her and her questions, which was an unexpected trait in a journalist in his experience.

Then he remembered the note and, picking it up, toyed a little with it. This was unexpected, but then God did move in mysterious ways, didn't he?

Chapter 45

SULLIVAN HAD ALSO been hard at work that Sunday. He'd been up at the crack of dawn to view what Jerry had sent across. He was tired, not having had much sleep, but as soon as he saw the file contents, tiredness left him and he was riveted by its drama.

The first statistic he saw was from Portugal where at least 4,815 boys and girls since 1950 may have been abused by priests and other church personnel. He looked closer wanting to know where this figure came from. It had been a panel of experts hired by Portugal's own catholic bishops reported by Die Welt's on-line site called 'dw.com/en/portugal'. It was a six-person commission, primarily funded by the catholic church itself, but the relationship with the bishops didn't seem to have been very good since its Chair, child psychiatrist Pedro Strecht, threatened that he would be the first to walk out if the church tried to intervene in what was to be an independent process. Not a good start!

Once their report was released, the bishops then turned around and refused to remove named abusers from ministry, then saying they would only compensate victims if courts ordered them to.

"Extraordinary," muttered Sullivan. "They set this panel up, then refused to abide by its decisions." He read on. The Portuguese catholic church, however, did promise to 'build a memorial to victims'.

"I'm sure they would have appreciated that," said Sullivan sarcastically.

He skipped down to France, another very catholic country although with a secular streak. Here a major report by a commission in France, reported in Newsweek, had revealed around 3,000 priests and religious officials had sexually abused more than 216,000 children since 1950.

"Unbelievable," muttered Sullivan again. He was beginning to feel sick at the enormous number of victims involved, lives marred forever. And for what?

"What did the Vatican say," he scanned the following page to find it. Here it was: 'The Pope feels pain over the findings, and expresses hope for a path of redemption'.

"A path of redemption for whom?" asked Sullivan. "The victims? They need compensation and probably a lifetime of counselling. The priests? They need to be prosecuted, no question. The church? A new Reformation without a shadow of a doubt."

He grunted. "If it was a corporation, the CEO would be sacked or pressured by shareholders and press alike to resign."

The head of the inquiry said that the church had shown 'deep, total and even cruel indifference' towards victims. Even today, the abuse had not been eradicated and he called for the victims to be compensated and for reforms within the church.

What country was next? Ah yes, Ireland. This would attract readers since many were of Irish descent. What do we have here? Sullivan turned over page after page of abuse and cover-up. He was astounded and sat back wondering how on earth could all this have happened on a little island with such a small population without anyone saying anything. He needed a break and a shower, not that it would wash away the sense of disgust he felt at what he had been reading.

Having dressed, he looked in his refrigerator in the vain hope of finding something for breakfast. He viewed the contents with a large sigh, shut the door and went out in search of coffee and bagels. It was a sunny Sunday for a change, and the world was going about its relaxed Sunday business. He looked around at families, retired people, middle-aged folk like himself, many out for breakfast and wondered if any were catholic. Did they know what he knew? If they did, were they so wedded to their religion that they would look the other way, keep putting their money in the offering, keep supporting catholic charities, where possible abuse was still going on?

In the queue, he had to remind himself that he was seeing the underbelly of a large organisation and the majority of priests were good, decent and compassionate towards their flock. So why didn't they speak out? He finally ordered his breakfast to go and what he hadn't eaten and drank on the way back, he finished quickly at his desk.

He took a deep breath. Now for Ireland in detail.

The Ryan 2009 report, released by the Irish government (www.gov.ie), found that sexual and psychological abuse was 'endemic' in catholic-run schools and orphanages in Ireland for most of the twentieth century, resulting in several criminal cases exposing the extent of horrific crimes and details of how hundreds of priests abused thousands of children over decades.

"These priests must have known each other," said Sullivan. "It's inconceivable that one paedophile priest didn't know what another in his own diocese was doing."

He read on. By this time, the reporter was getting anaesthetised to these numbers as each country that Jerry had researched and sent over seemed to be worse than the previous one. How many more countries were there?

Back to Ireland. Here was a real case, a real story which he could use better than mere statistics. He settled down to read the story as reported by the Belfast Telegraph.

Father Brendan Smyth abused over 140 children over four decades. Originally born in Belfast, he was arrested but dashed across the border to the Republic to escape justice where he was on the run for three years. An extradition request was lodged with the Irish government which was completely mishandled leading to the collapse of the Irish government.

Sullivan did a double take. "A paedophile priest actually caused a government to collapse!" It was the revelations of Smyth which led to several inquiries set up in both the Republic of Ireland and Northern Ireland.

The Ryan Report looked into child abuse in institutions run by religious orders. It detailed horrific neglect by these bodies who were left to look after children. Rape and sexual assault of children were routine. They were kicked, physically assaulted, and forced to carry out hard labour. More than 90% of witnesses reported being physically abused.

Next, the Ferns Report. This was solely about abuse in one single diocese, Ferns. It documented more than 100 allegations of child sexual abuse made between 1962 and 2002 against 21 priests in the diocese.

"They definitely knew each other," muttered Sullivan. "It was a cabal. I bet they shared the kids between them." He swore.

Addressing how the allegations were handled, the report stated that between 1960 and 1980, Bishop Donal Herlihy treated child sexual abuse by priests in his diocese exclusively as a moral problem rather than an egregious crime.

Next was the Murphy report. How many more reports were there?

This one investigated allegations of child sexual abuse by priests in the Archdiocese of Dublin over the period 1975 to 2004. Judge Yvonne Murphy examined complaints about the alleged sexual abuse of over 320 children. The report consisted of three volumes, cost a total of 3.6 million euros and stated that the four archbishops, John Charles McQuaid, Dermot Ryan, Kevin McNamara, and Desmond Connell, who were serving during that period, handled complaints 'very badly'. One of the priests who admitted his abuse, stated he did so more than 100 times and another did so fortnightly for 25 years, and along with clergy, the Irish police (Gardai) were also accused of covering up the scandal.

It was indeed scandalous. Sullivan had to take a break. He knew this would make a great mid-week special, but was beginning to be concerned that his readers might be so numbed by the dimensions of this, it might lead them to shake their heads and do nothing.

Suddenly, he knew he had crossed a line. He was emotionally involved with this story in a way that he hadn't been in previous investigations. He needed to draw back somehow and view it more objectively. Yes, there was room for outrage, but rational outrage, not the overwhelming emotional anger he was feeling at the moment. He had only met one mother of one victim in Chicago, not even the victim himself, and he had been emotionally drawn in.

He was a hard-bitten investigator who, supposedly, had seen it all. But he hadn't, until now. It had crossed his mind a few days ago that he ought to try to meet a victim to give him more depth in his writing. But not now. He didn't trust his emotions. Maybe it was because of his recent dinner engagement with his daughter, the first quality time he had with her for a long time. He still treasured it. If anyone was to harm her, he knew he would not be able to control himself.

This would have to be kept quiet. He didn't want Porter or Janice, for that matter, to know this part of his character. Perhaps they wouldn't regard it as weakness. No. He still wanted to be known as a dispassionate investigator – nothing could rock him. He still hadn't finished the document but already knew he would have to be careful how he wrote his copy. Porter would smell lack of objectivity a mile off.

What was the next country – let's make it the last. Italy? Surely not. The country which hosted the Vatican itself? Sullivan browsed through Jerry's copy. He was looking for the results of an inquiry similar to that in other countries. There was no national investigation. The only report he could find was one by senior catholic officials which covered only two recent years. That found 89 presumed victims and accused 68 people. Most victims were between the ages of 15-18 when the abuse took place.

"That's odd," thought Sullivan. "Not the usual victim profile."

He read on and it became all too clear. Sixteen of the victims were those the church considered as 'vulnerable' with claims involving inappropriate language, (whatever that meant) behaviour and touching.

"Ah!," exclaimed Sullivan. "Now it becomes clear. They took advantage of defenceless teenagers probably with a mental age in low single figures."

A further report was promised but with no timescale, so it was doubtful if it would ever take place.

"Evidently," muttered Sullivan, "the church still has a sense of being untouchable in Italy, when the exact opposite should have been true."

"Now," he wondered to himself, "are there any survivor groups like SNAP in Italy? They might shed some more light on what had been going on."

"Yes, here's one called Rete l'Abuso."

Francesco Zanardi was the president of this group and a clerical abuse survivor. Reuters reported that he had tracked more than 350 cases of paedophile priests in the Italian justice system, but there were no details of what they have been charged with, if anything. Sullivan was frustrated.

Italy seemed to be an anomaly in shedding any light on paedophile priests. Even the United Nations Committee on the Rights of the Child had criticised Italy for not sufficiently protecting minors from sexual exploitation. The committee had expressed concern about the numerous cases of children having been sexually abused by religious personnel of the catholic church and the low number of investigations and criminal prosecutions of those crimes.

Jerry had captured a quote by Paola Lazzarini, president of the group Women for the Church. She had commented that 'the catholic church is a hierarchical church, in which the chain of command is very clear, yet when it comes to abuse, personal responsibilities become vague'.

"You're telling me," muttered Sullivan. "I can see the headline now," he said under his breath. *Paedophile Priests Operating Under the Nose of the Pope*, or something like that."

He continued to examine the detail. "Ah! Here's another story which will be useful." It concerned a Father Gianni Bekiaris, reported by 'complicit-clergy.com'. A survivor had accused him of years of abuse starting when he was eight. Although he was subject to a church trial which recognised the priest's guilt, he was never defrocked. In fact, according to Jerry, he continues to celebrate Mass today, even in the presence of minors.

"Wow," exclaimed Sullivan. "What's a church trial? I need to find out, but it sounds like a sham."

As an addendum, Jerry had added in the Italian section that a priest in Argentina had been convicted of sexually abusing deaf children and had been sentenced to at least 40 years in prison having been previously accused of abuse in Italy, but not sanctioned by the Vatican.

"OK. I've read enough," said Sullivan to himself. "It's the same story over and over again. It's institutional abuse, tolerated and covered up on a global scale."

Chapter 46

MONDAY MORNING. NEITHER Sullivan nor Janice knew what the other had been doing over the weekend. Each might have thought the other would have visited friends and family, gone to a gig, or otherwise have taken it easy. They alone had been working hard on their stories, consciously or unconsciously, trying to outwit the other. Knowing that a competitive spirit had been building, Porter was beginning to have some concerns. Perhaps, he should have told each that the other was working on an important story, rather than ordering Janice not to call Sullivan back. This morning, he would have to watch their corner closely.

He planned to arrive surprisingly early at the office just in case. It was always good practice, he thought, for a boss to do the unexpected just to keep everyone on their toes. Others in the newsroom, used to having the place to themselves, looking on with some dismay as he strode through into the Holies. Something was up! The gossip was about to begin not that Porter minded. They could chatter all they liked but he wanted to make sure his investigators didn't fall out. They were earning the paper a lot of money and, unbeknown to them, he was on a bonus.

Sullivan arrived first and, as Porter saw him, made to go over to him to mention Janice's story before he got the wrong idea. But then saw Janice come in right behind him. Ah! Perhaps they've already talked and there's no issue. He decided to stay in his office.

"Do anything interesting over the weekend?" Sullivan greeted Janice, cheerfully.

"Went to the opera," returned Janice, laying her notepad and recorder on her desk.

" My word! We are going up in the world," said Sullivan pleasantly.

Janice looked up. No sign of sarcasm, just gentle banter. Unlike Sullivan. She knew he was going to be brought down to earth at some point but that was Porter's issue. It was his decision to keep Sullivan out of the loop, so it was his responsibility to calm potentially troubled waters.

"Sullivan is like a dog with two dicks this morning," she announced when she opened the door of the Holies. "Are you going to tell him, or am I?"

Porter sighed. "Go back out and, in a minute, I'll call you both in." Janice went back to her desk. Sullivan didn't even look up or question why she wanted to talk to the boss.

Sure enough, Porter yelled across for both of them to come in. He was not at all certain how to play this. When they were both settled, he said,

"Shut the door, will you," he said to Sullivan who was last in.

"Now I know each of you have worked on something over the weekend. Sullivan go first."

Sullivan looked up sharply, first at Porter then at Janice, who merely lifted her eyebrows and shrugged.

"Sullivan," said Porter trying to command the room, "What have you got? I haven't told Janice what you've got, neither have I told you what Janice has got. I want an update from each of you. Now."

Sullivan obediently outlined the various conversations with him and Jerry culminating in the deal. Excitement then took hold as he outlined what he had with the suggestion that, in his opinion, it merited another mid-week special. Janice whistled in the appropriate places to show support for him.

"How much have you written up?" asked Porter.

"I've got ten related top stories ready to go with a load of other back-ground," responded Sullivan confidently.

"OK. We can certainly think of another special," said Porter. Sullivan looked pleased.

"OK. Janice, now you."

Janice started the story of her weekend. "I got a message from your PA late Friday afternoon after I had left the office. It was someone claiming to be the Pope's private secretary who had just resigned and had come to Boston." She paused as she saw Sullivan's mouth drop open.

She hurried on. "I checked him out every which way, and he's genuine."

Before Sullivan could jump in, Porter asked her, "Why on earth would he come to Boston?" Janice then told the story from meeting at Starbucks to the interview.

Sullivan, who had been quiet as he had listened to what Janice had to say, now spoke up. "Was the message specifically for you or just for the newsroom?" He was suspicious that Janice had been given the story over him.

"He got my name from the by-line on the Arata story and asked for me personally."

Porter jumped in. "We know what we want to do with Sullivan's story. What do we want to do with this one?" The editor-in-chief was trying to clear a path for a joint decision that would keep everyone happy. Yes, he could make a decision and mandate something, but wanted a harmonious office and decided that a joint decision would fulfil that objective.

However, Sullivan didn't want to move so fast. "Why wasn't I, as the senior investigator, given this information?" Janice did quietly mention the message she had left on his phone, but it was left to Porter to say, "That was my call. I wanted your total attention on the stuff from the UK."

Just at that moment, Janice's cellphone rang. She looked up. "May I take this?" Porter nodded hoping that would end the meeting. She stepped out and while Porter tried to call a halt, Sullivan was having none of it. Janice could see a red-faced Sullivan raising his voice and Porter looking distinctly uncomfortable.

After a minute, a white-faced Janice re-entered and as both men looked at her, Porter asked, "What's happened?"

Janice looked at Sullivan. "You remember Kevin and Kevin's grandmother?" He nodded. "Well, she's been arrested."

"On what charge," asked Sullivan as she sat back into her seat.

"She tried to kill the priest who abused her grandson."

"Shit," exclaimed both men simultaneously.

"Wait a minute," exclaimed Sullivan, "How did she know who he was?"

Janice was now close to tears. "It was the laptop."

"What about it?" asked Porter.

Light was beginning to dawn on Sullivan. "Shit," he said again. "Don't tell me, he left everything accessible on it."

Janice nodded. "And I just took it back to her like I promised."

"Do we have any liability," asked Porter.

Both reporters looked at him incredulously. "OK, OK." He held his hands up. There was silence in the office for a moment. Then Porter said, "Whatever you think of the circumstances, it's a story until we figure it out."

He turned to Janice. "Get down there and see what's happening. Call me when you know – and keep Sullivan in the loop as well."

That ended the meeting.

Janice returned the call intending to say she was on her way. It went unanswered, of course. The African-American grandmother's cellphone was now in secure police possession along with her other personal effects. Dora Webster was not an unintelligent lady and, in normal circumstances, she could be a little feisty. Janice was desperately hoping that she would know not to say anything without a lawyer present but if she had deliberately gone to attack the priest, she could be in a lot of trouble.

She would almost certainly be arraigned in court within forty-eight hours, so Janice wanted to get there today so she could have some time with her. She had no idea whether she would be allowed to see her, but she was determined to try. She had heard that a friend didn't have a right to see someone in a police custody suite, so she would have to be circumspect in her approach to the officers. Her lawyer would, most likely, be a public defender – lovely people but overworked and not always able to provide the defence their clients needed. But she couldn't afford anyone else and there was no pot of gold at the end of a criminal trial.

She quickly went home to change and pack an overnight bag, then it was down the freeway as fast as she dared to New Jersey. More thoughts tumbled through her mind as she drove, scarcely noticing where she was on the road. If there was no access to the police custody suite, she would have to wait and see which state jail she was sent to. Most likely it would be the Edna Mahan Correctional Facility for Women. Janice didn't know much about the state law in New Jersey but she was sure there must be some mitigation possible. Either Dora's mental state, provocation in terms of what was done to her grandson, or maybe something else the lawyers could drag up. She didn't know.

She arrived at the Bridgewater Township Police Department where she presumed Dora was currently being held. She looked at the place and guessed that she wouldn't be here very long but be taken to a larger police department building. In fact, she may have already been moved. She went in and asked to see Mrs Dora Webster. It seemed to be a relatively informal place unlike some of the larger city departments. After a few questions about who she was, the custody officer confirmed that a Dora Webster was in custody and allowed her through but not before sharing his opinion of the case.

"These paedophile priests piss me off," he said. "If it was me, I'd......" she never heard what he would do because he never got around to completing the sentence. Out of another door came a male plain clothes detective.

"You here to see Webster?" he asked.

"Yes," Janice replied. "I'm probably her only friend."

"Well, she certainly needs every friend she's got," said the detective. "You're lucky. She'll be out of her tomorrow morning." And he continued walking on out of the entrance door.

"Where's she going?" Janice shouted after him. No response.

"Do you know where she's going?" she asked the custody officer.

"Nope," he said.

The suite door was opened and she made her way down a short corridor. A distinctive smell reached her nose and she grimaced, thinking that Dora had to live with this for the rest of the day and throughout the night. There were only a few cells. Most were empty although she guessed they would be filled by midnight.

A cell door opened and there was Dora sitting on a wooden bench looking quite disoriented.

"Hello Dora," greeted Janice.

The lady looked up. Janice was shocked at how frail and worn out she looked, even from the last visit. Her eyes were blank as if she couldn't focus.

"It's me, Janice," The cell door banged shut and the lock slid across.

There was the beginning of recognition. "You rang me earlier this morning. I came straight away."

"Yes, Janice. From the paper?" Dora now seemed to wake up.

"That's right. Can you tell me what happened?" asked Janice quietly.

She then told the story of how she was feeling very low yesterday thinking about Kevin and decided to get his laptop out to see if she could make sense of the suicide.

"I thought that if I could understand what made him do it, I could rest easy."

"What happened?"

"Well, I began to look through what was on the computer and came across a diary of sorts. It didn't give many dates but it talked about his friends and this one priest."

"Is the laptop still at the house?"

"It was but the police may have taken it by now."

"Did Kevin identify the priest and detail exactly what he did?"

"Oh yes. Sometimes in excruciating detail." She broke off at this point and began sobbing. "He groomed Kevin by pretending to protect him from some white boys who were bullying him. Then ....."

Janice said nothing but laid her hand on Dora's shoulder and waited for her to regain some composure. She was, however, thinking about her culpability in taking back the laptop with all the details readily available. In her defence, she thought to herself, Dora had never given any indication that she might try to attack the paedophile priest.

"What did you do?" asked Janice.

"I knew where the boys club was and it was obvious who the priest was. Kevin had described him. He was a smarmy-looking man. I just went up to him, asked him if he was Father Graham. He said yes. I said that he had killed Kevin and I stabbed him."

It was said in such a matter-of-fact voice that Janice was startled.

There was a knock at the door and loud male voice shouted, "Three minutes."

"Dora. I'm going to try and get a decent lawyer for you. So say absolutely nothing to the police, do you hear? Nothing." Dora nodded.

"You will probably be arraigned in court tomorrow and transferred somewhere else. Call me when you get the chance and tell me where you are and I'll come and update you on what I've managed to do."

Dora nodded again. Janice gave her a hug and began to leave. "By the way, what about your church friends. Have they been to see you?"

"Never told them."

This time Janice nodded and made her exit. Not only was she thinking about the next legal steps, but also how she could write up the story to support the woman. She had ideas about both.

Chapter 47

BACK AT THE office, Sullivan had been working on stories to fill his mid-week special while Porter informed the lawyers that he was going to do it with stories from another legal jurisdiction. They weren't thrilled and sent over a message advising the editor not to go ahead. Porter ignored them. He was getting emotionally involved as well. Who wouldn't be?

The issue for Sullivan, wasn't the number of stories he could get out of the copy that Jerry had sent over, but how to get a different angle for each. The pattern was virtually the same country by country. It was taking all his experience and guile to find the right approach for each story. But he had a gap. Just enough for a stand-alone story on the mysteries of a catholic church trial!

This was something else. Rather than an adversarial system, it seemed to be based on old Roman civil law – an inquisitorial system with judges leading the investigation. The defendant has a favourable presumption in law meaning that the defendant will win by default unless a majority of the judges are convinced with moral certainty of the petitioner's case.

"So just a few hands need to be greased," thought Sullivan cynically.

The more the reporter read, the more confused he became. There were lots of different tribunals depending on how far up the bureaucratic chain the case went. Then, there were the appeals which could be decided by a neighbouring diocese. For example, a case in the diocese of Springfield, Massachusetts would be appealed to the tribunal of the Archdiocese of Boston, but a case originating in the Archdiocese of Boston would be appealed to the tribunal of the Archdiocese of New York, by agreement between the archbishops of New York and Boston.

Sullivan was losing the will to live and began to think there was no story here. But he needed to fill some more space. Perhaps he would look up Wikipedia and just do a factual piece, then get Arata to check it. Problem. He was Janice's contact, so convention and respect said he would have to go through her. He didn't want to ask Janice for a favour but would Arata respond to him? He'd give it a go.

"Father Arata, this is Sullivan from the Gazette. I'm a colleague of Janice."

"What can I do for you?" asked Arata warily.

"I wanted to write an explanation of ecclesiastical courts. Actually," he ploughed on, "I've kind of written it just from internet research and wondered if you could check it for me?"

"Mr Sullivan, I had a deal with Janice and I fulfilled it. I believe that concludes our business."

The phone went dead and Sullivan swore. He had all but forgotten the altercation in the Holies earlier. He hadn't even given any thought to Janice, or Kevin's grandmother for that matter. Now he envisaged her reaction to what he had done and desperately tried to convince himself that it was not his concern. His ability to compartmentalise had been finely honed over decades and it didn't let him down now. It was in the interests of the Gazette after all. This edition was going to be much better than the first and he was going to make it happen. Not that it was a competition.

Janice didn't come back into the office that day, but made a call to Porter outlining the situation in New Jersey and saying she would write up a draft of the story overnight. Normally, she would have asked Sullivan to look at it to make sure it had the right balance of objectivity and drama, but it seemed their relationship had changed and it was Porter she now looked to. She wrote up the story quickly, the words flowing easily. With a few amendments after a re-read, she emailed it off to Porter and set her mind to pursue another path which had occurred to her on the return journey.

Late Sunday afternoon in his hotel room, Douglas-Scott looked at Janice's note and decided to make the call. When the phone was picked up by someone calling themselves Arata, he tried to explain himself.

"Hello, my name is Douglas-Scott and I was given your name by Janice Munroe at the Gazette."

There was a pause on the line. "Are you latterly of Rome?" Arata asked.

"Er. Yes, as a matter of fact I am, but no longer."

"Where are you?" asked Father Arata.

"I'm at the Comfort Hotel, here in Boston."

Another pause, as if Arata couldn't quite believe what he was hearing.

"Father, you must come over to the late Cardinal's residence. I'll send a car. It should be with you in about twenty minutes, traffic permitting."

"Thank you. That would be kind."

Forty minutes later, Father Douglas-Scott was being escorted into the magnificent building still in his civvies, to meet Father Arata dressed in his cassock who looked at his visitor carefully as he walked in.

"My word, it is you," he exclaimed. "My dear man, come this way." He turned to the chauffeur and asked him to take the Father's suitcase to the guest suite.

"Father, Have you eaten this evening?" Arata asked.

"Er. No, I haven't."

"I haven't either. Let's eat together."

Over the meal, Arata introduced himself more fully, talking a little about the late Cardinal, but being circumspect about views on the current state of the catholic church. Douglas-Scott reciprocated about his recent history but was rather more open about why he had resigned, how he had come to meet Janice, and that he was considering renouncing the priesthood.

Arata then felt he could share a little of his own misgivings so that by the end of the evening, the two men discovered they had much in common and the discussion turned to what could they do to provoke change.

During their discussion, Arata's phone rang. It was Janice.

"Apologies for disturbing your evening," started Janice. She still couldn't decide how to address him. Was it Arata, Father, or Gino? She decided to avoid them all.

"Good evening Janice. Good of you to call. Your friend and I were having a lively discussion."

"Glad to hear it," replied Janice. "I need to ask a small favour of you."

"Anything in my power," said Arata.

"I seem to recall that when the Keating affair exploded a few years ago, your father helped the archdiocese finance the compensation that was needed. Is that true?"

"Yes, I believe he did."

"Does he still do that sort of thing?"

Arata paused. "Is this request for your newspaper?" he asked circumspectly.

"No, no," replied Janice and went on the explain Dora Webster's position down in New Jersey.

"Yes, he might be able to do something. Here's his number. You're welcome to say that you've already spoken to me."

"Thanks. Much appreciated." She rang off and immediately rang Arata Sr. who let his cellphone ring out because he didn't recognise the number. Janice was half expecting it and left a brief message just outlining who she was and that she had spoken to his son. The entrepreneur was waiting for the message to determine whether he wanted to answer his phone to a stranger on a Sunday evening.

He was intrigued to see what this journalist from the Gazette wanted and even more where his son fitted in.

"Ms Munroe. What can I do for you?" he asked, giving nothing away.

"Mr Arata, thanks for taking my call." Janice was as solicitous as she could be, quickly outlining the situation in New Jersey.

"I'm trying to find a firm of civil lawyers who will sue the catholic church for the abuse of Kevin Webster by this priest. It's possible the diocese might need some finance if the compensation we obtain is large enough. Also, I need some criminal lawyers to defend Mrs Webster. If I can make enough noise, one way or another, we might find a jury who will fully understand the mitigation here. "

The opportunity was not lost on Arata Sr. but it wasn't his style to jump straight in and offer his services, though he immediately saw a way he could help Mrs Webster and possibly himself.

"Ms Munroe. Would you allow me a little time to give this some thought?"

"Of course, Mr Arata. But I don't think we have a great deal of time."

"Will twenty-four hours work for you?"

"I think that will be just fine," replied Janice.

"By the way," said Arata in closing, "I do know an excellent firm of criminal lawyers in New Jersey who might be able to act for Mrs....."

"Webster," prompted Janice.

"Yes, Mrs Webster. I will contact them if that's appropriate?"

"Certainly. Currently, she has to rely on public counsel. They are well-meaning, but I think this case will prove to be beyond them."

"I think you're correct, Ms Munroe. Leave it with me and I'll get back to you within twenty-four hours."

The conversation finished with Arata in deep thought. He could easily see how this could come together but, nevertheless, it would be complex to make all the finances stack up. The compensation award had to be large enough to pay the lawyers and himself, with maybe a little for Mrs Webster. The issue was that the costs of the lady's defence would have to be incurred before he knew the outcome of the compensation claim. However, he was so furious with the mess his church was in, he began to think whether he might take on that risk himself. He couldn't afford to involve Rossi who would be just another element of cost for something he could do himself.

He made his first call to De Luca in Chicago. He suspected he would not be interested but might know a firm in Jersey he had links to.

The call was answered almost immediately. "Hi Arata, what can I do for you?"

"Apologies for calling on Sunday evening," said Arata, knowing full well that lawyers in his class worked 24-7 which is why most of them were rich but divorced, some two or three times. He quickly explained the situation. He was looking for a firm specialising in criminal law that could defend Mrs Webster and another firm specialising in compensation claims, if possible, against the catholic church. As a minimum, the latter would need to pay for the former, hopefully with some left over for the lady in question.

"I'll speak to my colleagues tomorrow and come back to you by lunchtime."

"Thanks, De Luca. Knew I could rely on you." With that, he put the phone down leaving De Luca wondering where his fees were in this deal.

For Sullivan, it was now mid-afternoon and he finally looked up from his computer having taken most of the day to line up all his stories. They would need to go to Porter but he believed his editor-in-chief owed him, so was not anticipating too much blowback.

Janice was making her way into the office having spent the morning editing her copy of the New Jersey story and following up a suggestion Porter had made for a tie-up with a New Jersey paper which also belonged to Meyer's newspaper empire. There was no money in it for the Gazette, but Meyer would appreciate it and, more importantly, it might help to form public and potential juror opinion about Dora Webster's case.

She had debated whether or not to come in at all, she was that tired. But she wanted to try and mend relationships with Sullivan if she could. Well, she could try. Sullivan was already in when she arrived and feeling rather pleased with his progress, even if the piece about church trials still lacked a fact check. He was feeling bullish. Wikipedia couldn't be that wrong, could it? He would use that as his base and just publish.

He listened off and on to what Janice had been going through over the past twenty-four hours and, privately he was impressed with her, although refused to acknowledge it. He made some positive noises although keeping his distance physically and verbally.

Porter called her in for an update, then gave her a copy of Sullivan's stories for the mid-week special.

"Read it and get back to me with any comments by five, please." He then told her to go home. Sullivan watched the body language of the couple. He knew, but they didn't know that he knew.

Chapter 48

DE LUCA WAS as good as his word and, by lunchtime, Arata Sr. had the names of two legal firms in New Jersey with contacts already lined up. He called Janice, who was at the office, and asked her where the defendant was located so a visit could be arranged.

"I'll make a call. If you send me the name of the lawyers who will defend her, I'll warn her that they will visit." Sullivan looked over at her but made no comment.

It seemed that the police didn't know where she had been taken after her arraignment. Not their business any more. As far as their detectives were concerned, it was a slam dunk. Evidence had been passed to the prosecuting authorities. Nothing more for them to do. So it was the beginning of a number of calls to the District Attorney's office to try to find someone that was both interested to help and could access the information. Janice was not family and so it was easy to ignore her.

Eventually, she had to persuade a clerk to call the police station for them to confirm that she had been the only visitor Mrs Webster had received. Once confirmed that there was no other family, Janice finally got her name listed as 'next of kin', clearance that enabled her to discover what she had suspected. Dora was in the Edna Mahan Correctional Facility for Women. Now she was official.

A call to the Correction facility got nowhere. They didn't know who she was and were not bothered to try to find out. Evidently, their computer records had not been updated with the latest batch of criminals assigned to them. So she called the lawyers, mentioning Arata's name. Again a blank until she mentioned Dora's name, then a lady was put through who introduced herself as the principal lawyer who would lead the defence, but she didn't know who Janice was. Five convoluted minutes later, the links of the chain were finally sorted out, although the lawyer, Ms Kristin Adams, was hesitant when she learned that Janice was an investigative journalist.

Janice suggested they meet prior to seeing Dora together at the Correctional facility. Ms Adams agreed, if only, Janice suspected to try and control what she might write in the Gazette. The lawyer agreed to make the appointment at the prison once she heard how Janice had been given the run-around. A final text to Arata to confirm all the arrangements had been made and she sat back in her chair confident that everything had been done to give Dora the best chance of being cleared. She knew there would be a civil claim against the catholic church running parallel to the criminal case and she determined to keep her eye on its progress. That was likely to take more time than the criminal case but, together, this was going to make a great story, whatever way it turned out.

She cast an eye over towards Sullivan, wondering what he was thinking. These days, he wasn't saying much. He was keeping himself to himself. The only comment she had made to Porter about Sullivan's stories was the church trial one which, she said, was a bit confused – almost as if he didn't really understand it but had just done a copy and paste job. It was up to Porter to decide what to do and he had decided to leave it as is. The special was now on the streets and she determined to congratulate him, hoping that might melt the icy atmosphere that had enveloped their corner of the office. As far as she knew, nobody else had noticed the temperature drop, or if they had, didn't care. Her cellphone pinged with a text. It was Father Arata.

"Thought you ought to know. Someone called Sullivan from your office called me yesterday to fact-check a story for him. Afraid I declined. Hope that doesn't embarrass you."

Janice read and re-read it. Her blood was beginning to boil. This was against all Gazette protocols where key contacts were carefully nurtured by the one who had the relationship and all approaches were to be made through that individual. Sullivan had broken that rule and with it, any remaining trust Janice had in him. If he had come through her, he might have got the fact-checking he wanted and, in her opinion, needed. As it was, in his arrogance he hadn't done a basic check and they had probably lost an important contact, perhaps crucial in their campaign against paedophile priests.

She sat at her desk outwardly silent but inside fuming. She didn't want to have an open row with Sullivan in the office, nor to march into Porter lodging a complaint. It was late afternoon by now and, after a quick email to Porter saying she would be in New Jersey the following day, she upped and left without a word. Sullivan didn't care. He was the goose that kept on laying golden eggs for the paper. Porter wasn't going to sack him in the middle of such a lucrative campaign as this one. In any case, if he did go, he would take his knowledge and reputation to a competitor. That wouldn't go down well with Meyer which meant that Porter's own job might be at risk. The editor-in-chief would have to come down on his side, he was sure, rather than pander to his mistress. He would bet $1000 that Meyer didn't know.

The following morning Janice set off for her meeting with Kristin Adams. A lukewarm reception was anticipated from the lawyer but, being official next of kin, gave her a strong position to be involved in everything. The journalist wasn't going to take any nonsense from the lawyer. She had two objectives: to secure the best outcome for Dora and, secondly, to write up a series of stories with the minimum of legal interference.

"Good morning, Ms Munroe. How are we?" asked Ms Adams rather patronisingly as Janice was met in front of the plush reception desk at the firm's offices.

"We are very well and looking forward to see how you perform," replied Janice, putting the onus firmly on the lawyer.

Kristin Adams smiled as she led the journalist up to an interview room on the seventh floor. When coffee had been offered and accepted, Ms Adams opened her legal pad and began questioning her with two other colleagues alongside also taking copious notes. Janice outlined as succinctly as she could who Kevin Webster was, how he had been groomed and abused, the details on the laptop and her history with Dora, his grandmother.

"Where is the laptop?" asked Adams, immediately Janice mentioned it.

"The police have it," replied Janice.

Adams sighed. "We will get sight of some of it in discovery but would have been much better if we could have interrogated it earlier."

"But we don't and therefore we can't," Janice snapped at Adams.

There followed a prolonged private conversation between all three legal minds at the end of the room, leaving Janice to begin making her own notes on the first story she was going to release. Eventually, Adams returned to the table while the other two left the room.

"I think we have all we need for the moment. Shall we go and visit Mrs Webster? I've made the appointment for two o'clock."

Dora Webster was glad to see Janice and was waiting in an interview room specifically used for lawyer/client meetings. They hugged while Kristin Adams looked on, slightly bored and impatient to move on.

"This is Ms Adams," said Janice as she introduced the lawyer. "She's going to give you the best defence possible. There's a lot of mitigation here," she added.

Kristin Adams interrupted, "If you could leave the legal stuff to me," she said to Janice pointedly, who simply winked at Dora allowing the lawyer to do her thing. Thirty minutes later, the same questions had been asked and answered. After a perfunctory, "Thank you. I'll be in touch," from the lawyer, Dora asked Janice to stay behind for a few minutes. Ms Adams frowned at her exclusion, but had to withdraw while the two women, now firm friends, had a little time to themselves.

"She seems a little...." Dora stopped, looking for the right word.

"Formal?" suggested Janice.

"Yes. I suppose so," replied Dora. "Can she do this?"

"If anyone can, she can," said Janice, with more confidence than she was feeling.

"OK." Dora breathed a big sigh. "I suppose there's no chance of getting out of here?"

"I'm afraid not," replied Janice sympathetically.

There was a knock at the interview door and a guard arrived to escort Mrs Webster back to her cell.

"Can you go to my house and feed the cat?" asked Dora.

"Sure. Where's the key?"

Dora Webster looked a little embarrassed. "Under the flower pot next to the door."

"OK. I'll let you know how I get on and try to keep you updated," promised Janice, as her friend was bundled out of the room. She followed and caught up with Kristin Adams, both making their way out in silence.

When they were in the car, Janice said, "Just so you know, I will be writing about this case in the paper as part of our campaign about paedophile priests."

It wasn't a question and the lawyer didn't say anything except, "I thought you might. Perhaps you could send me a copy."

After Sullivan's mid week special, Janice commandeered the following weekend front page with the Dora Webster story. It was a human story of someone who had been tested to the limit and charged with attempted murder, while the priest who was guilty of the abuse, and indirectly the suicide of her grandson, was still free and under the protection of the catholic church. Janice put all her emotions into the copy and left it to Porter to weed out anything that went too far. He left it as it was.

Once she was back in her own car, Janice headed to Dora's home. As she approached, she could see something was wrong. The door was already open. She went up the stairs quietly and immediately saw that it had been completely turned over. Drawers had been emptied in the sitting room with their contents all over the sofa and chairs, the television had gone, utensils and crockery from the kitchen had been scattered over the floor and the upstairs was in a similar state of disarray. No sign of the cat.

It wasn't her home, but her legs were just as wobbly with shock as if it had been. She was close to tears. Who could have done such a thing? She pulled herself together and began to wonder how had they got in. She remembered the flower pot and went outside to look under it. No key. Some knew or it was a lucky guess. Back inside, she cleared a chair and sat down to survey the scene and think. Her initial thought was that the police had turned it over looking for more evidence, but surely they wouldn't have left the door open or stolen the TV? No, it was likely to be those white teenage boys who had previously racially bullied Kevin. She called the police station to explain what had happened, but as soon as they knew whose home it was, it didn't look like any priority would be given to investigate the break-in, even when Janice reminded them she was a reporter. Neighbours either side didn't answer when she knocked on their doors. Either not bothered or scared that the same treatment might be meted out on their homes.

She carefully shut Dora's front door without any key to lock it, and made her way home. It was so unfair. She had already determined that Dora didn't need to know this and that she would come back over a weekend with some help to clear up if the police had not been.

Chapter 49

DOUGLAS-SCOTT SPENT A comfortable night at the Cardinal's mansion and, over breakfast the next morning, informed Father Arata that he had decided to go back to the UK.

"I have also been giving some thought about how we might further the cause we both believe in," said Father Arata. "It occurred to me in my devotions this morning that perhaps you might delay your trip for a few days?"

"What did you have in mind?" asked Father Douglas-Scott absent-mindedly tucking into breakfast.

Without answering the question directly, Father Arata asked. "Do you know when your interview with the Gazette will be published?"

"No, I don't. I shouldn't think they would leave it very long. Why?" Douglas-Scott was now intrigued by what his friend had in mind.

"The Gazette is a Boston paper and, although its stories will be picked up by other media, it occurred to me that there might be a way of turbo-charging the message, if you'll forgive the expression."

"Ah!" replied Douglas-Scott, beginning to see where Arata was going. "You're talking about TV."

"Would that be so bad? Of course, we would have to get Janice to mediate this. It wouldn't be appropriate to do this ourselves. And we would have to ensure the interviewer was sympathetic, but I think she could do that, don't you?"

Douglas-Scott was not sure. "I don't want to imply any personal criticism of His Holiness."

"No, of course not. It's the organisation as a whole that needs to examine itself."

"You're right about that," agreed Douglas-Scott.

"In fact," continued Arata, "you would be helping His Holiness in his fight against the regressive forces that seem to run the Vatican."

Arata could see the possibilities were gaining traction in his friend's mind. "Think and pray about this today during your devotions. It would be a shame to miss such a great opportunity."

Douglas-Scott found himself wrestling with the issue for most of the day, weighing the pros and cons and desperately praying for divine guidance. God seemed not to hear. At lunch, he had still found no peace but delayed purchasing any airline tickets to London Heathrow. He felt he needed to call Janice. He trusted her.

"Good afternoon Janice," came the polite greeting of the priest.

"Afternoon Father," replied a surprised Janice, still in her VW travelling back to Boston. "What can I do for you?"

"Er. Can you tell me when my interview will be published?"

"Possibly this weekend. Our mid-week special is out today which might interest you."

Douglas-Scott smiled. "I will certainly buy a copy."

"Sorry, it wasn't a sales pitch. It has a section on church trials and I'm not sure my colleague fact-checked it thoroughly enough."

"Oh. In that case, I will give you some feedback." He paused. "Will it be this weekend?"

The signal was lost for a few moments. "Sorry, I lost you there."

"Are you driving?" asked the priest.

"Yes, but I'm hands-free. What did you say?"

"Will my story be published this weekend?"

"We have a number of stories that are competing for the front page this weekend and yours is definitely one of them. Why?"

There was a longer pause and Janice was wondering what was coming next. Eventually, the priest answered. "Father Arata and I have been debating something and I wanted your input."

"Yes, what was it about?" Janice decided to slow down so she could concentrate on the conversation. Something was worrying the priest.

"He suggested," another pause. "And I'm not certain about it."

"What did he suggest?" asked Janice beginning to wonder what on earth was coming next.

"Whether it might be a good idea to time your publication with a TV interview. In his words, it might 'turbo-charge' the message." The priest anxiously waited for her reply.

Janice's mouth dropped open. This was the last thing she might have expected from these two priests.

"What a brilliant idea," she exclaimed.

"You think so?" asked Douglas-Scott.

"Certainly. We should do it." Janice was now thinking on her feet. "We'll need to get the right interviewer and do it in the right place, not in a studio, in my opinion," she added.

"Very well," said the priest. "I trust you to make the arrangements."

"I'll be back in touch," said an excited Janice who now speeded up, anxious to get back and talk to Porter.

Just as she was approaching New Haven, traffic began to slow down and eventually it all ground to a halt. Having just passed an exit, she either had to make it to the next exit and use her satnav to join the 95 further north, thus bypassing the congestion with all the other vehicles trying to do the same, or wait it out. She decided on the latter and whilst she was waiting, decided to call Porter and ask him out for dinner that evening.

"Hi Porter, what are you doing this evening?"

"I thought you were in Jersey?" he questioned.

"I was. I'm now in a traffic jam south of New Haven."

She could hear him grunt down the phone as he considered the proposal. "Is this business or pleasure?" he asked finally.

"A bit of both. I have an exciting opportunity to talk to you about."

She was expecting another grunt but didn't get one. He sounded quite positive.

"Great. I could do with some good news."

"Why? What's happened?" she asked, a little concerned.

"Sullivan's happened, that's what," was the response.

"What's he done now?"

"Didn't fact-check one of his pieces, that's what. And I was the mug who let him get away with it."

Janice stifled her chuckle. "Someone complained?"

"That priest you interviewed, that's who. The Pope's ex-private secretary, no less."

She had to laugh out loud at this point. She just couldn't keep it in.

"Something funny?" grunted Porter.

"It's good to know the demographic of our readership is going up," she said with as straight a face as she could muster. "Actually, it's him I want to talk about tonight."

"He's not my favourite person at the moment. How is it that every time you interview a priest, they write back in and say almost the exact opposite they said in the interview?"

"They're complicated people, priests," said Janice, and rang off.

The traffic began to move slowly just as she got a text. "Same time, same place." She smiled.

The congestion had delayed her such that she didn't enter the outskirts of Boston until six o'clock. No time to call in at the office, so straight to her apartment to rest, shower and change before going out. She began thinking about whether she might do the interview herself. It didn't have to be live so if she, or he for that matter, made any mistakes, it could all be edited before being transmitted. It depended on the TV station and Porter, of course, but a new career without Sullivan sounded good. It might even enable her and Porter to be more open about their relationship. That thought led her into thinking about such a relationship. Was it possible? Was it desirable? Was it what she wanted?

She arrived five minutes after the time allotted, to find Porter already studying the menu, which was odd because he had ordered the same mains each time they had been there together. They greeted one another warmly but not romantically. Each seemingly needed to test each step a few times before stepping out – just in case.

They ordered and, as the waiter moved away, Porter said, "Let's get business over first, shall we? By the way, what is it with you and priests? Do you fancy them or something?" Janice could see he was being light-hearted in a Porter-type way.

"He rang me as I was driving back."

"Is he still here, in Boston then?" asked Porter.

"Yes. He's staying at the Cardinal's mansion with Father Arata."

"Of course he is," replied Porter sarcastically.

"Anyway, he wants to do a TV interview in conjunction with the publication of our story."

Porter had been wiping his lips with his napkin. There it stayed for at least twenty seconds. Janice counted them. It was a long time.

"Bloody hell," exclaimed Porter when he finally came to. "How the hell do you do it? One exclusive after another."

Janice smiled modestly. "We need to find a station and....."

Porter interrupted. " Meyer is in the process of buying one and this would be a great way to launch it."

"I thought I might do the interview?" continued Janice tentatively. "He knows me and I think would open up more to me."

"But you have no television experience," countered Porter.

"However, lots of experience at interviewing people," she argued.

"Sounds like you want a new career." Porter looked at her suspiciously.

"Maybe. It might help you out with Sullivan." She didn't finish the sentence with, "and our relationship." He would have to come to that conclusion himself.

He was saved from answering immediately as the mains arrived, they having dispensed with any starters.

"I'll take that under advisement," he said with a mouth half full of steak. For a few minutes, they concentrated on food, each thinking about what next and the possibilities that might hold.

"Has Meyer bought this TV station yet?" asked Janice.

"Don't know," replied Porter. "But I'll find out when I've finished this last mouthful."

He took out his phone. "What's up, Porter?"

"Have you bought that TV station yet?"

"Not quite. Why?"

"I may have your first exclusive if you move swiftly," promised Porter, who then proceeded to outline the opportunity that Janice had brought to him.

"She's smart, that one," Meyer said.

"I agree. She also wants to do the interview."

"Does she?" Meyer's voice rose a few notes.

"When is this guy thinking of moving on?"

"I think he'll stay for a couple of weeks but not much longer."

"OK. I'll get back to you."

The phone went down and Porter turned to Janice. "I think he bought the whole package."

She smiled. "Now pay up. Business over."

Chapter 50

THE CURRENT OWNER of the TV company wanted more money than Meyer was willing to pay and so negotiations had stalled. Now the situation had changed. This interview could launch the new station with a huge audience, plus monies from syndication rights. It was a once-in-a-lifetime opportunity and he would be willing to pay a little more. The trouble was, he didn't have a little more. Maybe if Arata would come up with his investment quickly, then he believed he could seal the deal.

"Meyer, good to hear from you." Arata was always pleasant even when he was about to disappoint someone.

"Arata, how are you?"

"Well. What can I do for you?"

"I know your investment in my venture was predicated on your opportunity with the catholic church, but I have an updated proposal to put to you."

"I'm listening, Meyer."

"My editor at the Gazette, Porter, had just rung me. Janice Munroe, who I believe you know, has secured an interview with the ex-private secretary to His Holiness, the Pope."

Arata was a little taken aback. "I'm impressed. I thought she was a smart lady."

"The thing is, they have lined him up for a TV interview which I want to do on my station. It would be timed to go out in conjunction with the Gazette story."

"Now that is interesting. Quite a coup for you, Meyer." Arata was already smelling an opportunity, but as usual, was playing hard to get.

"I'd like you to reconsider your investment based on the projected audience, advertising, and worldwide syndication rights."

"I see," said Arata, not giving anything away.

"It's going to be a great opportunity for both of us." Meyer's excitement was understandable but not a great negotiation stance. Arata reckoned he could easily up the percentage ownership with the same level of investment.

"Can you get me some numbers?" Arata asked evenly, having already made up his mind he was going to invest.

"Sure. I can get you them by close of business tomorrow."

"Thank you," replied Arata, thinking the man must be desperate. He immediately contacted Mattia, his son-in-law, and briefed him on what he wanted, then settled down with a warm feeling in his bones.

Sullivan didn't have any warm feelings. Porter, having received Douglas-Scott's letter taking issue with some of Sullivan's copy, had given him a severe dressing down about putting forward text which has not been externally verified.

"If this blows up further, both your job and mine will be on the line. And I happen to like my job, so guess who will be leaving." Porter was leaving nothing unsaid.

"I tried but the deadline caught me." Sullivan was twisting and turning.

"Who did you try to contact?"

"Father Arata," admitted the reporter.

"But isn't he Janice's contact?"

"She wasn't around. Haven't seen her in days."

Porter looked like thunder. "Haven't you heard of a phone? You ****ing moron. You've published stuff which doesn't stand up to scrutiny, you tried to use another journalist's contact without asking, and you've probably lost us a valuable contact who was on our side. Get out!"

Sullivan left the office, tail between his legs, and went to the pub to drown his sorrows. It had been a long time since he had gotten drunk, but this time that's exactly what he intended to do. He knew his judgement had been wrong and the only warm feeling he had was that of alcohol gradually permeating his system. By nine o'clock, he was starting to feel nauseous. He couldn't hold his liquor as he used to be able to.

"Must be getting old," he muttered to himself as he started another pint. It was ten o'clock when the inevitable happened. Charles, the black bartender, came over and sat next to him. They knew each other well since Sullivan had been drinking here for decades, ever since he started working at the Gazette.

"Sullivan. Time to go home," he advised. "Shall I call you a cab?"

"Thank you, Charles," said the beery reporter, slurring his words. "I don't need a cab. I'm perfectly fine." He began to get up with Charles putting out a steadying hand which Sullivan dispensed with.

"I'm perfectly fine," he repeated, half falling over the table. He staggered outside to be greeted by a cold shaft of air which sobered him a little and he began to make his way back to his apartment, usually only twenty minutes drive away. Some sing when they're drunk, Sullivan merely swayed. Not a good thing to do when the sidewalk became narrow due to scaffolding.

It all happened so quickly. One minute he was on the sidewalk and the next he was on the ground with lights flashing around him. At first, they were yellow headlights but soon they turned red and blue. He knew somewhere inside that it meant either police or ambulance, maybe both. But he had no idea what they had come for. As he looked up from the road, he noticed a clear night and lots of stars. Someone was standing over him and he encouraged whoever it was to look at the stars.

"Aren't they pretty," he mumbled.

He felt a hand feeling his legs and someone asking him, "Does it hurt?"

"What a stupid thing to say," he thought until that hand reached his knee when he yelped out in pain. At that point he realised he was lying down and unsuccessfully attempted to get up.

"Woah," said the paramedic who then shouted to his partner. "Bring the stretcher – I think he's broken his leg."

Sullivan continued to protest as he was loaded into an ambulance and taken to St Elizabeth's hospital, affectionately known as St Es, located in the Brighton neighbourhood which, serendipitously, had a catholic foundation. He was quickly assessed to have one broken leg just below the knee with other minor cuts and abrasions. He was admitted after insurance documentation had been taken and next of kin had been informed.

When Linda, his ex., and daughter arrived after the hospital's phone call, he was still sleeping off the effects of the binge drinking he had indulged in. Chloe looked concerned whereas Linda shook him hard to wake him up and, by the look on her face, was ready to give him a hard time. Sullivan moaned and groaned as he reacted to the shaking, gradually waking up. He stared at them, then at his surroundings as if he had no memory of what or why.

"You were drunk and passed out when you walked into some scaffolding," Linda said quite harshly.

"Nice of you to come," muttered Sullivan gradually returning to his sardonic best.

"You fell into the road and a truck just missed you," she finished off.

Chloe, on the other hand, was more gentle in her concern. "Are you OK, Dad?" she asked.

Sullivan was now struggling to get to a sitting position without much success and, finally, giving up.

"My leg hurts," he complained.

"It would do," was Linda's riposte. "It's broken."

" I can't stay here. I've got stories to write up."

"You could try getting up and walking out of here," replied Linda. "It'd be a laugh for everyone."

"Mom," interrupted Chloe, "give Dad a break." Turning to her father, she asked, "Why did you get drunk? It's years since you pulled that one."

Sullivan began to think back and began groaning again. "Where's my phone? I need to call Porter."

"Why?" asked Chloe.

"Because I messed up big time."

"I expect Janice will be along soon," she said.

"I doubt it," muttered Sullivan again.

"Why?" asked Linda, with an accusatory voice.

"We aren't getting on at the moment," replied Sullivan.

"Why does that not surprise me?" said Linda. "Look, we need to go. Glad to see you're not at death's door." And she marched off.

"Bye Dad," said Chloe and planted a kiss on his forehead.

"Thanks, love," he responded. "Let's go out again soon?"

"Of course." And she was also gone.

A nurse found his cellphone but said he could only use it in a non-clinical area. A pleading smile from Sullivan and a promise to make only one quick call did the trick.

"Sullivan, where are you?"

"I'm in hospital."

"What? Stop ****ing about! I need you in here."

"I really am in hospital," repeated Sullivan.

There was a pause on the line and Porter's tone changed. "What happened?"

"I was on my way home, struck my head on some scaffolding and fell on the road."

"How on earth?... Oh no. You were plastered!"

"Only a bit," admitted Sullivan. "Anyway, I'm at St Es and, apparently, I've also broken my leg. But I can still type," he added.

"Shit," exclaimed Porter thinking about work. Then, being the caring boss he sometimes was, he said, "I'll call in on the way home."

He immediately called Janice. It was the night after so he was pleasant, even warm.

"Hi Janice, Sullivan got drunk and is in hospital with a broken leg."

"Pardon?"

"Sullivan....." started Porter.

"Yes, I heard. What happened?" Janice was concerned.

"The old Sullivan. I suppose he's never been off the wagon, but he really fell off last night."

"Why?"

"Maybe my fault. I gave him a real bollocking yesterday afternoon about ... well, quite a few things. Anyway, he went out, got well pissed and one thing led to another, I guess."

"Where is he?"

"St Es, in the Brighton neighbourhood."

"OK. I'll call in tonight. Any news from Meyer?" Janice was anxious to have her début TV interview."

"No, but I said Douglas-Scott wouldn't be staying in town for very long."

"OK. I'll get back to him and say we're arranging it and it shouldn't be long. It's not like he's paying for a hotel any more."

Janice made a quick call to the priest who was quietly calm about it all, which helped her to calm down after the news about Sullivan. All they could do now was wait.

Chapter 51

IN JERSEY, THE claim against the catholic church for the actions of the Father Graham had been submitted. The lawyers had a retired detective on their books to delve into the past of everyone they sued. Every corner of their lives was turned over, every favour called in, and every possible witness prepared to testify was identified. Marek Wyszynski, known as Wizz to his friends, was a grade 3 detective from New York City. He could have retired to the golf course since he had all the money he wanted from his police pension, except he didn't like golf. He had wanted to retire at the earliest he could, aged 50, having already been shot twice. Fortunately, with no lasting impacts to his health but you never knew. Each year, the reactions got slower and he decided to get out while he was still alive, but he lived for the job. This position suited him well.

He was a catholic but assured his boss that this was not a hindrance, rather the reverse. If he had his way, these perverts would go straight to jail for life. He had three grandchildren, too young to be groomed by any priest, but he had advised his son and daughter to bring up their children on a catholic-light faith – diet catholicism, if you will.

Digging into Father Graham was not difficult. He already knew about the Diocesan Year Book and started his investigation there. Although he was not aware of the pattern of behaviour that Cardinals had adopted, he soon saw the familiar pattern. Discretely visiting each parish where the priest had been assigned, his behavioural signature was soon identified. He would establish youth clubs for boys, hiring local halls if the church premises didn't have one. Basketball, baseball and soccer were favourites. From the evidence of angry parents spoken to, he easily established half a dozen who would be willing to testify against the priest.

His full name was Father Graham Wilson, but the civil case named the Cardinal as representative of the catholic church. He was aware of the sexual abuse perpetrated by the priest and, knowingly, moved him on from one parish to another after a suitable few months of 'gardening leave'. As soon as Wizz produced his evidence, the lawyers contacted the police and Father Graham was arrested and charged with sexual abuse with named and unnamed minors. This arrest, they knew, would considerably help the civil case. While the lawyers concentrated their efforts on identifying measures to ramp up the compensation claim, the date for the criminal case against Dora Webster had been decided by another court. It would begin in eight weeks.

Ms Kristin Adams conveyed the news to Janice via a one line text message. Nothing about how her defence was looking and nothing about how Dora was feeling. Janice had been sending her friend letters, but she was not getting any replies causing her to wonder if her letters were not being passed on or perhaps Dora was sinking into depression. A visit was not possible at the moment for with Sullivan out of action, she was having to do the work of two. Her latest story had already been approved by Porter and she knew it would go out this weekend in conjunction with their sister paper in Jersey. She hoped this would have a major impact on public opinion in that State. She wanted to continue to push the story but couldn't settle on a new angle.

That opportunity came from an unexpected source.

"Ms Munroe," announced Kristin Adams and carried on without giving Janice a chance to answer. "I thought you should know that following the break-in at Ms Webster's home, the landlord has given her notice to quit."

"What?" replied a stunned Janice.

"What do you want to do?" questioned the lawyer.

"What do you mean?"

"You're the official next of kin. How do you want to store or otherwise dispose of her belongings?"

Janice was still trying to comprehend how a person could kick someone when they were already down. One of the neighbours would have informed the landlord about Dora's situation and he decided he didn't want either a convicted criminal living in his property or that property vandalised because it was empty.

"I don't know at the moment." She said, then added, "One thing I do know is that we shouldn't tell Dora yet. It will devastate her and, hopefully, the civil case will provide her with some funds to start again."

"I'll text you the landlord's number and you can make the necessary arrangements with him."

The line was cut and her phone pinged with the incoming text.

"Bloody lawyers," muttered Janice. "She probably charged $50 for that minute."

The conversation with the landlord, if it could be called a conversation, lasted less than the lawyers phone call. As soon as he knew Janice was the next of kin, he said, "Empty the place within 48 hours or I will."

Janice was about to try and negotiate when the call was cut. She was angry that nobody cared a jot about this lady, even the lawyer. She determined that at least the landlord would feature in next week's edition, anonymously, of course but with a few hints here and there.

She had to speak to someone who could finance the removal and storage of Dora's possessions. Porter had to be the one. Maybe he could get Meyer to cough up since he was making a lot of money out of them at the moment. She looked up from her desk and saw Porter was with Mackie, his Finance Director.

"Maybe they both need to be in on this," she thought.

She knocked on the door which was shut and before Porter could complain, she had started.

"I need to speak to both of you," she said.

Porter looked annoyed, whilst Mackie was intrigued that someone from the news floor would barge into the Holies uninvited.

She hadn't prepared her pitch so it just came out in garbled fashion. "Dora Webster is on remand and the landlord has evicted her and we have twenty-four hours to get a removal and storage solution in place."

Mackie looked blank as if to say, what on earth has this to do with the Gazette. Porter knew but didn't want to promise anything. Janice had to up the pressure.

"We're making a lot of money out of her situation, as is our sister paper in Jersey. We cannot be seen to stand by and see her lose everything." There was the faintest hint of a threat there which wasn't lost on the editor-in-chief.

"Look here, Janice..." he started.

"Why don't we get Meyer to finance it? He wants to launch his new TV station using me. Explain that it is very important for me. He'll agree."

Mackie looked appalled at the blackmail suggestion, while Porter suddenly saw his way out. Janice read his face and went for the close. "It needs to be today. I'm happy to begin ringing around to try and find someone who will do it."

Porter nodded. "OK. I'll get it for you."

"Don't forget, we'll also get some good coverage for our beneficence in our own papers. Good, eh?" She shut the door behind her and left Porter to explain to Mackie what on earth happened in that three minute meeting. But Janice was happy.

Back at her desk, she began to troll the internet for removal and storage companies near Bridgewater, New Jersey. She asked the first company a price without specifying the short timescale, just to get an idea of the cost of such an operation. Then began to search for someone who could do the job tomorrow within a reasonable premium. She noted down some silly prices before coming to Bryants, an African American business. Janice thought Dora would approve. She booked their van and used her credit card trusting Porter would come up with the goods. She asked for an invoice to be sent to her immediately, which they did. So far, so good.

Porter's office was now empty of visitors and she approached, but this time respecting his position and waiting for an invitation to enter. He nodded his head.

"I'm sorry for earlier," she started as she entered. Porter waived her away.

"He said yes." The editor-in-chief sat back in his chair and chuckled. "What else could he say."

"Here's the invoice," said Janice. "I've paid it on my credit card."

Porter reached out his hand to take it. "Just watch out. He's likely to give you a hard time when he next sees you," he warned.

Janice nodded, then asked, "Can you find out by how much the circulation of the Jersey paper has increased due to our stories?"

"Sure," said Porter not quite realising why Janice was asking. "Mackie will have that." His voice trailed off as the penny dropped. "Nice," he said. "You'll go a long way."

Janice smiled.

Having filed her Dora Webster landlord story for the next edition, she decided there was time to drive down and visit her friend without the lawyer being present. She called ahead and this time there was no issue. Their systems had caught up and she was known to them as the official next of kin.

It was obvious immediately Janice entered the visiting hall that Dora was not coping with prison very well. In fact, the reporter was quite alarmed at what she saw.

"Dora, you don't look well," said Janice.

"This is a terrible place," replied Dora looking around anxiously. "If I have to come back here, I don't think I'll be able to carry on."

"I must say, it looks pretty grim," said Janice empathising with her. "Has Kristin Adams, your lawyer, been to see you?"

"No, no one."

"Have you received my letters?"

"No, nothing."

"What?" Janice was furious. "I'm so sorry. You know, I suspected that something was wrong when you didn't respond so I made copies." She passed them over and Dora clutched at the bundle of paper. "Don't worry, I'll get it sorted before I leave."

"What about the lawyer? Can they get me out of here?"

"I'm afraid the law courts are very slow. They're going to process it through a Grand Jury first, then they set a date for the trial which will be in Somerset County."

She was not going to tell her that she had not heard from Ms Adams, but she made a mental note to call Arata to get some pressure exerted. In her opinion, they should be requesting a hearing to release Dora, since she posed no flight risk but she was no legal expert. It was something she was going to take up with Ms Adams in person.

"The priest, Father Graham, has been arrested on criminal charges and we are also suing the catholic church. I'm writing about both in my paper and we have a sister paper who is running the stories here in Jersey."

Dora began to smile a little. "I thought I'd been forgotten and just left here."

Janice reached out to touch her hand. "Never," she said emphatically.

"Soon there won't be anyone here who reads a paper who won't know what you've been through and why."

"I thought there were rules about what you could write about an upcoming trial?" asked Dora.

"Yes there are. We have to be careful how we write the story," She winked at Dora.

There was the beginning of a scraping of chairs as prisoners and visitors were getting up to leave in response to prison officers enforcing the end of their allocated time.

Janice wanted to support Dora one last time before she had to go. "Please take care and be positive. I have a good feeling about this. I'm going to make some phone calls as soon as I reach my car."

Dora smiled a little as she was hustled away whereas Janice wanted to let rip at someone, anyone. First in line was the lawyer.

"Kristin Adams please,"

"I'm afraid she's in a meeting at present," came the anonymous reply.

"Of course she is," came the caustic reply from Janice. "Ask her to ring me before close of business. Today!" She then gave the required details and cut the line.

She wasn't going to wait for a return call which might not come, so she called Arata. He was also in a meeting but his secretary said she would interrupt and let him know you had called.

"He should call you back within the hour," she said. In fact, he called back within five minutes. Janice explained her concerns and asked whether he could put some pressure on the partners of the law firm to improve communication, principally to their client. He said he would do it right away. She could envisage what would be happening inside the law firm and was counting down to see how long it was before Ms Adams called her. She bet on two minutes but after ninety seconds her phone rang.

"Hello Ms Munroe," came the voice.

"Good of you to call. I know how busy you are," said Janice, sardonically.

"What can I do for you?" the lawyer asked bluntly.

Janice wasn't expecting an apology, but perhaps a change of tone. Clearly, a more conciliatory approach was not going to happen.

"I called to see Dora today and she said you had not been in touch and she didn't know how her defence was progressing." Janice saw no need to beat about the bush. She wanted to be blunt and secure some plain speaking from Adams.

"It's coming on well," said the lawyer.

"That's not good enough," started Janice trying to keep her temper under control. "Where, in your priority list, is keeping your client informed and, more to the point, involved?"

"Ah. Yes. I had intended to go yesterday, but something came up."

"It had better be something to do with our case, and I checked. You were not on the visitor's list." Janice was getting worked up now.

"It happened before I had chance to make the request. But the Grand Jury date is happening shortly. Of course, Ms Webster won't be able to attend."

"Something came up? What actually happened?" asked Janice.

"I'm afraid that's confidential," said the lawyer defensively.

Janice made the pause a little longer before she released her last onslaught for this call. "Ms Adams, you're skating on very thin ice. Let me make this crystal clear. I want you in that prison, at least once a week from now on in, keeping Dora fully informed about your progress and a written copy to me each Friday."

She then hung up and realised that she had been holding her breath for what seemed a long time. A few deep breaths and she relaxed into her car seat ready to make the journey back to a cheap motel for the night. Tomorrow would be a big day. Dora's house was going to be emptied and she wanted to be there to take charge.

Chapter 52

Sullivan sat up in bed with his leg in plaster, reading this weekend's Gazette. It was Saturday and he noted, without any pleasure, that this was the second front page in a row about the lady in Jersey who had tried to kill a paedophile priest. Porter was losing it. Letting Janice get away with whatever she wanted to put on the front page. He could feel his blood pressure rising so he put the paper down and reached for his headphones. He was an oldie who was still wedded to his vinyl collection. Streaming was not for him and his old Chevy had no place for an iPod or anything new-fangled like that. But he did have some music on his phone – a nod to modernity. He pressed the buttons and Dexter Gordon's *I'm a Fool to Want You*, came up, nearly seven minutes long. He lay back, listening to the soothing tones of the tenor sax that always worked to reduce his stress.

Long before the end of the track, he began to think about Porter, Janice and their relationship. He knew they'd had a fling earlier when Porter got divorced but this one seemed more... measured, more serious. In truth, he had no problem with it but if it was affecting Porter's judgement, that would be different. And the current indications were, that it was.

Listening to his music made him feel relaxed and tired, so he settled down with his eyes closed and began to doze. It was strange. He was doing no exercise, no real work and yet he continually felt tired. The medics explained it as an accumulation of stress and work over years, meaning that his body was now taking the time it needed to recover. One nurse suggested that this episode might have been a blessing for if he had not been forced to slow down and give his body time to recuperate, he would almost certainly have been heading for a heart attack. He wasn't sure about the blessing bit for, although the severe headaches were receding thanks to his medication, his head still hurt.

Well, he'd be out on some sticks in a day or two and couldn't wait to be back in the office assuming his usual senior place. There had been lots of time to think in hospital and he had been generating ideas to move the campaign on which he wanted to share with Porter; that is, if Porter had calmed down. So what if one priest had written in with critical comments? He was sure no one else would have noticed and readership was still steady at a new high. People were still keen to follow the story. But not for much longer if Janice kept getting her way.

His daughter, Chloe, came in and gave her father a friendly shove. Sullivan immediately opened his eyes, smiled and took his headphones off. There was something more important to him than Dexter Gordon, after all!

"Hi Dad," Chloe greeted him with a hug. "Feeling better?"

"The leg is fine, although I'll have to walk with sticks for a while."

"That'll be a sight to behold," she said, smiling.

"Thanks for coming in. Really appreciate it." Sullivan was anxious to maintain good relations with his daughter, even if his ex. wasn't interested.

"When are you being discharged?" she asked.

"Should have been tomorrow but I need meds and, for some bizarre reason, the pharmacy isn't open on Sunday, so it'll be Monday."

"I'll bring the car."

"You can drive?" asked Sullivan surprised.

"I'll forget you asked that," Chloe replied. "Give me a text half an hour before you need me and I'll meet you outside," she said as she kissed him on the cheek and left.

"Bloody hell," said Sullivan under his breath. "Where have I been for the last decade?" He made himself a promise that this relationship would not fail.

The following weekend edition of the Gazette was provisionally headlined with the Douglas-Scott interview. The proviso was that Meyer did the deal and bought the channel. It was not done yet, though. Porter was getting anxious and had asked Janice for an alternative front page just in case, but not about Dora.

"We can't do it three weeks in a row. Readers will think we've run out of stories." As an addendum, he added, "We haven't, have we?"

"Of course not," Janice answered more positively than she was feeling. She went back to her desk and began to troll through her notes to find a story with another different angle, which was not easy. The trajectory of the story had to be sorted that day because in the morning she was off to New Jersey. It would be an early start since the removal company wanted it to be done and in storage by lunchtime; fitting in two jobs in one day was the clear ambition. Back to today's task. Sullivan probably had more stuff on his computer and, although she could have obtained his password properly, she decided to refrain, rightly thinking it would worsen relationships considerably.

So she started investigating any and all internet stories about the catholic church, of which there were very many, some she knew about and others not. She found paedophile activities in Australia, South America, and virtually every country on Earth. No surprise there. Then came across a story about victims in the US who didn't want financial compensation. This caught her attention. Apparently, they were prepared to give up their rightful financial compensation for specific concessions from the catholic church, such as publishing a list of all known offenders, putting confidential church documents into the public domain, setting up a hotline for people to report clerical abuse and policy changes to better protect potential victims. This had happened in Montana after the diocese did the usual to protect their assets, then went bankrupt. There was no report to demonstrate how far the church truly went to discharge these settlement agreements.

It was a good story in the making though, so she spent time talking to local media, prosecutors, published court reports, and anyone in the catholic church she could contact to validate the internet report and get publishable quotes. She had wanted to make a call to Douglas-Scott to warn him of the weekend as the probable date of the interview and decided to ask him about the Montana situation.

"Hi Father Andrew," she greeted him, a bit more informally this time.

"Hello, Janice, are you well?"

"Er. Well enough, except my colleague has broken his leg so I'm a little busier than usual."

"Sorry to hear that," was the solicitous reply.

Janice jumped in before having to talk more about Sullivan. "We're currently thinking that the TV interview will be sometime this weekend if that's OK with you?"

"Yes, that will be good. I want to go back to the UK to see my sister and her children shortly so that timing is good."

Janice didn't want to press the point about the timing probabilities, so began to talk about the interview itself.

"I'm thinking we will just go through the interview in the same order as before, but I will plan to ask more adversarial questions, giving you the opportunity to expand on your current beliefs, if that's alright."

"That's fine. I shall enjoy the cut and thrust," replied the priest. "I should be grateful if Father Arata could attend, in the background of course. He's been very generous with his accommodation and time."

"Of course. I'll let you know the exact timings shortly." Then Janice added before Douglas-Scott left the line. "By the way, what do you think about dioceses accepting non-monetary conditions at court hearings when being sued?"

"Woah! Did you just doorstep me on the phone?" It wasn't an annoyed reaction, but definitely surprised.

Janice was just as surprised at his knowledge of 'doorstepping'. "Sorry about that. Force of habit," she said, hoping that hadn't tarnished the relationship. "It's just that I've come across something that the diocese of Montana is doing. It may be that Father Arata knows about it," she replied.

"OK. What sort of conditions?" he asked. Janice then outlined what she had found out about Montana. He agreed to look at it but there was no promise to provide a comment.

"Damn." Janice kicked herself. She was picking up Sullivan's habits. Her fault. She put the bones of the story together but didn't yet file it.

It wasn't until Tuesday that Meyer gave the thumbs up to Porter. It was to be a Saturday night show, the headline name yet to be decided. He had his researchers working on other celebrities to be interviewed on succeeding Saturday nights but was throwing everything at the first night with an interview with the Pope's private secretary. Producers at the station were extremely doubtful about a rookie TV interviewer for such a crucial slot. They had their own man who, they claimed, would do the job well. Because the whole future of the station relied on this interview with an enormous amount of money at stake, Meyer succumbed to pressure and called Janice into the studio for a screen test, fortunately for Friday morning.

Wednesday morning saw Janice furiously driving her VW back down Route 95 to Dora's home. The bad news was that the removal crew had already started; the good news was that the cat had reappeared. The men were working quickly, with Janice just as anxious to leave late morning as they were. She did a quick rifle through the drawers in Kevin's room just in case anything had been missed, thinking where a teenage boy might hide his treasures. Nothing. A quick look in the closet, now empty, revealed nothing except a broken bit of plasterboard.

Just as she was turning to leave, she looked back at the crack in the plaster. There were no other cracks and it looked odd. She stepped back and put a finger into the hole, felt something and when she had tugged a little, pulled out a memory stick. She looked at it with amazement, not quite believing what she had found but hoping it was a copy of what was on the laptop. She quickly put it in a pocket and went to see if the removal men had finished. They had.

"Have you seen the cat at all?" she asked one of them, cursing herself for not putting it in her car when she had the chance.

"Yep. Gave it some food in the kitchen. Looked like she was hungry," he added, as an obvious cat-lover.

"I'll have to take it back with me. What do I need," she asked.

He looked at her before leading her into the house and gathering up all the cat paraphernalia that Dora had accumulated. "It's a her," he said, knowingly as Janice looked aghast at all the stuff she would have to pile into her car.

"You take good care of her," warned the removal man. "She's getting on a bit and she needs to be looked after properly."

Janice was now regretting her promise to look after the cat. With her lifestyle, and living in an apartment, she was not at all sure how this was going to work out. At least, she was on the first floor. Nevertheless, into the car went cat and all, the cat albeit in a pet carrier. She would have to work it out somehow. It slept much of the way back, or least, didn't make any noise until she began to reach the outskirts of Boston. She hoped to God it was trained otherwise it was going to a cattery. In fact, now she thought about it - not a bad idea. I wonder how much it costs?

On arrival, she began to carry everything into her apartment when a neighbour, who she had only met once or twice, saw her with the cat and came over to stroke the animal.

"What a lovely cat," she said. "Have you just got it?"

"No," replied Janice, thinking quickly. "I'm just looking after it for a friend who's moving."

After more cat talk, which Janice completely failed to understand, she managed to get away. Once inside, she put some food, water and the litter tray out in the kitchen, then sat down to look at the story she was building. The cat would have to sort itself out. Now the story was on, she could relax a little, but a text from Porter said that he still wanted it to be filed by noon tomorrow, Thursday, just in case. She worked solidly on it for a couple of hours, assuming that she wouldn't hear from Douglas-Scott and got it into some sort of shape. She knew if she had another week she could do a lot better, but tonight she was deadbeat. She forgot about the cat and dragged herself off to bed.

The next morning, Janice was astounded to find the cat had snuck up on her bed in the night and was still fast asleep. She had overslept by about an hour after the stresses of yesterday. So after a quick shower and breakfast, she replenished food and water and left her apartment, arriving at the studios in downtown Boston promptly at ten o'clock. The show's producers met her and took her straight to a studio where she was given lines to say while a gaggle of onlookers, including some critics, watched in the production control room where the composition of the outgoing programme would take place. The director of the show was scrutinising Janice closely. Her face and manner were fine so she got the job much to the disgruntlement of the resident interviewer. The discussion then revolved around her ability to do the interview live. The fact that she had done an interview before and knew the interviewee was in her favour, but it was still a huge risk and eventually, was judged to be too much and the decision was taken to record it.

It didn't bother Janice. She knew she could do it and left the studio to prepare her 'adversarial' questions, knowing that the front page of the Gazette was already in place. When she got home, the cat was nowhere to be seen. She swore and left the door ajar for the remaining light hours hoping that it might return before dark. She resolved was to get a cat flap installed although it would ruin her door forever.

Chapter 53

THE TWO PRIESTS were having a deep discussion which had started with Douglas-Scott sharing Janice's request with his friend. Arata didn't know anything about the church in Montana and so looked at the internet report about the archdiocese with interest. On the one hand, he didn't want to see the catholic church penniless but, even with the compensation payouts, they were far from that. On the other hand, he couldn't agree with financial manipulation which deprived victims of the compensation which, potentially, allowed them something of a normal life. In truth, while money was probably the only way the legal system could measure the impact of criminal harm, most of the victims of clerical abuse would never live normal lives ever again. But the lawyers were happy.

"What do you think?" asked Douglas-Scott.

"If I was looking at the matter of compensation objectively," said Arata carefully, "I would be looking for an agreement with enough financial compensation to provide on-going counselling for the victim, plus some of the non-financial measures which would begin to kick start change within the church."

"But that's not what either set of lawyers would be looking for," replied Douglas-Scott cynically.

"So, these complainants must be doing it without lawyers?" questioned Arata.

"Then, they're not likely to get any financial compensation," surmised Douglas-Scott.

"I guess that's their choice," observed Arata. He looked up from the computer and turned to face his friend.

"Changing the subject, how's this interview going to go down with Rome?" quizzed Arata.

"Not very well," admitted Douglas-Scott.

"Do you think it will make any difference?" Arata didn't sound hopeful.

"No," replied Douglas-Scott bluntly. "If a massive paedophilia scandal hasn't caused senior clerics to re-think where they're taking our church, I'm not sure anything will."

"Then why are you doing it?" Arata was perplexed.

"Because I need to be true to myself," responded Douglas-Scott. "I intend to resign when I've done this because I see no sign of any of the old men wanting reform."

Arata stared at him. Douglas-Scott saw his astonishment at the term 'old men'. "I don't mean to be derogatory," he continued. "But it's the younger men who can see the future – their future – while the older men continue to be locked into their tradition and how things have always been."

"There's some truth in that," admitted Arata. "But sacrificing yourself ....." He stopped as his friend smiled.

"I'm not sacrificing myself, I'm liberating myself." Arata still looked puzzled. "I can do no more than I am going to do. After this, I will be toxic and the big guns at the Vatican will embark on a crusade to discredit me and drag up all sorts of half truths and falsehoods to 'protect the church'."

"Surely not," protested Arata.

"Wait and see. Every organisation, religious or secular, church or business, will go to any lengths to protect itself. It wants to continue to exist and to do that it must protect its reputation. The catholic church thinks it must exist for it's theology says it is the only true church, though many younger men don't believe that any more.

"You don't believe that?" asked Arata.

"I think that's the past. There are lots of devoted Christians who are not catholics. I'm sure God is big enough to accept them."

"Maybe," Arata was grudging in his response, as if Douglas-Scott was now going beyond where he was happy to go.

"Are you confident," Douglas-Scott was testing his friend, "that Christians who are not catholics will be rejected by God?"

"I suppose not," Arata was beginning to squirm a little. "I suppose when you put it like that. But surely the catholic church has a duty towards its own communicants. If they lose faith, then ......"

"Of course, but we are not doing our duty very well, are we?"

"Don't you believe that the great majority of priests are doing a great job?" asked Arata.

"I certainly do. And it is they who are being let down by the small minority of perverts. Sorry to use that word, but unhappily, that's the truth. I believe the Vatican must take measures to pro-actively weed them out without delay."

"I can see why you needed to step away," said Arata glumly.

"If you sense God wants you to stay, then you must," encouraged Douglas-Scott. "It will be up to you to work from the inside."

"Yes, I think that's still my path, although my father would dearly love to see me get involved and, eventually take over, his business."

"Someone said once that a priest is not just for life. I think he meant that it stretched beyond this life, but I think it also means that it doesn't have to be for life."

"But the oath we both swore?"

"Loyalty to the Pope and the catholic church?"

"Yes."

"What if you believe that the catholic church is in deep disarray and the Pope seems not to be able to do anything about it?"

"Ah! You're talking about Gamaliel in Acts 5:39."

Douglas-Scott grinned. "Not a perfect analogy, but good enough." He got up and went over to hug his friend. "You are a great friend and I've come to admire you greatly. I hope you will continue to think well of me. In the meantime, I must retire for there's a little TV interview coming tomorrow and I need to spend some time in prayer beforehand."

Arata Sr. was becoming a little impatient with the progress of the civil claim against the catholic church in New Jersey relating to Dora Webster. He knew the criminal trial of attempted murder was now fixed in the court's calender and if the other case didn't move along, he was in the unenviable position of having to bridge the gap between the criminal lawyers fees and the projected compensation coming from the civil lawyers. He needed some reassurance so he called the partner of the civil firm.

"Morning, my name's Arata and I believe De Luca from Chicago mentioned my name in respect of the compensation claim for Kevin Webster."

"Morning Arata, yes he did. How can I help you?"

"Can you update me on progress, the chance of the claim being successful and the probable amount that might be awarded?"

Arata was nothing if brusque when it came to business. It was appreciated by the lawyer, to whom time was money and who billed his customers in ten minute slots.

"Progress good. Got our best investigator on it and has found lots of evidence of inaction by this diocese with regards to errant priests and some great witnesses of Father Graham's misdoings. So, a great chance. As to the amount....." The lawyer tailed off.

"I'm sure you know," continued the lawyer, "that this church has a track record of hiding its assets prior to filing for bankruptcy."

"Know it very well," said Arata. "Is that what they are going to do?"

"Not clear yet, but we are trying to outflank them on this one if we can, before they do it."

"OK. As you know, I'm underwriting this, so I'd like a weekly update please."

"You shall have it," said the lawyer.

With that, the conversation finished with Arata just a little less unhappy. He needed to be in control and he wasn't. He was still agitated, money meant a lot to him especially as he had inherited nothing and made all he had by his own efforts. Then an idea occurred – perhaps his son might be able to get into the catholic hierarchy in this archdiocese to find out what was going to be their financial strategy.

"Gino, how are you?" Arata Sr. was sounding more upbeat than he felt.

"Father, good to hear from you," replied his son warily.

"I'm sure you've heard about the claim being pursued in regards to Kevin Webster down in Jersey?"

"I have," replied Arata Jr.

"I wonder if you could do me a favour." He then explained his role at the behest of Janice Munroe from the Gazette. He figured that mentioning her would help soften the cautious reaction he already sensed from his son.

"I'm financing the action and hoping that a successful claim will pay for the defence of his grandmother."

"Oh. I see," replied Junior, beginning to realise what might be at stake for his father. "How can I help?"

"Could you try to use any contacts you have within the church down in Jersey to find out whether they intend to hide their assets and declare bankruptcy?"

The priest was dubious. "I'll try. But I don't have any contacts there." Then a thought occurred. "Maybe Douglas-Scott may be able to help. He will have some influence I'm sure as the Pope's ex private secretary."

"Do what you can. I'd be very grateful. If they do pursue this strategy, there may not be sufficient funds available to pay compensation."

"Understood."

Arata Jr. sat back in his chair, for a moment thinking how much his father stood to lose. It was unlike him to put his own money on the line for someone else. Maybe there was hope for him yet. Douglas-Scott had retired for the night, so this would have to wait until after the interview.

Chapter 54

THE RECORDING WAS scheduled for Saturday morning. Janice had arranged for a cab to pick up both priests and transport them to the studio where she and the producers would be ready to welcome them. She hadn't had much time to make a relationship with the staff at the TV studios, feeling as if she was in a goldfish bowl and a little nervous. The producer and studio manager had a copy of her notes and knew the order the interview would take.

She and her interviewee were in the Green Room having just come out of make-up. Then she remembered the cat. "Bloody cat!" A quick apology to the priest for her unseemly outburst and, after a quick explanation, gave Porter a call to get someone round to see if it was outside the front door. If it was let it in and put some food out. Almost immediately, they were called in.

Being on the other side of the camera was very different. She walked around the set for a few minutes to familiarise herself with the layout. The backdrop walls which had been set up for an interview seemed very flimsy and only six feet tall, just enough for the close-ups. A runner dashed past her across the floor to remove some pictures on the backdrop relating to yesterday's basketball coverage, replacing them with blown-up pictures of the Pope, the late Cardinal and other large photographs relating to the catholic church. Boston was home to a large catholic community and the studio wanted to show its support, probably not knowing exactly what Douglas-Scott was going to say although the Gazette interview had already been on the streets for twelve hours.

They sat down on the chairs provided, Janice with her notes on her lap whereas Douglas-Scott, in his priestly robes, was expected to take part without such prompts. Make-up staff rushed in to put last-minute touches to the foreheads and cheeks and the first take got underway. As Janice worked her way through Douglas-Scott's early career, she began to get instructions in her ear to move on to the Vatican days. From then on there was quiet. Most in the studio were probably catholics at one time or another, but all were fascinated to hear what went on in the Vatican behind closed doors. So far, so good. Before they came to the current situation, someone shouted "Cut" and everyone had a break, except the studio staff and producers who were in deep conversation.

The protagonists left the studio and went back to the Green Room when Arata came over to congratulate both.

"Mesmerising," he said. "This will be watched by millions."

Staff were beginning to eat what Janice thought were snacks but, as she looked at her phone, she saw it was lunchtime. The time had flown past. She hadn't thought to bring anything, but Meyer had. He came over to them followed by a young lady who had food and drink for them all. Meyer shook them all by the hand.

"Father Arata, good to meet you. I know your father, of course," he said.

Arata mumbled, "Of course." Then in a louder voice, "Pleasure to meet you."

"And this must be our guest," said Meyer smiling widely. "It's a pleasure to meet you, sir." The media mogul was piling on his appreciation, and why not? He stood to earn a fortune from the programme. His marketing staff were making the most of the launch: advertisements, sponsorship deals and rights agreements across the US and round the world, including Italy.

Douglas-Scott merely nodded and shook Meyer's hand. "And, of course, our interviewer. Ms Munroe, you are doing an excellent job if I might say so. I might have to ask Porter to let you go." He laughed as did Janice, though not as effusively.

"Please enjoy lunch. I have to go but I'm looking forward to watching the show tonight." With that Meyer took his leave. While they all tucked into their lunch, Douglas-Scott asked Arata how Meyer knew his father.

"I suspect my father knows every businessman in the city and maybe beyond," he said apologetically. Janice made no contribution to the conversation. She was thinking about the possibility of changing her career.

Sullivan was still in his hospital bed desperate to get out. He did think of just packing his bag and leaving, but he needed meds. His mind was buzzing with ideas, not at all interested in the 'interview', although he was interested in any adverse reaction to criticism of the catholic church. If it was considerable,

Janice might be toast. Porter would have to let her go or admit their relationship was more than just business. Then he would have no competition. And no, he hadn't read the Gazette that weekend, deliberately. Saturday evening seemed quiet to him. No one came into his room. No one passed by. It was almost as if everyone was watching the wretched interview. Well, let the chips fall where they will. He would survive. He sat up and moved to the edge of the bed, reached for his 'sticks', slotted his hands on the rests and hobbled to the restroom. Looking left and right, every television was on the same channel.

"They must be making a fortune out of this," he thought. "I wonder how much Janice is making out of this? Perhaps she'll end up doing this rather than returning to the paper."

It was on the return journey that he overheard some of the 'cut and thrust' that Janice had promised the priest. He lingered outside his room listening to the TV in the next room. It was the point when she was challenging him about his criticism of the 'old men'. The next room had two beds in it and, it seemed, both men were watching with some passion. One was being a little vocal about the criticism of the 'old men', expressing the view that they had the experience to guide the church, while the other, a much younger man, expressed the contrary opinion with just as much fervour. Each followed up their opinions with stories, personal or otherwise, which attempted to back up their stated beliefs. If this was a microcosm of the city and its environs, then the Gazette could certainly push into that.

Then, ruefully, he realised that Janice would be writing these stories, possibly for weeks to come, just riding a wave of disparate opinion amongst their readership. Letters would be flooding in from both sides. The paper would become the centre of the debate. Readership would rise again and she would become the name associated with the clerical abuse campaign, when it had been he who had broken the story in the first place. The senior investigator settled back in bed and decided to watch. He had to know what he was up against.

He was reluctantly impressed by how Janice questioned the priest, not letting him get away with bland assertions but interrogating him over them. However, the priest certainly knew his stuff and was an excellent communicator. Somehow, without criticising the Pope or any individual, he managed to make a compelling case for reform of the church, certainly as far as errant priests were concerned.

"You've said you're looking for change," Janice was coming to the end of the session. "Perhaps there are two kinds of change: transformational change and incremental change. Which do you want and which do you think you might get?"

The priest laughed. "Change is not a word spoken about much in the Vatican. It's all about protecting the church. In the last century, it was from communism, hence the quasi-support for fascist Germany. Today, it is probably more about secularism."

"What does the Vatican fear about secularism?" asked Janice.

"You might not remember," answered Douglas-Scott, "that in the 50s and 60s, countries such as Spain, Portugal, Italy and Ireland, in particular, were almost ruled by catholic prelates. The priest was god. He heard confession and knew everyone's secrets. Very powerful. Not something you would want to lose."

"We know things have changed in those countries, so what has been the church's response to secularism?"

"The way the Vatican seeks to protect the church is by doubling down on its traditions, doctrines, and history."

"So no change, then?" persisted Janice.

"Pope John was the last Pontiff to realise things had to change. He was quite clear about what he wanted Vatican II to accomplish i.e. the defence and advancement of truth, catholic truth. But he realised that to do that mindsets had to change, both in the Curia, in dioceses and parishes across the world. I believe we are at another moment now. I hope we grasp it."

Janice paused to let the comment sink in, allowing Douglas-Scott to add another.

"Have you listened to an album by Sting called Sacred Love?"

She was thrown off guard for a moment, but quickly collecting herself asked, "You mean the pop artist who was with the Police?"

"Yes," confirmed the priest.

Janice heard the producer in her ear, "Where's he going with this?" It was a one way line and obviously a rhetorical question. Janice didn't have a clue and was thoroughly taken aback that the Pope's ex-PS would know about a Sting album.

The priest continued. "There's a track on it called, 'Let's forget about the future and get on with the past.'" He was smiling to have taken Janice off guard for a moment and added, "I don't know for sure, but I think Sting may have been a catholic at one time. It's very perceptive."

There was a rustling throughout the studio at this revelation so much that the studio manager had to hold his hand up to silently ask for quiet.

Janice heard the producer again in her ear, "Wind up please." So Janice pulled out her copy of that weekend's edition of the Gazette so that everyone could see, and quoted part of his interview where he said he wanted to support the Pope.

She simply asked, "So do you think what you have said here, pointing to the Gazette, and tonight will have been interpreted by the Pontiff as support or a stab in the back?"

He replied with an open face, "With all my heart, I hope the Holy Father finds it supportive."

Janice concluded by saying, "Father Douglas-Scott, thank you." There the interview ended, the credits rolled and, in the studio, the lights went off. Discussion that evening all around Boston, across the US and around the catholic world, would surely continue.

After the recording session had finished mid-afternoon, Janice breathed a great sigh of relief as she and the priest took off their mikes. She had warned him earlier, whilst they were in the Green Room, not to say anything further until they were off the set, just in case anyone in the studio had the idea of keeping the mikes live, hoping to get a tasty extra from the ex-private secretary to the Pope. They were met back in the Green Room by Father Arata who, full of emotion, gave both of them a lingering hug.

On the way out, Janice asked a question of both priests which she didn't want to bring up in the interview but which was intriguing her.

"May I ask you one final question?" she asked.

"Are there any mikes around," joked Douglas-Scott.

Janice smiled, then posed her question. "There seems to be a reluctance among the clergy to recognise civil authorities. Where does that come from?"

"That's a good question which needs more time to answer than we have right now," said Douglas-Scott. "Maybe we could get to that another time. I must confess to being rather tired after your grilling." He smiled so that Janice didn't take it personally. She let them go.

Neither priest wanted to see the broadcast in the evening, the recording had generated enough stress for one day. So for the evening, they dined in the Cardinal's dining room with Arata having told the Cardinal's chef to excel himself one final time before Douglas-Scott flew out of Boston for London the following day. Porter invited Janice for an evening meal both as a congratulatory celebration and as an occasion to find out whether a new career was on the horizon.

After the evening broadcast, Sullivan mischievously wondered what Sunday sermons various catholic priests in Boston would try to deliver the following day. As he thought about their difficulties, he indulged himself with a chuckle or two. Their congregations would certainly be talking about the interview, some on one side, some on the other. Very few would have no opinion whatsoever. It was the hot topic of the day, but for how much longer before everyone moved on?

As he lay in bed, he dug out his phone again from where he had hidden it from the nursing staff. Douglas-Scott had mentioned Ireland in particular, so he began looking at catholic stories from Ireland. Perhaps Jerry had missed something. If not already, the catholic church was becoming something of an obsession for him. He scrolled through stories on his phone cursing the hospital for not allowing him to use his laptop. At least he had his phone.

Jerry had missed something. There it was. But it was not about paedophile priests, which was why he had not included it in his tranche of research. As he began to read, he felt the familiar emotions of indignation and anger. This reinforced his obsession. God, what a church!

This BBC story related to the so-called, 'Magdalene Laundries' of Ireland which was a catholic institution which was thankfully wound up in 1996. During these years, 30,000 Irish women and girls were forcibly confined in these institutions, being labelled 'fallen women'. Most had become pregnant and given birth outside marriage, which for the catholic church, was a terrible sin. No mention of the men who had got these women and girls pregnant! The inmates were forced to clean clothes and scrub floors seven days a week with no pay, had their hair chopped off, and were prevented from speaking. Their names were also changed so that no one in the outside world would be able to find them.

Sullivan had thought he had already seen the worst that the catholic church could do, but he realised he was wrong. This was surely horrendous. These women and girls were deemed flirtatious or promiscuous and were often the victims of rape and sexual assault inside these prisons. There was another institution – mother and baby homes for mothers who had babies out of wedlock. The regime was similar, cruel and vengeful. Sometimes, inmates were trafficked to other laundries either to prevent someone from finding them or because they had become too difficult to handle. In the 1950s, up to 1% of the entire population of Ireland were in such institutions.

"But where was the Irish government in all this?" he asked himself. "Surely criminal offences were being committed daily."

It seemed from the article that the Irish state was involved at least passively, in consenting to catholic doctrine and practices, not wishing to challenge the all-powerful catholic church. But finally, a formal apology for the survivors and compensation of 100,000 euros for each surviving victim was offered from the Irish government. There might have been some compensation from the catholic church, but Sullivan couldn't find any mention of it.

He bookmarked the story and turned off his phone. This was happening in the 'enlightened' Western world. It was surreal, more likely to be a story from Iran or Afghanistan. From a gleeful sense that he had come across another story to feed to his readers, he now felt depressed and dispirited. A melancholic mood came over him as he ruminated on human nature, religion and power.

Chapter 55

BACK AT ST. Es, Sullivan had received his meds, although he had to wait until mid-morning. His patience was wearing thin and was about to get thinner. His daughter had arrived on cue to chauffeur him to the office. He desperately wanted to keep good relations with his daughter who had been estranged for so many years, but much as he wanted to keep his mouth firmly shut, he seemed to have no control over it.

"When was it you passed your test?" he asked.

"Just sit tight and say nothing," replied his daughter, who had been thoroughly briefed by her mom, his ex.

"I was just asking," he pleaded, not very convincingly, holding his hands tightly on his sticks and his feet pressed down firmly on the floor of the vehicle.

He arrived at the office without any mishap but with Sullivan stressed and sweating. He kissed Chloe on the cheek and expressed his thanks, asking whether he could take her out again later.

"Sorry Dad. I'm out with my boyfriend tonight."

"Boyfriend?" stuttered Sullivan.

"Yes, Dad. It's what girlfriends have,"

"And what does this boyfriend do?"

"He's a police officer."

Sullivan turned round, "He's what?"

She smiled at his discomfort and drove off. He stood on the sidewalk and watched as she drove away. "My God," he said under his breath, "she'll be married soon. To a police officer! And I could be a grandfather within a few years." He shook his head and went through the doors of the Gazette. Jimmy, the security man, looked up and stared at him.

"Don't say anything," warned Sullivan. The man smiled and put a finger to his mouth. He went up in the lift for the first time in his career. He arrived in the newsroom resplendent with his joggers and sticks. No fanfare, no clapping of hands. It seemed hardly anyone had missed him. Even Porter wasn't in the Holies. He shuffled over to his desk and sat down and looked across to Janice's desk, wondering where she was. She didn't seem to report to him any more.

Janice had woken up that morning in her own bed. She had enjoyed the meal with Porter which had allowed her to wind down after an amazing but highly stressful day. But she wanted to go back to her place and not have to think of anyone else. Porter understood, kissed her on the cheek and said,

"See you in the office tomorrow." She looked at him and smiled. "Yes, boss."

Although tired, Janice didn't sleep very well. Probably too tired. Odd replays of the interview raced through her mind as her brain decided to mix it all up and take away her success. It was all a mess. Everyone thought she had failed miserably. She should stick to the Gazette. She woke with a start at five o'clock after her brain decided to release another thought. The bloody cat! She had forgotten all about it and it wasn't there when she got home. If someone had let it in as she had asked, they must have let it back out and locked the door so it couldn't get back in. She still hadn't yet organised a cat flap.

She broke out into a sweat. There was little chance of getting to sleep so she got up and looked around the house just to make sure. No cat. Although it was still dark, she opened her back door and switched on the outside light in the vain hope that the feline would be there, somewhere. It wasn't. She thought about leaving some food out but any animal could come and eat it. It wouldn't demonstrate that Dora's cat was close by.

Grabbing some juice, she sat down at her desk to remind herself of what was going on in her life. She had been so taken up with the interview that everything else had faded into the background. She began to make a list:

- The cat and cat flap.
- Dora's case – court case in a few weeks.
- Contact Ms Adams – where's the weekly brief?
- Visit Dora before court, but after talking to the lawyer.
- More copy needed for next weekend's edition - build on reaction to interview.

- TV or Gazette – the future?
- Porter – what do I want?
- Sullivan....

Her pen stopped as she thought of Sullivan. What should she do? If she was going to stay with the paper, they had to get on somehow. She thought again about how a move to TV would solve a number of relationship issues. Then she was interrupted. A faint meow from the door caused her to jump to her feet and rush to the door. Sure enough, outside was Dora's cat waiting patiently to come in.

"Am I glad to see you," said Janice, opening the door but resisting any temptation to pick the thing up. "I expect you'd like some food?" A bowl of food was all ready next to the litter tray. First item n the agenda for the day – organise to get a cat flap. She discovered a likely contractor who was nearby and a quick message to him, albeit at 5.30am meant that she could tick one item off her list.

Now in a much better mood, she began to write her draft copy for next weekend. She didn't yet know the extent of the city's reaction to the interview, but she could easily articulate both sides of the argument. She wrote with that in mind, trying to pick a middle way which wouldn't alienate readers on either side. Nevertheless, the headline and first paragraph had to be punchy other-wise it might not be read. By the time she had finished, it was time to shower and breakfast before heading into the office. Her jacket was hung up by the front door and as she slung it over her shoulder while having a final glance in the mirror, she felt an object in her jacket pocket.

"Shit," she exclaimed as she withdrew the object. A memory stick. "Shit," she repeated having completely forgotten to post it to Ms Adams.

Arriving at the office, the first thing she did was to download the contents onto her desktop and, without even looking at the subject matter, she grabbed a jiffy bag and label and quickly hand-addressed it. A quick note stuffed inside said that she had just found this at Dora's house and hoped it would be useful. A little economical with the truth, but she was not going to put herself in debt to that lawyer.

Sullivan watched this urgency with some interest. "Important?" he asked.

Janice looked at him and decided to play it straight. "Yes. It's a memory stick that Kevin hid in his grandmother's home. I'm hoping it finally nails that priest and he spends a good part of the next decade in some prison somewhere." She almost spat out the words, surprising herself with her vehemence.

"By the way, how are you? I hear you've been through the mill over the last week or so." It was said without any edge and it seemed Sullivan hadn't taken it any other way.

"I'm OK," he responded evenly. "Well done on the interview, by the way. You're quite a star now," he observed.

"Thanks. It was quite stressful, actually," she replied. "But good to be back to normal."

"Thought you might want to do that full-time, instead of being here?"

"No one's offered me a job and, besides, the main reason it came over so well was that I knew the man and had interviewed him before for the paper. That probably won't happen again."

There was a pause in the conversation. "Still," continued Sullivan, "just once a week wouldn't be too onerous."

Janice shrugged, she had no more to say on the subject. She settled herself to interrogate Kevin's files when Sullivan suddenly said quietly, "I know."

Without looking around, Janice replied, "You know what?"

"I know about you and Porter."

Janice froze momentarily, then tried to shrug it off. "Not been stalking again, have we?" she asked sarcastically.

"There's a reason why relationships are forbidden between a senior and more junior member of staff here," stated Sullivan.

"Is that so?" said Janice now turning around to look at her colleague. "And what kind of relationship do you think we have?"

Asking such a full-on question seemed to stop Sullivan momentarily in his allegations.

"Go on," pressed Janice, her tone of voice now becoming quite ominous.

"Well," started Sullivan, deciding he had to finish what he started, but thinking that he might have got all this wrong. "I know you had a fling when he first got divorced and I know you've recently had evening meals together."

"Is that it?" asked Janice, now quite aggressively.

"It doesn't take a genius to see how easy it would be to go further," said Sullivan, sounding as if he was already defeated.

"So you're the relationship genius, are you?" asked Janice, knowing how Sullivan had botched up every relationship with women he had ever had.

"No need to be so sarcastic," said Sullivan. "And never with anyone at the paper."

"It is a vicious allegation with no basis in fact. But now you've mentioned it, perhaps I will invite Porter round to my place for some nooky."

Sullivan stayed quiet. What had started as a peaceful conversation between colleagues was now anything but. It seemed there was no way back from this. Janice was fuming with indignation and now unable to concentrate on anything. She just sat in her seat pretending to read what was on her screen but thinking furiously about the situation. Porter was in his office. She could march in there giving Sullivan the message that she was going to complain, she could sit there and try to get on with re-reading her draft for next week's front page, or she could go home and work there.

In the end, it was Sullivan who struggled to his feet and made his way slowly to the editor-in-chief's office. Janice watched him go, wondering what he was going to say. He wasn't in there long. When he came out, he returned to his desk, switched off his computer and, without a word, hobbled out of the newsroom. He sat in reception downstairs waiting for an Uber to take him home.

Meanwhile, as Janice looked over to Porter, he signalled to come in.

"Can't the two of you get on?" he asked once Janice had come in, but already knowing the answer.

Father Arata had a problem. His father. Yes, he had asked Douglas-Scott whether he would contact the Cardinal in the Jersey diocese. The man from Rome thought it might be best if it was done before the interview but unfortunately, the Gazette was already on the streets. And yes, he had got straight through to the Cardinal by virtue of his past position. It had been a tricky conversation.

"Your Eminence, thank you for taking my call."

"A pleasure, Father. What can I do for you?"

Douglas-Scott hesitated, a little for effect. "I have heard since I have been in the US, that there are some legal tangles that are affecting your archdiocese."

"Yes, there are. But we are tackling them in a spirit of goodwill." The Cardinal didn't elaborate on what a 'spirit of goodwill' meant.

"I've also heard that some archdioceses in the US are indulging in," he paused again, "shall we say dubious financial engineering, thereby reducing the value of assets by which to pay compensation to victims." There, he had said it. Either he was going to be told it was none of his business or he would be assured that would not be the case in his archdiocese.

In the event, it was neither of these.

"May I ask what your interest is," asked the Cardinal suspiciously.

"I'm sure you are just as concerned for the reputation of the church as am I, and also the Holy Father," he added. "If the press were to get hold of such practices, it would not look good."

"Of course," rejoined the Cardinal. "I agree."

"I hope you didn't mind my call. Unfortunately, I'm flying to London on Monday, otherwise, I would have loved to have visited you."

"I wish you a pleasant flight," said the Cardinal.

Father Arata ruminated on the conversation as Douglas-Scott relayed it to him. It sounded positive but, now the interview had gone out, he wasn't sure whether the Cardinal's tentative agreement would stand. Anyway, he had to call his father.

"Ciao Gino," said Arata Sr. "You have news?"

"Yes. Father Douglas-Scott was happy to call the Cardinal and he agreed it would not be good publicity if indeed they did secret away their assets."

"Excellent," said his father.

"But...." said his son.

"I thought there might be a but," interrupted his father.

"That agreement was made before the broadcast interview he did. I'm not sure if such an agreement will still stand." The priest was apologetic.

"Yes, I understand," said Arata Sr.

"But I have had an idea which may be useful to you."

"What's that?"

"The Gazette did a spread not very long ago about this very subject. There might be a way to use a copy of that paper to good effect in Jersey?"

"Nice idea, Gino. Let me think about it. Ciao."

Chapter 56

THE FOLLOWING MORNING, the two priests went off to the airport driven by the Cardinal's chauffeur with Arata in his cassock and Douglas-Scott in jeans. Understandably, he wanted to be as anonymous as possible but whether that objective would be achieved Arata thought was doubtful, although the Boston Red Sox baseball cap would certainly help his disguise. He received a little extra attention as he passed through passport control but no one blinked an eye through security and, once he had skipped the pleasures of duty-free, he was finally able to relax.

"Don't bother to answer," said Porter to his rhetorical question about his investigators' relationship with each other. Janice was kept standing until he signalled her to sit down.

She sat down. He gave a deep sigh. "Sullivan has resigned."

"What?" This was the last thing she had expected. "Why?"

"Why do you think?" Porter looked at her. "Why the hell can't you two get on? You used to be able to."

"We were having a civilised conversation today but then he went completely off-piste."

"How?"

Janice squirmed in her seat a little. She explained his accusation and her response. Porter was silent and looking out of his window. Janice waited.

"If Meyer offered you the interview job, which I don't know whether he will," he quickly added, "would you take it?"

Janice could see where the chips were falling. It did make sense but if it didn't work out, where would she go. Porter was looking at her carefully.

"I'm speaking as your boss, not as your...er....friend," he said.

"With a couple of provisos."

"Which are?"

"That I get a year's contract and that if they want rid of me, I can come back here."

"Woah. No problem with getting your job back here, but the other? That's way above my pay grade."

"Meyer won't want Sullivan to go. He's the golden goose and he knows the competition will snap him up so it would be in Meyer's interests to keep Sullivan here. But I've probably already made him lots of money without any payment, so it's a toss-up."

Porter grunted. "I knew you were a smart lady," he said. Then broke into a smile. "If we pull this off, we could have evening meals together regardless of whether Sullivan is peeping in at the window." Janice also smiled.

"I'll make the call," said Porter, "and let you know." Janice was dismissed. Back at her desk, she gave her front page copy another look-over, emailed it to Porter when she was satisfied, arranged a visit at the prison, and set off for Jersey.

"I hear you've been busy," remarked Dora, once she and Janice had been put together.

"How did you know?" Janice expressed some surprise.

"The interview was carried on CNN and I managed to watch it as it was pertinent to my case."

Janice looked at her. She was a lot brighter than she had seemed during the last visit. "I hope it was good viewing," said Janice.

"It was excellent. You're a natural. You managed to be sensitive but pugnacious at the same time, not letting him get away with anything."

"Well, it wasn't quite like that. I wanted to put the other point of view to give him a chance to defend the catholic church."

"But it was obvious that there was no defence when it came to paedophile priests."

"I agree," said Janice. "Moving on – your cat is with me, safe and well in Boston."

"Thank you. I was going to ask you. She prefers Go Cat, by the way."

"I'll make sure to get some," replied Janice. "So. Have you seen your lawyer recently?"

"Yes, she came in last Friday and said the Grand Jury stage was complete and it was all going well."

"Did she give any details?"

"Not really, except that a copy of the laptop would have been good, but the police and prosecution have that." Dora began to lose her positivity until Janice said,

"You'll never guess what I found when I went to your house?" Janice stopped suddenly. She nearly said 'to oversee the removal company', until she remembered just in time that Dora knew nothing about her house being repossessed by the landlord.

"What?" asked Dora.

Janice looked around to make sure no one was listening, then dropped her voice to a whisper. "In Kevin's closet, there was a bit of plaster and plaster-board missing."

"Yes. I'd always planned to get that fixed, but never got around to it," said Dora also lowering her voice.

"Just as well because when I put my finger in there, I found Kevin's memory stick."

"He had a memory stick?"

"Yes and I suspect he downloaded everything that was on his laptop."

"My goodness me. That means we have a copy of his laptop." Her face visibly brightened.

"So I've sent it to Ms. Adams but I haven't heard back from her. It could be a game-changer."

"Good news, at last," said Dora. "And just in time."

"What do you mean?" asked Janice.

"The trial has been brought forward to next week," said Dora. "I assumed you knew."

Janice was cursing Ms. Kristin Adams quietly but also feeling guilty for forgetting to post the memory stick earlier. Her face betrayed nothing. "It doesn't matter. When next week?"

"Monday."

"I'll be there," said Janice.

On the way out of the facility, Janice felt her phone vibrate in her pocket. It was the lawyer informing her, by text, of the trial date at the Somerset County Superior Court the following Monday morning at ten.

"That bloody lawyer had better do better with the court than she has with me," said Janice out loud as she was walking out to her car.

Porter was on the phone to Meyer hoping to find some solution to the personnel problem he had. He didn't want to admit to the media mogul that Sullivan – the golden goose – had resigned, but was hoping that Meyer would hire Janice, allowing him the upper hand when he contacted Sullivan. But the German was playing it cagey.

"She did well, no doubt about it. But we haven't finalised our schedule yet. I haven't yet decided that a Saturday night interview is viable. I mean, how many top celebrities can we get? It might start well, but I don't want it to fizzle out with third-rate guests."

Porter was getting desperate. "What if, instead of putting her on the payroll, you took Janice on a self-employed basis? Obviously, you'd have to give her reasonable notice, but then you're not committed to having another person on the payroll. It would be more payment by results."

"You're sounding as if you want to move her on?"

"God, no. But I can see the synergy between what we publish at the weekend with what you interview on Saturday evenings. It worked very well last time. She would write the story for the Gazette on Friday, then do the interview on Saturday."

"What about Sullivan?"

"I don't think he'd make a very good interviewer," said Porter, tongue in cheek.

"Very funny," replied Meyer. "I'll think about it."

End of conversation.

Sullivan waited in reception much to the amusement of Jimmy who, it turned out was a bit of a comic. So until his Uber arrived, the journalist had to endure:

"What do you call a guy who has broken all his arms and legs?"

"I don't know," said Sullivan, not really paying attention.

"An ambulance! Jimmy doubled over as he laughed. Sullivan was unmoved.

"What do you get when you cross a busy road with a broken leg and a blindfold?"

Sullivan sighed, hoping that Uber wouldn't be very long.

"Hit." Another round of laughter.

"I think I need a smoke," said Sullivan, and took the opportunity to make his way slowly through the revolving doors to the pavement. As he smoked, he thought again about what he had done. Did he mean it? What was he going to do? Would Porter just carry on with Janice? If so, he would have to try the competition. No, he really didn't want to do that. Working at the Gazette was comfortable. At his age, he didn't want to start over with new people, new processes, and having to prove himself all over again. So why had he told Porter he was resigning? Of course, he hadn't written anything down yet, so it wasn't a real resignation, was it? But could he carry on with Janice still in the office? Maybe he had been out of order but he wasn't going to play second fiddle.

At that moment he saw two young nuns walking past in their black and white habits. He took a double take at these girls having always assumed nuns were much older.

"I suppose everyone has to be young once," he mused. As he looked closer, he realised that they were not much older than his daughter. Why on earth would they be wasting their life? There was so much to live for. His mind went back to the Magdalene Laundries of Ireland.

"I wonder how many of those nuns were young like these two? Surely they must have known that something was seriously wrong." Then a horrible thought crossed his mind.

"What happened to the babies?" If they took in pregnant girls who weren't married, what happened to the babies, if the girls were working in the laundries seven days a week? He remembered that the report spoke of mother and baby units. Maybe they were transferred there?

His reporter's nose was twitching. He could smell a scandal here, knowing what he did about the Magdalene Laundries. He was about to turn around and march back into the newsroom and dig out the details at his desk, but then realised he had resigned.

Here was his Uber. He stubbed out his cigarette, got in and went home.

His leg was aching as he went up to his apartment. He needed some meds immediately, then some sleep. It occurred to him as he was dropping off, that perhaps he ought to request a regular check-up, after all, he was entitled to one, even though his recent hospital stay probably cost a fortune. Ahhh. Sleeping in his own bed, waking up when he wanted, no one wanting to prod or poke him and food to his taste. It was good to be home!

It was way past nine the next morning when his cellphone rang, disturbing a pleasant dream about ….. he couldn't remember. It was Porter.

"Sullivan, have you calmed down from yesterday yet?"

The reporter struggled to get up and swing his legs over the side of the bed. "Well, I may have been a bit overwrought from the hospital experience, but something needs to be done."

"I agree," said Porter.

"What are you going to do?"

"I agree that you were overwrought and in the cold light of day, probably didn't mean what you said."

"Oh," said Sullivan. "So you're not going to do anything?"

"I didn't say that, but I'm the editor-in-chief and I'm not going to be held to ransom by anyone."

Sullivan said nothing so Porter continued. "Something will be done and I will make some changes. No one will like everything, but this newsroom is a team and I can only have team players. I need to know from you within the next twenty-four hours, whether you're going to be a team player or not."

Sullivan still said nothing. Porter was sweating on the other end of the call. Had he been too hard? Would Sullivan back down?

"I can give you that answer right now," said Sullivan. Porter anxiously waited. "I'll be a team player and I've got a story."

"I'm glad to hear it," said Porter. "See you back in the office tomorrow and we'll talk about the front pages." He cut the call before overwhelming relief showed in his voice. He knew it was not entirely over yet, but he had won the first round and a smile played around his face.

Chapter 57

FATHER ARATA HAD just heard that a new Archbishop was to be appointed to the Boston archdiocese. That wasn't news since the vacancy meant that someone would eventually be appointed. What made it news was the speed at which this particular appointment was to be made. Such an appointment could easily take up to six months to make and was a complicated process, as are most involving the Vatican. Many parties have input to the process: neighbouring bishops, the faithful, the apostolic nuncio, various members of the Vatican Curia, and the Pontiff himself, all might have a role in the selection.

Perhaps, because of all the negative publicity that the Gazette had given the catholic church, the Pope had decided that the post couldn't remain vacant for long. Father Arata remembered one of the remarks that Douglas-Scott made before he left. It was to watch for a pattern in the appointees to senior clerical positions in the church. So Arata had been watching, not just for his own potential future, but to try to discern what His Holiness was saying to his church through these appointees since he would have the final say on the candidate.

The priest decided to call his friend in the UK. He was halfway through dialling his number when, at the last minute, he remembered the time difference. It might be late evening across the pond, but he felt sure that Douglas-Scott would still be up and about. He was.

"Good evening, my friend," Douglas-Scott greeted his friend.

"Good afternoon to you," rejoined Arata. "You remember that before you left you said to watch out for senior clerical appointments?"

"Yes, I remember," said Douglas-Scott.

"Well, after only a few months, I'm going to get a new boss."

"Congratulations."

"Whether that will be the case is a moot point," said Arata. "The point is, he's in his late sixties."

"Oh!" exclaimed Douglas-Scott. "That doesn't sound good."

"Same old, same old." Arata was disappointed. "It was to be expected, I suppose."

"Sounds like there has been some successful lobbying," replied Douglas-Scott.

"I was hoping that he would be a reformer and His Holiness would have heard the cry."

"He might turn out to be a good man," replied Douglas-Scott, "Who is it?"

"Someone from the Mid-West, I heard. I thought His Holiness could appoint who he wanted?"

"There's a limit to what he could do if there is a swell of opinion within certain factions. But he will meet with them personally at the Vatican and I'm sure he will convey his wishes."

Arata was quiet. A 'good night' from Douglas-Scott brought an end to the call, leaving Arata a bit less positive about his future.

Janice had the all-clear from Porter to go to the first day of Ms Webster's trial in Jersey providing there was a good story to come. Janice had no idea about the story. She just wanted to be there for her 'next of kin' and to scrutinise the lawyer. Something inside wanted Ms. Adams to fail abysmally but that would mean Dora would be found guilty and jailed. That was a luxury too far. Privately though, Janice was of the opinion that unless the lawyer came up with legal issues with the prosecution case or overwhelming mitigation, it was a slam dunk. After all, she did try to kill the priest and had already confessed to it, so it was as open and shut a case as ever there was. Janice was not hopeful.

She was not allowed to see Dora – lawyers only. She could only give a little wave from the public area but Dora didn't seem to see her. Her eyes were downcast and her demeanour defeatist. Janice was angry that Ms Adams had not prepared her properly. Surely she should have been told to look positive and confident of the right verdict, but what did she know? She couldn't do anything now since the dice was already rolling and it would land where it would land.

Opening statements were predictable and told Janice nothing knew. No mention by either party of the laptop or its contents which, she thought, must come later during the cut and thrust. At the close of business, she felt that she had wasted her time. There seemed to be no story here until the final verdict, unless.....

After the call from Porter, Sullivan remained on the edge of his bed thinking about what he wanted to do. And what he wanted was to file a story about catholic nuns and the babies that they inherited from the pregnant girls they took in. Shuffling as best he could on his sticks, he got himself back into the office. No one took any notice because no one knew anything was amiss. Even Porter, who saw him drag himself in, dropped his eyes again and let the reporter get on with what he wanted to write.

Sullivan's nose had picked up the scent of a cover-up and he was going to blow the conspiracy wide open. He felt like this every time a potential scandal was about to be uncovered. This was his job, his destiny. This was where he belonged. No one was going to stop him. He turned on his desktop and started looking for Irish mother-and-baby institutions. As his imagination was running rampant, he envisaged catholic nuns involved in child trafficking, perhaps for cash but with the best of motives, of course.

Ah. Here it was. It all came to light in a place called Tuam in County Galway. Hundreds of babies had been found buried in a mass, unmarked grave. Sullivan stopped.

"What?" he exclaimed out loud. "This can't be. Surely nuns can't be murdering hundreds of babies?"

The exclamation caused a few heads to turn in the office. "Sorry," he called out. Who was reporting this? He looked at the by-line. It was the BBC. Reasonably reliable, he thought. He carried on reading.

The institution mainly housed women and girls who had become pregnant outside marriage, widely viewed as shameful and socially unacceptable throughout most of the 20th Century in Ireland. It prompted the Irish government to set up a wide-ranging investigation into the operation of mother and baby homes, in a bid to shed light on the lives and deaths of thousands of former residents.

"Thousands!" exclaimed Sullivan again. "What the hell has been going on?" More staff in the newsroom looking up this time. Sullivan didn't even bother to apologise this time. He was on to something and like a hound following a scent, he was going to corner and catch his prey. He kept reading.

This mother-and-baby home was started in 1925 in a former workhouse in Tuam. Although owned by Galway County Council, it was run by catholic nuns – the Bon Secours Sisters. For the next 36 years, it housed unmarried mothers and their children during a period when such women and girls were ostracised by Irish society and often by their own families if they became pregnant outside marriage. It was a serious sin. Abortion was even more serious.

"Bloody theology," exclaimed Sullivan. "Who's to say what is a sin and what isn't? And if this is the result of theology, I'm sure God doesn't approve. And where were the men who got these girls pregnant? Where were they?" He made a note to get a catholic view. Who? He didn't know yet. He couldn't contact Father Arata because he had already been hauled over the coals for contacting him, and he wasn't about to do that again. Anyway, he'd work that out when he got the story straight. He kept reading.

Tuam was just one of several similar institutions in which about 35,000 single mothers gave birth. Research showed that, on average, a child from the home died every two weeks between 1925 and 1961. These deaths took place during a period when Ireland had a 'very high infant mortality rate' mainly due to various diseases.

"Unbelievable," Sullivan was appalled and delighted at the same time. Appalled that kids his daughter's age were having their babies taken away with many of them dying and delighted because his obsession with knocking the catholic church was vindicated yet again. It was like taking candy from a baby. He began to wonder whether that was the fault of the Irish state or the nuns not being medically trained or perhaps inadequately supervised by the catholic church. Most likely, the church fully endorsed what the nuns were doing. More reading.

Having fallen into a dilapidated state, the Tuam mother-and-baby home was shut and its remaining residents transferred to similar homes around the country, but no records were kept of where the Tuam babies were buried. Remains were eventually found in a large underground 'structure' which was divided into twenty chambers relating to the treatment or storage of sewage or wastewater.

Sullivan held his head in his hands. "They threw them into their septic tanks. Can't be surely? Dropped them in? Lowered the bodies down on ropes? How?" The reporter was past saying he'd seen it all. Every day of this investigation seemingly brought new horrors from the catholic church.

"Probably said a prayer as the babies bodies were dropped and concealed from prying eyes. Bit late to pray," added Sullivan, rather devoid of any knowledge of catholic doctrine. There were no official records of any of these deaths lodged either with the state or within their own order.

"That confirms it," said the reporter exultantly. "They were concealing the truth. There was a conspiracy between the nuns, maybe between nuns and priests, perhaps even between them and the Irish state. Unbelievable!" said Sullivan now shaking his head.

There was a comment from the current Taoiseach (Prime Minister), a man called Enda Kenny who described the burial site as a 'chamber of horrors.'

"This is directly from the Middle Ages," muttered Sullivan. "Maybe that's where the catholic church still is?" Thoughts were racing through his mind. Where were the priests supposedly supervising these nuns? Were the nuns just obeying orders? How many babies were born to girls already in these homes were the result of priestly abuse? A few years ago, he would have laughed such suggestions out of court, but now? Maybe it was a conspiracy imposed by the priests on the nuns? But nuns wouldn't turn a blind eye to all of this, would they?

"Unless," he thought, "they were told they were doing God's will?"

There were eighteen such institutions in Ireland during this time, another one at Bessborough in County Cork, reported by the Irish broadcaster, RTE. More than 900 children died while resident here and it is still not known where the vast majority are buried. Sullivan did a quick calculation. If all eighteen had the same number of deaths as Bessborough, that made 16,200 child deaths in total.

The Sisters of Bon Secours were on record as offering their 'profound apologies' to all the women and children who lived at the Tuam home, their families and to the people of Ireland. The order admitted its nuns,

"did not live up to our Christianity when running the home. We acknowledge in particular that infants and children who died at the home were buried in a disrespectful and unacceptable way. For all that, we are deeply sorry."

Sullivan sat back in his chair, his mind in a whirl. What a completely warped attitude to sexuality and intimacy by the catholic church. Totally dysfunctional. Young mothers and their sons and daughters forced to pay a terrible price for the catholic church's legalistic doctrines.

"I wonder if they thought that these kids, born out of wedlock, were somehow evil or tainted and were deliberately allowed to die?" Again, a question he would not have given any credence to a few weeks ago. But now......

"I bet," said Sullivan carrying on talking to himself, "that there are still nuns and priests in the catholic church who think this was the right thing to do."

Sullivan turned his attention to getting a catholic view on all this. Instead of finding a person, he decided to find a book entitled, 'Catholic Doctrine for Dummies'. Of course, such a book didn't exist, but others did. He discovered that it was Augustine of Hippo who postulated that human beings were born into sin from the beginning – the doctrine of Original Sin. This has been embedded in all western religion, both catholic and protestant.

"How on earth did the catholic church manage to keep this doctrine going when the faithful became more educated, more scientific." Sullivan mulled this one over. He then read that the Eastern church never took on the idea of Original Sin, but rather embraced a doctrine of what might be called Original Blessing – that all creation, human and non-human, reflected the image of the Creator.

Interesting, but this didn't really help in the construction of his front page story. He wondered what his Dad would have made of it, but he was dead. However, his Mom wasn't.

Chapter 58

JANICE WAS DESPERATELY trying to find a story in the proceedings of the first day of Dora's trial until she realised that the real story was in another court-house not far away, where Father Graham and the catholic church were on trial. Suddenly, the awful truth struck her. The memory stick. She should have sent it to those prosecuting this paedophile priest. She didn't know to whom she should send a copy. A quick call to Arata Sr.

"Hi Janice," greeted Arata Sr. now on quite familiar terms with the reporter.

"Can you tell me who is leading the prosecution case against Father Graham?"

"Father who?" asked Arata Sr.

"The priest who is being prosecuted for abusing Kevin Webster. You know, Dora Webster's grandson."

"Ah. May I ask why you want to know? I don't want some front page exposé which would damage the case." Arata Sr. was initially suspicious of everyone. It was just how he was.

"I've found a memory stick where Kevin has detailed what this priest did to him."

Suddenly Arata Sr. was alert. "Really?"

"Yes really," said Janice, a little put out.

Arata Sr. then gave her a phone number which she called and, mentioning Arata's name, broke the explosive news to him. It took a few seconds for Aaron Mulligan, the attorney, to realise what Janice was saying.

"We've already started the trial," he said.

"I know. That's why I'm calling you. It's also being used in the defence of Ms. Webster, Kevin's grandmother. I can't believe you didn't reach out to the law firm who is defending her."

No reply was forthcoming from the embarrassed attorney.

Janice continued. "Text me your email address and I'll send it over. It's a large file. It'll be quicker than trying to get anything out of that firm."

"Who are they?" asked the attorney. Janice told him and he sneered with disdain.

"You don't seem to like them," commented Janice.

"That's putting it mildly," replied the attorney. "Right, I've sent my personal address over. Can you do this right now?"

A few touches of her keyboard later and she replied, "On its way. Good luck."

He replied, "We may have to ask for a continuance."

Petty squabbles between defence law firms were par for the course, as were difficulties between defence firms and prosecuting authorities so she took no notice of the attorney's contempt. Often the latter moved into the former after a suitable time in position, especially if their careers showed signs of peaking. But she had her story. She could weave both together convincingly, thus continuing to support Dora and expose the catholic church.

Sullivan was on his way to visit his mother. He usually managed to make the journey to Richmond, Virginia for Thanksgiving. Now he thought about it, did he go last year? He couldn't remember. But usually most Christmases, with a few exceptions over the last couple of years. He always felt a little guilty but he didn't regard himself as a bad son, just incredibly busy. Investigative journalism was his lifeblood and nothing got in the way of that. At least that's how it had been. But now a new relationship with his daughter was changing him.

He began to think about his Mom a little more. She was getting on in years now – must be eighty, he thought. In reality, she was nearly ninety, but still as sharp as she'd always been, at least she had been when he had last spoken to her, which was...... he couldn't quite remember. He began to wonder how she was managing on her own. Now he thought about it, didn't she have a double hip operation a few years back? Yes, but he couldn't get away to go and see her. It had been right at the time he had struck gold with the Keating revelations. There was no way he could have spent time away from the office.

It was an eleven-hour drive to Richmond, so he decided to take a Jet Blue flight; only two hours flight time from eleven until one o'clock in the afternoon. He hired a small Toyota on his expense account and drove from the airport to the house where he had grown up and his mother still lived. She had refused to move even after his father had died. At two o'clock he was parking his ride next to an American Foursquare house commonly found in Virginia and other parts of the East Coast. These homes were built in the early 1900s, but his father had looked after it well. He sat outside for a few moments looking at the square or rectangular shape with its hipped roof and wide front porch. It hadn't had much attention since his father had passed away. Perhaps he should again suggest she move, but he knew the firm but negative riposte he would receive.

He had phoned earlier so she knew he was coming but didn't know exactly why. There had to be a reason, for her son rarely did anything without purpose and usually to do with his job. She would wait and see. Her hearing was still good and that was a knock on the door. She galvanised herself into action as fast as she could. Mustn't keep the busy man waiting.

"I'm coming," she yelled as she made her way leaning on her trusty frame. It took her fully two minutes to get to the door.

"Why didn't you just come in?" she scolded him.

"Sorry," he replied with some embarrassment as he saw the struggle his mother was undertaking.

He gave her a gentle hug before she turned to replace her steps whilst he shut the door and followed her meekly into the sitting room where news was exchanged after he had made her and himself a drink in the kitchen. She expressed some pleasure when he told her of his renewed relationship with her granddaughter but she was waiting for him to get to the point. It wasn't long in coming.

"Mom. You remember that exposé we did about the priest who had been abusing his altar boys?"

"Yes, I remember," his mother replied.

"Well, we've found a lot more. Priests all over America, all over Europe, indeed all over the world."

"It's disgusting," said the eighty-nine year old.

Sullivan settled himself down now he had introduced the topic. "There must be something wrong with their theology, or traditions, or something. I mean, how can this be happening all over the world?"

The old lady paused as if surprised her son was raising this as the topic he wished to discuss. After a moment's thought, she said, "I'm not an expert on the catholic church. Haven't you got anyone else to ask?"

"I'm interested in what you think," said Sullivan, leaning forward. "After all, you and Dad know about these things."

"I do remember something," she said after thinking a little. "It was Cardinal Heenan, who was the top catholic in the UK. He was asked once what word he would use to describe the catholic church." She stopped.

"What did he say," asked Sullivan, anxious to hear.

"Authority."

Sullivan sat back. "That says it all," he remarked. "Some priests, even bishops, take their clerical authority as permission to do whatever they want, knowing that they can always have confession and have it all go away."

"But it's not just them," said his elderly mother.

"What do you mean?" asked Sullivan.

"What about those tele-evangelists?" She saw her son's face drop as she moved away from the catholic church. She carried on. "And the Episcopal church, with probably other smaller ones too. I don't think any were on anything like the same scale, but it'll happen wherever you get a power differential, be it in church, politics, TV and film, or big corporations. Powerful men like to take advantage of those who look up to them."

Sullivan stared at his mother. She was still as sharp as a needle. He was enjoying this conversation but he wanted to focus in on what he had come to ask.

"You know the Bible better than me," he started. "Can I ask you some questions about what catholics believe?"

She looked at her son. "I guess you're not going to church any more, then?" she asked.

"No. I think I've gone off all things church," Sullivan replied.

His mother grunted a little bit of displeasure. "I suppose that's understandable," she conceded. "Anyway, ask me what you came here to ask?"

"Much of the power of a local priest is his 'supposed' authority to forgive your sins, no matter what you've done or how many times you've done it. Where does that come from?"

"Your father would know better than I, but I think it's partly based on a verse in John's gospel where Jesus says to his disciples: 'If you forgive the sins of any, their sins have been forgiven them; if you retain the sins of any, they have been retained.' They believe that apostolic succession came down from Peter to the Pope, down to archbishops and bishops, and even to the lowly parish priest.

"But you and Dad never believed that?"

"No, of course not."

"Why?"

"You can't just take a verse like that out of its context and make it mean whatever you want it to mean."

"What does it mean then?"

"You have to remember that none of what is in the Bible, whether Old or New Testaments, was written **to** us. It was written **to** other people; the Jewish people in the Old Testament and mostly to Gentile converts in the New."

"You've lost me now, Mom," said Sullivan.

"They all lived in a different time, in different cultures."

"Are you saying that none of it is relevant to us?"

"Of course not. The Bible may not have been written **to** us, but was certainly written **for** us."

"So we have to look at the context of what is being said," said Sullivan, the light slowly dawning.

"That's what I believe, and that's what your father thought. Some might disagree."

She laid back in her chair looking exhausted. She picked up her tea. "Son, this tea is cold. Could you warm it up please?"

Sullivan got up and took the cup into the kitchen, glad for the moment to think about what his mother had said. He didn't think that the Gazette would do theology but there was certainly food for thought here. He took the heated tea back into the sitting room, where his mother had fallen back to sleep with her mouth open and some faint snoring could be heard. He looked at his watch wondering how long she would sleep and should he stay. He decided to stay for an hour but, if she slept longer he would leave a note explaining that he would come back soon. This time he meant it.

In exactly an hour, he penned the note and left the house to make his way back to the airport. He had work to do.

Chapter 59

JANICE'S STORY ABOUT the various legal processes in New Jersey was relegated to page three. She understood that readers needed a rest from full-on page one exposés week after week, but she was disappointed especially as Sullivan's story about wider catholicism got a centre spread. He had managed to find some internet articles both for and against catholic doctrine and Porter seemed quite impressed with the balance he had achieved. He was back in favour.

Still no decision from Meyer about the TV job for Janice which was causing Porter some angst, not just because of the relationship between his investigators, but because he wanted to firm up some other changes he wanted to make in the newsroom. He looked out of his office to see Janice and Sullivan working away but now with desks slightly shifted, so they weren't looking at each other.

He shook his head, unable to understand what was so serious that these two would hardly speak to each other. His phone rang. He looked at it. Meyer. What did he want?

"You'll be pleased to know that I've made a decision," he announced as if Porter, by some weird osmosis process, was able to know what he was talking about.

"About Janice and the Saturday night interview spot?" he asked, hopefully.

"Sorry, no." said the mogul.

"Then what?" asked Porter rather impatiently.

"I've decided to purchase another paper," he said.

"OK. That's nice for you, but what's that got to do with me?" Porter felt frustration rising.

"It's in Providence, Rhode Island, just down the road from you."

"Which paper? There's already a few in that region?"

"Top secret, at the moment," said Meyer conspiratorially.

"Oh!" said Porter, not really interested.

"I want you to be editor-in-chief for both papers with a local editor in each location."

"Oh!" said Porter again, now with a renewed interest.

"Do you want the job?"

"Sure, if the deal is right," replied Porter.

"I'm very pleased with what you've done at the Gazette and I'm suggesting that Janice become the editor in Boston and....." Porter could see where this was going.

"Sorry to interrupt. I'd like to visit the paper in Providence when that's official and then decide how to proceed with my staff."

Meyer chuckled. "I have no problem with that," he said. "You know, I trust you implicitly." There was a click as Meyer's phone went dead. Porter knew the continuing trust of his publisher was in direct proportion to the continuing profitability of the paper, but he felt sure there was a tidy sum in the Meyer trust bank at the moment. This revelation meant there was a lot to think about, but nothing he could immediately do. Nothing was going to be said to any staff because, knowing Meyer, it might all collapse.

Janice spent day two of Dora's trial in another courthouse. She wanted to assess how the prosecution of Father Graham and the catholic archbishopric was progressing and hopefully speak to the attorney who now had Kevin's laptop files.

It was a lot more interesting than the previous day. The prosecution was continuing to set out its case with brutal rationality. She guessed the emotion would come later. It seemed their investigator had done his job well with a host of uncomfortable questions for the representatives of the catholic church. At four o'clock, the judge called an end to the day and Janice introduced herself to the attorneys outside the courtroom.

"Excuse me, who is Aaron Milligan?"

"I am," said a slim, well-manicured middle aged man. "Who are you?"

"I'm Janice Munroe. I sent you the laptop files."

"Good to meet you," he said hurriedly and offered his hand which Janice shook. "Sorry, I need to get back to the office. Can I leave you in the hands of my investigator?"

Before Janice could answer, he had pivoted away, signalling to a burly sixty-year-old who nodded and came over to Janice to introduce himself.

"Hi, I'm Marek Wyszynski, Wizz to my friends. I understand it was you who got the laptop contents."

"Hi, Wizz. From today's proceedings, it sounds like you've already done a thorough job for your employers."

"Thank you, but I'm not an employee just a humble freelancer. However, I've had a glance at the contents of the files you sent over and they're dynamite."

"I'm hoping it will enable you to up the compensation claim," said Janice.

"Why?"

"Because Kevin's grandmother is being tried on attempted murder of your defendant in a courtroom not too far from here and she will need to have some money to start over."

Wizz lifted his eyebrows. "That's tough," he said. "These men are scum, and I say that as a catholic myself. But I have no input in how such monies get parcelled out."

"Of course. I've also sent the laptop contents to the lawyers defending her, so I'm hoping that they can use it to help the jury see the mitigation," explained Janice.

"Have you asked my attorneys to send any other stuff to the lawyers over there?"

"That's not going to happen," explained Janice. "There's no love lost between that firm and your attorneys, but does that mean you have other stuff that might be useful?"

"Let's not talk here," he looked around to see who was still in the vicinity. "What about meeting up later for a drink? I might have something you could use."

Janice had no hesitation in accepting the invitation. Whatever he had, she wanted and would do anything, or almost anything, to get it if it looked useful. At seven o'clock, or just a few minutes later, she arrived at the VintEdge Wine Bar in Somerville, just out of Bridgewater. She was a little surprised at the exterior which seemed rather generic but, as she entered, she was pleasantly surprised. Inside felt like a sleek Manhattan wine bar with modern decor and comfortable seating. Wizz was already sitting at the bar with a beer and saw her in the mirror at the back of the bar. Without turning, he raised his hand to acknowledge her presence. Hardly the 'come-on' she was half expecting, but the night was yet young.

"What'll you have?" he asked as she sat on the next bar stool. As she didn't drink beer, she asked for her usual – a white wine spritzer. For the next ten minutes, they danced around each other, part small talk and part enquiring into each other's past. Janice was happy to participate in the give and take but wanted to get business over and make her mind up about whether pleasure would follow or not.

"So what have you got for me?" she asked.

Wizz refrained from the playful comment which immediately came to mind, and answered seriously. "I can't pass on any research which I've already passed to the prosecutors. That would be unethical. But I do have some stuff which recently came to me from witnesses who were late in returning my calls."

"And?" Janice was getting a little impatient.

He took a memory stick out of his pocket and laid it on the bar. He put his hand over it as Janice reached out. "You have the details here, but you have to make them your own. I can't be associated with it. Is that clear?"

"I think I can do that," said Janice, changing her hand to an open one, inviting Wizz to pick up the stick and place it into her hand. As he did, the touch of male flesh on female flesh hit them both. It was almost as if their bodies had already made a decision and it was up to their wills to confirm it.

As if he wanted to ignore the physical electricity, he began asking more about the Gazette and how she had become entangled with the Websters. She felt freer to talk at length about the crusade the paper was on, how she had never met Kevin, but reading the contents of the laptop felt such an abhorrence at the grooming that she had determined to do everything she could to right the wrong that had been done to the family. Wizz listened without interrupting which was a good sign for Janice. No male that she had ever known, including Porter, could do that. Without knowing anything about him, except what he had deigned to share with her at the beginning of the evening, she determined that she liked him.

It was soon apparent to him that she had only planned a day's visit and it was now nearly ten. An invitation was extended and accepted. Wizz lived a

ten-minute drive away and both cars convoyed to his swish top-floor apartment where the man of the house produced some champagne which Janice
put aside for later.

Meanwhile, in Rome, the Douglas-Scott interview had certainly shone
a light into the Holy See and, where the Pontiff could previously only see
obstacles, he was witnessing cracks in the traditional wall of conservatives
and the beginning of a divergence of thought. Factions had begun to emerge
so that His Holiness could now begin to see who might be potential modern-
isers. The traditionalists were, predictably, opposed to Douglas-Scott's views
and expressed their opposition with some force, whereas some others, from
unexpected quarters, were willing to discuss a different vision of where the
church might be at the end of the decade. Clear fault lines had been exposed
which, with care, His Holiness thought he might be able to exploit.

He maintained a dignified silence on the issues as muted discussion began
in the corners of the Vatican. The truth was that he had always agreed with
many of the views his English PS had espoused but had decided that 'slowly
slowly' was the best strategy to achieve progress. It meant going at the pace
of the slowest but many of them were, in reality, pushing to go backwards.
He had to admit that his tenure up until now had not produced much of
note, rather had been beset by scandal upon scandal. He wanted to change the
narrative and here was his opportunity. In his mind, he began to formulate a
strategy to move the church forward.

His current PS, an Italian priest called Albertelli, who was well connected
within the Vatican, seemed to be more progressive than conservative although
His Holiness was well aware that, up until now, rarely did anyone within the
walls voice what they truly thought, rather what the person they were talking
to wanted to hear. No truer than when talking to Peter's successor. But things
were beginning to change.

Even so, the dark arts of politics were being used without mercy by the
conservatives headed by the Congregation for the Doctrine of the Faith, the
rock on which many Popes, who wanted change, had foundered. Traditionalists
saw danger signs and began circulating completely unfounded rumours to
La Republica and any other media who would listen. In the meantime, His

Holiness invited those who he thought might follow him, for prayer and discussion in his private chapel one by one.

Chapter 60

SULLIVAN WAS KEEN to get back to the newsroom but had no idea how he could incorporate what his mother had told him into a story that would pass the Porter test. He spent the night thinking about it and woke up the next morning no further forward. He put it all on the back burner and got over to the office. Janice wasn't in. Porter was but paid scant attention until two beefy Boston police officers came into the office full of intent. Porter had, at that very moment, picked up the phone to hear Jimmy, the security man, advising him of the unannounced visit. He saw the policemen make a beeline for Sullivan with the whole newsroom stopping work to watch, whilst Porter quickly stepped out of his office and brushed past everyone to reach the investigator's desk.

"What's going on?" he demanded of the uniformed officers.

"Please stay back," one of them firmly advised.

"I'm the editor-in-chief and I want to know what's going on?"

"Mr Sullivan here is under arrest and we have orders to take him to the precinct."

Sullivan himself seemed to have lost his voice and was looking around completely disoriented. Porter again tried to get some kind of explanation.

"What for?" asked Porter raising his voice.

The same officer now turned to the editor and faced him squarely in an almost threatening manner. "Please stay back, otherwise you will be arrested for obstruction."

Porter started to get agitated before realising that the officer meant what he said. So he turned to Sullivan.

"Don't worry Sullivan. We'll get to the bottom of this."

By this time, the other officer had cuffed the journalist and began to lead him out of the newsroom with everyone staring at the exiting party, some taking videos on their phones. Porter hadn't moved, gaping at the threesome as they moved out of the door. At that point the room erupted with noise, each asking another if they knew what Sullivan had done. If they didn't know, as good journalists, they began to speculate. Must be serious.

Porter yelled at everyone. "Show's over. Back to work." He faced his newsroom. "Not a word outside this room until we know what the hell's going on. The last thing we need is the competition to get a whiff of this." He looked sternly around. "If I find anyone has, even to family and friends..." He drew his finger across his throat. He went back to his office and immediately called the precinct, but no information was forthcoming.

An hour later, Janice walked in after her extended evening with Wizz. She headed straight to Porter's office and marched in.

"What the ****'s going on?" she shouted to Porter.

"Shut the door," ordered Porter. "And how did you know?"

"Jimmy downstairs told me," she replied.

"Shit," exploded Porter. "I forgot about him." He grabbed the phone and made his views very clear to the man who protested his undying loyalty to the Gazette.

"I don't believe that for a minute," murmured the editor-in-chief. "He'll tell someone, that's for certain."

"Tell him what," pushed Janice, still waiting for an explanation. Porter explained what had happened just an hour ago and that he knew no more.

"This is an attack on the paper and I'll get a front page ready." Despite her deteriorating relationship with Sullivan, she saw it as an attack on all of them.

Porter was quiet. "You know Sullivan just as much as I do." He paused. "We don't know what the hell he's done yet. Get down to the precinct and try to find out. Call me when you get more and, if it's serious, I'll get on to the lawyers for advice. Unfortunately, they're not a criminal practice so it'll be yet another set of money-chasing suits. And I guess I ought to call Meyer." By this time, he was more talking to himself. Looking up, he saw Janice.

"Are you still here?" he asked, and she quickly headed out.

Sullivan allowed himself to be led out of the offices, even giving Jimmy a wink. He was thinking hard. The uniforms were not speaking to him, just carrying out their orders so it was someone higher up who was responsible. His obsessive mind had already pinned the blame on someone in the catholic church who had taken a dislike to his crusade against paedophile priests and the catholic church in general. He began to grin to himself that this was going to make a great front page. Content with these thoughts he settled down in the back of the Ford Crown Victoria as it made its way to the precinct where he was processed and put in an interview room.

As he sat waiting for someone to interview him, he began to formulate the angle of his story. *"Top Journalist Arrested for Exposing Catholic Paedophiles."* Not bad, he thought, although he knew headlines were mostly a sub-editor's job. Maybe *"Catholic Church and Police Conspiracy."* He liked that one. Porter was on his side and maybe Janice would have to admit he was top dog.

His watch and phone had been taken from him, but he guessed he had been in the room for about twenty minutes. He knew the form. It would be at least an hour before someone deigned to enter the room. Asking for a lawyer never entered his head, after all, he was innocent and definitely in the driving seat. He would make sure that whoever came in, knew it. It was thirty minutes before a young detective came in. Sullivan smiled thinking a junior had been sent in to cut his teeth on a 'pain in the ass'.

"Are you a catholic?" he asked. The journalist was in first with his question.

"Excuse me?" said the detective looking a little confused.

Sullivan repeated his question. The man answered. "No. Why?" This was not the response the investigator was expecting and he began to retreat in his thinking.

"I thought the reason I was here was because of the stories I've been writing for the Gazette?"

The detective stared at him. "What stories?"

Now Sullivan was becoming disoriented as his whole thesis was falling apart.

"Why am I here, then?"

"First, I need to read you your rights," said the detective who proceeded to advise Sullivan of his right to a lawyer etc. etc.

"I don't understand. What have I done?"

"Someone has reported that you were seen drunk in a public place and our enquiries have confirmed that."

Sullivan sat back and blinked a few times as he struggled to understand what was going on. "You mean that incident where I banged my head a few weeks ago?"

"Yes," and the detective read out the date, time and location of where Sullivan had collided with some scaffolding on a sidewalk. "Is that correct?" he asked.

"Yes," said Sullivan beginning to catch up. "But that's not even a misdemeanour in Massachusetts. And besides," added Sullivan, now warming to his argument. "no officers were called. No breath test was taken. No crime committed." He finished triumphantly.

"Mr Sullivan, you are accused of being a public danger or nuisance leading to a charge of disorderly conduct."

Sullivan stared. The detective went on. "Which, I think you'll find, is a crime. What have you got to say?"

Sullivan was not normally at a loss for words, but his mouth opened with no communication coming forth.

"Mr Sullivan, have you anything to say?"

"This is ridiculous. What evidence have you got?"

"We have video footage from two passers-by that you were so drunk that you fell into the road causing a hazard."

"Who?"

"I can't say, but it's definitive. We can't have people drunk and disorderly and causing a public nuisance."

"This is nonsense. Someone's out to get me."

"And who might that be?" asked a disbelieving detective.

Sullivan had catholics uppermost in his mind, but no individual name to blame. So he thought better of making wild accusations and began to think a bit more clearly. The detective was asking him if he had anything more to say.

"No," said the investigator lamely. "I need to make a call."

He phoned Porter and explained the situation with a plea that he'd like to avoid having a criminal record. Porter called Janice, who hadn't had any cooperation at the precinct and filled her in on Sullivan's predicament. Janice was surprised, then not surprised. "It was only a matter of time," she said to Porter who grunted his agreement and immediately moved on to talk about next Friday's front page.

"What have you got for Friday?" asked Porter.

"I can write something up on the Jersey situation if that's what you want?"

"I want a stunning front page, and I only have one investigative reporter," Porter snapped back, then repented. "Sorry," he said and began to curse Sullivan. "This is his problem, not the paper's responsibility. I can't pay for this." Porter was mumbling to himself.

Janice took the opportunity to move back to her desk and assess what she had for the next edition. Porter, in the meantime, left a message for Meyer and contacted the paper's lawyers to ask them to call Sullivan and offer him some advice. They reluctantly agreed but only after Porter demanded to know what else their substantial retainer was for and slammed the phone down. He had washed his hands and felt bad for it. Sullivan was going to have to sink or swim on his own.

A junior at the Gazette's legal firm was dispatched to visit Sullivan and get him out. As it happened, this young lady was recently out of law school, had some training in criminal law and knew that this episode was quite unusual. As it was the first 'case' she had been given, she wanted to make it count. Sullivan's usual misogynistic thoughts kicked in as he saw a girl just out of law school who had been dispatched to help him. Such thoughts were quickly scattered as she explained that there was no case.

"I haven't seen the videos, but they do not prove any level of inebriation. There is also an opportunity to sue the scaffolding contractor and/or the city authorities for not providing lights on the sidewalk under the scaffolding for the safety of the public."

"Great. So can I get out of here?"

"I shall demand your release right now." She got up to leave the interview room and added. "By the way, don't get any hopes up about any compensation. It's just a tactic to show we're serious about getting any potential prosecution dropped." As she left the room, Sullivan began to think again about who had taken the videos and who had authorised his arrest on such flimsy evidence.

He arrived back in the newsroom that afternoon to cheers and waving of papers. He smiled whereas Janice grimaced, thinking there would be no stopping him now. The conquering hero returns unscathed! He went in to see Porter.

"Thanks for sending that lawyer. She was only a few years older than my daughter but knew her stuff."

Porter looked at him, not knowing that the lawyers had actually sent someone, but happy to take the plaudits. They didn't come often, especially from Sullivan. "You're welcome," said the editor-in-chief. "So what's the situation now?"

Sullivan outlined how he was able to walk away with the police not progressing with any case. "That's because there was no case. Someone was out to get me."

Porter looked sceptical. "Who?"

"I don't know. The videos sent in were anonymous. I guess they recognised me and decided to have a go."

"Is there a story here?" asked Porter.

"Not unless I can find who took the videos, why, and who at the precinct decided to arrest me."

"Until you do, perhaps you could get together with Janice and get me a front page for Friday." Porter put his head down, indicating the meeting was over. Sullivan went back to his seat and turned his desktop on. Janice looked across wondering whether to say anything.

"Are you OK?" she asked after a minute or two.

Sullivan pushed his chair back. "Yep. Pretty scary at first though."

Janice saw a slight change in his demeanour that indicated their relationship might be salvageable. "I bet," she said supportively.

"Have you got anything for this Friday?" he asked.

"Not punchy enough," she replied, bringing him up to date with what was going on in Jersey.

"Same here," he said, then looked hard at her. "So no mega dollars in TV then?" he asked.

"Doesn't look like it," she replied. "Perhaps we'd better pass on this week. I might have something better next week."

They both settled at their desks after a civil conversation. Maybe the relationship ice had been broken for now. After a few more minutes, Janice said, "I could make a call."

Sullivan turned around. "What for?"

"To try and find out who authorised the arrest."

"Sounds good," Sullivan was hesitant, not sure if he wanted a favour from

Janice. "Who will you call?"

"Arata. He knows anyone who's anyone in Boston."

"I thought Arata was a priest?"

"But his father, Arata Sr., is a catholic businessman who seems to be well connected." Sullivan could see a story here. "OK. See where it goes." Then added, "Thanks."

Janice looked through her phone log, found the number and made the call. Predictably, it rang out as it had done previously. She left a brief message and waited to see if he would call back. It was towards the end of the day when she received the return phone call.

"Ms Munroe, how nice to hear from you." His solicitous tones belied a suspicious mind. "To what do I owe the pleasure?"

Janice explained how Sullivan had been arrested on a trumped-up charge and wondered if he had any connections at the precinct which would elucidate who had authorised the arrest and what might have been the motivation. She and her colleague suspected some catholic angle but they didn't know for sure.

"I'm not sure I can help, but I will give it some thought." His reply wasn't a surprise since she knew him to be a cautious man.

Sullivan looked across and she shrugged. "Maybe," she said.

Chapter 61

Dora's trial was nearing its climax and Janice wanted to be there. She left Sullivan to talk to Porter about any input for Friday's edition and set off for Jersey intending to stay over with Wizz and be at the criminal court in the morning. He was pleasantly surprised to get her call and was more than willing to facilitate the stay-over.

It was a pleasant meal, this time at Janice's expense, at which each gently probed the other about their lives so far. They both agreed it was unusual for a journalist and even an ex-police officer to be together. Nevertheless, it seemed to be working for each, especially as their interests in the two cases they were following were mutual.

"Do you really think Dora will be found not guilty?" asked Wizz, dubiously. "After all, she did do it and confessed to it. That's a slam dunk where I come from."

"I'm hoping not," said Janice. "It all depends on the jury. If they are emotionally moved, they can make the right decision, even though it won't be the legal one."

Wizz wasn't convinced, but left it at that. As far as he was concerned, the law was the law. He changed the subject to the trial he was involved in.

"I think we'll get a unanimous guilty verdict against the church and I have high hopes of a large compensation payout."

"How much?" asked Janice.

"Again, depends on the jury. The information I was able to gather was damning, but you can never tell."

They both lapsed into silence, finished their coffees and made their way back to Wizz's apartment. He offered a bourbon nightcap which she accepted although not her usual tipple. It had the desired effect. Janice woke first and gave a smile at the sleeping Wizz opposite her. As she got up to shower, the smile changed to a frown as she began to think more seriously about Wizz, then about Porter, then Wizz again. What did she want? She certainly didn't want to live in Jersey, so what did that mean for Wizz? And anyway, he had shown no sign of wanting the relationship to go further. But she knew herself, and if she continued to see him, there might be no going back. Porter would be disappointed, she knew, but developing a serious relationship with the boss was not necessarily a route to eternal happiness.

Wizz was now up and moving, suggesting he take her to his favourite breakfast venue which he did and they both enjoyed. Both were anxious to get to their respective courts since Janice had said she would be driving back to Boston once the court had adjourned for the day, but not before a tender hug and kiss outside the restaurant.

Dora's case was on the back burner of her mind until she parked the VW and began moving towards the courthouse. She saw her lawyers at a distance but, with no inclination to greet them, pressed forward into the courtroom to take her seat, somewhere she hoped would enable her to make eye contact with Dora. It wasn't long before a voice announced the arrival of the judge and there being no legal issues, the jury was summoned. Janice knew this would be the last day, for summing up began. The prosecution outlined the seriousness of the crime, mentioning the fact that the accused had already confessed several times. She had confessed that she was guilty and that the law must take its course. It was short and to the point, making clear to members of the jury that emotion cannot trump legality. The defence, however, poured on the emotion. After all, they had nothing else in their bag.

As part of the judge's direction to the jury, she said that it was up to them to determine guilt or innocence and not to recommend sentencing. That was the responsibility of judges who had to follow sentencing guidelines. It was up to the jury. As they were sent away to deliberate, lawyers and other 'hangers-on' went out to find lunch. Wizz called Janice to say that in their trial the priest had been found guilty of sexual assault and the catholic church would inevitably be found guilty as well.

"It's a pity that news didn't arrive before our jury retired," said Janice, a little despondently.

"There might be a way," said Wizz, conspiratorially.

"How?" asked Janice, eager to swing the jury in Dora's favour as much as she could.

"The legitimate way is to get the defence lawyers to get the news to the judge in his chambers. Whilst you can't get to the jurors for the verdict, you can get to the judge for sentencing. Sometimes, if it is a guilty verdict, the judge may delay sentencing if he or she wants a further report."

"And the illegitimate way?"

"Loiter by the courthouse and hope that either someone goes in with food or drink, mention it to them and hope they say something."

"Hmm," reflected Janice. "Jury tampering is a crime, right?"

"Certainly is," replied Wizz.

The call was cut and Janice quickly thought she could do both. A call to Ms Adams quickly passed on the news of Father Graham's legal guilt and left her to decide what action to take. Hopefully, she would do the right thing. She picked up a newspaper lying on an empty restaurant table and headed back to the courthouse to loiter. When anyone came close to moving in, she would lift the paper and exclaim in a raised voice, "Wow, that catholic priest has been found guilty."

Nobody asked to look at the paper, but most turned to look at her as they went in. At about three o'clock, people began to reassemble having been told that the jury had finished their deliberations. She quickly wrapped up her newspaper and dropped it in a nearby bin, joining the stream to enter the courtroom. No one had long to wait before the foreman of the jury was asked for their decision.

"Not Guilty."

There was an audible gasp from the courtroom, Janice included. She glanced at Dora who either hadn't heard or it hadn't registered, for her face was unchanged. As the judge turned and gave her permission to leave, she still didn't seem to understand that she was free to go.

Her attorneys gathered around to congratulate her while the prosecutors gathered up their papers and left the building. Janice suddenly realised that Dora had nowhere to stay and wasn't in any condition to fend for herself. Going back to Boston that evening might have to be shelved. She quickly called Arata, gave him the verdict and said she was taking Dora to a hotel for a few nights while she found a new rental. Predictably, the call went to voicemail, but she knew Arata would listen, understand and get back to her at some point. In the meantime, Janice would have to use her credit card again.

There was a complete melee outside the courtroom as excited reporters waved phones in Dora's face and cameras clicked incessantly as she appeared, escorted by a female officer. Janice pushed her way forward, mouthed 'thank you' to the officer and grabbed Dora's arm propelling her through the throng towards her car parked around the corner. She had no intention of allowing Dora to release any parts of her story to some other hack. The crush followed and only relented as Janice shut the doors and put her foot down.

"Dora, you're free," said Janice as she drove off with some sideways glances at her friend. She wanted to be upbeat and excited for her friend. Dora rewarded her with a weak smile. The trial had taken a major toll on her mental health and, it seemed to Janice, that a full recovery might take some time.

"Come with me. Let's go and have something to eat." Dora allowed herself to be led out of the VW with Janice still talking, trying to be as normal as possible. As they walked up towards the restaurant, Dora began to look around for the first time as if she finally realised that she was not going back to prison. They settled themselves down and ordered, with Janice searching for a way to tell Dora that she had been evicted and couldn't return to her home.

"I've booked a hotel for tonight as a treat," said Janice, knowing she couldn't keep this away from her friend much longer.

"I want to go home," said Dora, halfway through a doughnut.

"The thing is," Janice started hesitantly.

"What?"

"I'm afraid your landlord couldn't hold on to your home. He didn't know how long you would be away." Janice was painting what she thought was the best picture for Dora. Suddenly Dora came to life.

"I might have known it," she said bitterly. "But I'm well rid of him. He was a creepy bastard." Janice was taken by surprise at this sudden vehemence and took it as a good sign that Dora's mental health might not be as bad as she thought.

"What about my stuff?" she suddenly exclaimed.

"Don't worry," said Janice. "I've got it all in storage."

"And who's paying for that?" Dora seemed back to her combative self and Janice smiled.

"The catholic church," she answered, waiting to see how Dora would react.

"What?" Dora looked incredulous.

"Father Graham has been found guilty of crimes against Kevin and other boys and we are working to claim compensation from the church."

"Oh," said Dora. "I didn't know." Then, as she thought about it added savagely, "I hope he rots in jail."

The pair were silent as they finished the food until Dora spoke up. "How much?"

"I don't know yet. It has yet to be decided and I want to write up your story to add pressure to the claim." It may not have been the whole truth but near enough for Janice.

"Before we go, let me make a phone call to a hotel. Is there one near where you used to live?"

"Make it one near to the church I go to and I'll begin to look for a place so I can walk on a Sunday morning."

Janice began to relax as she could see that Dora was taking responsibility for her future. In the back of her mind, she had been dreading having to go back to Boston with Dora not capable of making decisions.

TripAdvisor came up with several recommended places. Janice immediately ruled out cheap motels and chose a Comfort Hotel, since the one that Douglas-Scott had stayed in Boston seemed to be good, and Arata was paying in the interim. Whilst Dora was settling in, Janice went out to buy some overnight necessities for her friend, then spent two hours recording an interview with Dora about her whole experience. At about nine o'clock in the evening, Dora ran out of energy and Janice left to travel back to Boston.

As soon as she got into the car, she called Porter who answered in his gruff voice.

"It's gone nine in the evening," he grumbled. "Where are you anyway?"

She broke the news saying her story would make a great front page, and maybe, another interview for Meyer.

Porter changed his tone and congratulated her. "Well done. It's too late for a major splash this weekend, but write up a teaser for this weekend and a longer piece for next weekend and I'll speak to Meyer in the morning."

With that settled in her mind, she started back, with a sudden thought. "Bloody cat! I hope it's alright."

Chapter 62

ARATA SR. RECEIVED the message Janice had left but didn't call back. Rather, he called Aaron Milligan, the lead lawyer running the case against the catholic church.

"Aaron, I understand that the priest in question has been found guilty?"

"Afternoon Arata. News travels fast. I don't think that even social media has published this yet." He laughed.

Arata ignored the comment, the lawyer still enjoying the afterglow of victory. "Where are we on the issue of compensation?"

"I understand you have other lawyer's fees to settle, but we're not there yet."

"How much are you asking for?" Arata was not giving up easily.

"One million US," replied the lawyer.

"Give me an estimate of your fees."

"Can't do that yet. I'm sure it will be in the range we've previously discussed. If not, I'll contact you with details."

Arata grunted and cut the call. He made some quick mental calculations in his head. Even if that amount was awarded, the catholic church paid up, and both legal firms billed the expected amount, it would only leave $350k. After storage costs and his commission, Mrs Webster would be able to pocket about $300k. Yes, that was acceptable. It would be sufficient for her to buy an apartment and have some funds left over. Still, he called De Luca at his Chicago office and, although nearly six thirty, knew he would still be at his desk billing some unfortunate client.

"De Luca. I've just been talking to Milligan in Jersey."

"Evening Arata," said the lawyer, used to Arata's bluntness.

"It looks like they've won their case against that priest and the catholic church. Do you think you could have a word to go easy on the fees? I want as much as possible to go to the lady, Mrs Webster."

"I thought they had given you a ballpark?" questioned De Luca, not wanting to touch the holy ground of professional fees.

"They have, and as long as it stays there, I'll be happy."

"I'm sure it will," reassured the Chicago lawyer.

"That's good," said Arata, leaving De Luca in no doubt that the businessman was not going to accept any 'extras'.

He sat back wondering how he had got himself into this situation where he was bankrolling two court cases to give some money to someone he had never met and probably never would. Sure, he might get something out of it, but then risk deserved reward. It was that lady journalist. She had really got to him. He had to admit that he had never done anything like this in his whole life before, but she had managed to persuade him. No mean feat. Perhaps, he was just getting old and losing his touch. Now, she wanted him to find out who was responsible for Sullivan's arrest. No, he was not going to do it. They were the investigators. They should do their own dirty business. He had done enough for them. It was time to get back to real business.

There was very little conversation during the evening meal except the obligatory congratulations to the cook – his wife. He was just about to retire from the table when his phone rang.

"I've told you before, Arata, no phones at the table. It's a rule."

He looked at the phone. It was his son. "It's junior."

"That's nice," said his wife, quickly changing her mind. "We don't hear enough from him."

"I wonder what he wants?" murmured Arata Sr.

"Perhaps, he just wants to talk to his parents," stated his wife, contradicting her husband. "You always think people have ulterior motives," she added rather accusingly.

Her husband put it on speakerphone. "Hi son, you're on speakerphone and your mother is here."

"It looks like I've got a new boss," announced Arata Jr.

"That's nice," said his mother using her favourite phrase again.

"Who is it? Do you know him?" asked his father.

"No, and no. But I'm told he comes from the mid-west and is in his late sixties."

"Is that good or bad?" His father was anxious that his son moved on in the church.

"Probably not good for reforming the church," answered Junior.

"Does the church need reforming?" contributed his mother, who liked to think the best of everyone.

"I think so," said her son. "But I suspect he has been appointed to steady the ship after all the Gazette revelations."

"That's good, isn't it?" commented his mother.

Her husband butted in. "Will he have already contacted major catholic supporters in the city?"

"I'm sure of it. He will want to hit the ground running. I understand he's quite a formidable figure."

"The church needs someone like that," interrupted his mother again.

Arata Sr. had heard all he needed. "OK. Let us know when he arrives and whether you're going to be moved."

"Will do."

"Goodbye," shouted his mother quickly, but the call had already ended.

Arata Sr. was already moving from the table to his study while his wife looked on disconsolately. He called Janice.

"The new Archbishop, probably soon to become a Cardinal, seems like a hard-liner being sent here to get things on to a firmer footing after your revelations."

"So, do you think he was behind the arrest?"

"Don't know for certain, but my son says that he will have already spoken to influential catholic people in the city."

"Is the Chief of Police a catholic?" asked Janice.

"Does it snow in winter?" responded Arata, sarcastically. "Anyway, that's all I've got. The rest is up to you." He hung up, happy to have got that off his chest and resolving not to get involved with the Gazette any further.

Janice had no evidence but perhaps a way forward for Sullivan. She had made the call and that was it. Sullivan was now on his own. The following morning she updated him on Arata's information but with no further offer of help. She reinforced this by getting her head down, busily attending to her burgeoning email inbox. Sullivan muttered his thanks, recognising a growing dependence on his colleague and her contacts which had to stop. He needed to do this himself. But where to start?

He glanced at the time on his desktop and concluded it was time to go home. He would put on one of his favourite CDs and, with a glass of Jack Daniels, he was sure inspiration would come. Sullivan lived a bachelor's life, at least as far as cooking was concerned. He just didn't do it. So with a Mexican take-out on the passenger car seat, he coaxed his Chevy home. After a long shower, he put the food in the microwave and ate it whilst watching CBS News.

He thought of a FOI (Freedom of Information) request to the police but doubted that would provide the information he needed even if they did reply. It would also have the effect of alerting the police department that the Gazette was not letting the matter drop. That could be positive or negative. He could try to persuade Porter to get the paper's lawyers to issue the request. It would certainly have more bite, not coming directly from the Gazette, but they would surely suspect the source. Whatever the response to either of these approaches, it would still enable him to write a story highlighting the police department's refusal to release the requested information or their prevarication, depending on the response. *"Police Deny FOI Request"* or *"Police Prevaricate over Solicitor's FOI Request?"*

No. He was not happy. There had to be a better way. He took out his 'snitch' book - his special Filofax with all the names, email addresses and cell-phone numbers of anyone that might be useful to him.

"I need to go through this one day," he muttered to himself, as he saw a few people he knew had already passed away. He got to the end, closed the Filofax with an annoyed grunt and got up to choose the music. It was to be John Coltrane's Blue Train album which prompted him to pour the stiff Jack Daniels he had promised himself. He sat down in his favourite chair and had his epiphany. Chloe's boyfriend! Of course! His excitement suddenly went off the scale, then subsided as quickly as it had arisen. Maybe he wasn't her boyfriend any more. Young people these days got through relationships like.....he didn't know. They were a mystery to him. But he needed to find out and, if they were still together, find a way to get the information he wanted whilst at the same time, not jeopardising his newly resurrected relationship with his daughter. Tricky, especially as he had never met this man. Perhaps, he could invite both of them out to dinner just to develop a relationship with him a little. Test the water. Maybe exchange phone numbers … no, that would be creepy. But dinner, yes.

"Hi Chloe, how are you doing?" Sullivan was upbeat.

"I'm alright Dad. Are you fully recovered?"

"Totally," assured Sullivan. "And off the drink for the time being."

"Glad to hear it. What can I do for you?"

"Thought I might ask you and your... er, boyfriend to dinner one evening?" Sullivan held his breath. "You know, as a thank you for sorting me out at the hospital."

"I didn't really do anything." It was a mild protest.

"Well, I appreciated it." He paused, waiting for her answer.

"Sure. I'll ask him and see what dates he has. He has shifts that are usually difficult to change."

"Of course. I'll look forward to that."

Sullivan breathed a sigh of relief although he knew if Chloe told her mother, she would instantly suspect his motives. So he determined not to mention anything on the dinner date. The objective was just to establish a rapport with him and gain his confidence. The approach could come a little later. He tried to persuade himself that he was in no hurry, but he was. He could smell a great story as well as getting some revenge.

Now he began to think about it, maybe Porter wouldn't allow him to write it since it involved him. That meant Janice would do it. Hmm. He had no qualms about the quality of what she would produce. It was just a bit galling to chase down a story and have someone else write it. No. He would write it and if Porter wanted to put Janice's name on it, so be it. It was important that journalists were not blackmailed or intimidated in going about their work. After all, he was standing on the moral high ground.

A quick Jack Daniels, by way of celebration, and time for bed.

Chapter 63

JANICE WAS STRUGGLING with the cat and desperate for Dora to find a place. She wasn't bothered about the cost of the storage – it wasn't her cost, although she did recall that it was on her credit card.

"Hi, Dora. How are you getting on with finding a place?" Janice was trying not to give any impression of urgency but was not succeeding.

"Sorry, Janice. I know the hotel bill is mounting. I've seen two places I like and am just about to phone one and sign up."

"How does the landlord seem?"

"Nice, but you can never tell. He doesn't want his property to remain empty because that means he's losing lots of dollars."

"Will you have enough to put down a deposit?"

"Just. I haven't collected my Social since....." She stopped.

Janice gave her a moment to recover, then tried to assure her that more money was on the way. "I'm told by the lawyers that now the catholic church has been found guilty, the court will determine the compensation level quite quickly."

"How much will that be?"

"To be honest, I have no idea," responded Janice diplomatically. "There are two sets of lawyers to pay, but I would expect five figures."

"That would be nice." Her voice sounded as if she didn't believe it would happen.

"Let me know what your new address is and your moving-in date and I'll arrange for your furniture to be delivered."

"No. I can do that. You've done enough. I'm very grateful."

"OK. Tell me when the date is and I'll bring your cat back."

"How is she?"

"She's great. Looking forward to seeing you, I'll bet." Janice didn't elaborate. "Oh, and make sure that you check the hotel bill and charge it to my card which I've already given them."

"I don't want you to pay for all this." Dora had no option but didn't want

Janice to think she was taking it for granted. "I'll pay you back."

"Don't worry. It'll all come out in the wash," said Janice, thinking what a stupid thing to say. "Anyway, I have to go right now. Take care."

Porter was in his office when Meyer phoned about the possibility of Janice doing another interview, this time with Dora Webster.

"Porter, remind me of the story with this Mrs...."

"Webster," cut in Porter, annoyed that Meyer had not even given the idea any thought. He proceeded to give his boss a quick summary of who she was, who the grandson was, what had happened to him, what she had done and how she ended up prosecuted but found not guilty.

"I'm holding the story for you so we can release the weekend you broadcast. But we've got to make our minds up now. It has to be this weekend or every other paper will have the story when it's ours." Porter didn't care about Meyer's TV channel. He just wanted to go ahead and publish. The interview request was a favour to Janice.

"I think it's going to be a no. We've already got this Saturday sewn up."

"No problem," said Porter, happy to have finally got a decision. "By the way, what's happened to that paper in Providence you were after?"

"Still negotiating," said Meyer.

Porter replaced his handset with a little more force than usual. He saw Janice at her desk, tapped on the glass of his office and beckoned her in.

"You can use the phone, you know," suggested Janice.

"Hmm," grunted Porter. "Meyer has turned down the idea of the interview, so I want the story in this weekend before any other bastard publishes it."

Janice looked a little disappointed but shrugged it off. "Sorry," said Porter, seeing her a little dejected. He tried to soften the blow for her. "Personally, I think it would have been great, but I'm not a media mogul." He pursued his lips. "Shall we have dinner tonight?"

"Sorry. I need to finish this story and tomorrow I'm going to Jersey to take her cat back and maybe get a bit more to flesh out the story."

"OK." Porter was the one looking disappointed this time.

Just as Janice got back to her desk, Sullivan's cellphone buzzed. Chloe, hopefully with a date.

"Hi, Chloe,"

"Hi, Dad. Can you make this Friday at six? Tom is on lates."

Two days. "Perfect." Sullivan was delighted. He had been reconciling himself to waiting for a week, maybe two. "See you at our usual place?"

"Dad, we've only been there once," chuckled Chloe and she put the phone down.

He began to whistle at his desk, something he never did. Janice looked up but said nothing. Something or someone had made him happy.

"Hope it lasts," thought Janice, concentrating on writing the Dora Webster story for Friday. She was trying to write it as she had done for the Douglas-Scott spread and began to realise there were big gaps in her knowledge of Kevin, his mother, their relationship, how Dora had got drawn into looking after him, etc. etc. She sketched and re-sketched out her question headings, before heading out of the office for an early start to Jersey the next morning.

Mid-evening came and Janice was settling down to watch a movie when Dora phoned to say she had signed up for a new apartment.

"That's great news, Dora."

"Yes, I'm pleased," she said, sounding positive and excited. She gave Janice her new address explaining that she could move in immediately.

"You won't have any furniture until the storage people deliver. Look, let me give you their number and call them tomorrow to see when they can deliver. Again, they have my credit card but get a copy of the statement please."

"OK. Thank you."

"Anyway, I want to come over tomorrow to fill out some history for the article I'm writing. I'll meet you at the hotel mid-morning and we'll go out for lunch."

"I should be treating you," said Dora.

"Don't worry. This is on expenses," said Janice airily.

When Janice arrived at the hotel the next day, a few people were milling about outside the front entrance. She took no notice and went through to collect Dora. However, when they both tried to step out of the hotel, a far bigger crowd had gathered and surged forward as soon as they saw Dora, shouting aggressively with placards calling for Dora to go to prison and supporting the catholic church. Both women were taken aback by the presence of the crowd and the anger they could see in their behaviour. Janice quickly drew Dora back into the lobby and suggested she sit at the back out of the eyeline of the protesters. She wanted to quiz the demonstrators knowing this would add more flavour to her story and take a few photo shots for good measure. It emerged that, while it was privately arranged, certain unnamed catholic priests had not discouraged it.

After about ten minutes, Janice emerged back into the hotel asking the concierge if there was a back entrance. There was, and they made their escape with Janice seeking to support a tearful Dora.

"Take no notice," Janice counselled as they made their way. "They are a rent-a-mob. Ordinary people voted you not guilty because of what had been done to Kevin and you."

They took an early lunch and lingered at the table so that Janice could go through all her talking points. It took some time with frequent stares from staff, prompting Janice to order more and more coffee refills. Dora had hardly eaten anything and not drinking a great deal either, still anxious and despondent after suffering abuse as they exited the hotel earlier. She had to be continually encouraged to talk about things she wanted to forget, but Janice wanted to finish writing the story that evening, so she pushed until about four o'clock when Dora called time. She was exhausted.

As they moved back towards the hotel, Dora grabbed Janice's hand for security.

"Don't worry. I'm almost sure they will have gone by now," said Janice, and squeezed Dora's hand to reinforce her presence but also to pull the grandmother along a little. As they rounded a corner, they could see that the protesters had gone which gave Dora some relief until she began thinking about the following morning.

"Don't forget you're moving out shortly and," she added, "you now know where the back door is. Use that." As they were passing the hotel concierge, he called to them and passed an envelope with 'Mrs Webster' scrawled on the front. Janice was immediately on her guard, taking it on behalf of her friend who was still finding it difficult to come to terms with what her new life would be like.

While upstairs in her room, Dora was being encouraged to think more about moving into her new home, partly as a distraction from the envelope but also to move her into a more forward-thinking mode. After all, she would be getting her cat and furniture back. It would be a new start. It wasn't immediately clear that the strategy had worked, so she didn't stay long. She gave Dora a hug and asked her to call as soon as she knew a moving-in date when she would bring the cat. Janice was not a social worker and didn't want to become one.

Once in her car, Janice opened the envelope to find an exaggerated threat to Dora's safety. She mulled over the option of involving the police knowing that some might not be in favour of helping this particular lady. Whilst it was directed to Dora not her, Janice didn't feel it was serious, so she kept the envelope in her pocket. The prospect of two burly uniformed policemen cross-questioning the elderly lady would, almost certainly in Janice's estimation, have been as bad as meeting the mob outside the hotel earlier. She didn't want Dora to go through that experience on her own, and she had a story to complete and file.

Chapter 64

IT WAS LATE when Janice parked her VW and went to her apartment's back door to find the cat meowing outside the door.

"You've got a bloody cat flap at great expense," she said angrily to the cat. "Why not use it?" She decided again that she was not the sort of person to have pets and would be very glad to get this animal back to Dora. She opened the door, put some Go Cat down with some fresh water, locked up and went straight to bed.

In the morning, the cat had gone, presumably through the cat flap. She shrugged and made her way into the office intending to go over the Dora story once again before filing it with Porter. Sullivan came in shortly afterwards and grunted his greeting. However, he didn't look as grumpy as he sounded. His head was up, his eyes bright and he looked like he had a story. Janice decided she should try again to resurrect the relationship.

"You've got a story?" she queried. Sullivan turned and smiled.

"Not yet, but I've found a way to pin down who ordered my arrest."

"Do tell," she said, but Sullivan just put his finger to his nose. "Plausible deniability," he said and turned on his desktop.

It was a Friday. That weekend's edition was out, so it was a day for mopping up the untold emails which came in for both of them, mostly a waste of time, but then doing expenses (not a waste of time) and other housekeeping chores. No liquid lunch together – the relationship hadn't been restored to that extent yet. Besides, Sullivan was trying to keep his alcohol intake down as much as he could reasonably be expected to. He left at four thirty with Janice calling out, "Good luck," although she had no idea where he was going or who he was meeting.

Sullivan wanted to be at his best for his date with Chloe and her boyfriend so needed time to get ready and be at the restaurant before they got there.

"Hi, Chloe," he greeted her as she and Tom walked in.

"Tom, this is my Dad," Tom, still in civvies, put his hand out.

"Good to meet you, sir," said Tom.

"Please, call me Sullivan. Everyone else does, including my family." He laughed.

The meal went well, with Sullivan answering Tom's questions about his job and, much to Sullivan's surprise, agreeing with a lot of what the Gazette had been printing. The journalist was beginning to feel confident of his ground but contained himself admirably until at the end when Chloe excused herself to freshen up.

"Tom, may I ask your advice? As a police officer, I mean," started Sullivan. Tom began to look uncomfortable, but the journalist ploughed on. "Chloe might have told you that I was recently arrested but not charged with anything. Does that mean I still have a criminal record?"

"Yes," said Tom. "I'm afraid it does. Chloe told me and from what she said, it sounded a bit odd."

"What can I do about it?" asked Sullivan.

"I'm not a lawyer, but you could consider having your records expunged or sealed, I suppose," said Tom. "Being arrested but not charged is grounds for expungement."

"It was a little odd, like someone was getting at me for the job I do. I'd like to know who authorised it."

"Paperwork wouldn't necessarily say who made it happen, just the officer who implemented it," explained Tom.

Sullivan was quiet, hoping Tom might offer to look at the paperwork for him. He didn't. Just then Chloe came back and announced they had to go so Tom had time to change into uniform before doing his shift.

"Off you go," said Sullivan. "Good to meet you, Tom."

"Thanks, Mr Sullivan," said Tom, shaking hands, and off they went leaving the investigator not much further forward, a check to pay and not a little disappointed. He waited five minutes to give time for them to get away, then got up and made his way home. The night was still young so he sorted through his vinyl collection to determine what to put on the turntable. Tonight it was going to be Charlie Parker, starting with a track called The Bird, his nickname. He began to write up a story as if he knew who had set him up. He was confident he would get to the bottom of it sooner or later. Further shots of Jack Daniels helped him to lose track of time and it was way past midnight before he turned in.

Very early the following morning, before he was fully awake, his cellphone buzzed, meaning that a WhatsApp had arrived. His mind registered the message but he was in no hurry to look at it or reply. His head ached as he rued the alcohol he had indulged in the previous evening. Rubbing his eyes, he pulled himself out of bed and staggered into the shower, allowing the hot water to fully awaken him. He began to think about the day ahead. Saturday. Nothing to do except try to make further progress on his next story. He couldn't be bothered to go out for breakfast, so just had a strong coffee and promised himself a substantial lunch if he made progress on his story. He looked over what he had written the previous evening and scrapped the lot. What on earth had he been drinking?

Then he remembered the WhatsApp. He quickly looked at his cellphone. There it was or, in this case, there it wasn't. It had been deleted. He looked again at the cellphone number. No, he didn't recognise it and it wasn't in his contact list. A mistake maybe.

Janice was also having a lie-in, but not because of alcohol. She had been up and down to Jersey too many times and it was catching up with her. Her cellphone had also buzzed. For her, a text. This one from Dora saying she was moving in that day. The journalist groaned and turned over in her warm bed not wanting to drive back down to Jersey so soon. As she lay thinking about getting up, she reflected on the upside; she could finally get rid of the cat. But there was no urgency for Dora was responsible for sorting out the removal company. So, after she had locked the cat flap to prevent the animal from escaping, she had a leisurely bath, then went out for breakfast as was her usual Saturday routine and only then did she assess herself as able to drive south with the cat in her basket.

She was on her way out when she stopped, thinking that Dora was bound to ask about money. She quickly called Arata.

Surprisingly, he answered instead of letting it go through the voicemail. "Good morning Ms Munroe. How are we this morning?"

Janice thought he was sounding particularly chipper this morning. Maybe some funds had come through. She hoped so. "Very well, thank you. I'm going back down to Jersey to help Ms Webster move into her new flat. She managed to put down a deposit from her Social which she had not collected since being charged, but she needs funds to live. How are we doing with the payouts?"

"Well," replied the entrepreneur, "I think we have some good news. The court awarded us $750,000. Whilst I haven't got the final invoice from the lawyers, I think she should expect to get $100,000 or so."

"Are lawyers that expensive?" asked Janice, gulping a little about the difference between the award and the payout to Dora.

Arata sighed. "I deal with these people all the time. You can't do without them, but they don't come cheap."

"I don't think I'll tell Dora about the $750,000."

"Perhaps that's wise," agreed Arata.

"There are some incidentals such as the removals, hotel etc. etc. but I've paid for those on my credit card. I'll send a copy of my statement to you when I get it."

"Of course. Perhaps you could send me Ms Webster's bank details. I don't know her financial situation but it might be good to mention that tax might be due and she should probably get some financial advice."

There the conversation ended with Arata both satisfied and, at the same time, rather uncomfortable. He had already worked out that his commission would be about the same as the payout to Ms Webster and for that, he was feeling a pang of guilt. A new experience, but nothing to worry about.

Janice set off with her good news. The roads were comparatively empty except for the truckers. They never stopped, it seemed. She arrived at the address Dora had sent, to see the removal company just finishing up. Janice entered fearing the type of mess that she'd experienced when she had last moved. But instead of furniture and boxes being scattered hither and thither, Dora had taken charge and the flat was quite well sorted although the grandmother looked worn out, sitting on her sofa. As soon as Janice brought the cat in, however, her face lit up and a new burst of energy was released enabling Janice to gather more background for her story. It was on her way out that she asked for the bank details prompting a conversation about the potential payout, tax and need for advice.

Janice departed leaving Dora to work out what she was going to do. She reminded herself again that she was a journalist, not a social worker and now she had her story. She was fond of Dora but knew she had already crossed the line of personal involvement and she wanted, needed, to extricate herself. The story would appear next weekend and she would move on.

It was Tuesday and both were in the office. Janice had already filed her story and was wondering whether that was the end of the paedophile priest crusade. Sullivan, on the other hand, was still wanting revenge for his arrest and desperate for its existence to be expunged. His mind kept returning to the missing WhatsApp message. He decided to call his digital fix-it contact. Iqbal was not a friend or a colleague, rather someone who was working out a favour to Sullivan for an investigation some time ago where his involvement had been kept out of the papers.

"Hi Iqbal," greeted a cheery Sullivan.

"Sullivan, this has got to stop. I'm not doing any more for you."

"Iqbal, I'm a reasonable man. Let's suppose this is the last one which makes us even. After this, I will pay for your services."

Sullivan heard a sigh at the other end and knew he had his man. "Last time," said Iqbal. "What have you got?"

"This morning I received a WhatsApp but didn't look at it until I got into the office. But then I found the sender had deleted it. I want to know what the message was."

"You're joking. You can't get into WhatsApp. That's what makes it so good."

"Ah," said Sullivan. "But I'm sure you know or can find a back door. I've looked it up and I know it can be done."

Iqbal was quiet, weighing up whether to acquiesce or stand firm. "You realise it means I have to hack your phone. Have you got anything incriminating on there?"

Sullivan thought about it. On the one hand, Iqbal might have access to his private files but, on the other, the very fact that he had hacked his phone could be used against him, unless he was recording this call. Decision made.

"Do it."

Chapter 65

As JANICE MUSED on what might follow the campaign they had been living off for months, her mind was taken back to the question she had asked Douglas-Scott after the TV interview. He had sidestepped the issue, saying he was tired but seemed quite alert to her. Why? He had all but invited her to discuss it another time. Perhaps, he wanted to speak without Father Arata close by in case his views embarrassed the Boston priest. Now he was in London she presumed, and maybe no longer a priest, which meant he might be able to speak more freely.

She determined to call him to ask whether he would speak to her on the subject. She set up a Zoom call for after lunch which would be early evening in London. She took her laptop into the office interview room and waited to see if he would accept the meeting. He did.

"Ms Munroe, how nice to hear from you," said Douglas-Scott, courteous to the end.

"Do I call you Father, or are you now just a plain Mr.?

He laughed. "Why not just call me Andrew."

"OK, Andrew. If you remember, at the end of the TV interview we did, I asked a question which you politely declined to answer."

"I remember, and I knew you would also. So you want to know about accountability in the catholic church?"

"Is accountability the issue?"

"Oh yes. Especially in relation to the paedophile priest issue."

Janice sat back, watching the ex-Private Secretary to the Pope on Zoom offering his explanation.

He fidgeted in his chair for a moment before starting. "Where ordinary people would see the sexual abuse of children as a heinous crime, the culture of the church sees these as the sins and failings of its priests."

"Yes, I've heard that before, but that is all priest-focussed. What about the children, the victims?"

"The focus of society in such cases would, quite rightly, be on the children.

But the culture of the clerical hierarchy means that the focus is always on the priest."

"But how on earth can grown men, bishops and archbishops, ignore what parish priests have done to children in their care?" Janice was getting rather worked up.

"Ms Munroe...."

"Please call me Janice," said the journalist interrupting.

"Janice, I'm not excusing or ratifying such behaviour. I'm simply stating the culture that exists."

"Apologies."

"I understand your angst. This is part of what needs to change. You see, where an ordinary parent would imagine the damage that could be done if this were their child, this culture cannot imagine how a parent would feel. This clerical bubble is completely self-focused and does not see themselves to be accountable to any civil authorities that might be a given for ordinary citizens."

"That's astonishing," interpolated Janice.

"I'm afraid that within this culture, accountability is never imagined as something we owe the people or secular authorities. Instead, catholic priests of whatever rank, feel they are somewhat exempt from that. The only true accountability owed by them is to the bishop, archbishop and ultimately, to the Pope."

"Good heavens. It's as though priests, bishops, archbishops, cardinals, whatever, think they still live in some medieval kingdom."

"Nicely put."

"So where did this culture come from?"

"Well, the culture came from medieval times, as you so eloquently put it. Even until well into the twentieth century, the priest was god in many countries, never held accountable."

"Really?"

"Oh yes. For example, Ireland, Spain, Portugal, Italy, even France to a lesser degree. Still is in Central and South America."

"That's astonishing."

"Not really. Nobody wanted to get on the wrong side of their priest. After all, everyone confided their sins, both major and minor, to the priest so that he could absolve them. He knew everything about everybody."

"So do you really believe that absolution from one priest to another, who happens to be a paedophile, makes it alright to go and do it again?"

"I wouldn't put it quite like that. Absolution doesn't imply it's alright to continue in sin, but I suspect most people, including priests, think the slate is then clean if they do the penance meted out, and feel able to continue because the slate can be cleaned again, and again," said Andrew.

"So why has it not been challenged and changed?"

"As I've said before, change is extremely slow when it comes to the Holy See. It believes it has little need to."

"Why? You would have thought that they would want to be seen to be squeaky clean."

"Allow me to get into a bit of legalese. Vatican City State is a sovereign legal entity, just as the UK or the US is. It has its own 'diplomats' called *nuncios* who live in embassies called *apostolic nunciatures*. However, it neither issues visas nor has consulates, has no alliances or extradition treaties. This is all explained on Wikipedia."

"Sorry, I don't see where this is leading."

"Simply this. As a sovereign country in itself, it recognises no accountability to any outside authority - financial, legal or moral. It is not a democracy. It is ruled by the Holy See – that is the Pope in conjunction with the various Vatican institutions. It can do what it likes with no opposition to hold its activities to account, thus secrecy within the walls abounds. It's how it has always been."

Janice was silent, not quite knowing what to say. They looked at each other on their respective devices before Douglas-Scott began again. "I do believe the current Pontiff is trying to change things but is meeting some obstruction. With the agreement of the other overseers of the Vatican Bank, he has already appointed a Chief from outside the walls, who is not a priest. That is a major step."

"But he's not doing much about clearing out paedophile priests," declared Janice.

"Not yet," admitted the former priest and Vatican insider.

"One last thing," said Janice, "what about allegations of links between the Vatican and the Mafia?"

"I believe that is all in the past. If you look at recent pronouncements, you'll see zero tolerance for them and their activities today. Personally, I don't believe it is a relevant issue any more."

"Is it true though, that some priests still baptise their infants, forgive their sins and still have links with them?" Janice was pushing her interviewee as far as she could, thinking this might be the last time she could do this.

"They are all God's children. Babies still need the services of priests as, I believe, we all do."

Janice gawped a little at this but said nothing. She had run out of questions but wanted to finish on a friendly note. "Thank you, er, Andrew. I wish you well and I owe you a debt of gratitude. I trust your hope of a renewed church comes to pass."

"So do I, but maybe not in my lifetime. Goodbye." With that, he switched off his device and she was left looking at her laptop wondering what on earth would she write about. Would it be upbeat about how the church was changing? Or a stinging rebuke of an institution that was anchored in the past? And how did people still flock to it and give it their money? She couldn't understand it.

Sullivan found himself kicking his heels in the office. He also felt that the paedophile story had run its course for the moment, but he wanted to find out who had sent him a WhatsApp and what it said. It could be another lead by someone who wanted to remain anonymous. He had hope that Iqbal would come through for him. His cellphone buzzed.

"The message just contained a name," explained Iqbal.

"So what was the name?"

"Frank McKinley."

Sullivan paused, rather dumbfounded. "Who the hell is Frank McKinley?"

"No idea," said Iqbal. "And I don't want to hear from you again."

"But who sent it?" asked Sullivan, but Iqbal had gone.

The investigator put the name into LinkedIn, as he had a tab opened to that site already. It was a useful search engine for professional people. As expected, there were hundreds of McKinleys, with many of them having the first name of Frank. He knew no way of narrowing the search since he didn't even know whether this person was in the US, let alone Boston. They could be anywhere in the world. So he put the name into his search engine. Again, lots of Frank McKinleys.

Janice came out of the interview room mulling over the conversation with Andrew Douglas-Scott. Sullivan was at his desk, head down, hand over his mouse but looking frustrated. She had seen that look a hundred times. Previously, she would have made a sarcastic quip but they didn't have that kind of relationship any more. She was not going to open any conversation. As far as she was concerned, it was his responsibility to make the first move if he wanted to repair their relationship.

He looked up as she sat down, closing the window he was examining. She assumed he didn't want her to see what he was doing and she was about to ignore him when he started a conversation.

"Have you got anything else on paedophile priests?" he asked openly.

She looked at him carefully, wondering whether to answer honestly or wind him up. She decided to give him the benefit of the doubt and answer honestly.

"I've just had the last conversation with Douglas-Scott who, incidentally, will shortly be renouncing the priesthood."

"What about?"

"Accountability in the catholic church."

"Sounds a bit heavy."

"Well, it seems to get to the heart of why the catholic hierarchy acts as they do."

Sullivan was paying attention now. "I'm not sure I understand," he said.

She looked at him and assessed he was genuinely interested, so she outlined the dialogue they had together. He sat back in his chair, gauging its news value.

"Probably not a front page," he responded, "but interesting all the same."

"I agree," said Janice. "Not sure where we go on the paedophile priest thing now. Have you got anything which would go with it?"

"No," Sullivan admitted. "I'm still trying to find out who authorised my arrest."

"So we have nothing for this weekend's edition."

"If I could find out, we might be able to establish some kind of segway between the two stories and then put some kind of conclusion together."

"What have you got so far?" asked Janice.

"Someone sent me a WhatsApp and then deleted it before I could read it."

"Did you recognise the number?"

"No. I don't know whether it's another story or linked to enquiries I've been making about my arrest."

"Hmm, that's difficult," said Janice. "Not easy to get into WhatsApp."

"It's not that," explained Sullivan. "I got Iqbal to hack into my phone to get the message."

"Whose Iqbal?"

"The guy who downloaded the data on Kevin Webster's laptop."

"Oh. And he can hack into anyone's WhatsApp account?"

Sullivan ignored the question. "Anyway, the message only contained a name."

"Which was?" asked Janice.

"Frank McKinley."

"I remember a Frank McKinley" Janice recalled with a faraway look.

"You know Frank McKinley?" Sullivan raised his voice a level.

"I'm just trying to remember," said Janice. "Yes, my father used to meet a Frank McKinley years ago."

"Is he local," asked Sullivan.

"Yes. He was someone from the Lodge."

Sullivan stared at her. "You mean the Masons?"

"Yes. My father used to be one, probably still is."

"Here in Boston?" queried Sullivan.

"This is where I was brought up. Now my parents live near New York."

Sullivan wasn't listening. "So why would someone send me the name of a mason?"

Chapter 66

THE CONVERSATION DRIED up, Sullivan staring into space trying to imagine a link between the masons and the catholic church and Janice trying to concentrate on her story, albeit with Sullivan's dilemma still on the back burner of her thinking.

Without looking up, she said, "It can't have anything to do with the catholic church. They condemn everything masonic."

"But the catholic clergy are a bit like the masons, aren't they?" persisted Sullivan.

"Not really," replied Janice. "Except both do charitable works...."

"And both are kinda secretive," interrupted Sullivan.

"Anyway, whatever the Vatican says, I guess it doesn't stop a catholic man from becoming a mason or vice versa," contributed Janice.

"I suppose not," replied Sullivan, thoughtfully.

"The only way to find out is for you to check this guy out. I've got a story to write." Janice turned to her desktop, reactivated it with a touch of her mouse and brought up what she had written so far about accountability in the catholic church.

Sullivan took the hint and settled himself down to troll through whatever he could find about all the Frank McKinleys in Boston who might be masons. Not an easy task since masons tended not to advertise themselves as such.

Porter could see his investigators working, if not together, at least not quarrelling. He desperately wanted to talk to Janice on a personal matter, but couldn't think of an excuse to call her into the Holies without putting Sullivan's nose out. And he didn't want another verbal explosion from him. So he just looked out of his office window at her. What did she think of him? If he became serious, would she back off? Was there another man on the scene?

He cursed himself for acting like a love-sick teenager and got his head down. There were things to sort out. He reached for his handset and pressed the code for Meyer.

"Porter," he sounded cheerful. The TV station must be doing well, thought Porter.

"Boss. Have you got a deal on the other paper yet?"

"You must be psychic," said Meyer in his gravelly German accent. "Signed with the lawyers early this morning. I've just sent you a note with the details."

Porter looked at his inbox and, sure enough, there was the email from Meyer.

"Have you decided how you're going to allocate your staff?" Meyer asked.

"Yes," replied Porter. "I'm going to ask Janice to take over in Providence. What's the situation down there? Who's currently in charge?"

"Nobody at the moment," replied the media mogul. "I need you in there asap."

"I'll be down there tomorrow," promised Porter.

"Good," said Meyer and cut the line.

Porter, a man of action, put aside his personal issue and called his FD.

"Mackie, you remember I mentioned some while ago that Meyer might be taking over another paper?"

"I do," said the dour Scot.

"I've just come off the phone with him and it's agreed. I'm forwarding a copy of the email he's just sent to me. It's down in Providence and I'm going to go down there tomorrow. Ring your counterpart and get him to email over a copy of last year's P&L, plus a breakdown of current costs, specifically salaries. I want them by the close of business today so I can look at them overnight. Oh, and let them know that I'll be visiting tomorrow. I want a full staff meeting at midday."

"Yes boss," said Mackie.

Porter wanted to see what potential financial and personnel chaos awaited him, but also how to pitch his offer to Janice. If he could do that before he left, he could invite Janice to an evening meal and put the proposition to her. Sounded like a good plan to him.

Her cellphone buzzed. When Janice saw who was calling, she got up and began to move to the coffee area, away from Sullivan before answering.

"Sorry, I've got plans for this evening," was the answer after he put his invite to her

"It's business as well as pleasure?" said Porter, hoping to attract her interest.

She hesitated. "Well, I'm going to see the Nutcracker at the Opera House," revealed Janice, who was beginning to get a taste for their productions.

"May I ask if you're going alone?" asked a still hopeful Porter.

Janice was still hesitant. Porter didn't strike her as a lover of ballet. Was he offering to come? Either he's desperate or it's important. "Yes," she admitted.

"May I come with you?"

"Really?" She was a little shocked.

"I'd love to. What's your seat number?" She gave it to him.

"I'll ring you back if I can arrange a seat."

Janice reviewed the call in her mind. As she walked back to her desk, without looking at the editor-in-chief, she wondered again what on earth he was up to.

She kept her head firmly down for the rest of the afternoon until Sullivan interrupted her.

"May I ask for a favour?" He sounded contrite.

Janice glanced sharply over at him to see if his face was as contrite as his voice sounded. It was.

"You can ask," she said, not giving anything away.

"It's a long shot, but could you ask your father if he has a cellphone number for Frank McKinley?"

Janice stared at him. Sullivan hurried on. "I can't think of any legal way of getting his number so I can check him out."

"That really is a long shot. I'm not even sure if either of them had cellphones in those days or if indeed they kept their original numbers."

"I'd be very grateful. I'm just chasing down every avenue possible," said Sullivan.

Janice was just about to lift her phone and make the call, when she said, "What's today?"

"Wednesday," replied Sullivan.

"He'll be at his swimming class this afternoon. I'll call him this evening." Sullivan wasn't sure if this was a put-off or if the old man really did have a swimming class on a Wednesday afternoon. However, he had no option but to express his thanks and wait until the morning.

After showering and eating when she got home, Janice almost forgot to call her father, such was her curiosity about Porter who, at that moment, was looking up The Nutcracker on the website to get some idea of who wrote it, what it was about, and anything else to enable him to make intelligent conversation with Janice. He discovered that it was a ballet rather than an opera which he had thought, considering it was put on at the Opera House. It was about a girl who befriends a nutcracker that comes to life on Christmas Eve and wages a battle against the evil Mouse King. Weird. He switched to YouTube which advertised the most popular tunes in the ballet and congratulated himself on recognising most of them. Wow!

"Hi Mom, it's Janice." She made the call with twenty minutes to spare before she had to go. The greeting was followed with five minutes of small talk which Janice was happy with for she hadn't called her parents for two or three weeks. At the end of a Q&A about work, health, and boyfriends (as her mom insisted on calling any man she mentioned), Janice asked if her father was there. He was.

"Hi Dad," Janice began. "Mom will bring you up to date with all my news," said his daughter hoping not to have to go over it all over again.

"Hope you've been following our recent campaign in the paper," she asked. He was always more interested in the paper and current affairs than his wife.

"Certainly have," he responded. "You're doing an excellent job." After more of the same, Janice finally launched her question.

"You may be able to help me on something," she said openly.

"Ask away," he said.

"We're doing some further investigations and have come across someone you used to know."

"Who is that?" asked her father.

"Frank McKinley."

There was a silence at the other end. "Not sure you want to mix with him," he said eventually.

"I agree. He wasn't a particularly nice guy, as far as I remember," said Janice.

"And the rest," said her father.

"Well, he's come up as a person of interest on something we're looking at. And I wondered whether you still had a contact number for him?" Janice held her breath.

"I used to. Hold on, let me see." It seemed to take an age and Janice was looking at the clock, knowing she had to leave the house in five minutes and glad she was already dressed and ready to go. Eventually, he returned to the phone.

"Janice, are you still there?" He sounded apologetic.

"Yes," she replied.

"I've got one number," and he gave it to her. "No idea whether he retained it. He definitely won't have the same phone he did then."

"That's great Dad. Thank you."

"Don't get directly involved with him. He's trash - as slippery as they come."

"Roger that. Have to go now. Love to you both." She ended the call feeling guilty as if she had used her parents. She had but made a mental note to travel down to see them soon. As she put the finishing touches to her hair, she heard a text come through. It was Porter saying he couldn't get a seat next to her but had ordered drinks in the interval at the bar on her floor. She smiled, then dashed out of the apartment,

Porter was not too disappointed to have to settle for a different seat for it meant not having to engage with Janice about the performance and making his lack of knowledge more public than she suspected. Neither opera nor ballet were to his taste, although he had to admit that he had never seen either. Anyway, he had another agenda for the evening and reckoned he could cover business and maybe personal stuff during the interval. Whether the lady would give him an immediate answer was another question. Before leaving for the Opera House, he had scoured the documents Mackie had sent to him, particularly the salary details, and knew he could offer Janice a good deal without upsetting other staff at the paper.

It was time for the interval and he came to the point fairly quickly and made his pitch. "I don't know what to say," she stammered, amidst the hustle and bustle of ballet-goers struggling to get their ordered drinks. "I need some time to think about it."

"It's a great promotion and only an hour and a half away. I'll continue to

edit here in Boston and give you a free hand. We could share stories and..."
He stopped himself going into the personal angle thinking she would deduce
that herself if it meant anything to her.

As she was now saying nothing, he continued. "I'm going down there
tomorrow to see the lie of the land and to get some impression of the staff
there."

"Were you thinking I might come with you?" enquired Janice.

"No," said Porter. "But if I knew how you were thinking by lunchtime, I
could potentially announce it. But if you need longer, that's fine."

"No pressure then," said Janice, sardonically. Porter smiled. The bell rang
and everyone began to go back to their seats for the final Act. He kissed her
quickly on the cheek and she went back to hers, whilst he surreptitiously went
home. Job done.

Janice viewed the second half but couldn't say she watched it. Her mind
was buzzing with what Porter had to say. She knew she wanted it, but still had
to go through the thought processes of what it would mean for her and her
life.

Sullivan was waiting at home for a call that never came. He didn't know,
didn't care, that Janice was out for the evening. For her part, the conversation
with her parents and the receipt of a precious cellphone number for Sullivan
was aeons ago. She was consumed with what her future might look like in
Providence, whereas Sullivan was consumed with waiting for a phone call. At
ten he started with a few Jack Daniels listening to some Woody Herman. He
thought the clarinet was a much under-appreciated jazz instrument, rather
overtaken by the saxophone. At midnight, he knew the call wasn't coming and
with a few choice expletives, he got ready for bed.

Janice was already in bed by midnight but far from sleeping. She hardly
slept at all that night, continually looking at her bedside clock wishing light
would dawn. She thought about the issues with managing other journalists,
especially if they were like Sullivan. Then the face of Wizz would pop into
her imagination, followed a little later by Porter. What did that mean? Then
back to Providence. Was she up to it? She wasn't confident. Why not stay in
a place she knew and was comfortable? She didn't know anyone down there

and knew she couldn't get too friendly with any in the newsroom. She began to understand why Porter increasingly wanted to see her. He was lonely and she would be as well. If she did link up with Porter, how would that work? It would be at weekends only. Was that enough? Not really. But then did she really want to settle down?

Chapter 67

SULLIVAN WAS MADE to wait for the result of Janice's call to her father until the following morning. He was depressed, thinking that no news was bad news, and not in a good mood. Janice came in with loads of make-up on but the bags under her eyes were still evident, even to Sullivan. One look at her and he decided to try to be cheerful.

"Wow. You must have had a great evening," he said, with the best of intentions.

She scowled in return and flung a piece of paper on his desk as she passed. It had just one cellphone number on it. Sullivan looked at it, open-mouthed.

"You did it," he exclaimed.

"It might not work," she said dismissively.

"But I might be able to track him, even with this."

Janice looked at him suspiciously. "You're going to get properly arrested, if you're not careful. Then it'll be curtains."

Sullivan didn't answer but concentrated on treating the piece of paper with as much respect as he would have done a hundred-dollar bill. He had that faraway look in his eyes as he began to envisage a conversation with Frank McKinley. How was he going to start? Would he say upfront who he was? Better not. So what would be the reason for the call? He'd have to think hard. He had one chance. Then another name popped into his head.

Iqbal.

He'd have to pay for this one. Should he run it past Porter, or do it and argue later when he was able to write up the story? He decided on the latter. If he had to take the cost on the chin, then it was worth it. He was going to get the bastards.

He rang his IT fixer. Iqbal didn't pick up, as Sullivan knew he wouldn't. So he left a message explaining that this time it was a 'proper job'. He knew that newspapers in the UK had been sued for thousands for employing people to hack celebrity phones. Indeed, The News Of The World, a paper owned by Rupert Murdock, had folded. In light of this, he wondered whether Iqbal would agree to do the job, even if he got paid. It was illegal after all. He would wait an hour or two and if he hadn't heard, he'd ring again, and again.

Janice moved to the coffee area. She didn't want to know what Sullivan was saying or doing. Even though she might be in Providence, if it all went wrong she wanted to truthfully say, "I know nothing." She was going to knock on Porter's door, but remembered he was down at the new paper. What was the time? He said by midday. It was eleven. She decided to text him and say she would take the job. Once she'd done that, it was as if a weight had been released from her shoulders and she began to smile. Her new life was about to start.

Her cellphone buzzed. It was Porter sending a thumbs-up. Then a longer text saying he had booked himself into an hotel for the night and that she could travel down. Why not stay over and he would introduce her to the staff the following day? Her smile was broader now. She responded with another thumbs-up.

She went back to her desk to find a deeply frustrated Sullivan not able to progress his investigation because no matter what message he left, Iqbal was not picking up. He was walking around muttering expletives and no one was going near him. Janice didn't blame Iqbal for not picking up, Sullivan could be a bully when someone stood in his way and it was not nice to see. She contented herself with the certainty of leaving the building permanently very soon. Hallelujah!

In fact, why didn't she leave now? There were no further responsibilities here. Her attention was now fifty miles to the south. Porter would have to break the news to Sullivan and anyone else interested. On her way, she received a text from Arata Sr.

"Sorry for the delay on arrest issue. No further progress except that many police officers are masons."

Janice took note then promptly forgot about it. She had other things on her mind.

Sullivan finally got a text back from Iqbal asking him what he wanted but not to phone. The investigator breathed a sigh of relief. He began to type in his text.

"Need to explore a cellphone no if still in use. How much?"

A return text came back quickly.

"No."

Sullivan stared at the brusque answer, his frustration almost boiling over. He threw his phone on the carpet where the casing was dislodged, landing under Janice's desk. She had already gone, so he was left to crawl underneath her desk himself bringing a few quiet sniggers around the newsroom. He put it back together again to find a WhatsApp had come through from an unidentified phone. It had a name, cellphone number and a cryptic message, "Call."

He looked at it. Another WhatsApp from another unidentified cellphone! He stared at it almost unbelievingly, then grabbed a pen and scrawled down the details before they disappeared. Where were these WhatsApps coming from? Were they linked to his investigation? Only one way to find out - he had to follow the trail, no matter where it led. He sat back in his chair and, automatically looked across to Janice's desk to ask her advice. Of course, she wasn't there. He noted that her desk was tidied as if she was going to be away for a few days. Strange. She hadn't said anything but then she probably wouldn't, Sullivan concluded.

But he needed someone to talk it through – the risks and benefits. Incidentally, where the hell was she? It was mid-afternoon and he was annoyed. She should be here. He looked across the floor to Porter's office. He was gone too. Coincidence? Of course not. The chief investigator was getting tired of being kept out of the picture as if he were the junior. This had to stop or he would go somewhere where he was valued.

Back to the job at hand. He called the number offered to him.

"Is that Sullivan?" the voice asked.

The reporter was taken aback and didn't immediately reply. So the voice repeated the question.

"Yes, who's this?" he asked.

"You don't need to know, but Iqbal said you had a job?" The voice had an accent which he couldn't place. Iqbal was clearly from the Indian sub-continent, but this could be Eastern Europe, maybe even Middle Eastern. The voice repeated.

"You have a job?" it asked again.

"Er. Yes," said Sullivan.

"Well, what is it?"

"I have a cellphone number which I need to explore."

"Ah. You need me to hack into a phone. No problem."

Sullivan, a little taken aback by the normality of hacking a phone, asked, "How much?"

"Depends on what you want."

"Right." Sullivan now sounded a little more assured in his request. "I want to know if it's still live, who it belongs to, both outgoing and incoming calls, texts and WhatsApps for the last month."

"Presumably, you want the content as well as the numbers?"

"Of course."

There was an intake of breath at the other end of the line, as if someone was weighing up how much he could charge for the task.

"As you came recommended, it'll be $500." The voice carried on before Sullivan could comment on the price. "I'm sure you understand the need for security." He then gave Sullivan the name and street of a small shop in downtown Boston. Ask the man for the key to box 7, place the cash in an envelope and return the key to the man."

"What about CCTV?" Sullivan didn't want to be identified.

"Don't worry. There is no CCTV in that street and the in-shop camera pictures get wiped every twenty-four hours."

"But...." A click on the line said that the conversation was over. Sullivan was going to propose a half up-front and the rest after the successful completion of the job. He sat thinking he would WhatsApp back to make his proposal, then thought, "What the hell!" If the guy was that security conscious, he would have taken the SIM card out of what, he presumed, was a burner.

He had a decision to make. Clearly, Iqbal had passed on the job to someone else and he had Iqbal's details, so maybe it wasn't such a leap of faith. But $500! There was no alternative. If he wanted to pursue the investigation, it was the 'Voice', or nothing.

It was now lunchtime, perfect for drawing out the cash. He took an envelope out of the office and headed out planning to go straight to the shop. He had a rough idea where it was but took fifty minutes of walking to get there – a lot healthier than thirty minutes in the Irish pub! It was a meandering fifty minutes as he window shopped on the way, even entering a shop or two just to confuse any subsequent examination of the CCTV. He paused outside a window display of menswear with slimline mannequins sporting clothes he would never buy. He moved on trying to contain his anxiety to get the envelope deposited. Inside was a message demanding the data by the end of the week, thus giving the 'Voice' three days. He walked straight back to the office $500 lighter, with no idea whether his money had been well spent.

Janice had gone home, packed for a night away and set off for Providence. She arrived mid-afternoon and took some time to drive around the place and get a feel for it, stopping at a news-stand to pick up a copy of all the local papers, including the Post, the one she was inheriting. She looked at hers first. The front page was well laid out but the story reminiscent of small-town America. She wondered if that was because there were no stories of note or whether that's what the locals valued. If the latter, she didn't rate her chances of staying very long. If she could transition it to something more like the Boston Gazette, then she'd work all hours to make it happen. She knew the 190,000 population of Providence City was not in the same ballpark as Boston but, the wider metropolitan area boasted 1.6m people although shared amongst all the other papers. She spent some time looking through them, ready to make a few knowledgeable comments at the midday meeting the following day.

Her expertise was in bigger stories and investigative reporting, which was what Porter wanted, she was sure. Whether it's what the readers and, hence the money men, wanted, she would find out very soon. Having covered most of the city and scanned the papers she decided to check in at the hotel, taking the papers with her. She would see what Porter made of them when he finally joined her. Fed up with waiting, she decided on a lazy bath and readied herself for the evening which would be on the Gazette's tab. Sitting in the bubbles, she also determined that after the midday meeting the following day, she would go down to see her parents in New York. There might not be much time over the next period, as she anticipated working 24/7 to get this job under her belt. They were owed a visit and she wanted to tell them about her new post in person.

When Porter eventually arrived, he was full of energy and optimism, partially because he was going to share the night with Janice whom, he had at last admitted to himself, he loved. He came into the hotel room and could see light under the bathroom door.

"Hi. I'm back," he shouted.

"I'll be out in a minute," was the response.

In the meantime, he took his jacket off and headed for the minibar to get himself a Bushmills. It was a little celebration he owed himself. Once Janice was out, Porter went in to shower and get ready for the evening. By the time each was ready, it was seven o'clock and they left for a mystery restaurant. It had sounded a good idea at the time but, on the way, Porter was getting nervous thinking he should have chosen something more American. Los Andes was a Peruvian restaurant serving Peruvian, Latin, Seafood, Spanish and Central American food. It had an excellent rating for food, service, value and atmosphere. He hoped it was well deserved, not that his whole evening depended on it. Not like a first date.

The elephant at the table was their relationship. The talk was all about the paper and more about the paper and its competitors. It was all business.

"They're a bunch of good people," he explained. "Just need some guidance and leadership, which they've been lacking."

"Anyone able to step up to some good investigative reporting?" asked Janice.

Porter's eyes twinkled. "I knew that's where you would go," he said. "Yes, two youngsters impressed me."

"Youngsters?" queried Janice.

"Well, thirty somethings," responded Porter and they both laughed.

Chapter 68

IF TRUTH BE known, His Holiness missed his English Private Secretary. The Pontiff had just finished his morning devotions when his mind unexpectedly turned to Father Andrew Douglas-Scott. He sincerely hoped he had not renounced the priesthood. After all, when a man is ordained as a priest, he receives this sacred character to act in the person of Christ and as His instrument for His Church. He recalled some of the conversations they had engaged in about paedophile priests and, in the context of this 'sacred character', he decided he must begin to deal with the issue more urgently. He decided to do something which, to his knowledge, Popes had never done before with a device which Popes had never possessed before.

Security demanded that he be accompanied everywhere in the Vatican as if there was any threat to his safety within the walls. He knew exactly why it was there and it wasn't anything to do with safety. On his way back from his chapel with his current PS, he suggested they move to the smaller office for a moment. He gambled that there was no listening device here which might overhear his phone call. He allowed his PS to stay in, for it would also be an opportunity to test his loyalty.

"Hello?" Douglas-Scott answered hesitantly, knowing it was the Pope's phone, but not who might be using it.

"Andrew. How good to hear your voice." The Pope was warm in his greeting.

"Holiness," exclaimed Douglas-Scott.

"I trust I have not caught you at an inopportune time?"

"Not at all, Holiness. Delighted to hear from you." Then a sudden thought occurred. "Are you well?"

The Pontiff chuckled. "Yes, Andrew. Very well. I wanted to talk to you about your future."

"Really? I was discussing it just the other day with my sister."

"Well. May I make a suggestion?"

"Please."

"First, are you still a priest? I remember you said you might take a drastic step once you resigned?"

"I'm still Father Andrew Douglas-Scott."

"Good. Now I've been thinking that I would like to move a little faster on that subject we talked about so often." His Holiness knew that Father Andrew would know what he was talking about and also pick up that he was a little constrained, meaning someone else was in the room.

Douglas-Scott was rather nonplussed for a moment. "Er. Yes. Of course," he stuttered. "How can I help?"

"The current Cardinal in Australia is in some difficulty and may well retire within a few years." The Pontiff paused before continuing. Douglas-Scott already knew that there were child molestation allegations against Cardinal George Pell.

"There is a vacancy for a Bishop there and I would like to appoint you to that position."

The unspoken implication of the request did not pass unnoticed by Douglas-Scott who remained silent.

"Andrew, I know it's quite a surprise, but will you pray about it and text me your response? I have to announce the appointment within days."

"Holiness, I am honoured but I have little pastoral experience." He heard a laugh at the other end of the phone.

"You sound like Moses when he was being asked by God to speak to Pharaoh."

"I could never compare myself to Moses,"

"Nevertheless, will you come back to me quickly?"

"Holiness, isn't the appointment of bishops a rather complicated process with many participants?"

"Usually, yes. But this is a special case. You'll have to charm those around you if they feel left out. It's my decision."

It was the answer to Douglas-Scott's prayer. He had been in a quandary ever since returning from Boston. Should he renounce the priesthood and be done with it all? What would he do? He didn't want to return to the FCO – that would be going backwards. Perhaps he should try and make peace with his ex. and see if she had really changed as his sister had implied. Now God had spoken.

"If you truly think I'm the right person for the job, I'll accept now."

"Excellent. In that case, get on a plane to Rome tomorrow. There are a few other bishops to be appointed in two days and you will join them."

The conversation ended with a satisfied smile on the face of the Pope and a 'what just happened' look on the face of Bishop-elect Douglas-Scott. The Pope tucked his phone in a pocket in his vestments, put a finger to his mouth towards his PS, and left the room for his office with a spring in his step whilst his PS looked on astonished.

"Good afternoon, my friend." The Bishop-elect was calling Father Gino Arata in Boston to give him a heads up with the news.

"Great to hear from you. How are you?" He was delighted to hear from his friend.

"I have some news which may stagger you."

"After all that's happened here over the past few months, it will take a lot to stagger me," responded Father Arata.

"I've just had a phone call from His Holiness."

"My goodness. Is he unwell?"

"My first thought too. No. He wanted to know if I was still a priest."

"And are you?"

"Yes, just. I've been struggling about what to do with no real answer. Then comes a phone call wanting to know if I would become a Bishop in Australia."

"What!" Father Arata could hardly believe his ears.

"And, get this. He wants to go faster in sorting out the paedophilia issue."

"That's a change then."

"I always knew that's how he really felt, but he wanted to try to do it under the radar. As soon as he says or does something, it's all back on the front pages again."

"The Curia won't like it."

"Neither will the majority of Cardinals. I think he's been quietly appointing younger Bishops who agree with us."

"Well, he's not appointing any younger Archbishops here. I've got an old traditionalist coming to Boston shortly and I'm expecting to be moved some-where else."

"The old guard has to go at some point."

"We'll be the old guard by the time they are all retired, defrocked, in jail, or dead. Anyway, congratulations. When you become Cardinal, let me know if there are any vacancies over there."

"Thank you. By the way, don't let Janice know directly. His Holiness wants to let Australia know first. You can tell her to watch for something amazing to happen, though. I'll give her a call as soon as it's made public. I owe her that."

Arata and Douglas-Scott were nowhere near the radar in Providence. Janice was concentrated on editing, heavily relying on two sub-editors who had been there a long time. For her, it was going to be evolution not revolution, but she did want change and it would begin with investigations. She tasked two younger men to search out stories which could grab the front pages and increase circulation and website traffic.

A phone call from Arata came as a shock and immediately drew her back into her former life in Boston. He had no idea she had moved and what he said made her hesitate to update him.

"Hello, Ms Munroe. I trust you are well." Father Arata was as solicitous as always.

"Very well, Father Arata." They had both inadvertently begun to use their formal titles again.

"I had a very interesting call from a mutual friend today."

"Really," said Janice, wondering which mutual friend this was.

"He suggested you pay attention to Vatican announcements in the next two days."

Now she knew who it was. "And how is Father Douglas-Scott?" she responded playing for time.

"Still a Father, apparently."

"That's a rather cryptic message, even for him," said Janice. "Nothing else you can tell me?"

"Apologies, but you might beat your old paper to the scoop." He cut the call. So he did know about the move! Where on earth did he get that information? It occurred to her that he would make an excellent investigator, but sadly that would never happen. But he obviously wanted to stay in touch. He still might make an excellent Vatican/Catholic watcher.

How to play it? She could do it all herself, showing her two protégés how it's done, or she could give it to them and see what they made of it. She decided to do both. It would be fun for her and a good experience for them to compare copy. But she was still a couple of days away.

Chapter 69

IT WAS ONLY forty-eight hours later that Sullivan got another WhatsApp from an unidentified cellphone with the one word, 'Pick up'. He didn't need a translation. Porter was back in the office but without Janice, which had the investigator wondering. No explanation, but he was way past thinking she would report to him. He told himself, he didn't care. He had been successful before Janice came along and he would continue to be, as long as Porter didn't get in his way.

He left his desk as untidy as it always was – it helped to disguise when he had just gone out for coffee and when he had just gone. This time, he had gone. He picked up his 'man bag' and exited the building. It was raining heavily. He swore and ducked back inside to ask Jimmy for an umbrella. He always had a stash of golf ones ready with Boston Gazette blazoned over them.

"Jimmy, do you have a plain one?"

The security man looked at him with a wry smile, as if he knew the reporter wanted to go incognito.

"Under cover, sir?" he asked winking.

"Just a plain umbrella, please," replied Sullivan, not wishing to engage in a long conversation.

Having thanked the security man for a much smaller item, he snapped it aloft and began to work his way downtown to the small shop with the umbrella held low to avoid any lurking cameras. He surreptitiously looked in at the shop window once he had arrived to see if anyone else was in there and, as it seemed empty, pushed the door which, in turn, allowed the entrance bell to alert the shopkeeper to a potential customer. The Asian shopkeeper poked his head around the back door and came out when he saw Sullivan, immediately proffering him the key to Box 7. Sullivan looked at him, wondering what sort of business was actually going on here but the man avoided his gaze putting the key directly on the counter as if wishing to avoid any chance of contact. Sullivan took the key as the shopkeeper moved into the back of the premises. He would claim to know nothing. The reporter's hands trembled a little as he fumbled his first attempt to open the door of number 7. A thick bundle of papers lay inside which made his heart skip a beat. He put in his hand to retrieve them and, having a quick look around to ensure the shopkeeper was not looking, had a quick look at the top sheet. It was a list of numbers and names which, at first glance, looked kosher to him. Without further examination, he stuffed the lot into his bag and exited the shop. He looked skyward to confirm the rain had stopped but then continued to keep the umbrella up in a vain attempt to disguise himself from any lurking CCTV in neighbouring streets. He was not going back into the office; total privacy was required to examine what he had got for his $500. He was desperately hoping not only to get to know who had ordered his arrest, but a great story and his $500 back from the Gazette.

He arrived through his front door, putting his bag on the table. He knew he had all evening to work through the wedge of papers now he had the haul to himself, so he was going to take his time. First, a drink. He deserved it. Then he ordered a take-out before settling down on the table to examine what he had.

Porter had left after breakfast to return to Boston, leaving Janice to go into the newsroom and introduce herself. The editor-in-chief had arranged for a nine o'clock meeting for all staff to meet their new editor. Janice decided to go in early and settle into her office, partly as an example and also to get used to her new surroundings. As staff began to arrive, they would see her already in and setting the tone of her editorship.

By and large, it was a good day. The older members of the team were understandably apprehensive but the youngish element were keen to show what they were made of, which meant that they could adapt and grow more than if they were Sullivans. She gathered the news team together separately to talk through what they were doing and how they might improve. A younger woman's touch as editor seemed to be better appreciated than that of the older man who had been there for years. There were lots of ideas, some of which Janice felt were immediately implementable. A flying start. A quick word with Porter in Boston reassured her and he seemed pleased with what she had accomplished.

Now the editor-in-chief had to announce the move to the Gazette staff. Most would take it in their stride but it was Sullivan who might need stroking. Porter decided to call him into the office before the general announcement. The chief investigative reporter walked into the Holies with a saunter that said he had something. Porter certainly noticed but decided to ignore it.

"Janice is becoming editor of another paper down in Providence," revealed Porter bluntly.

"What?" Sullivan was stunned.

"Is that a problem for you?" asked Porter, not quite knowing what was going through Sullivan's conspiratorial mind.

"Er. I suppose not. Just used to having her around," he said, in a non-committal sort of way. Changing the subject, he thought he might lay the foundation for claiming back his $500 from the paper.

"By the way, I'm still pursuing leads about who authorised my arrest and why," he said.

Porter looked at him sceptically. "You have some leads?" he questioned.

"Oh yes," affirmed the reporter. "May cost a few dollars, but I think it's going to be a great story."

"So?" said Porter. "I'm waiting."

Sullivan smiled a not very convincing smile. "All in good time," he said and exited the office with Porter gazing at his back as he went, questioning, "What's he up to now, and how much is this going to cost me?"

Two days later, Janice was interrogating the Vatican's website. She saw nothing except an announcement of new bishops to be consecrated. Hardly front page stuff …..... then she saw it. Bishop Andrew Douglas-Scott. Wow! She would never have believed it. The last thing he said to her was that he was going to renounce the priesthood. What had changed his mind? The Pope, presumably. It was interesting to her but, she reflected, it would hardly move the dial on her readership. Where was he going? Australia? Dull. It looked like a backwater appointment, until she remembered Cardinal George Pell and the trouble he was in for child molestation.

That's it! He's being groomed for the Archbishop's job and to clean up any lingering paedophile priest skeletons in the closet. Still not front-page stuff, though. How old is he? She would put him at forty-five. Still young. I guess having cleaned up there, he will be moved to a more important role as Cardinal, now with a specific reputation. But where? Where else? The US of course. Now she had her front page. She would put $1000 on it within five years. Is that why he appointed an older man to be Archbishop in Boston?

She was excited. Yes, change in the catholic church seemed slow, but these moves were amazing seeds for the future. Would her protégés get that far without her help? She doubted it, but it would be a good test for them. She then wondered whether Father Arata had got that far, for if Douglas-Scott did move to the US, Arata could look forward to some promotion.

Chapter 70

SULLIVAN NOW KNEW that there was considerable WhatsApp traffic between Frank McKinley and another number. That person seemed to be superior to McKinley, the tone of the messages indicated some authority. The content was intentionally obtuse but knowing what Sullivan knew, he could read between the lines easily. It was clear to him that there was a conspiracy between McKinley, his superior and another unspecified person to 'teach him a lesson', meaning Sullivan. Getting close, thought the investigator, but it was going to cost more money. He could ring the number of the superior and hope he or she identified themselves, but the superior's phone would have to be hacked to identify the third person in the conspiracy. Then he might need more legal means to blast his accusations over the front page. If Porter didn't insist on it, the lawyers certainly would.

Sullivan sat and scratched his chin. He was in the office and his scratching reminded him that, in his excitement, he had forgotten to shave that morning. Who cared these days anyway? He looked across at Janice's empty desk and realised that there would never be any more sarcastic comments about his clothes, lack of aftershave or anything else. He missed her. There was no one else he could talk to about his dilemma. A pang of guilt sprang up about his behaviour but was quickly stamped upon.

So what was stopping him from moving forward? Another $500? No, he would pay for it himself if it came to it. Legality? He could circumvent that with clever copywriting, implying involvement without actually accusing anyone of wrongdoing. So what was it? Was he losing his nerve? He spoke sternly to himself to 'get a grip' and as if to reinforce his determination, lifted his cellphone to call the superior.

"Deputy Chief's office," sang out the voice of a secretary. It was the 'Gotcha' moment Sullivan had dreamed of. He quickly cut the call hardly believing that the Deputy Chief of Police would not only have used his own cellphone, but given it to his secretary to take any calls.

"That stupidity is going to cost you your job," thought Sullivan. Now for the third person.

"Yes," said a monotone voice.

"You've just done a job for me and I have another." Sullivan didn't want to say his name, although he knew that both the 'Voice' and Iqbal knew who he was and were capable not only of hacking his phone but deleting, or even adding, messages to it.

"$500 and your instructions in the usual place."

"But...." The line was dead. No negotiation. In that case, he would ask for more than he needed. Maybe there were other stories he could wring out of his $1000 investment. Sullivan looked at his watch. Time to draw out more cash, walk to the drop-off point and stop for lunch on the way back. He was not a big spender, so his excitement was tinged with some reluctance at the cost he was incurring.

Over lunch, he began to think about the police involvement and what the relationship was between Deputy Chief McGowan and Frank McKinley. Both names had Irish ancestry and probably both were catholics, but that was hardly novel in Boston. Nevertheless, Sullivan's antennae were registering suspicion. As soon as he got back to the office, he began to dig into McGowan's history. He seemed to have risen through the ranks quite quickly but perhaps he was just a good officer. Not a crime. But there was something about charities he was involved with. One was definitely catholic, and there were pictures of him shaking hands with the previous Cardinal, Patrick Doughty. Others seem to be quite anonymous in their origins, but wait. Here was one openly run by the Masons who prided themselves in their charitable endeavours.

He sat back in his chair. What had Janice said about the Vatican at odds with the Masons? Maybe. But, as they had agreed at the time, there was no reason why an individual catholic shouldn't choose to become a mason, especially if it enhanced his career. The pieces weren't difficult to put together; that is, if they were the right pieces.

Predictably, Janice's protégés didn't make the connections she had. How could they since they didn't have the history, but once she had spelt it out she saw their excitement at the story and subsequent working together to come up with a front-page spread. It was a reminder of how it used to be with

Sullivan. She paused a little to daydream about when she started as an investigative journalist. Yes, she was going to enjoy it here.

Back to the job at hand. She was still able to access her Gazette account and, from that, managed to download various pictures which they might decide to use. She watched the 'youngsters' back at their desks working together as if it was their first big breaking story. Perhaps it was. Yes, she was just as excited as they were.

The Providence Post was a daily paper which brought different challenges for its editor than the cycle she was used to at the Gazette, which was also a popular weekend paper in Providence. The Post also tried to do something special for the Friday edition, with Saturdays generally devoted to a sports/property/what's on diet. Could she run head-on with the Gazette? She wanted to but felt the need to run the idea past Porter. After all, he was still editor-in-chief and she had only just started her editorship.

"Janice, how's it going?"

"Very well. Enjoying it."

"What can I do for you?"

"I don't want to overtly compete for the weekend readership with you down here, but if you haven't got a blockbuster, I may be able to prop up the coffers a little."

"What have you got?"

"I'd rather not say yet. We're working something up and I'll know when our 'youngsters' bring me their copy."

Porter grunted. "You learnt fast. Look, I trust you to do what you think is best for your readership. The only thing I ask is that you warn me about any weekend clash if we have a splash."

"Agreed," said Janice. "We've certainly got something brewing but I won't know whether it's this or next weekend."

"OK. Sullivan thinks he has a story about his arrest. Reckons it's a conspiracy."

"Sounds like Sullivan."

"He seems pretty cocky at the moment, so I wouldn't put it past him. But it's not for this coming weekend. It's free for you if you want it."

"I'm burning the midnight oil anyway, so I'll take it."

"No pressure," said Porter, smiling to himself. He knew exactly what she was going through.

Janice walked out of her office and over to her protégés. "Listen up. We're going this Friday."

The two 'youngsters' looked up and their faces dropped. "That means we've only got a day and a half," said one.

"I want your copy on my desk by close of business on Thursday."

"But..." started the other.

"Get used to it," said Janice. "I know you can do it."

She went back to her office with a smile on her face and started to draft out copy for some trailers during the week, putting some pressure on the advertising department to up their revenue. She knew a one-off would not be sufficient to encourage advertisers to part with much more money, but a good splash now would be a solid base for the next one.

Sullivan's cellphone buzzed. He snatched it up. Maybe it was the WhatsApp he was anticipating that would move his story forward. No. It was his daughter sounding a little uptight.

"Did you really ask me and my boyfriend to dinner just so you could ply him for police information? He's just told me what you asked when I had gone to the restroom."

Sullivan grimaced. He had hoped that it had gone unnoticed. Clearly not. Now he had a choice: did he come clean, deny the charge or make up some explanation? He typed back.

"No. I really wanted to thank you and be involved in your life as a Dad. When you went to the restroom, we were just chatting and I asked Tom whether my arrest would be forever on my record, because I wanted it taken off and he gave me some advice. That was it."

He was quite desperate to quell any potential break with Chloe. She was now the only family he had who would talk to him and he liked her, a lot. He admitted to himself that he had never been a good husband or a father; he had messed up his marriage and affairs, ignoring his daughter until it suited him or he needed help. He had ruined a good working relationship with Janice, now she had gone. He needed to change. But he also needed to get this story over the line. Perhaps then he could concentrate on what relationships he had left.

The buzz of his phone rescued him from making promises to himself that he probably wouldn't keep. He casually looked at it, thinking it was probably Chloe again. No. An unknown number with a curt two-word message: 'Pick Up'. His heart began to beat faster and one hundred per cent of his attention was now on his investigation. It was all-consuming.

He tried to walk out of the office in his normal, slouchy gait, giving no one any indication of the excitement he felt inside. Once on the sidewalk, he headed towards the shop, retrieved a package and quickly made his way back, head down. This time, he would go back to the office. Depending on what was in the bundle, he might want to talk to Porter.

He was now familiar with the way pages were laid out and began looking for any reference to a third person, possibly the one who started the conspiracy. He began by looking back to any texts or WhatsApps from the date of his accident to his arrest. Emails wouldn't give him a cellphone number and that's what he wanted. There were lots from the Chief to his Deputy as might be expected but nothing which allowed him to identify any third party. Then, there it was. A text from the Deputy Chief to his boss referencing an email from 'our friend'. Instantly, adrenalin started pumping. This could be it.

Sullivan began at the beginning, now searching through emails received by the Deputy from his boss with a thread from someone else. After an hour of searching, he found it.

"Thank you for taking my call recently. Prior to my taking up the post in Boston, I wanted to speak to key personnel in the Archdiocese to assess the state of the church after the recent onslaught you have had to endure. Your feedback was very useful and I believe we are on the same page."

It was obvious from the email address that the sender was the new Archbishop who was about to take up his post in Boston. He smiled because Janice had been warned by one of her contacts that he would be contacting key people in the city before being appointed. He continued to read.

"I fully intend to increase the pressure on those who would seek to harm the flock and I would welcome any support you may be able to give in this regard."

Hmm. There is certainly intent here, mused Sullivan, but nothing explicit.

Any actions taken in response were all on the shoulders of the police. Very clever. He looked at the thread from the Chief to his Deputy. Nothing, just asking him to come in 'for a word'.

So, who should he go for? The Archbishop who sowed the seed? The Chief who 'had a word' with his Deputy? The Deputy who contacted Frank McKinley? Or McKinley himself? He didn't have legal proof of anything. Even to write copy which simply posed questions would require the lawyers' acquiescence. He sat back in his chair frustrated. Although he now knew how the conspiracy had worked, he couldn't move on it..... yet.

Chapter 71

JANICE FINALLY HAD her front page and the Providence Post had its first real breaking news story which, although catholic in nature would, she gambled, entice other readers to part with their money, maybe for the first time. She was already setting up the follow-up story but needed to see how this edition went before deciding on what angle to use.

Her protégés were happy at their scoop but she pushed them to find more front page exposés to maintain momentum. She didn't want the paper to become too catholic-oriented because, although there was a significant catholic population, they were not in the majority and she wanted to position the Post well away from the Gazette, which already had a loyal readership in Providence. That was not to say she would shy away from piggybacking on any appropriate Gazette stories, giving them a different angle. Nothing was ever ruled out, but she knew she had to tread lightly.

Sullivan, in the meantime, had decided on the perilous approach he had to take before he could go into the Holies with a strong enough story, not only to get it over the line but to recover his $1000. If his strategy went wrong, the story was scuppered. On the other hand, if it went as he hoped, there would be one hell of an earthquake in the Police Dept. He decided to proceed down the conspiracy chain, starting with the Archbishop using information gathered from one to get access to the next, and so on.

Right, recorder at the ready. "Hello. Archbishop's residence." The male voice was firm but cultured.

"Good morning. My name is Sullivan from the Boston Gazette and we're publishing a story prior to His Eminence arriving here. I wonder if he could quickly comment on one aspect of it?"

A pause at the other end of the line. "Perhaps if you could email the question, then..."

"I'm sorry," said Sullivan cutting in. "Time is of the essence here, I'm sure you understand. His Eminence would surely like to create a good impression for our readers. It'll only take a minute."

Another pause. "Please hold."

Sullivan not only held the phone but his breath as he waited for the Archbishop to decide if he wanted to speak.

"Mr Sullivan, what can I do for you?"

Sullivan would have yelled out loud if he could, but he quickly restrained himself and answered in a measured tone. "Thank you, Eminence. It's only one question. Could you confirm that you have already spoken to several key catholic supporters in Boston including the Chief of Police?"

"Mr Sullivan. Whilst I appreciate your call, I must say that your past endeavours have not endeared you to the catholic church."

"We all have our jobs to do, Eminence. But I understand from other sources that contacting senior community leaders is standard protocol prior to taking up such an appointment?"

Sullivan thought he detected a sigh from the Archbishop on the end of the line. A further pause. "Mr Sullivan. Thank you for your call. I don't know who your 'other sources' are, but I don't wish to discuss church business with the Gazette."

Sullivan grinned. "I'm sorry to hear that, Eminence. It would look better to our readers, who I think are looking forward to your induction, if you were already talking to our community leaders."

"Well," he hesitated. "Of course I am and I'm looking forward to getting to know everyone."

"I appreciate you taking my call. Thank you, Eminence."

"Good day to you." The Archbishop cut the call.

The journalist would have 'high-fived' Janice had she been there, but she wasn't. His little victory, as he saw it, couldn't be shared with anyone yet.

Sullivan was desperately trying to keep his excitement under control as he plotted what approach to take with the Chief. His recorder was on.

"Chief's office." The female officer's voice was clear and firm.

"Good morning. My name is Sullivan from the Gazette. We're just about to publish a story about the arrival of the new Archbishop. I'd like a comment from the Chief before we publish if I can?"

"I'm sorry. You'll need to contact Media Relations for ....."

Sullivan cut in again. "Unfortunately, as always, time is of the essence and it's more a personal matter for the Chief. Perhaps you could tell him that I've just spoken to the incoming Archbishop on the same subject. I think you'll find he will want to speak to me."

A pause on the line. "Please hold."

Sullivan sensed he was on a roll. He was disappointed.

"I'm afraid, he is unable to speak to you. He kindly asks you to contact Media Relations."

Playing hard to get, thought Sullivan. A last attempt. "Perhaps you might be able to help me as there's very little time left. The incoming Archbishop has confirmed to me that he has spoken to several senior community leaders prior to his induction, including the Chief. Can you confirm that?"

"I can't, I'm sorry." She cut the line.

No matter. Sullivan had what he wanted. He rehearsed the line to himself. "The Chief's office would neither confirm nor deny...."

The call to the Deputy Chief would have to be different but immediate, since he was in no doubt that the Chief would shortly contact his Deputy, putting him on his guard. He switched the recorder back on.

"Hello, Deputy Chief's office." A male voice this time. Authoritative and measured.

"Good morning. My name's Sullivan from the Gazette...."

He was interrupted. "Allow me to stop you right there, Mr Sullivan. The Deputy's not here. He's at a town hall meeting. If you could...."

Sullivan interrupted this time. "Of course," he exclaimed, thinking on his feet. "That's why I'm calling. I'm supposed to be covering it, but I've forgotten where it is, and I'm late."

"You sure are," came the response. "But it's not due to finish at the City Hall for another hour or so. So, if you hurry...."

"Thanks," replied Sullivan. "I'm on my way." He immediately grabbed his coat and set off with the intention of doorstepping him after the meeting hopefully before he could get any messages from his boss. He started to walk fast but his stamina was far from what it should have been. He yielded to the protests of his body and hailed a cab. When he arrived, the meeting was still going on so he quietly let himself into the building. The Deputy Chief and the Mayor were on stage and about fifty in the audience. The policeman was dressed in his finest and certainly looked the part, but Sullivan thought he was rather young for such high office. Hopefully, not too used to dealing with experienced hacks like me, he thought.

The meeting ended with the gathering beginning to gather their coats and retreat, whilst the Deputy and the Mayor continued to talk together. Sullivan watched them shake hands and the Deputy moved towards the door where the journalist was waiting. He prepped his recorder.

"Excuse me, sir. Sullivan from the Gazette. May I ask you a question?" Before the Deputy had a chance to deny the opportunity, Sullivan continued. "We're doing a piece about the arrival of the new Archbishop. I spoke to the Chief's office earlier and she said you were the person to ask."

"Ask away," said the Deputy jovially.

"I've also spoken directly to the Archbishop of course, and he says that he has, quite properly, spoken to many of the senior community leaders of Boston including the Chief and possibly the Mayor." He had seen the Mayor approaching and thought to add her in to dilute any indication of jeopardy. "Has the Chief spoken to you about what the Archbishop would like to see when he arrives?"

Suddenly, the Deputy saw the danger. "I'm sorry. I have to get back to Schroeder Plz."

"The Chief did speak to you then?" persisted Sullivan.

"No comment," said the policeman.

"Do you know Frank McKinley, sir?" No answer.

"I have evidence that you contacted him after you met with the Chief. Is that right?" No answer. At this point, the Deputy got into his limo and his chauffeur drove him away from further embarrassment. The Mayor turned towards Sullivan with a puzzled look on her face.

"What was that about? He seemed quite rattled."

"I'm afraid he has every reason to be," replied Sullivan.

"What's he done?"

"Buy the paper on Friday," said a chuckling investigator.

Sullivan wasn't at all sure his story would be the front page that weekend. That would depend on how carefully he wrote his copy and what Porter and the lawyers would say. Taking on the catholic church was one thing. Taking on the police was something entirely different. He had to get it right. Time for one more call and then to squirrel himself away to draft his story.

"Hello." The voice was gruff, full of suspicion and with a faint Irish lilt.

"Hi, Frank. My name is Sullivan and today I've been talking to the Deputy Chief of Police, who's put you right in the middle of a shitstorm."

Sullivan thought it would be best to go in all guns blazing and grab Mr McKinley's attention before he had time to cut the call.

"Who's this?"

"It's Sullivan from the Gazette. You're being set up, by the way. I know the Deputy told you to get hold of those pics. But I'm not interested in you. I want to expose the higher-ups. I'm writing this story up for the front page as we speak. Will you talk to me?"

A pause. Sullivan held his breath. He had no compunction about slightly twisting one element of the truth, just to get to the whole truth.

"I'll WhatsApp you a time and place."

"It needs to be...." McKinley had gone before Sullivan could say "in the next 24 hours."

A WhatsApp came through moments later. "Lone Star Taco Bar, 8am tomorrow." Sullivan was happy, except he hated Texans only a little bit less than he hated tacky tacos.

"The things I do to get a story," he murmured.

He spent the rest of the day in the office putting together the first draft of his copy. He drafted and re-drafted until his fingers hurt. He knew he would have to change it in some ways, but it felt good to have thought through some of the language he could use and the different angles he might take.

Unbeknown to him, Porter was watching keenly from his office, noting how industrious his chief investigator was working. "He's really got something," he mused.

"Sullivan," he called out from his office door, then sat down again. The reporter looked up, annoyed that his train of thought had been broken. Nevertheless, he had to be polite to Porter to get his $1000 back.

He left his desk and went to see the boss.

"What's up?" he asked.

"Have you got anything for this weekend?" asked the editor-in-chief.

"Won't know for certain until tomorrow morning."

"It's Wednesday tomorrow. I don't need final copy until close of play, but I need to know if you have something and what it is. Otherwise, you lose the slot."

"Sure. It'll cost you, though," said Sullivan, exiting the office, anxiously wanting to get back to his computer.

Porter was intrigued. Usually, Sullivan was keen to boast about what he had, and what did he mean by 'it'll cost you'?

Chapter 72

DESPITE HIS DISTASTE of tacos, Sullivan was at the appointed place at the appointed time. He thought it might have been heaving with workers having breakfast but if there was to be a breakfast rush, it had probably already happened. He looked around the current haul of customers. No one beckoned to him and he could see no one who looked like Frank. He had a picture of McKinley from his research but he had no idea how long ago it had been taken. He could now be an old man with a bald head and long beard for all he knew.

He sat in the corner with his third cona coffee, waiting. More minutes went by. After nine, Sullivan was thinking that he was not going to show. Then he saw a man appear to the side and sit at an adjacent table.

"Just stay where you are," came a voice. "And tell me what this is all about."

Sullivan looked over and saw a faint resemblance to the photo. "You've aged," he quipped.

"So, what do you want from me?" said McKinley, not even looking towards Sullivan. "And where's your little girl? Janice, right? She give you my name?"

The reporter refused to take the bait, concentrating on getting his recorder ready, but knew it wouldn't catch anything said from the table which McKinley had chosen.

"Canny," thought Sullivan as he decided how to approach this unexpected twist. He fidgeted with the condiments and menus trying to deploy his recorder on the edge of the table where it might catch something he could use.

McKinley looked at his watch. "You have three minutes and then I have to go."

"Did the Deputy Chief contact you and ask you to get photos of me?"

"You know he did," was the monosyllabic answer.

"I'd like to hear you say it," pressed Sullivan.

"Yes."

"How did you get them?"

"It wasn't that difficult."

"Then how?"

"CCTV footage."

"Let me get this straight. The Deputy Chief passed CCTV footage to you?"

"How else was I going to identify who had the pics."

Sullivan was stunned for a moment. This was gold dust. "So you had the faces of those who took the photos....how did you track them down?"

"Again, not difficult."

"How?"

McKinley got up. "Don't use my name, otherwise there will be trouble." With that, he disappeared through the front door leaving Sullivan to grab his recorder to see if there was anything usable on it. Bingo! Yes, it was faint but definitely usable for Porter. Maybe not the lawyers though. He finished his coffee and exited the diner to head over to the office. He wanted to sit down and get his story straight with all the evidence he could muster. Porter would surely want to know where he got his information so he had to be a little circumspect about the hacking element.

He desperately wanted to get his story out there, so he called his editor.

"Yes, I have a story for this weekend. Hold the front page for me," he told Porter from his cellphone on his way back.

"Is it about your arrest?" Porter asked.

"Yes. I've just come from a key whistleblower who has confirmed what I knew from other sources."

"You have the evidence?"

"I have him on tape."

"Come straight in. I want to hear it all."

"But I haven't got the final copy yet," protested Sullivan wanting time to get his act together.

"Don't need that until close of play today. But I want to ensure it will stand up before you get your front page." Porter cut the call leaving Sullivan fuming. He decided to stop at one of his favourite coffee shops to jot down all the details of the conspiracy, who was involved, etc. before coming to the 'evidence' to substantiate his claims.

Porter was already thinking ahead. He wanted the story but was a little troubled because the crux of it was about the journalist who had investigated it and would write the copy. He wasn't at all sure he could put Sullivan's name on the byline. If the story held up, it wasn't a question for the lawyers but an editorial decision. In any event, he'd probably have to get legal cover since it all sounded a bit on the edgy side.

In the middle of his thinking, his secretary buzzed him.

"I've got the police on line one," she said.

"What! I suppose you'd better put them through," he relented, thinking what the hell had Sullivan done now.

"Porter," he announced himself to whoever was on the other end of the line.

"Mr Porter, this is Sgt. Bell from Traffic."

Porter butted in. "What has Sullivan done now?"

"Excuse me, sir. Who is Sullivan?"

Porter stopped for a split second. "I thought the call was about my reporter, Sullivan."

"No sir. I'm from Traffic in Providence."

Porter suddenly felt disoriented. "What?"

"I understand sir, that you know Ms Janice Munroe?"

"Yes. She's my editor for the Providence Post." Porter was now getting a bad feeling. "Why? What's the problem?"

The officer coughed. "I believe she had you down as her next of kin?"

Now Porter felt himself tremble all over. "Probably," he said faintly.

"Sir, I'm sorry to have to tell you that Ms Munroe was involved in a hit and run in the city last night."

"Oh my God," exclaimed Porter. "Is she OK?"

"She's been taken to the Andrew F. Anderson Emergency Center and the medical staff say she's currently in surgery."

"How bad is she?"

"I'm sorry sir. I don't have that information. May I suggest that you travel down. I understand she will be out of surgery in about an hour."

"Er. Yes. Certainly. Thank you, Officer."

Porter got up, told Layla, his secretary, to book him a hotel in Providence and find a phone number for her parents. Then he left the building. Sullivan looked up and saw him disappear through the office door at some speed. He called to his secretary.

"Where's he going?"

"Janice has had an accident," replied Layla.

"So when is he due back?"

"Not entirely sure, but certainly not today," confirmed Layla.

"But what about Friday's front page? We were meeting to discuss it at six."

"I'm sure he will be in touch." Layla was trying to placate an exasperated Sullivan who only had one thing on his mind.

"This is ridiculous. We have a paper to run and our editor-in-chief goes swanning off as soon as Janice has an accident. It's not good enough."

Layla, who was used to Sullivan's outbursts, had turned away and had begun working again. The senior investigative reporter stomped back to his desk to continue to work on his copy, though when his editor would make time to review it was anyone's guess.

Porter had no one at home to inform that he wouldn't be around that evening. He had been hoping that Janice might be that one. He unconsciously began praying before he jerked himself out of it. But why not? Didn't everyone pray in times of desperation? It might work. He would try anything, make any promise, to make Janice recover. But what if she recovered but was physically disabled? Or had PTSD and psychological issues? Or even needed round-the-clock care? He began to pray harder. Fortunately, there were no patrol cars on his route, as he proceeded to break every speed limit down the 93, then the 95 to Providence. He arrived at the hospital and rushed into reception after quickly parking his car. He was directed to a ward after saying who he was and showing some ID, with the proviso that the patient might not yet be awake. He didn't care. He just wanted to see her and be with her.

Sullivan wanted that Friday's front page slot and the 'close of business' meeting Porter specifically requested was obviously not going to happen. He was not pleased, knowing that Porter would inevitably require changes. He murmured under his breath.

"I'm wasting my bloody time here."

The more he thought about the editor-in-chief not doing his job by running after his lover, the more incandescent he grew. It morphed into his copy as he denounced the Archbishop, the catholic church, the Deputy Chief, McKinley and anyone else he could think of. Once finished, he emailed it to Porter, daring him to redact any of it and attempting to pull him back into the role he was paid for and one he should be fulfilling. The message that accompanied the attachments was brusque to the point of being rude.

It was six o'clock and the editor-in-chief was still sitting beside the bed of a very ill lady. Janice was still unconscious and the surgeons didn't know how long it would be before she regained consciousness, if ever. Porter was heartbroken for Janice and, if he was honest, for himself as well. He had been dreaming of their life together. He knew it was way premature but he couldn't stop himself. He had fallen for her in a big way and it was all he could think about.

Sullivan's email didn't help and he felt anger towards his employee for his selfishness and meanness of spirit. He looked back at Janice lying in the hospital bed. She hadn't moved since he had got here. He couldn't just sit here and do nothing so, with a great deal of mental effort, he opened Sullivan's attachment.

The investigator had gone home as soon as he had sent the copy. What was the point of staying? He had enough of being jerked around. Just as he got home, his cellphone buzzed.

"Sullivan, you are a ****ing idiot." Porter wasn't going to mince his words. He had to sound off to someone and it might as well be Sullivan. Before Sullivan could get a word in, Porter continued.

"Janice is lying at death's door and you are only concerned with yourself and your bloody copy. And, if this is all you've got, you can forget any front page. This is nothing but a rant and nowhere near professional journalistic practice."

Porter was not letting Sullivan off the hook and continued.

"Re-write it and, when you've got your act together, call me and talk me through the evidence you have for these serious allegations.... and it'd better be good." Porter cut the call.

Sullivan was stunned. Nobody had told him Janice's condition was so serious and he was beginning to regret everything he had thought and said over the last four hours. He was just about to blame Layla for not telling him when he realised that it was this instinctive reaction that had got him into so much trouble both at work and in his marriage and various affairs. He was dejected, despondent and dispirited, not feeling like doing anything to his copy.

He quickly texted Porter.

"So sorry. I didn't know. I know I'm an ***hole. How is she?"

Porter saw the text was from Sullivan – too early for him to have done anything to his copy. He was tempted to ignore it and let Sullivan stew, but he sighed, opened and read it. He nodded to himself. At last, Sullivan was joining the human race. But Porter was not letting up yet. He responded, ignoring Sullivan's abject apologies.

"It's 50:50. Not regained consciousness yet."

The message didn't cheer Sullivan up one bit. The truth was he was quite fond of Janice but his competitive instinct had pushed her away. He bitterly regretted his stupidity but too late, it seemed. He had to just suck it up and hope there might be a route to redemption.

He looked at his copy and pressed delete. The only thing he could do now was to write a dispassionate piece, sticking to the facts as he knew them and carefully choreograph his text to avoid any direct allegation where he was unable to cite legal evidence. Phrases such as 'sources close to'... 'rumours flying around say'.... 'possible conspiracy'.... together with a request for those who supplied the photos to contact the Gazette office, were now the basis of the article. He sent it off to Porter at nine o'clock, thinking that he might get a call in the morning.

The editor called him back within ten minutes.

"Talk me through the evidence you've got which you can't publish, and why?"

A subdued Sullivan explained the conspiracy he had discovered, omitting the hacking element, but knowing he would have to admit it at some point.

"How did you get to this conclusion?" There it was. Sullivan let out a heavy sigh, not knowing how Porter would react. He explained the deletion on his WhatsApp account and how he had asked his source to hack his phone to find out what the message said.

"You asked someone to hack your own phone?" Porter was incredulous. "And who is this magic person?"

"The same one who unlocked that boy's laptop for Janice. Suddenly, it opened up a trail that led to the Archbishop who confirmed he had indeed spoken to the Chief of Police, whose office declined to confirm that the Chief had instructed his Deputy to get to me through a third party, who I've met and is on record as confirming the order."

He neglected to mention that Iqbal had refused to hack the other phones and he had used someone who he didn't know and who could, potentially, blackmail him as soon as he saw the furore the article would surely provoke.

There was silence at the other end then, "I want to hear the recordings. Send them over."

"I'm not sure I know how to do that," admitted Sullivan.

"Find someone." Porter cut the call.

Janice could have done that for him, but that wasn't possible. How dependent was he on her? He shook his head. Who else? It had to be someone from the newsroom whom he could trust to keep his/her mouth shut if they listened, which they would, even if it was just curiosity. What about Mackie? He might know or know someone trustworthy who did know.

"Hi Mackie," said a quiet Sullivan. "Sorry to disturb you."

"Sullivan? What the hell do you want?" Sullivan grimaced as he thought of what he was about to ask.

"I guess you know what's happened to Janice?" Even now, Sullivan was using Janice to get what he wanted and he knew it, but there was no other way. Surely she would approve. Well, if not approve, grudgingly agree Mackie was the right person. After all, it was an emergency. Well, perhaps not really an emergency, but surely the right thing to do for the sake of the paper, of course. Sullivan was squirming inside but determined to keep going.

"Yes, what's that got to do with you calling me at home at ten o'clock at night?" At least Mackie hadn't put the phone down. A minor victory.

"Porter, quite rightly, rushed down to see how she is, but he's still working.

He's looking over my copy for tomorrow's front page from her bedside and wants to hear some recordings I've made which back up the story."

"Very interesting," said Mackie dryly.

"The thing is," Sullivan rushed on. "I don't know how to get the recordings onto an email or something to send it through to him." He paused. Mackie said nothing. "I thought you might be able to help or recommend a trustworthy person who could?" Sullivan finished with his most begging tone.

Mackie remained quiet as if deciding what to do. "What sort of recorder do you have? It's not an old analogue one is it?

Sullivan breathed a sigh of relief. The financial man was going to help. "No. No. It's a digital one. Janice made me throw my old one away."

"Thank God for Janice," said Mackie. "Right, have you got your recorder and laptop wired up? In easy steps, Mackie took him through the process and, with a few mistakes from the analogue reporter, it was done.

"Mackie, I'm very grateful. You've saved the front page," said Sullivan, wanting to pay tribute.

"I'm overwhelmed," replied a sarcastic Mackie.

Sullivan stayed up to see if Porter wanted to discuss anything but, by midnight, had heard nothing so he went to bed. It would be Thursday tomorrow and everything would need to be in place as early as possible.

Chapter 73

PORTER HAD TEMPORARILY fallen asleep in his bedside chair. He was awakened by an older couple who came through the door with real concern on their faces. He dragged himself to his feet assuming they must be Janice's parents. They were. He introduced himself and gave them an update as far as he knew, offering his chair to the mother who looked quite feeble. The nurse was hovering, encouraging them to go home overnight and come back in the morning. Porter offered them his hotel room, saying he would stay at her bedside as there was only room for one. After a discussion between husband and wife, they decided they would take the hotel room and come back in the morning.

As they were having their discussion, Porter thought he heard the buzz of his cellphone, so as soon as they had gone, he turned to his phone and saw that Sullivan had sent through some files which he assumed were the recordings, together with a rider to say some were a little faint. He stirred himself to listen, starting with the Archbishop and finishing with a male who spoke on the condition he was not identified. He heard Sullivan agree.

Porter was no novice in the investigative journalism game and knew risks needed to be taken to uncover a story. He recognised the language Sullivan was now using in his copy and, overall, thought it stood up. Nevertheless, at one o'clock in the morning, sent the whole package to the lawyers with a request for a response by ten the next day.

He was just closing his eyes again when he thought he heard a stirring from the patient. He crouched over her, calling her name quietly. She was looking alternately pale and grey with her arms twitching spasmodically in her induced coma. Her eyes didn't open nor did she make any sounds. Had he just imagined it? Anyway, he took it as a good omen and settled himself back in his chair in a slightly better frame of mind. Perhaps she would recover consciousness by the morning. She didn't.

Janice's parents arrived at nine and stayed with their daughter, Porter having grabbed another chair from a neighbouring room then disappeared to the coffee shop to see what was on offer in the way of breakfast. Not a lot. He satisfied himself with a sausage roll and a large black coffee. Just before ten, he got a call from one of the Gazette's lawyers.

"Morning Porter. I've looked through your package and I've heard the recordings, but nowhere is there any detail about how these persons were identified in the first place?"

Porter suspected that Sullivan had used various devious means to identify who to call but didn't want to block the story.

"Just standard investigative journalism," replied Porter vaguely.

"Hmm." The lawyer was not altogether happy.

"We've been here before," said Porter. "In fact, at the beginning of every story, there are contacts, whistleblowers who give us information but don't want their names publicised." Porter was on Sullivan's side and wanted to get this over the line. He could see a few follow-ups in the coming weeks and didn't want to lose that opportunity.

"I suppose so," grunted the lawyer. "But Sullivan can't post it in his name. Somebody else needs to be on the byline."

"Yes, I thought that myself," agreed Porter.

"I'll have to email you with my reservations, of course," finished the lawyer.

"Of course," Porter smiled. He knew the score. The story was a go and, together with the prospect of Janice waking up later, he was happy. The package was emailed to his production team, copy Sullivan, and told them to run with his story for this weekend's edition but with his name on it.

"Let's see what a shitstorm this provokes," he said to himself, not just referring to the response of the Archbishop or Police. He decided that he needed some fresh air, so exited the hospital and took a fifteen-minute walk reflecting on what the medics had said earlier that morning.

He had been woken up at some unearthly hour by medics who had come to do their checks and was asked to leave for about ten minutes. The senior doctor had come out and reported that she seemed to be nearer consciousness than the previous evening.

"It could be this afternoon, evening or even tomorrow. We don't know for sure."

Porter, anxious to ask a dozen questions, was stopped by the medic saying,

"Sorry, we just don't know what state she will be in. She suffered a serious concussion to her head, so you'll have to be very patient."

He had wondered whether to let her parents know when they arrived, but decided not to say anything. It was all conjecture and no point in lifting hopes yet. He updated both newsrooms as to the prognosis for Janice last night, so he felt able to concentrate on business for a few hours. The Gazette was sorted so he turned his attention to the Post. One of the sub-editors had been asked to step up and he explained to Porter that they had a Vatican scoop as their front page. Porter was intrigued and began to understand the cryptic conversation with Janice the previous day. He read the copy with some fascination, knowing some of the background. He congratulated the two who had put it together and gave it his blessing once he had taken the opportunity of putting a column next to it about the hit and run, appealing for help in tracing the driver. After an hour or so on the phone, Porter was satisfied that it was all under control, at least for this week.

Sullivan didn't see the finished front page until that morning as he was on his way for his usual Saturday breakfast. He was astonished to see Porter's name on the story and not his. His immediate and instinctive reaction was to swear profusely, gathering a number of angry looks from other customers in the restaurant, some of whom had their children with them. He turned around, mouthing 'Sorry' to the tables immediately around him, not really concerned whether they accepted his apologies or not. It gave him the opportunity to calm down, realising it was probably at the insistence of the lawyers. He tried to satisfy himself that at least he got the story out and he would wait for the backlash with some pleasure. But he still had to talk to Porter about his $1000. He didn't intend allowing that to go unpaid. After all, there were going to be a series of follow-up stories that would make the paper a lot more dollars than that.

His thoughts turned to Janice, and satisfaction over his story quickly turned to guilt as he recalled his behaviour towards her. He had a sudden thought. Why not drive down to Providence? Yes, he felt he needed to be there. If he started now, he could be there in an hour or so.

He arrived at about eleven and made his way up to a room expecting

Porter to be there, but an older couple were sitting silently next to a bed. He quickly gave his apologies and backed away, saying he was looking for Janice Munroe.

The man got to his feet. "This is Janice's room," he said, calling after the new visitor. "Are you from the paper?"

Sullivan was on his way out of the door in embarrassment after going into what he thought was the wrong room. He stopped and turned around. "Yes," he said. "My name is Sullivan."

"Ah. Yes, Janice has spoken about you."

Sullivan was at a loss for words thinking that Janice would have probably made lots of derogatory remarks about him. He tried to deflect. "Er. Are you her parents?"

"Yes," said her father. "I'm afraid there's not much news. She's still unconscious."

Sullivan took a closer look. He hardly recognised her with all the tubes. She also had her head shaved with many stitches in evidence alongside a large gauzy bandage.

"I'm so sorry," he mumbled and shuffled his feet as if his body was trying to leave the room.

"I'm glad to meet you," said her father, moving over to shake his hand. "She had a very high opinion of you. She said it was you who broke the story about the paedophile priests?"

"Er. Yes, I did but she did just as much, if not more, to expose them."

"Well, she'll be glad you're here."

Sullivan didn't quite know what to say, an experience that had only happened a few times in his life. Her mother stayed quiet, her eyes fixed on the bed, but her father continued, "Mr Porter is downstairs in the coffee shop."

"I'll go and find him," said Sullivan, glad to get out of the room.

"We said we'd call Mr Porter if there was any change," her father called out after him.

Sullivan walked slowly back downstairs rather confused. She hadn't bad-mouthed him, rather the opposite. He found Porter who immediately exclaimed,

"What are you doing here?"

"Thought I'd come over in case she came to," he said. "Just met her parents."

Porter grunted. "I suppose you'd better sit down."

Investigator and editor didn't have much to say to each other, which was good news for Porter. Sullivan was not an easy person to get along with and he preferred to keep the relationship to a business one. The last thing he wanted was for Sullivan to bring up the subject of his relationship with Janice.

Then, at two in the afternoon, Porter's phone went. He listened and immediately started for the stairs, not bothering with the elevator. At first, Sullivan didn't react but, as he saw the speed with which his boss was moving, decided that something was happening upstairs. They both burst into Janice's room as the nurse was talking.

"Her vitals are improving," the nurse was announcing to the posse that was now invading the room. "But please give her space and time."

At that moment, Janice began to blink and try to move her head. The nurse moved towards the bed, keeping everyone away from getting too close. Her mother was nearest, trying to attract her attention but it seemed Janice couldn't focus and soon closed her eyes. Everyone waited in silence with eyes totally focussed on the patient, waiting for more movement. After a few more minutes, the eyes opened again and her lips began to move but without any sound. The nurse leaned forward and gave her a short drink of water. Now her eyes were taking it all in. She looked past her parents and saw Porter and began to smile a little. Then she saw Sullivan and continued to smile.

"OK, everyone. I want you all to move away," said the nurse firmly, allowing the patient time to thoroughly wake up and understand where she was.

"Porter." came a croaking voice, hardly audible. Everyone looked around. The nurse hurriedly changed her instructions. "Whose Porter?"

Porter came forward a little. "You may stay for a little longer," said the nurse. "But don't push it. She must be allowed to recover very gently at this stage."

The others left and Porter came closer, putting his hand on hers and squeezing gently. They both smiled at each other before she squeezed his hand, closed her eyes and drifted off with a sense of contentment on her face.

Chapter 74

ALL HELL WAS breaking loose at Police HQ with the Chief on the warpath, the whole of his force having read the front page of the Gazette. He called his Deputy Chief in.

"How the hell did Sullivan get this information?"

The Deputy, now only concerned with retaining his job since being door-stepped at the town hall meeting, put the blame squarely on Frank McKinley.

"He could only have got these details by hacking my phone."

"Can you prove it?"

There was no answer from the Deputy.

"Get out." The Deputy started to move out when the Chief shouted after him. "And if you can't prove a hack, you'd better ensure McKinley is in the frame. Find him and bring him in for questioning."

The door to his plush office was now shut and the Chief began to think. There was no doubt that he was going to come under some criticism so it was damage limitation time. The new Archbishop would have seen this already so decided to get ahead of him.

"Eminence, I take it you have seen the front page of the Gazette today?"

"I have."

"We have a leak somewhere," said the Chief, being somewhat economical with the truth.

"I trust you can fix it."

"We've launched an investigation," replied the Chief hurriedly.

"Hmm. Depending on what the next story is will determine whether I am able to take up the post in Boston," said His Eminence.

"I think Sullivan's aim is at us," said the Chief, trying to comfort the cleric.

"I don't think that at all," rejoined the Archbishop Emeritus.

Sullivan had only released a fraction of the story he intended to publish. The Archbishop Emeritus of Boston was right. There was more to come. Much more, and it was definitely aimed at him. Sullivan saw this whole catholic conspiracy as corruption of the worst kind and he had returned to the office ready to pen the next story. It had the desired effect from Sullivan's point of view, for it transpired a few weeks later that the Archbishop would not be coming to Boston, neither would he be promoted to Cardinal. The brief conversation with His Holiness revolved around both stating their desire 'to protect the church'. In the obtuse way such dialogue was conducted, it was never directly mentioned but the Archbishop realised that his retirement was now required.

The Pontiff made no further comment to the Archbishop, but remembered Douglas-Scott's comment about 'old men'. Now Peter's successor was forced to delay any appointment to Boston until the continuing story had played itself out and the Gazette had moved on. Perhaps a younger man would be best after all.

The Deputy Chief was unable to find McKinley who had moved out of state immediately after his meeting with Sullivan. He was hunkered down with other masonic friends down in Rhode Island and not to be found despite police efforts. If truth be known, the Deputy didn't try that hard for he knew McKinley would finger him and the implications might be worse than those he expected. It was not long before the Deputy was moved to another force and lost a level of authority, but the Chief managed to stay on in the job due, it was rumoured, to a close relationship with the Mayor, something which Sullivan thought he might look into at some point.

Janice was recovering well physically although, as she began to remember more and more of what had happened to her, she became inexplicably tearful at odd times. Her doctors explained that this was not unusual and would gradually improve, but that she should not go back to such a stressful job straight away. Porter took a fortnight's leave with Meyer's blessing leaving the shop in the hands of his most experienced sub-editor. However, that didn't stop him from asking to receive early sight of each front page on a Thursday morning which gave him an opportunity to comment before it was put to bed.

Janice, however, would take a lot longer to recover before resuming editorship of the Post. She came back to Boston temporarily and decided to move in with Porter, but still retain her apartment. It troubled her that whilst the stolen car had been found, the perpetrators of the hit and run had not. In her more energetic spells, she started to look at data on these crimes, plus the impact they made on the victims and their families. It might make a story one day, but hardly the sort of front pages she was used to.

What might, if she dared let Porter read it, was that opinion piece she had quickly written after her first interview about paedophile priests. She read it through again and, with a few amendments, decided that it still stood up so one evening, hesitantly, allowed Porter to read it. With a few perceptive comments, he declared it ready to publish.

"But," he explained. "I've generally steered the Gazette away from 'column-ists' publishing their opinion pieces."

"I'm thinking of the Post," countered Janice. "As a daily, we could start to make the Saturday edition more of a weekend paper than it currently is."

"You're the boss but, in my humble opinion, it's not a front page scoop, more a centre spread where you could refresh your readers on the Gazette campaign and position your piece alongside."

Janice nodded and they both fell into silence. Porter could see that even such a brief conversation had wearied her. It was to be a long road back.

Back in the Gazette newsroom, Sullivan showed no signs of slowing down. He just kept going but, despite the circulation impact of his arrest stories, never recovered his $1000. Porter explained, with half a smile, that to do so would make him party to an illegal activity, even though his name was on the byline. However, the senior investigator did get the raise he was after. He declared himself satisfied as was Mackie, now the paper was back to one investigator.

The Pontiff began to move his modernising agenda a little faster, or at least as fast as it was possible with many Cardinals around the world joining senior Curia prelates quietly slowing it all down. It would have been frustrating had not the man in white known this would happen and kept his expectations low. His job was to sow seeds which another would see germinate, another water and probably yet another reap only a small harvest. Such was the Papacy.

Chapter 75

IT HAD BEEN three weeks since Janice had moved back to Boston. Ten o'clock in the morning and she was just finishing getting dressed. This was now her routine. Porter's fortnight's leave had come to an end, so he had left hours ago for the Gazette office. Her cellphone rang and a glance at it revealed an anonymous number. As a journalist, she would have answered it straight away thinking it might be a story, but now she was hesitant. Her energy levels, whilst improving, weren't yet sufficient to re-enter the stressful world she had temporarily taken leave of. She waited for it to go to voicemail.

She took herself and the phone to the kitchen to get some fruit for breakfast especially bought in by Porter. He was trying to take good care of her. There was no urgency to listen to her message. With food and a coffee inside her, she then decided to dial up her voicemail.

"Ms Munroe, this is Detective Reardon from Providence police. Perhaps you could ring me back on this number at your convenience." She stared at the cellphone for a minute or two with any number of possibilities running through her mind – most not very pleasant. She left the kitchen and settled on an easy chair in the lounge and rang the number.

"Thank you for calling back, Ms Munroe. May I ask if you know a Frank McKinley?"

Janice shook her head as if to clear it, then hesitantly answered, "Yes."

"May I ask how?"

"Well, my father used to know him, years back."

"Can you tell me when you last met him?"

"I've never met him."

"He seems to know you," continued the detective, "and holds some kind of grudge against you."

Janice was confused. "That's impossible."

"The car we found had been reported stolen and completely wiped clean, except for just one fingerprint on a key fob which had been thrown away. We matched it to a Frank McKinley who, at present, is still on the run."

Janice was quiet.

The detective continued. "I'm afraid it doesn't seem to be an accident. We believe you were targetted."

Then it clicked. Sullivan. She was furious.

Acknowledgments

WHILST THIS STORY has been set in Boston, my fictional Boston Gazette in no way reflects the professional equivalent of the Boston Globe who originally broke this story. Their investigators deservedly won a Pulitzer for their persistence and courage, and a multi-Oscar nominated film called 'Spotlight' was then released.

In order to maintain distance from the real investigation, I refrained from either seeing the film or reading the original book called 'Betrayal' whilst I was writing.

It may seem petty, but I have kept the word 'catholic' and 'church' without their capitals.

I also owe thanks to other media who pursued the story and provided valuable background in their reporting. In no particular order they are:

Patheos	The ConversationUK	Guardian
BBC News	Irish News	New York Times
CNN	nbcnews.com	Washington Post
NPR Illinois	nj.com	La Republica
crimemagazine.com	Newsweek	Die Welt
Belfast Telegraph	complicitclergy.com	RTE
churchandstate.org.uk		

Others who selflessly gave their time to review various iterations of the manuscript are:

Simon Porter	Phil Everest	Sandra Daplyn
Ray Aiken	Dustin Lees	Ros Dakin